Trapped in a shadowy deep space maze of politics
and death—where mysteries deepen by the hour...
and rules change with no warning.

HELLBURNER

The new thriller by Hugo Award winner C. J. Cherryh

"Excellent. . . . Cherryh, who evokes more tension and
danger in one verbal confrontation than most writers can
manage in a dozen space battles, maintains a fast
pace throughout."

—*Publishers Weekly*

"One of the finest writers SF has to offer."
—*Science Fiction Chronicle*

"Marvelously skillful." —*Philadelphia Inquirer*

"Cherryh's gifts are many: she creates believable,
sympathetic and altogether imperfect characters and
scrambles them well, creating gut-wrenching
interpersonal conflicts and tensions."
—*San Diego Tribune*

"C. J. Cherryh writes intelligent, realistic science fiction."
—*Columbus Dispatch*

"[Cherryh's] singular ability to create a believable vision
of a spacefaring future is exceeded only by her talent for
populating that vision with 'real' people."
—*Library Journal*

"Cherryh has the unique gift for making her words and
her people so real that we can never forget them."
—**Lester del Rey**

"Cherryh's short, reverberant sentences have the feel
of the best tough-guy detective fiction, and she
is marvelously skillful in establishing her
characters' motivations."
—*Cleveland Plain Dealer*

"One of the finest prose stylists in the field."
—**David Drake,** author of *Hammer's Slammers*

more . . .

"Winning science fiction . . . [by] one of the genre's best authors. . . . Her action-filled tales are in the best science-fiction tradition, and are invariably thoughtful glimpses of a future where the technology changes but humans don't."

—*Sacramento Bee*

"Fast-paced and engrossing."

—*Bookwatch*

C.J. CHERRYH

HELLBURNER

WARNER BOOKS

A Time Warner Company

WARNER BOOKS EDITION

Questar® is a registered trademark of Warner Books, Inc.

Cover design by Don Puckey
Cover illustration by Don Maitz
Hand lettering by Richard Nebiolo

Warner Books, Inc.
1271 Avenue of the Americas
New York, NY 10020

A Time Warner Company

Printed in the United States of America

Originally published in hardcover by Warner Books.
First Printed in Paperback: June, 1993

10 9 8 7 6 5 4 3 2 1

CHAPTER 1

STOCKHOLM is a city of islands and gardens, a
stunningly eclectic architectural mix, from the
Rigsdagshus to the 23rd century Carlberg Museum,
from the restored Riddarsholm Kyrka to the
Academy gardens...

Founded in the mid 13th century, the city of Stockholm holds abundant evidence of a thousand years
of Baltic seafaring tradition, plus a lively nightlife
centered in modern Gustavsholm—

Ben indexed through the motile pictures and the text, the
statistics about rainfall and mean average temperature which
the Guide cautioned a visitor did not in any sense mean a
constant temperature. Useless statistic—unless one contemplated Antarctica, where a mean temperature of −57° C and
an average hours of sunlight only slightly better than Sol
Station core meant Ben Pollard had no interest in McMurdo
Base. Ben Pollard had seen a good deal of cold and dark
and rock in his life. *Old* rock. This 13th century business

amazed him. The whole damn human race dated itself in eighteenths of Jupiter's passes about the sun, to the astonishingly recent number of about 10k such fractions, if you took the oldest cities. ASTEX R2 out in the Belt had been a skuz old place and a friend of his had sworn it had seen better days just in *his* lifetime, but when Ben Pollard thought *old*, he thought in millions. The rock he'd handled out there was *old*. Humankind was a real junior on those terms.

He sipped real orange juice, imported up from the blue, cloud-swirled globe you could see at any hour on channel 55, along with the weather reports anywhere in the motherwell.

Weather—was a novelty. Real weather. You got weather in a station core when they were blowing cold rock down the chute. You got condensation in your spacecraft and you swore like hell and wiped and dried and tried to find the source of it. But in the motherwell condensation fell out of the sky in frozen balls or slow flakes or liquid drops depending on the low level atmospheric temperatures, and k-wide clouds threw out electrical discharges that made it a very bad notion to stand (the Guide said) at the highest point of the landscape.

Daunting thought.

The Guide said 70% of the Earth was water.

The Guide said water in the oceans was 10k meters deep in places, and because it wasn't frozen, Luna's gravity pulled it up in a hump of a wave that rolled around the globe and washed at every shore it met, enough to grind up rock into beaches.

All that unfrozen water. Gaseous nitrogen and liquid water that made all that sparkle when the sun hit the wrinkles on it that the Guide said were waves.

He planned to stand on a beach and get a good close look at that unfrozen water. On a clear day, when there were no lightnings. You could do it from the station. You could be there while you were here, but VR was a cheat, you could be a whole lot of places that weren't real. He wanted to stand at the edge of the ocean and watch the real sun disappear behind the real world, at which point he figured he would really believe he was standing on a negative curvature.

The Guide said some spacers got dizzy, with the horizon going the wrong direction. There were prescriptions for vertigo. There were preparatory programs. But hell, he'd monkeyed around the core at R2, and stared straight at the rotation interface. That had to be worse.

The clock on the screen said: 0843 June 14, 2324. And there was plenty of time this morning for coffee. Dress maybe by 0930h. Exams were done, the last score was going up today, but, hell, that was Interactive Reality Sampling and he had that one in his pocket, no question, no sweat. Probably set the curve: him or Meeker, one or the other: just let the UDC get *that* score, and Stockholm was in his pocket for sure, motherwell assignment in the safest, softest spot in the service except Orlando. Stockholm was where Ben Pollard was headed, yeah! soon as the interviewers could get up to station.

Hell and away from the Belt, he was. Here you didn't jam two guys into a fifteen by six, hell, no, Sol Station and Admin? You got a whole effin' fifteen by six .9 *g* apartment by *yourself*, with a terminal that could be vid or VR whenever you opted. If you qualified into the Programming track in the UDC Technical Institute, you got an Allotment that afforded you 2c/d Personals per effin' seven-day week, which meant oj that was real, coffee that was *real*, red meat that was *real*, if you had the stomach for it, which Ben personally didn't—you lived like an effin' Company exec and had a clearer conscience. And if you could get that onworld posting, your tech/2 graduation rating equaled a full UDC lieu-tenancy in the motherwell, with an Army first lieutenant's pay to start, full grade technical/1 promotion guaranteed in a year, and access with a capital A to all the services that pay could buy. You knew there was a war out in the Beyond, but it wasn't going to get to Earth, that was what they were building that Fleet out there to stop—and even if it did nobody was going to hit the motherwell, humans just didn't *do* that. You were safe down there. You'd be safe no matter what.

He'd got his graduation With Honors, he was certain of it; he'd sweated his Security verifications, but they'd come through months ago, and nobody had come up with an objection; he'd sailed through the Administrative Service exams four weeks ago, and the only complication in his way now was the formal interview, as soon as the personnel reps from the various agencies could get seats on a shuttle up here—funding time and some legislative hearing in Admin had had the shuttle up-slots jammed with senators and brass and aides for the last three days; but that was thinning out, thank God. The agency interviewers might turn up by the end of the week, after which time—

After which he could book himself a seat for Earth on whatever assignment shook out—maybe even take his pick: Weiter had dropped him a conspiratorial word that he had three different computer divisions fighting over him, including strategic supply modeling and intelligence, and the prestigious AI lab in Geneva (which was for his personal ambitions a little too scientific and academic—give him something with a direct line to politics, God, yes. There was money in that, and a protected paycheck).

Money. A nice apartment down where you navigated a perceptually planar surface at a 300kph crawl, when he was used to thinking in kps and nanosecond intersects. Life on Earth went so much slower and death came so much later for a man who had money, brains, and position.

He'd had a partner back in the Belt, Morrie Bird, who had used to talk to him about Colorado, and cities and sunsets and Shakespeare. Bird had set a lot of personal store by Shakespeare. Bird had thought Shakespeare was important to understand. So when it had turned out of all things that he was going to the inner system, he had made it a certain point to see this Shakespeare guy—translated tapes, of course. V-vids, where you could wander around and watch the body language. And Bird had been a hundred percent right: Shakespeare really helped you figure Earthers. Blue-skyers. People who had never felt null-g, never seen the stars all the way to forever—different people, with numbers hard to figure; people who thought they had a natural right to orange juice and gravity, people who (the Guide maintained) felt the moon tides in their blood.

Getting the right numbers in a new situation absolutely mattered. On Earth air was free and ship routes and energy were what the old Earthers had fought bloody wars over. Sincerely skewed values—but you had to think about that two-dee surface constantly, and it was limited that way. Finite. Finite resources. Shakespeare helped you see that— helped you see how certain old Earthers in control of those resources had thought they could run your life, the same as Company execs. And how these king-typos always talked about God and their rights, like the preachers on R2's helldeck, who snagged you with tracts and talked to you about free-shares in their particular afterlife and argued whether the aliens at Pell had souls. Only these old kings had been the preachers *and* the law *and* the bank.

Long way to come, from the Belt, from Company brat in a Company school learning nothing but Company numbers— to figuring Shakespeare and human history. But there it was, the motherlode of all living stuff and the home of human-kind back when humans had been as backward as the Downers at Pell—Earth was full of museums, full of artifacts, pots and tombs and old walls graffitied with stuff that was supposed to make you live forever. The Guide said so.

Most of all, it was the motherlode of information, data, old and new. And the right numbers and enough data on the systems that ran the Earth Company and the United Defense Command could make him rich; rich made a man safe, and got him most everything Ben Pollard could put a name to.

Visitors to Stockholm may be impressed with the Maritime Museum or the Zoological Garden in Haga Park. . . .

A planet that wasn't a radiation hell was a novelty. Earth with its completely outsized moon was a novelty. And life thriving at the *bottom* of a gravity well was a radically upside down way of thinking. Life that made good wine and food that wasn't synth, a surface where plants grew and cycled the O_2 and the CO_2 on sunlight and dark; the habitats where animals lived. Fascinating concept, non-human things walking around where *they* decided to walk and looking at you with unguessable thoughts going on behind their eyes. People searched the stars for life, and there was all this life on Earth, that blue-skyers took for granted, and ate, if it didn't look too much like people.

He wanted to see a zoo. He wanted to look at a cow or a dog and be looked back at, when he'd never expect to see any real thing more exotic than miners on R&R and bugs under a lab scope.

Humans had existed such a scarily short time. With this war going on in the Beyond they seemed scarily fragile.

He wished he could talk to Bird about that. Bird had had a peculiar perspective about things. He wished he could really figure out what Bird had been, or recall half that Bird had said over the years. There was so much blue-sky attitude he still couldn't get the straight of. Baroque, was the word. Curves all over their thinking, like gold angels on the old buildings, that didn't have a damn thing to do with useful—

The message dot flashed on the corner of the screen.

God, it *could* be the interview notice. His fingers were on the Mod and the 1 to Accept Mail and the Dv and the 3 to Print faster than he could think about the motion.

It said:

TECH/2 Benjamin J. Pollard
CTS/SS/UDC 28 BAT 2
0852JUN14/24 SN P-235-9876/MLR
Report to FSO-HQ, 0930h/ref/Simons

Fleet Strategic Operations? *Fleet* Ops?
What in bloody hell?
MRL. Automatic log. No way to pretend he hadn't gotten
the message. No way to query the CO. Weiter would tell
him it was a report-to, he didn't have the answer, and he'd
effin' better answer it and find out what the Fleet wanted
with a UDC lad, hadn't he?
It *wasn't* an interview. God, no. Fleet Strategic Operations didn't need a UDC programmer tech/2 with a Priority
10 for economic/ and strategic/supply modeling. Did they?
Shit, no—the damn tight-fisted legislature insisted on
trying to interface the UDC EIDAT with the Fleet's Staatentek
system through the EC security screen, that was what. The
Fleet Staatentek system tried to phone the UDC's EIDAT
4005 to ask for available assignees, and the 4005, behind
the EC's security cloak, spat up a UDC Priority One
assignee for a Fleet data entry post—
But you couldn't ignore it. You didn't want to face the
interviews with an interservice screw-up or a Disciplinary in
your record. Damn the thing!
No second cup of coffee. He drank the half he had left
while his fingers tapped up the station map and asked it
where in hell FSO-HQ was on the trans system from his
apartment in TI 12 for a 0930h appointment.

9:15 2 green to 14, blue to 5-99: pass required
for entry.

Hell and gone from TI, and it was already 9 o'clock. Ten
effin' minutes to shave, dress and find his copy of his rating,
which clearly said UDC Priority Technical/2, before the

Fleet grabbed him and stuck him at Mars Base doing data entry in Supply.

He burned the beard off, pulled on his dress blues: never wear fatigues to an interservice glitch-up. He had to talk to officers, no question, before this one was straightened out, maybe all the way up the effin' C/O/C in the UDC *and* the Fleet. It could be a long day.

Envelope from UDC Technical at Geneva in the brief-case, where it belonged. He put it in his breast pocket.

Never a friggin' situation without a last friggin' minute complication. God, he didn't know why things like this happened to him. His interview appointment could come through at any hour, he *didn't* want Meeker to grab the first slot—first effin' thing he was going to do if they gave him Geneva was put the shove on that damned EC Software.

He checked his watch. 0908. Five minutes to walk to the trans. Orders *in* his pocket. Yes. And out the door.

Trans was packed. A whole wide-eyed batch of shiny new C-1's with their entry tags and their hand-baggage occupied all the seats, and Ben clung with an elbow about a pole and punched buttons on the hand reader, running down the applicable rules on interservice transfer apps.

Wasn't any reason to sweat it. Couldn't be. Weiter'd shoved him through three levels in a year. . . . He was Weiter's fair-haired baby, best Weiter had ever had in the department. Him and Meeker, neck and neck all the way. No *way* Weiter wouldn't go up the chain for him.

Green 14. He made the transfer and lost the C-1's—thank God. He got a seat, sat down and read.

Right of appeal. Ref: Administrative Appeal, Sec. 14. . . . Through chain of command in service of origin.

In service of origin. Which meant the United Defense Command, which *wasn't*, never mind Fleet Captain Conrad

Mazian's performance at the UN, going to let the Fleet get its hands on whatever it wanted.

Blue line now. Institution blue. The walls outside the spex in the doors grew skuzzier and skuzzier and the air that sucked in when the doors opened was cold and smelled of oil.

Descent into hell, Ben thought. Like R2 all over again. He sat in his dress uniform and watched the scenery, dark tunnel and grim flashes of gray-blue panels and white station numbers as the trans shot past stops without a call punched. Thump of the section seals. He could almost smell helldeck, all but hear the clash of metal and the hard raucous beat of the music echoing down the deck. He smelled the peculiar taint of cold machinery and kept having this most damnable feeling of—

—belonging in the dark side, living on the cheap, getting by, scamming the Company cops and *knowing* he could always slip through the system, knowing far more about the company computers and access numbers than the Company thought he'd learned. Him and Bird. —And Sal Aboujib.

Damn.

Helldeck wasn't a place you'd miss. He was someone else now. Spiff uniform and a tech/2's collar pin. Clean fingers—in all senses. He didn't do a thing illegitimate with the computers he worked with. He didn't know anybody who did, no, *sir,* didn't even dream about that h-word near the Defense Command computers.

He'd got away with it. Was still getting away with it. He'd dumped the card on R2, and it had never surfaced; he'd *gotten* his security clearance. He'd gotten his rank. Nobody was going to screw that up. Nobody could have found anything to screw him now . . .

5-99. The sign outside the doors said: SECURITY AREA. RESTRICTED. SHOW PASS.

He got up and got out in a beige, plain hallway, *warmer* here, thank God, it wasn't going to freeze his ass off or have him shaking when he was talking to the desk. He straightened his coat, clipped his fancy-tech reader onto his belt and walked up to the only door available, under a security array that was probably reading his respiration rate and taking notes.

He put his card in the slot: the door clicked and opened. Fleet Security occupied the solitary desk in the foyer; beyond it was a potted silk palm, an abstract picture, and another beige windowless door.

"Pollard," the officer said, with no attention to the protocols in the rulebook. Or his face. Just the readout on his screen. "Benjamin J. You're carrying electronics."

"Reader."

The officer held out his hand. Ben surrendered it and watched the officer turn it on and punch buttons.

"Fancy."

Break his effin' neck getting here and this cop-type stalled him playing games with a piece of expensive and delicate equipment. He said, "I've got an appointment at 0930."

The guard said, "HQ," and motioned with the back of his hand. "Lieutenant Jackson."

Jackson, was it? Fleet Lieutenant. Which, in the much-argued and protested Equivalencies, was a rank just under Maj. Weiter's; and one over his. Ben drew himself up with a breath, thinking, with part of his brain: Son of a bitch deep-spacer Attitude, and minded for half that breath to make an issue of interservice protocols; but the rest of his brain was still wondering if the Fleet could have any legitimate interest in him and hoping all he had was a pocket full of EIDAT-screwed orders. So he saluted, got a flip of the hand and walked to the inner door, that clicked open on a long bar of a desk and a sober-faced clerk who said (efficiency, at least) "Lt. Pollard?"

"Yes." Manners. Finally. He took the offered escort to a side office. Jackson took the salute, offered him a seat. Young guy. Pleasant, serious face.

Better, he thought.

"Thank you, sir."

Jackson folded his hands on the desk, "Lt. Pollard, —I'm sorry to be the bearer of bad news: a friend of yours has been involved in an accident."

"*Friend* of mine?" That was a complete mental shift. He honestly couldn't think if he had a friend. Not lately. Bird was dead. *Sal?*

"Name of Dekker," Jackson said and Ben all but said, *Shit!* before he remembered he wasn't in the Belt and swallowed it.

"Fatal?"

"Serious. He's asking for you."

"For *me?*" He was vastly relieved it wasn't Sal. Distressed if Dekker'd gotten in trouble. He didn't hate Dekker. Not really. Dekker had enlisted with him, gone off into some secret pilot training program . . . real hot piece of equipment, Dekker had said.

Jackson said, "His doctors feel it might be some help, a familiar face. . . ."

He thought, Oh, God, I don't want to do this. I don't want to see the guy again— I *hate* hospitals . . . I don't *like* blood—

But there it was, the brass had made a humanitarian move, no way to explain all the old business between them—it could drag up too much he didn't want on record; if Dekker had killed himself in some top-secret operation he was sincerely sorry, and if he was all Dekker could dredge up for a request—well, hell, the guy had saved his neck, sort of, back in the Belt—

And cost Bird's life, damn him, however indirectly.

"Sorry to drop this on you," Jackson said.

"Not a problem. Truth is, we weren't friends. —But I guess I owe him to drop over there."

"I've got a travel voucher for you."

"Travel voucher."

"B dock."

"Oh, now, God, wait a minute—" B dock wasn't on Sol One, it was on an auxiliary station three and more days out, on Sol Two. Ben reached for his pocket, right then. "I can't do that. I'm sorry. This is a priority rating. There's an agency officer coming for an interview this week. I can't leave."

Jackson laid an envelope on top of his. "There's a B dock shuttle leaving at 1205. That's your travel voucher and your leave. It's already signed and cleared."

"Sir, —that's six *days* even if I get a same day turnaround." He gingerly eased his letter from underneath and laid it gingerly to the side, in Jackson's view, where the United Defense Command logo showed. "This is from HQ Geneva. It says I'm a military priority."

"This one's from Captain Keu, in this office. On a classified priority. You're going."

"Dekker isn't a friend of mine!"

"He's listed you as next-of-kin."

"We're not related! God, —he's got a mother right here on the station, Astrid, Ingrid, something like that. Talk to her!"

"He's in a classified program. Only certain people are approved for contact in a next-of-kin emergency. You're it. You're not to call anyone. You're not to talk to anyone. Your CO will be advised simply that you're on humanitarian leave—"

"I'm UDC essential personnel!"

"Show me an assignment."

Shit!

"So you're going."

"What about my interview?"

"That's not my information flow. I'll log it as a query."

"Look, this is important. If I miss this slot I could wait six months!"

Jackson shrugged. "We all have our hardships, lieutenant."

"Look, this is a screw-up. It's an absolute screw-up. God, Dekker and I don't even *like* each other."

Cold as a rock. "I don't have that information. Transport will pick up your baggage at your quarters. Just leave it. Report to the shuttleport by 1145."

"It's near 1030 right now. It's twenty minutes to quarters—"

"I'd be on that shuttle, Lt. Pollard. When you get to B dock, report directly to the FleetOps office on the dock, give them this pass and they'll see you get straight to the hospital. Don't mistake that instruction."

"Listen, —sir, you know what happened—Dekker wrote me in as a joke. He never thought they'd be using that information. It's a damn joke!"

"If it is, I'm sure they'll straighten it out at the other end. I'd be moving, lieutenant." Jackson stood up and handed him the two envelopes as he rose. "Good luck."

"Yes sir," Ben said, took his papers and his orders, saluted the son of a bitch and left.

Collected his reader from the front desk, and made a fast, desperate consultation of the trans schedule while he was walking to the doors.

Twenty minutes to his apartment, thirty to the shuttle dock, ten to pack. If he risked a phone call to Weiter to request a rescue, it was a 90% certainty that Weiter couldn't do a damned thing against FSO before 1145 *or* later and he'd be screwed with Weiter for putting *him* in a Position. You didn't crack a security screen. Not if you hoped to keep your clearance in UDC computer tech.

They'd get him back in maybe six days?

Hell. Six days too late if he was on humanitarian leave on B dock when the UDC filled the Stockholm post. He'd get the scraps, the cold left-overs after Meeker got posted; and Hamid; and Pannelli— The next best choice he had was to appeal to Weiter when he got back and hang on as staff til something else came through, oh, six months, seven, eight months on, who knew?

Dekker had screwed up, the Fleet was evidently about to

lose its investment in him—and, not in his most copacetic state, Dekker had asked for him?

Ben thought, with every thump of the trans on its homebound course: I'll kill him when I get my hands on him, I'll fuckin' kill him.

CHAPTER 2

BFN hated institutions, *hated* hospital smells and institution colors and most of all he didn't look forward to this, in his first hour on B dock. He felt like hell, he'd slept in a damn cubbyhole of a berth hardly larger than a miner-ship spinner, his feet had swelled, he'd had sinus all the way: he'd spent too long in the null-*g* in his life and his body had a spiteful overreaction to the condition. They didn't issue pills and stimsuits for a three-day shuttle trip, no, that prescription's not on your records, lieutenant, sorry... If you'd just checked with medical—

It was damned well going to be on the record when he left Sol Two. Talk to the doctors in this hospital, get some damn good out of this end of the trip ... because he meant to be on that shuttle on its turnaround tonight. Six hours was plenty of time to see Dekker, and get out of here.

—after three days of floating in a three-berth passenger module on a cargo shuttle, ahead of a load of sanitation chemicals and spare parts. He'd had no one to talk to but a couple of machinists who were into some vegetarian religion and hooked on some damn VR game they wanted to explain to him; and he had had ample time to drift weightless in the dark and think—too much time to imagine this meeting, and what kind of damage a pilot could take in an accident. Missing limbs. Blood. He hated blood. He really got sick at his stomach if there was blood . . .

They'd had some sort of missile test that had gone bad out here. Nobody said what. There'd been a lot of long faces in Technical. A lot of emergency meetings last week. Dekker couldn't have been involved in any missile test. A pilot trainee didn't have anything to do with missile tests. Did he?

Jackson had done the talking. But why in hell did a Fleet captain sign the order and bust him out here? What was Dekker that the Fleet cared? The Fleet was fighting for its life in the Appropriations Committee. Dumbass pilot cracked up and UDC Priorities got overridden—for *humanitarian* reasons?

Not in the military he knew. That was the tag end that had disturbed his sleep and his thinking moments all the way out here. Their high-level interest in this affair was what had his stomach upset, as much as the stink of disinfectant and pain and helplessness in this place. He didn't like this. God, he didn't like this, and if Dekker wasn't dead he was going to strangle him bare-handed for writing him into that damned blank.

God, he was.

Reception desk. He presented his orders to the clerk and got a: "Lt. Pollard. Yes, *sir*," that did nothing for his stomach or his pulse rate. The receptionist got him a nurse, a doctor, and Dekker's attending physician, all in increasingly short succession. "How is he?" Ben asked the last, bypassing long introductions. "What happened to him?" and the doctor said, starting off down the hall:

"No change."

"So when did this happen?"

"That's classified."

* * *

More white coats. More people leaning into his face. They wanted him to open his eyes, but Dekker knew the game. They wanted answers to fill the blanks they had on their slates, but they wanted their own answers, the way they wanted the case to be.

Company doctors. He'd been here before. And they wouldn't listen. He asked, "Where's Cory?" because sometimes he couldn't remember what had happened, or he did, but it was all a dizzy blur of black and lights. The ship was spinning. He fought to get to the controls, because he had to stop that spin, with the blood filling his nose and choking his breath, and his hand dragging away with the spin, his grip going—

"Cory? You damned bastard, *stop!*"

But sometimes he came loose from that time and he was in hospital, or he was going to be, soon as Ben and Bird got him there, and they would lie to him and tell him there never had been a 'driver ship and he never had had a partner named Cory.

The Company had lied to him. They said he was hallucinating, but it was all lies. And sometimes he thought the hospital was the hallucination, that it was all something his conscience had conjured to punish him for losing his grip on the counter and for losing the ship.

For losing Cory.

And Bird.

Sometimes he was back in the shower, and sometimes tied to the pipes, because he was crazy, and he couldn't figure out how the ship had come to the hospital.

Thirty days hath September, March eleventh, and November. . . .

There were green coats now. Interns. He hoped for Tommy. But Tommy wasn't with them. "Where's Tommy?" he asked. "Why isn't Tommy on duty? —God, it's afire, isn't it? Meg? Meg, wake up, God, don't die on me—"

"Ens. Dekker, you have a visitor."

"I don't want any fuckin' visitor. Get away from me. Get out of here."

"Ens. Dekker, —"

"Tell him to go to hell! I don't want any damn Company lawyer! —Put Tommy back on duty, hear me? I want Tommy back." They grabbed hold of his arms, they were going to put the restraints on. Tommy wouldn't do that. Tommy would ask, Are you going to be quiet, Mr. Dekker? and he would say, Yes, yes, I'll be quiet, and Tommy wouldn't use them.

Wouldn't. But Tommy wasn't with them. And they did. They told him then if he wasn't quiet they'd have to sedate him. So he said, "I'll be quiet," and shut his eyes.

"Dekker," Ben said. And he opened his eyes. Ben was leaning over his bed. Ben was in uniform. UDC. That was different. But odder things happened in this place. He didn't blink. Things changed if you did. Finally he said, "Ben?"

"Yeah."

There was a ship out there. He remembered that. "Ben, we've got to go back. Please, we've got to go back, Cory's still out there—"

Ben grabbed a fistful of his collar, leaned close and said, in a low voice, "Dekker, shut it down right now or I'm going to kill you. You hear me?"

He said, "That's all right." He *felt* Ben's hand on him. He *saw* Ben's face. He knew where he was then, Bird was asleep and Ben was about to beat hell out of him. But that was all right. He really liked Ben, most of the time. And there hadn't been much to like where he'd been.

What could a guy do? Ben disengaged himself, and Dekker caught his hand. He pulled free and got out of the door to get his breath.

The doctor was out there, several doctors this time. "He knows you," Dekker's surgeon said. Higgins was his name. "You're the first person he *has* recognized."

"Fuckin' hell! Then he's cured. I'm out of here."

"Lt. Pollard," another doctor said, and offered his hand. "Lt. Pollard, I'm Dr. Evans, chief of psychiatry."

"Fine. Good. He needs a psych. That's all that's going to help him!"

"Lt. Pollard, —"

"Look, what do you want from him? The guy's schitz, completely off the scope. He doesn't know where he is, he doesn't know what happened—"

"Lt. Pollard." The psych motioned off down the farther hallway. "There's coffee in the lounge. You've had a long flight."

The psych wanted him to sit down and be reasonable, which he was in no mood to be. But coffee appealed to his upset stomach and his sleep-deprived nerves. And it was not at all a good idea to have a psych telling the local CO you'd been hysterical. You didn't need *that* on a record behind another service's security screen. So he went with the psych, he went through the dance—"White or black, sugar?" "That's enough, thanks,"—until he could get the weight off his feet, sink into a chair and try not to let Evans see his hands shake while he was drinking.

"So what happened to him?" he asked, before Evans could fire off his own questions.

"That's what we want to know."

"So how'd he get like this?"

"That's another question."

Deeper and deeper. Ben stared at the doctor and scowled. "So a door got him. Is that it?"

"A simulator did."

Flight simulator? Dekker? "Hell of a simulation, doctor."

"Didn't lock the belts, strong dose of sedative in his bloodstream."

Shit. Pills again.

Evans said: "We'd like to know how he got there."

Or maybe not. "You mean somebody put him there?"

"It's one possibility."

"Guy has a talent for making friends. Yeah. There's probably a dozen candidates."

"Why do you say that?"

Psych question. He thought, Because he's a fuck-up. Because he has this way of getting himself in trouble and slapping the hand that helps him. But that led to more questions; and screwed Dekker worse than he was with this guy, to whom he owed nothing yet. He said, finally, "Say I didn't really know him that well."

"He listed you as next-of-kin."

"It was a joke. The guy's full of them. Lot of laughs."

"We don't rule out suicide."

Dekker? he thought. Dekker? Suicide? The idea was more than unlikely. It upset him. And he didn't figure that, either why they could think that—if they knew Dekker, which they might not; or how Dekker could come to that—here, in this place that swallowed people down without a word.

"You don't agree?"

He shrugged. "It's not him. It's just not him."

You didn't come from where Dekker came from—didn't survive what he'd survived—and check out like that—in a damn sim. Something wasn't right, not with the questions, not with Dekker lying in there thinking he was back in the Belt, not with this whole max-classified operation that took a will to live like Dekker's and put him in that bed, in that condition.

Dekker had looked at him like he was what he'd been waiting for, and said, to his threat of killing him barehanded, That's all right . . .

Every time you got near the guy there was a disaster, Dekker attracted disasters, you could feel it, and, God of all the helldeck preachers, he wanted on that shuttle tonight. Do this effin' job, get Dekker to figure out where he was, and when he was, make him talk to the psychs, and get out of here while there was still a chance of making that interview—and getting out of this mess.

"I'll talk to him," he said.

"You're sure you're all right about that?"

Another psych quiz. Correct answer: "A long trip with no information, run in here straight from the mast, I was a little shaken up myself." He tossed off the rest of the coffee, got up and pitched the cup into the bin. "I'm fine to talk to him. What do you want out of him?"

"His health."

"Yeah, well, he'll pull it out. Knock him down and he bounces."

"Don't stress him, lieutenant. I really don't advise another confrontation. He's been concussed. We want to keep that blood pressure under control."

That was about worth a laugh. Dek was already stressed. Dek was in an out-of-control ship in a 'driver zone with his partner lost. He said soberly, "I've no intention of upsetting him."

The doctor opened the door, the doctor walked him back to Dekker's room and signaled an orderly for a word aside in the hallway.

Ben walked on in, pulled a chair over and sat down by Dekker's bed. Dekker's eyes tracked his entry, stayed tracked as he sat down, he wasn't sure how focused. Dekker had been a real pretty-boy, a year ago, fancy dresser, rab hair, shaved up the sides. Still looked to be a rab job, give or take the bandage around the head; but the eyes were shadowed, one was bruised, the chin had a cut, lip was cut—not so long back. The hollow-cheeked, waxen look—did you get that from a bashing-about in a simulator a few days ago?

"You look like hell, Dekker-me-lad."

"Yeah," Dekker said. "You're looking all right."

"So what happened?"

Dekker didn't answer right off. He looked to be thinking about it. Then his chin began to tremble and Ben felt a second's disgusted panic: dammit, he didn't want to deal with a guy on a crying jag—but Dekker said faintly, shakily,

"Ben, you'll want to hit me, but I really need to know—I really seriously need to know what time it is."

"What time it is?" God. "So what'll you give me for it?"

"Ben, —"

"No, hell, I want you to give me something for it. I want you to tell me what the hell you're doing in here. I want to know what happened to you."

Dekker gave a shake of his head and looked upset. "Tell me the time."

Ben looked at his watch. "All right, it's 1545, June 19th—"

"What year?"

"2324. That satisfy you?"

Dekker just stared at him, finally blinked once.

"Look, Dekker, nice to see you, but you really screwed everything up. I got orders waiting for me back at the base, I got a transfer that, excuse me, means my whole career, and if you'll just fuckin' cooperate with them I can still catch a shuttle in a few hours and get my transfer back to Sol where I can stay with my program. —Dek, come on, d' you sincerely understand you're screwing up my life? Do me a favor."

"What?"

"Tell the doctors what happened to you. Hear me? I want you to answer their questions and tell them what they want to hear and I don't, dammit, I want to be on that shuttle. You want me to call them in here so they can listen to you explain and I can get out of here?"

Dekker shook his head.

"Dekker, dammit, don't be like that. You're a pain in the ass, you know that? I got to get back!"

"Then go. Go on. It's all right."

"It's not the hell all right. I can't get out of here until you tell them what they want to know! Come on. It's June 19th. 2324. Argentina's won the World Cup. Bird's dead. Cory's dead. We came out here on a friggin' big ship neither of us is supposed to talk about and Gennie Vanderbilt is top of the series. Do you remember what put you here?''

"I can't remember. I don't remember—''

"Because you climbed into a friggin' flight simulator tranked to the eyeballs—does that jar anything loose?''

A blank stare, a shake of the head.

Ben ran a hand over his head. "God.''

"It's just gone, Ben. Sometimes I think it's the ship again. Sometimes it's not. You're here. But I thought you were before. What are they saying about the sim?''

"Dekker, —'' He gave a glance to the door, but the doctor-types were conferring outside. He said, in a low voice: "You're not hooked on those damn pills again, are you?''

Dekker shook his head. Scared. Lost. Eyes shifted about. Came back to him.

"Ben, —I'm sorry. Please tell me the time again.''

He didn't hit Dekker. He leaned forward and took Dekker's hand hard in his despite the restraints and said, very quietly, "It's June 19th. Now you tell me the year, Dek. I want the year. Right now. And you better not be wrong.''

Dekker looked seriously worried. A hesitation. A tremor of the lips. "2324.''

"Good. You got it memorized. Now there's going to be a test every few minutes, hear me? I want you to remember that number. This is Sol Two. You had a little accident a few days back. The doctors want to know, that's not so hard to hold on to, is it?''

"I can't remember. I can't remember, Ben, it's just gone . . .''

"Shit.'' He had a headache. He looked at Dekker's pale, bruised, trusting face and wanted ever so much to beat him senseless. Instead he squeezed Dekker's hand. "Dek, boy, listen. I got a serious chance at Stockholm, you understand me? Nice lab job. I'm going to lose it if you don't come through. I really need you to think about that simulator.''

Dekker looked upset. "I'm trying. I'm trying, Ben. I really am—"

Something was beeping. Machine up there on the shelf. Doctors were in the door. Higgins said, "Lt. Pollard. He's getting tired. Better leave it. —Ens. Dekker, I'm Dr. Higgins, do you remember me?"

Dekker looked at *him,* and said faintly, "Ben?"

"You do remember him," Ben said. "Hear me? Or I'll break your neck!"

"Don't go."

"He'll be back tomorrow."

"The hell," Ben said. "Dekker, goodbye. Good luck. I got to catch a shuttle. Stay the hell out of my life."

"Lieutenant." That was Evans. "In the hall."

He went. He got his voice down and his breathing even. "Look, I've done my job. I'm no doctor, you're the psych, what am I supposed to do?"

"You're doing fine. This is the first time he's been that sure where he is."

"Fine. I've got orders waiting for me on Sol One. I haven't got time for this!"

"That's not the way I understand your orders. You have a room assignment—"

"I haven't got any room assignment."

"—in the hospice a level up. It's a small facility. Very comfortable. We'd prefer you be available for him 24 hours. His sleeping's not on any regular pattern."

"No way. I've got a return order in my pocket, my baggage is still right back there in customs. Nobody said anything about this going into another shift. That wasn't the deal."

"Nobody said anything about your leaving. You'd better check those orders with the issuing officer."

"I'll check it at the dock. I'll get this cleared up. Just give him my goodbyes. Tell him good luck, I hope he comes out all right. I won't be here in the morning."

"Hospice desk is on level 2, lieutenant. You'll find the lift right down the corridor."

Ben had been there a while. Ben had told him—

But he couldn't depend on that. Ben came and Ben went and sometimes Ben talked to him and told him—

Told him about an accident in the sims. But if it was a sim then maybe people he thought were dead, weren't, even if they told him so. The doctors lied to him. They regularly lied, and Tommy didn't come back. They kept changing doctors, changing interns, every time he got close to remembering. . . .

Only Ben. Ben came and he started to hope and he knew that hope was dangerous. You didn't hope. You just lived.

Ben asked him was he on drugs. He had been once. He had been crazy once, now and again, but Ben and Bird had pulled him out. The ship was spinning. Cory was out there alone, and somebody had to pull him out—

Ship was spinning. Pete was yelling. And Cory—

Ben said he would kill him if he was crazy and he hoped Ben would do that, if he truly was, because he didn't want to live like that.

Ben said remember. But he couldn't remember any specific time in the sims. He could remember an examiner giving him his C-3. He could remember the first time he'd seen the boards. Remembered pushing beams at Sol. Supervisor had said all right, he could do that: he was under age, but they needed somebody who wouldn't ram a mass into the station hull. His head was bandaged, his ribs were. His knees ached like hell, he thought because he had hit the counter, trying to hit the button, but he wasn't sure of anything. You blinked and you got green numbers and lines, and if you followed them too far you never came back. Midrange focus. Back it up, all the way inside.

There'd been an accident and the ship had blown up. And his partners were dead. Or maybe never existed. It was a sim. Bright ball of nuclear fire. And he was here and they were in it, and it was all green glowing lines out there, whipping and snaking to infinity.

He remembered faces now. People he thought he liked— Bird. Meg and Sal. Cory, and Graff. Pete and Elly and Falcone. Faces. Voices. Falcone yelling, Hey, Dek, see you tomorrow.

But Falcone wouldn't. Elly wouldn't. They never would.

"You damn bastards!" he yelled. *"Bastards!"*

Interns came running, grabbed hold of him. "No," he said, reminded what happened when he yelled. "No. *Tommy!"*

"Get the hypo," one said, and he got a breath, he got a little sanity, said, "I'm not violent. I don't need it. It's all right. Let go, dammit! Get the doctor!"

They eased up. They stopped bruising his arms and just held him still.

"Just be quiet, sir. Just be quiet."

"No shots. No damn shots."

"Doctor's orders, sir."

"I don't need one. I swear to you, I don't need one."

"Doctor says you're not getting any rest, sir. You better have it. Just to be sure."

He looked the intern in the face. Big guy, red face and freckles, lying across him. Out of breath. So was he. And two other large guys who were leaning on him and holding his legs.

"Sorry," he said, between breaths. "Don't want to give you guys trouble. I really don't want to. I just don't want any shot right now."

"Sorry, too, sir. Doctor left orders. You don't want to be any trouble. Right?"

"No," he said. He shook his head. He made up his mind he had better change tactics. Agreeing with them got him out of this place. It would. It had. He couldn't remember. It was only the drugs he had to worry about.

"Just hold still, sir. All right?"

"Yeah," he said, and the hypo kicked against his arm. Stung like hell. His eyes watered.

He said, "You fuckin' get off me. I can't breathe. Let me up, dammit."

"Soon's you shut your eyes, sir. Just be quiet. You loosened a couple of John's teeth yesterday. You remember?"

He didn't remember. But he said, out of breath, "I'm sorry. Sorry about that. I'm better. A lot better."

"That's good, sir."

"Friend of mine was here," he said. But the drug was gathering thick about his brain. He said it again, afraid he might not remember when he waked. Or that it hadn't happened at all.

He went to sleep when they drugged him and he waked up and he never knew where or when. He was going out now. He felt it happening. And he was scared as hell where he would wake up or what would be true or where the lines would lead him.

"Ben," he cried, "Bird. Ben, come back— Ben, don't go— they killed my partners, Ben, they fuckin' killed us—"

"This isn't validated," the check-in clerk said, and slid the travel voucher across the desk in the .6 g of 8-deck. "You need an exit stamp."

Ben took the voucher with a sinking heart. "What exit stamp? Nobody said anything about an exit stamp. There's no exit stamp in the customs information."

"It's administrative, sir. Regulation. I have to have a stamp."

"God. Look, *call* Sol One."

"You do that from BaseCom," the clerk said. And added without expression: "But you need an authorization from your CO to do that, sir."

"And where do I get that?" You didn't yell at clerks. It didn't get you anything to yell at clerks. Ben said quietly, restrainedly: "My CO's on Sol One—I need the UDC officer in charge."

"This is a Fleet transport voucher."

"I know it is," Ben said. "But this uniform is UDC. Is it at all familiar to you? Where's the UDC officer in charge?"

The clerk got a confused look, and focused behind him, where someone had come into the office, to stand in line was Ben's initial reckoning; but whoever it was said, then, "Lt. Pollard?"

Voice he'd heard before. A long time ago. He turned around, a little careful in the .6*g*, saw a blue uniform and a black pullover, a thin, angular face and nondescript pale hair. Brass on the collar.

The trip out from the Belt. The *Hamilton*. And Jupiter's well.

Graff. Fleet Lt. Jurgen Graff. Carrier pilot, junior grade.

"There's an office free," Graff said, meaning very evidently they should go there. Now. Urgently. A Fleet lieutenant wanted to talk to him, and he was stuck on Fleet orders in something that increasingly felt like a deliberate black hole?

"I've got a flight out of here at 1800. They're talking about an exit stamp. I need some kind of clearance."

"You don't have a flight out of here. Not this one."

He slowed down, so that Graff had to pull a stop and look at him. "Sir. I need this straightened out, with apologies, sir, but I've got a transfer order waiting for me back on Sol One, I was told not to communicate with my CO, I'm *not* Fleet personnel. I understand the interservice agreements, but—"

"Five minutes."

"I'm UDC personnel. I want to see a UDC ranking officer. Sir. Now."

"Five minutes," Graff repeated. "You don't want your friend screwed. Do you?"

"My friend— Sir, I don't *care* what happens to my *friend*. I've got an appointment waiting for me back on Sol One, and if I lose it, *I'm* screwed. I'm just a little uneasy about this whole damn arrangement, —sir. This isn't what I was told."

"There's another shuttle out the 22nd. 2100 hours."

Ben caught a breath. Three days. But Graff's moves meant business and you didn't argue a security matter on the open dock—no. Even if it was blackmail. Extortion. Kidnapping.

Graff waited. He came ahead. He went with Graff into a freight office and Graff waved the lights on.

"Yes, sir?" he said.

"We need him," Graff said. "We need him to remember."

"Sir, I just graduated from TI. If I'm not back there for the interviews they're going away. They're going to assign those slots and I'm stuck teaching j-l programming to a class full of wide-eyed button-pushers, —sir. Excuse me, but I've not been in contact with any officer in my chain of command, I've gone along with this on the FSO's word it had notified my CO. I'm not sure at this point I'm not AWOL."

"You're not. You're cleared."

"I've got your word on that. I haven't seen any order but the one that had me report to the FSO on One. What have you done to me?"

"You have my word. I'll get a message to your CO."

"You mean they haven't?"

"I'll double check. We've played poker, haven't we, Mr. Pollard?"

"Yes, sir." Days of poker. Him. Dekker. Graff. No damn thing else to do on a half-built carrier.

"This is poker," Graff said. "For the major stakes. How *is* he?"

"What does it matter? What's he into?"

"Say I need him sane."

"He's never been sane."

"Don't joke like that. In some quarters they might take you seriously."

"I am serious. The guy's good, but his tether on reality's just a little frayed."

"Maybe that's what it takes to do what he does."

He stood there close to Graff, looking into Graff's sober face in this very unofficial office and suddenly wondering who and what Graff was talking about and what Dekker *did* regularly do that had put him where he was. He said, carefully, "Dekker got lost out in the Belt. Banged around a lot. Real disoriented."

"We know that."

And how much else? Ben wondered. God, how much else? News didn't escape the Belt. Security didn't let anything get out. Even yet. Everything about the mining operation out there was under wrap. You didn't know how much the Fleet might know. Or what tiny, inadvertent slip would let them guess what they'd done back there and what they might have been involved in that might screw his security clearance for good.

"I knew this man a handful of months. I've seen him like this before—when he first got out of hospital on R2. I can't make him make sense til he wants to make sense. I couldn't then. Nobody can."

"You made a good advance on it. Three days, lieutenant. I want him to talk."

Breath came short. "Do I get to beat it out of him?"

"Let's be serious, lieutenant."

"What am I supposed to be asking? Have I got a clearance to hear it? Or what happens when he *does* talk? What am I looking for?"

"As much as you can know—and it's not been released yet—there was an accident. Dekker wasn't in it. Friends of his were. Dekker's crew was lost."

"Oh shit."

"Top command subbed in another pilot with Dekker's crew on a test run. The test didn't go right. Total loss. Dekker was hospitalized, treated for shock. The day he got out—he either climbed into a simulator under the influence of drugs or something else happened. It's a matter of some interest—which."

Ben chewed his lip. Missile test, they'd said on Sol One.

Tech committee meetings. Place crawling with brass and VIPs. Hell. "So isn't there an access record?"

"Computers can be wrong. Can't they?"

Ben's heart rate picked up: he hoped to hell there wasn't a monitor hearing it. He tried to think of some scrap to hand Graff, for good will's sake. He finally said, "Yes. They can be."

"I want him functioning," Graff said. "Say you're on interservice loan—at high levels. It could be good. It could be bad. To take maximum advantage of that . . . you need to deliver." Graff pulled a thick envelope from his jacket and held it out to him. "He listed you next-of-kin. So you have a right to see this."

"I'm not his next-of-kin. He's got a mother—"

"She's specifically excluded. Don't worry. There's nothing in this packet outside your security clearance."

He took it. He didn't want to.

"I wouldn't leave that material lying about unattended," Graff said, "all the same. —You've got your quarters in hospital. I can't order you not to use the phone. But if you do, if you contact anyone else, do you understand me, you're not behind our screen any longer. Take my personal advice: get back to the hospital and stay there—and don't use that phone."

He looked at Graff a long, long moment. Lieutenant j-g. Carrier command officer. A tech/1 to a tech/2's rank. But he had the impression Graff was leaning on some executive and clandestine authority to do what he was doing. It was in Graff's tone, in the clear implication he should avoid his own chain of command.

"Whose office does this originate in, sir? You mind to tell me how official this is? Who's in charge?"

"Ultimately, the captain."

Two and two suddenly made four. Keu. Sol FSO. He looked Graff in the eyes and thought—I don't like this. Damn, I don't. He said,

"Is your captain the only authority that's covering me?"

Graff said, "No."

Conrad Mazian? The EC militia commander who was romancing his way through the UN hearings? "In which service, sir? I want to know. I need to know that. I want orders in writing."

"Ben. Take my word. I'd go back to quarters, immediately, if I were you. I'd stay quiet. I'd do everything I could to finish my job. If I were in your place." Graff opened the door, and shut off the lights. "If you need me, for any reason—tell Dr. Evans."

The keycard worked, at least. The room in the hospice was an institutional cubbyhole with a bunk, a phone, an ordinary flat-vid.

And no baggage.

Delivered, customs had said. Customs had showed him the slip. Delivered at 1500h. God only where.

He set down the soft drink he had carried up from level 1. He looked at his watch. 1845h.

He picked up the phone and went through hospital downside to call customs.

"This is Lt. Benjamin Pollard. I was just there. My baggage isn't here. Is it still being delivered?"

"Who did you talk to?"

He sat down on the bed. He pulled a vending machine sandwich from his pocket, laid it on the table by the soft drink, and pulled out the customs claim ticket. "The claim number is 9798."

A pause. *"It's been delivered, sir."*

"You didn't deliver it to HOS-28."

"That's what's on the ticket, sir."

"That's not what's in HOS-28, soldier. I want to know where my baggage is right now."

"That's all the record I have, sir. You could check with Lost Baggage at 0700."

"This shift doesn't find baggage, is that it? It just loses it?"

A moment of silence. *"I'll make a note of it, sir."*
"Thank you."

He punched out. He did not break the phone. He took a sip of his soft drink and unwrapped the sandwich.

No official assignment, no cafeteria open at this hour, no card with food privileges. He had fifty on him. Period. And Mr. Lieutenant j-g Jurgen Graff and his unnamed captain hadn't seen to that detail.

God, he didn't like the feeling he had. Bet that Graff *had* contacted Maj. Weiter? Hell if. Bet that the UDC knew where he was right now?

He looked at the phone and thought how he could call the UDC CO here. He could do that. He could break this wide open and maybe be a hero to the UDC—or get caught in the middle of something, behind a security screen that didn't have Stockholm anywhere inside it. A screen confined to *this* place. Right now he could plead total ignorance. Right now he had a transfer order signed by Keu and a Security stamp on it and he could plead he had regarded the order exactly the way it said in the Interservice Protocols. And he could do what they wanted and get out of here.

Dammit, he didn't know why Dekker was crazy. Anybody who wanted to fly little ships and get shot at was crazy. If even the simulator could half kill a guy—

He could have said get Dekker off the drugs. He could have said don't sedate him—but Dekker knew too much about him, damn him, Dekker knew enough to babble things that could end up on *his* record, if Dekker got to talking to the psych; and if Dekker had told certain things to Graff, God—Graff could have been sifting everything he had said against information he had no idea Graff had, and weighing it for truth. Graff could have had technical backup doing it, bigtime, interactive logic stuff you had no good chance to evade without a clearer head and a calmer pulse rate than he had had in that interview—

God only, what Dekker had involved himself in. Or why someone might have wanted Dekker dead.

Or what might happen if he picked up that phone right now and tried to get through to the UDC office—via hospital communications.

He didn't know enough about how the lines were drawn here. He didn't *want* to know enough. Do what Graff wanted and be on that shuttle on the 22nd, that was all. Any way he could. And if the UDC did land on him—spill everything immediately. Total innocence. No, sir, they showed me orders, they said it was cleared—

Somebody subbed a pilot on a test run? And somebody put Dekker into a simulator drugged out of his mind?

Bloody hell.

He pulled out the envelope, from inside his jacket. Opened it and pulled out cards and pictures, a couple of licenses and old IDs.

Flight certification. Picture of Dekker and three other people. Group shot. All in Fleet uniform. Woman and two guys besides Dekker. All smiling. Arms over each other's shoulders.

Old vid advert for a truly skuz sex item. God. We all have our secrets, Dek-lad, . . .

Picture of Sol Station. Picture of a couple of people outside a trans station. Picture of Mars Base from orbit. If there'd been any of Cory Salazar, Dekker had lost those, a long time ago.

Datacard. The phone had a reader, but he shoved the card into his own. Personal card showed vid rentals. Commissary charges. Postage charges. Bank records. Bits and pieces of Dekker's life since they'd parted company. Lad had 5300.87cc to his account and no debts. Not bad. Not rich either.

The other datacard was old notes and mail. Not much of it. Notes from various people. One letter months ago from Ingrid Dekker. Four, this last year from Meg Kady.

So Meg did write him. He would never have figured Meg for the letter-writing kind.

Would never have figured Meg for a lot else, either.

He keyed up Meg's last letter, scanned at random through what must have cost a Shepherd spacer a mint to send:

. . . can't complain. Doing fine. I'm working into the crew, got myself onto the pilot list . . .

Sal and I dropped into The Hole, just on a look-see. Maybe it's what we are now. Maybe it's just the place is duller. It doesn't feel the same—

So what does? he thought, and thought about Sal, and good times in the Hole's back rooms. But Sal Aboujib probably had herself a dozen guys on a string by now, swaggering about in rab cut and Shepherd flash, visiting pricey places like Scorpio's—if Scorpio's still existed. Sal had her a berth, had her a whole new class of guys to pick from. And Ben Pollard never had gotten a letter from Sal Aboujib. A hello from Dekker once, months ago. He'd said hello back. Only communication they'd had. And it was on here. *Hope you're doing all right. Everything fine.* Only longdistance letter he'd ever gotten, tell the truth. And what did you answer, to people you didn't want to be tied to? Good luck, goodbye, Dekker?

Bills. Note from one Falcone—*Dek, we don't like it either. But nothing we can do right now. They want a show. We'll sure as hell give them one.*

He skimmed back to the letter from Ingrid Dekker. A short one. *Don't come here. I don't want to see you. You went out there by your own choice and maybe it wasn't any of it your fault what happened, but things are hard enough, Paul, and I don't need any more trouble. Stop sending me money. I don't want any more ties to you. I don't want any more letters. Leave me alone.*

Shit.

He set the reader on his knee, gave a deep breath, thinking— Shit, Dek —He'd grown up on his parents' insurance himself, both of them having been so careless as to take the deep dive with their whole crew. At first he'd really resented them doing that, thought if they'd given a damn about their kid they wouldn't have been that careless, but he'd stared into Jupiter's well himself once—and he *knew* how subtle and sudden that slope was, in the pit of his stomach he knew it, now, and dreamed about it, on bad nights.

But his mama had never written him a letter like this one, and in that cold little spot marked Who's left to care, he guessed why Dekker might have written him as next-of-kin: Meg with her letters about how she was working into the crew and everything was going fine for her—Dekker wouldn't risk having another woman writing him, saying, Get out of my life, you skuz. Dekker already knew what Ben Pollard thought. And if Dekker was in trouble that needed a next-of-kin—whose life was he going to interrupt, who might remotely even know him?

He cut the reader off. He sat there in a cardboard cubby of a room with no damn baggage and for a moment or two had remorseful thoughts about Paul Dekker. Wished maybe he'd written a line or two more, back then, like—hell, he didn't know. Something polite.

What friggin' time is it?

Two *months* in a miner-ship with Dekker off his head asking him the time every few minutes. So here he was back there again—locked into a hospital with Dekker. One part of him felt sorry for Dekker and the other panicked part of him still wanted to beat hell out of the fool and get out of here. . . .

Dammit, what am I supposed to do with this damn card? Why didn't Graff give this stuff to the psych?

Sub in another pilot, did they? Why, if not Dekker's attitude? And *who* did it, if not the CO who's supposed to want this stuff from Dekker? Real brand-new ship, Dekker said once. That's why the Fleet had wanted him. He'd been real excited about it—wanted it more than anything in his life—

And a crew's dead and Dekker's screwed like that?

He sat there on the side of the bed desperately, urgently, wanting off Sol Two, he didn't at the moment care where. This whole deal had the stink of death about it.

Serious death, Sal would say.

No shit, Sal. What do I do with the guy?

CHAPTER

3

"MR. Graff, urgent word with you. Down the hall. Sir. Please."

0645 and the breakfast line in the green room was backed up to the door. Hardly time for coffee in the fifteen minutes before he was due in Tanzer's office and Jurgen Albrecht Graff punched white coffee instead of black for his stomach's sake. "Can it wait?" he asked without looking at Mitch, and caught the cup that tilted sideways and straightened it in time. Held it while it filled.

"No, sir. A number of us want to talk, sir. Urgent business."

Spit and polish. From Mitch. There was no one else in the rec nook of the mess hall and no reasonable chance of being overheard in the clatter of trays. "Tanzer wants to talk, too. I have an appointment in fifteen."

"Hell." Mitch was Shepherd, aggressively Shepherd, shaved up the sides, couple of earrings. Bracelet. "I swore you'd be there. Sir."

Graff lifted out the cup, said, "All right, five," and stole

a sip as he walked with Mitch out the main door and down
the hall to the conference rooms. Door to 6a was open.
Mitch's tech crew was there, Pauli and Jacoby, Jamil and
his longscanner, Trace. Graff recognized a delegation when
he saw it. Tanzer had said, Don't discuss the hearings.
Patently that was not the intention here.

Mitch shut the door. "Sir. We're asking you to get one of
us in front of the committee."

"Won't happen," Graff said. "No chance. You want to
get a haircut, Mitch?"

"Hell if."

"That's an Earth committee. Blue-sky as they come.
They won't communicate."

"Yeah," Jacoby said. "Is that why Tanzer killed Pete and
Elly? Couldn't let a Belter pull it off?"

"Ease off, Jacoby."

"They won't let us in hospital. You seen Dekker? You
seen him, lieutenant?"

Pauli muttered: "Wouldn't be surprised if Tanzer ordered
him put in that machine. Didn't want him at the hearings."

"Shut that down," Graff said. "Right now."

Mitch folded his arms, set a foot on a chair, and said,
"Somebody better hear it. They didn't want any Belter son
of a bitch in front of the cameras. Dekker couldn't fly it?
Then why didn't they sub the *crew*, ask them that!"

"Mitch, I hope somebody does have the brains to ask it.
But there's nothing I can do. They're not going to ask me
that."

"Hell if, sir! Tanzer's pets are killing us. You want me to
shave up like a—" Mitch looked at him—him and his
regulation trim, and shut the epithet off unsaid. "You get
me in front of that hearing and I'll look like a UDC
accountant."

"Mitch, I'm in a position."

"You're in a position. You're running safe behind shields—
sir. We're the ones with our ass on the line."

Pauli said: "And they can't automate these sumbitches any further. Why don't they ask somebody who knows?"

"The designers will. Staatentek's here. They'll ask. That much I'll get a chance to tell them."

"Ask 'em about the sim!"

Female voice: Trace. "They're not interested. This is going to be a whitewash start to finish."

"The designers have to talk to us, Trace. We'll get our word in."

Mitch said: "The *engineers* have to talk to us. The execs and the politicrats won't and they have the say."

"Mitch, I can't listen to this."

"Tanzer is a hidebound blue-skyer son of *a* bitch who thinks because he grew up with a rulebook up his ass is a reason to try to tell any spacer his business or to think that the salute-the-logo dumbasses they've pulled in off the Guard and the system test programs could do the job with these ships—"

"They can fly, Mitch."

"Yeah, they can fly. Like Wilhelmsen."

"Nothing *wrong* with Wilhelmsen. Listen to me— Shut it down, and listen: if we have a technical at work, we want to find it, we don't want to whitewash *that* either. We have something more at issue here than Wilhelmsen."

"Yeah," Pauli muttered. "Tanzer."

Mitch said, "Nothing wrong with that ship. Everything wrong with the pilot. And they aren't going to find the solution to what happened to Wilhelmsen in Tanzer's fuckin' *rulebook*. Sir."

"Let's just find out, shall we?"

"Just make the point with them, lieutenant: Wilhelmsen wasn't set with the crew. Wilhelmsen should have said not ready, *he* was the pilot, he had the final say-so, demo be damned. It was his *responsibility* to do that."

"Yes, it was his responsibility, but it wasn't in his judgment to do it, or he would have done it—the guy's dead. He got it the same as the rest, Mitch. Let's give the experts a chance to figure out what.''

''What chance have they got, if they're not getting the information? Their *experts* are blue-sky as Tanzer is!''

Jacoby said: ''It's the At-ti-tude in the UDC brass. They murdered Wilhelmsen and Wilhelmsen murdered that crew, that's what they need to hear!''

''All right! All right! But there's nothing I can do to get you in there right now, and if you act the fools and screw this, they'll pull those design changes and you'll be flying targets. Now leave it! Get off my tail! Give me a chance! *That's* the order. I've got a meeting.''

There was quiet. It wasn't a happy quiet. Graff handed the coffee to Mitch. ''You drink it.'' He started for the door in a dead silence and looked back. ''It's my life too, guys. You shit me, a carrier's gone. *Program's* gone. You understand that?''

They weren't used to hearing Helm Two talk like that. Not at all. There were sober faces.

Mitch said, ''No offense, lieutenant.''

Graff passed a hand over his close-cropped hair. Said, ''Hey, I have to deal with 'em, guys,'' and ducked out, with an uncomfortable feeling of being square in the middle— merchanter and neither Shepherd nor regular UDC. Not part of the rab the EC had exiled to the Belt, not part of the EC, either, in the sense the rab had resisted it—didn't even understand the politics in the '15, but he was getting to.

Fast.

They'd hauled the Shepherd pilots into the Program for their expertise. They weren't eighteen-year-olds, and they damned sure weren't anybody's boys. You didn't use that word with them. Didn't *lead* them, no way in hell. You fed them the situation and showed them where it was different from what they knew. You showed them the *feel* of it, and let it sink into their bones and they *showed* the interactive systems new ways to conceptualize. They designed a whole new set of controls around the Shepherds, and software to display what they saw in their insystem-trained heads.

Explain that to Col. Glenn Evan Tanzer, of UDC R&D. God, he wished the captain were back here, that *one* of the captains would turn up; Kreshov hadn't shown insystem for weeks; and exactly how it happened that one of the captains wasn't here at B Dock, at the same time a stray investigative subcommittee had outflanked Keu at Sol and gotten here unchecked—he didn't know. He couldn't even swear FleetCom was secure from the UDC code experts. Shepherds thought so, but he wouldn't commit any more to it than he had.

Not now. Not lately, in Sol System, where the enemy was mindsets that wouldn't understand the realities in the Beyond. The Belt was closer to The Beyond than it was to Earth.

And closer to it than Tanzer by a far shot. Always Tanzer—who'd been sitting here in R&D so long they dusted him.

0657. By the clock on the wall. He walked down the corridor, he walked into Tanzer's office, and Tanzer's aide said, "Go right in."

He did that. He saluted, by the book. Tanzer saluted, they stared at each other, and Tanzer said, "Lt. Benjamin J. Pollard. Does that name evoke memory?"

Shot across the bow. Graff kept all expression off his face. "Yes, sir. Friend of Dekker's. Listed next-of-kin on his card."

"Is that your justification for releasing those records to Sol?"

"Captain Keu's orders, sir. He sees all the accident reports."

"Is this your justification for issuing a travel voucher?"

"I didn't issue the travel voucher. Mr. Pollard's presence here isn't at my request."

"Lt. Graff, you're a hair-splitting liar, you're a trouble-maker and I resent your attitude."

"On the record, sir, I hardly think I can be held accountable—"

"That's what you think. You're sabotaging us, you're playing politics with my boys' lives, and you have no authorization to bring in any outsider or to be passing unauthorized messages outside this facility to other commands."

"That is my chain of command, sir. Dekker is my personnel, and Keu is my commanding officer. Sir. I notify him on all the casualties. What Captain Keu does is not in my control. And if the question arises, I will testify that in my opinion Dekker was not in that simulator by choice. Sir."

Tanzer's fist came down on the desk. "I'm in command of this facility, *Lt.* Graff. The fact that your commander saw fit to leave a junior lieutenant in command of the rider trainees and the carrier does not give you authority over any aspect of this operation, and it does *not* give you authority to issue passes or to take communications to anyone outside of BaseCom, *do you understand me?*"

"Where it regards your command, yes, colonel. But I'm responsible to Captain Keu for the communications he directly ordered me to make and which I will continue to make, on FleetCom. Lt. Pollard is here on humanitarian leave in connection with Fleet personnel. He's Prioritied elsewhere. He's here temporarily and he has adequate Security clearance to be here."

"He's also UDC personnel."

"He's under interservice assignment. On leave. And not available to R&D."

"A friend of Dekker's. Let me tell you, I've had a bellyful of your recruits, and I'm sick and tired of the miner riffraff and psychological misfits washing up on the shores of this program. Your own captain's interference with design has given this program a piece of junk that can't be flown—"

"Not true."

"—a piece of junk that works in the sims and not in the field, lieutenant, because it doesn't take into account human realities. That firepower can't be turned over to adrenaline-high games-playing freaks, Mr. Graff, and that machine can't rely on the 50%'ers on the sims—how many ships are you going to lose on that 50%? Four billion dollars per ship and the time to train the crew and you're going to gamble that on 50% of the time the pilot's nerves hold out for the time required? We're pushing human beings over *their* design limits, and they're dying, Mr. Graff, they're ending up in hospital wards.''

''Wilhelmsen didn't die of fatigue, colonel, he died of communications failure, he *died* of not working with his own crew. He schitzed—for one nanosecond he schitzed and forgot where in hell he was in his sequence. There's an interdict on that move—it's supposed to be in the pilot's *head*, and it failed, colonel, *he* failed, that's the bottom line. Dekker—''

''Dekker ran that same flight on sim and he's lying delirious in hospital. Don't let me hear you use that word schitz again, lieutenant, except you apply it to *your* boy. There's the problem in that crew. There's the troublemaker that had to prove his point, had to shoot his mouth off—''

''Dekker didn't run that sim. And the word is *concussion*, colonel. From the impact of an unsecured body in that pod. He didn't *forget* to belt in.''

''He was suited up.''

''The flightsuits keep your *feet* from swelling, colonel: Dekker's been exposed to prolonged zero *g*. The other crews say—''

''He was up there on drugs, lieutenant! Read the medical report! He was high on trank, he was in possession of a tape he had no business with, and he and his attitude got in that pod together, let's admit what happened up there and quit trying to put Dekker's smartass maneuver off on any outside agency. There wasn't one.''

''I intend to find out what did happen.''

''Do you? Do you? Let me lay this word in your lap: either you come up with proof that'll stand up in court martial, or this investigation is closed. Dekker climbed into that pod on drugs, because he has an Attitude the same as all the other misfits this facility's been loaded with, he believes he's cornered the market on right, he's a smartass who thinks his reflexes make up for his lack of discipline, and if you drop that chaff in the hearing you won't like the result. If you want this program to fly, and I assume you do, then you'd better reflect very soberly what effect your appearance and your testimony this afternoon is going to have on your captain's credibility—on the credibility of your service and the judgment of its personnel. Don't speculate. Keep to the facts."

"The facts are, Dekker saw what was happening, he called the right moves. It's on the mission control tape. . . ."

"You're so damned cocksure what your boys can do, mister, but it's easy to call the right moves when you're not the one in the pilot's seat. *You* won't sit those controls. *You* won't fly those ships. *Will you?*"

Fair question, except they'd been over that track before. "That's exactly the point. I'm not synched to a rider crew. Cross-training would risk both ships."

"The truth is, lieutenant, your *Fleet* doesn't want its precious essential personnel flying a suicide ship, your Fleet won't let go of its hare-brained concept before it stinks. Your Conrad Mazian isn't a ship designer, he isn't an engineer, he's a merchant captain in a ragtag militia trying to prove it's qualified for strategic decisions. This ship needs interdicts on a pilot that's stressing out."

"That ship needs its combat edge, colonel. If Wilhelmsen had had an AI breathing down his neck he'd have had one more thing on his mind: Is the damned thing going to take my advice or not? At what mission-critical split second that I happen to be right is it going to cut me out of the loop? You can't cripple a ship with a damned know-it-all robot snatching control away because the pilot pushed the g's for a reason that, yes, might be knowingly suicidal, for a reason that wasn't in the mission profile. Besides which, longscan's after you, and what are you going to do, give a Union longscanner a hundred percent certainty an AI's going to interdict certain moves? If he knows your cutoffs, he knows your blind spots. If he knows you can't push it and he can, what's he going to do, colonel?''

"When the physiological signs are there, you're going to lose that ship, that's a hundred percent certainty, and nobody else is going to be exceeding that limit.''

"Wilhelmsen was leaning hard on the Assists. He could have declined that one target, that's inside the parameters, that's a judgment a rider's going to have to make. But he'd have looked bad for the senators. He wanted that target. That's an Attitude. There's a use for that in combat. Not for a damned exhibition.''

"Wilhelmsen was saving the program, lieutenant, saving *your* damned budget appropriation, in equipment that's got six men in the hospital and seventeen dead. You don't push machines or human beings past the destruct limit, and you don't put equipment out there that self-destructs on a muscle-twitch. The pilot was showing symptoms. The AI should have kicked him out of the loop right then, but it can't do that, you say he can't have it breathing down his neck—a four-billion-dollar missile with a deadman's switch, that's what you've got—it needs an integrative AI in there—''

"Watch the pilots cut it off. Which you can't do with that damned tetralogic system you're talking about, it's got to be in the loop talking to the interactives constantly, and no matter the input it got after, its logic systems are exactly the same as the next one's, same as the ships are. The only wildcard you've got is the humans, the *only* thing that keeps the enemy longscanners guessing. The best machine you've got can't outguess the human longscanner—why should you assume they're going to outperform the pilot?''

"Because the longscanner can't kill the crew.''

"The hell he can't!''

"Not in that sense.''

"Your tests don't simulate combat. That's what we've

been telling you—you keep concentrating on the fire rate, always the damned fire rate and you're not dealing with the reason we recruited these particular crews. Nobody at Lendler Corp has been in combat, none of your pilots have been, the UDC hasn't been, since it was founded—your tests are set up wrong!''

Not saying Tanzer himself hadn't been in combat. Red in the face, Tanzer got a breath. ''Let's talk about exceeding human limits, lieutenant: what happened out there was *exactly* why we've got men in hospital over there who can't walk a level floor without staggering, it's why we've had cardiac symptoms in men under thirty, and those *aren't* from four-hour runs.'' A jab of the finger in his direction. ''Let me tell you, lieutenant, I've met the kind of attitude your command is fostering among the trainees. Show-outs and ego-freaks. And I wish them out of my command. You may have toddled down a deck in your diapers, and so may Mazian's ragtag enlistees out of the Belt, but how are you going to teach them anything when they already know it all and you acquired your know-how by superior genes? You can't lose 50% of your ships and crews at every pass. 96% retrievability, wasn't that the original design criterion? Or isn't that retrievability word going to be in the manual when we put this ship on the line?''

''If a Union armscomper gets your numbers you have zero retrievability, colonel, that's my point. You have to exceed your own numbers, you have to surprise your own interfaces in order to surprise that other ship's computers and that means being at the top of the architecture of your Adaptive Assists. The enemy knows your *name* out there. Union says, That's *Victoria*, that's Fitzroy or Graff at Helm, because *Victoria* wouldn't go in with Helm Three. They know you and they know your style, and it's in their double A's, but you innovate and they innovate. One AI sitting on top of the human and his interfaces is like any other damn AI sitting on top of the interfaces—there aren't that many models, the enemy knows them all, and the second its logic signature develops in the enemy's intelligence about you, hell, they'll have a fire-track lying in wait for you.''

"Then you'd better damn well improve your security, hadn't you?''

"Colonel, there are four manufacturers in friendly space for this tetralogic equipment and we can't swear there's not an Eye sitting right outside the system right now. Any merchanter who ever came into system could have dropped one, before the embargo, and it's next to impossible to find it. Merchanters are your friends and your enemies: that's the war the Company made, and that's what's going on out there—they don't all declare their loyalties and a lot of them haven't got any, not them and not us. They'll find out the names. They'll find out the manufacturers and the software designers. They'll learn us. That's a top priority—who's at Helm and who's in command, and if it's even one in four brands of tetralogic—''

"All the more reason for interchangeable personnel.''

"It doesn't work that way! You don't go into an engagement with anybody who just happens to be on watch. You *try* to get your best online. No question. You don't trade personnel and you don't trade equipment. You haven't time at .5 light coming down off jump to think about what ship you're in or what crew you're with. I'm telling you, colonel, my captain has no wish to raise the substitution as an issue against your decisions, but on his orders, as judiciously as I can, I am going to make the point that it was a critical factor. We can*not* integrate a computerized ship into our operations. In that condition it *is* no better than a missile.''

"You haven't the credentials to say what it is and isn't, lieutenant. You're not a psychiatrist and you're not a computer specialist.''

"I am a combat pilot. One of two at this base.''

A cold, dark silence. "I'll tell you—if you want to raise issues this afternoon, I'm perfectly willing to make clear to the committee that you're a composite, lieutenant, a *shell* steered by non-command personnel and an absentee captain, and you clearly don't have the administrative experience to handle your own security, much less speak with expert knowledge on systems you've never seen. I've held this office for thirty years, I've seen all sorts of games, and your commanding officer's leaving that carrier to subordinates and your own abuse of your commanding officer's communications privileges is an official report in *my* chain of command. This is *not* the frontier, this is *not* a bare-based militia operation, and if your service ever hopes to turn these trainees into competent military personnel you can start by setting a personal example. Clean up your own command and stop fomenting dissension in this facility!''

"I do *not* accept that assessment."

"Then you can leave this office. And if you are called on to testify, you'll be there as one of the pilots personally involved in the accident, not as a systems expert. You'd be very unwise to push past that position—or you'll find questions raised that could be damned embarrassing to your absentee superior and your entire service. I'm talking about adverse publicity, if you give grounds to any of these senators or to the high command. Do you understand that? Because I won't pull any punches. And the one security no one can guarantee is a senator's personal staff.''

"Are you attempting to dictate my testimony, colonel? Is that what I'm hearing?''

"In no wise. Give my regards to your captain. Good *day*, lieutenant.''

Something had come loose. Banging. The tumble did that. Dekker reached after the cabinet, tried to get to the com.

Hand caught his arm. Something shoved him back and he hit pillows.

Bang from elsewhere.

"Hey, Dek. You want eggs or pancakes?''

He couldn't figure how Ben had gotten onto the ship. Ben had rescued him. But he didn't remember that.

"Eggs or pancakes?"

"Eggs aren't real," he said. "Awful stuff."

"They're real, Dek-boy. Not to my taste, living things, but they're real enough to upset *my* stomach. Eggs, you want? Orange juice?"

He tried to move. Usually he couldn't. But his arms were free. He stuffed pillows under his head and Ben did something that propped the head up. Ben went out in the hall and came back and set a tray down on the table, swung it over him.

"Eat it. That's an order, Dek-boy."

He picked up a fork. It seemed foreign, difficult to balance in .9 *g*. His head kept going around. His arm weighed more than he remembered and it was hard to keep his head up. But he stabbed a bit of scrambled egg and got a bite down. Another. He reached for the orange juice but Ben did it for him, took a sip himself beforehand and said, "We got better at Sol One."

Maybe it was. Maybe he was supposed to know that. Ben held the cup to his lips and he sipped a little of it. It stung cuts in his mouth and it hit his stomach with a sugar impact.

"Keep it up, Dek-boy, and they'll take that tube out."

He didn't know there was a tube. Didn't know how Ben had gotten here. Or where they were now. Didn't look like the Hole at all. Didn't look like R2 hospital. He reached after the fork, took another tentative nibble at the eggs. God, he was weak.

"Where's Bird?" he asked.

"What year is it, Dek-boy? I warned you there'd be a test this morning."

He shut his eyes. Opened them and Ben was still there. In this room. He recalled something like that. Ben was going to beat hell out of him if he missed.

"2324."

"Good boy. Have some more oj."

"Can't." His stomach suddenly felt queasy, when he thought about that number. Number had to be wrong. He waved the cup away and watched Ben drink it.

Ben, in a UDC uniform.

He was going crazy. It was 2324. Ben didn't belong here.

Ben said, "You remember Meg and Sal?"

"Yeah. Sure."

"Meg writes to you, doesn't she?"

"Yeah, sometimes."

"Real love affair."

"We're friends."

"Yeah," Ben said. "You looked it when you said good-bye. Remember saying goodbye?" He took an envelope out of his pocket. Held up a handful of cards and pictures. "Remember these?"

He'd seen them before. They'd lied to him, the doctors had. They made all these things up. They told him they were his, he'd thrown them across the room.

Now Ben had them. Ben held up a picture of him with people he didn't remember and he couldn't look at.

"What are their names?"

He shook his head.

"Woman's Elly?"

The name jolted. Elly was dead. Pete and Falcone.

"Pete?"

Guy on the right. Big grin. Pete smiled like that. Pete had his arm over the shoulder. But he couldn't remember the photo.

"Which one's Pete?"

"I don't know." But it was a lie. Ben just didn't belong with them. Everything was scrambled. Cory and Ben and Bird. He was afraid Meg was going to be in that picture if he went on looking at it.

Blood. Exploding everywhere. Beads floating, fine mist.

He squeezed his eyes shut. The eggs didn't sit well at his stomach. Everyone in that picture was dead. He was in there too.

"Who's the other guy?"

"Falcone."

"Said not to worry about him. Didn't he? Left you a note? You remember?"

He shook his head. He shoved the table away, tried to get up. Ben pushed him back against the pillows and a stabbing pain went through his skull.

He grayed out for a moment. When he came back Ben was quietly finishing his toast. Ben said, "You ready to talk now?"

The cup hit the grid. Sideways. Two out of five. Graff lifted the cover up and righted it before the coffee hit, collected his overdue morning caffeine and turned in the general noise of the end of breakfast, straight into Villy's intercept.

UDC Flight Chief. *Captain* Alexandro Villanueva—senior test pilot for the UDC, who said, all friendly, "Hear you and the old man went one this morning."

Fast. Must have ricocheted off Tanzer's wall, Graff thought, and shrugged in mid-sip while Villanueva stuck his card in the slot and punched up a coffee. He said, "We differed."

Villanueva rescued his cup. "Damn thing."

"Ever since they changed the cups."

Villanueva took the coffee out and let the cover drop, said, quietly, "You know, back when we were doing the A-89, we had one of these runs of trouble. Lost twelve guys in six months. The old man just sat in that office and filled out the reports: you never saw him crack—but it broke him up. Same now. He wants to pull this program out. But we've got to come out of this with an answer. A right answer."

"Redesign isn't it." He got on well enough with Villanueva. Villanueva had started out calling him son—never did think he'd quite gotten the man out of the mindset. Gray hair on Captain Villy, legitimately come by, rumor had it: handful of crack-ups and a few pieces of luck—if dealing with Tanzer daily didn't do it. They kept trying to promote him to a desk, God only wish he'd get Tanzer's post and run the whole program, not just test ops—but Villy kept on making test runs himself, one of the UDC pilots who had real respect among the Shepherds.

"Graff," Villanueva said, "dammit, we're vulnerable on this project, we're real vulnerable. Politicians are gathering like sharks. I know the old man's hard to deal with. But let's not hang the differences out in plain sight today."

He thought about Mitch. About the frustration among the Shepherds, who wanted to fight Tanzer. And that did no good. "They won't likely ask me anything but where I was, where the targets were. That's all in the electronic record. Cut and dried, isn't that the expression for it?"

Villanueva stood there a moment. Just looking at him. He expected Villanueva to say something in answer, but instead Villanueva walked off with his coffee and didn't look back.

Maybe he should have given more back. Used a different expression. Read the signals otherwise. He didn't dislike the man, God knew he didn't dislike him. The man had been trying to say something, but somehow in the inevitable screw-ups between blue-skyer and spacer—he had the feeling the signals had gotten fuzzed.

Villanueva went over to a table with his own men. Sat down. Graff walked over to the other side, where a couple of the Fleet's own gray heads inclined together. Demas and Saito. Nav One and Com One—no credence at all to the Equivalencies that the Fleet had had settled on them. *Commdr.* Demas, as happened. But Nav One meant it was Demas did the major share of the course plots, with the backing of eighteen techs interfacing with scan and longscan at any given instant, which meant that a prototype carrier on a test run knew so precisely where it was and where everything else was that a Lt. j-g at Helm couldn't screw up if he worked at it.

Except with a wrong word to the UDC R&D chief.

"Think I just picked a wrong word with Villy. Does 'cut and dried' describe what they're going to ask at the hearings?"

Com One said, her almond eyes half-lidded, "Probably. 'Rigged' might too. On, is the man?"

Demas said, "A lot On. Deep in. Drink your coffee, Helm. Present for you." Demas laid a bolt on the table. Fat one.

Damn. "What is that?"

"That, J-G, is a bolt. It was lying next the wall in a dark little recess in the carrier's main corridor. Where the construction crew just installed the number eighteen pressure seal."

Thing was good as a bullet lying there. "I want to see the count sheet. I want the last crew that worked in there. Damn those fools!"

"Station labor. Gravitied brains. What do you ask?"

Ben said, "You remember Graff?"

"Yeah," Dekker said.

"What do you remember?"

"The trip out from the Belt. Here."

"Good boy. Where are we?"

"Sol Two," he said. Ben told him so. He had to believe what Ben told him: Ben was the check he had asked for, Ben was what he got and he had to believe everything Ben told him—he told himself that, this morning. Ben showed him pictures and showed him letters in the reader, that he remembered reading. The ones from Meg, the note from Falcone, the morning—

The morning they pulled him off the demo and put somebody else in.

Nothing you can do, Falcone had written. Left the note on the system. Came back like a ghost—after the accident. After—

"You remember where the sims are?"

"Which ones?"

"You tell me."

He felt tired, wrung out. He lay back in the pillows and said, "Couple downside. They're all the procedurals." Tried to think of exact words and remembered Ben was a licensed pilot too. "Ops stuff—stuff you need your reflexes for—it's in the core."

"Null-*g* stuff."

"Null-*g* and high-*g*." His eyes wanted to drift shut. His mind went around that place as if it were a pit. He could see the chamber in the null-*g* core, the sims like so many eggs on mag-lev tracks, blurring in motion. Lot of *g*'s when they were working. . . .

"When's the last time you remember using the sims in the core?"

Difficult question for a moment. Then not so hard. "Watch before the test. Wilhelmsen and I—"

"Wilhelmsen."

"He was my backup."

"Friend of yours?"

Difficult to say. "Chad . . ."

"Wilhelmsen?"

He nodded, eyes shut. "Son of a bitch, but he was all right. Didn't dislike him. We got along."

"So they subbed him in. You watch the test?"

He didn't know. Completely numb now. But the monitor on the shelf was showing higher points to the green line.

"You went into shock. They put you in hospital."

Wasn't the way he remembered. Wasn't sure what he did remember, but not that shock was the reason. No. He hadn't seen it.

"They give you drugs in the hospital?"

He nodded. He was relatively sure of that.

"Give you a prescription when you left?"

"Dunno."

"They say they did."

"Then I guess they did."

"You guess. Were you still high when you left the hospital? Did you have drugs with you?"

"I don't remember."

"What time of day was it?"

"Don't remember, Ben, I don't remember." But something was there, God, a flare on the vid, a light the cameras couldn't handle. Plasma. Bright as the sun. Pete and Elly, and Falcone and the ship.

"You all right?" The monitor was beeping. "—No! Let him alone. It's all right! Leave him the hell alone."

Orderly was trying to intervene. He opened his eyes and looked toward the door, trying to calm his pulse rate, and Ben leaned over and put his hand on his shoulder. Squeezed hard.

"You get in that sim by yourself?"

"I don't know."

"Somebody put you there?"

"I don't know. I honestly don't know, Ben. I just can't remember."

"Come *on*, Dek, *think* about it. You got into the core. You remember that? You had to get that far. What happened then?"

He shook his head. He kept seeing dark. Flashing lights. Green lines and gold. Heard Cory saying, Nothing you can do, Dek, nothing you can do . . .

They were back in The Hole. In his room behind the bar. Had a drawerful of pills. . . .

He put a hand over his eyes, then stared at the ceiling and looked over at Ben again to be sure where he was and when he was. But the black kept trying to come back and the lines twisted and moved.

'Driver ship, a k long. Loads of rock going to the Well at tremendous *v*.

Cory was dead. Dead a long time. So was Bird. He thought that Bird was dead. Fewer and fewer things were coming loose and drifting.

He pressed his hands over his eyes until it made sparks of color in the dark of virtual space. Red. Phosphenes. Was that what they said the lights were?

Spinning, of a sudden. He grabbed the bed.

Ben said, "God, watch it!"

Something was beeping. Ben said, to someone at the door, "He had a dream, that's all."

"Want you there this afternoon," Graff said to his Nav One; and to Saito. Saito said,

"This won't be like our procedures. An answer-what's-asked. This is Earth. Don't mistake it."

Graff took a sip of cooling coffee. "I couldn't. The old man hasn't sent us a hint, except Pollard, and Pollard doesn't know anything. I don't know if that's a signal to raise that issue or not—but I can't understand the silence. Unless the captain's leaving me to take the grenade. Which I'd do. Little they could do anyway but transfer me back. But he should tell me."

"No grenades," Demas said. "—No chance of Dekker talking?"

"Pollard's honestly trying. All I know."

"You sure he's the captain's? He could be Tanzer's."

Graff remembered something he'd forgotten to say, gave a short laugh. "Pollard's a native Belter."

"You're serious. Tanzer knows it?"

"Knows he's a friend of Dekker's. That has him the devil in Tanzer's book. What's more, this Belter claims he's a Priority 10 tracked for Geneva."

Demas' brows went up.

Graff said, "Bright. Very bright. Computers. Top security computers."

"Tanzer can't snag a Priority like that."

Saito said, "Not without an authorization. I doubt Tanzer can even access that security level to realize what he is."

"The captain set up Pollard with a room in the hospital. I told him to stay to it and Dekker's room and keep his head down. With a security clearance like that, he understands what quiet means, I think. He's got an appointment waiting for him—if he can get out of here before he becomes a priority to Tanzer."

"You signal him?"

"Every word I could prudently use. There were some I didn't. Maybe I should have. But he's UDC. You don't know where it'll go, ultimately."

"No remote chance on Dekker?"

"No chance on this one. Too much to ask. They've requested the log. They're going to ask questions on the carrier—they'll want to ask questions about the trainees. But they won't talk to them. They're not scheduled. Trainees don't talk to the EC. Trainees they're designing those ships around don't talk to the committee because the committee is only interested in finding a way that doesn't admit we're right. Another schitzy AI. Another budget fight."

"The Earth Company makes a lot of money on ship-building," Demas said. "Does that thought ever trouble your sleep?"

"It's beginning to."

The captain wanted to bust Demas up to a captaincy. Demas insisted he was staying with Keu. The argument was still going on. The fact was Demas hated administration and claimed he was a tactician, not a strategist, but Demas saw things. Good instincts, the man had.

Saito said, quietly: "Committee will be predominantly male, predominantly over fifty, and they won't understand why the captain didn't leave Fitz in charge and take me and Demas with him. *That's* what you're dealing with."

Fitzroy, Helm One, was answering questions for the committee at Sol One. Graff said, glumly: "Tanzer's threatening to make an issue out of *their* command rules."

Demas shook his head. "Let him make it. That'll get me to the stand surer than the nav stats would. And I don't think he wants that."

One could wish. But one couldn't get technical with the legislative types. With the engineers, yes. "They'd talk to

Demas. But the engineers couldn't talk policy to the legislators. Couldn't get through their own management."

"I keep having this feeling they're going to blindside us."

"You'll handle it. No question. Easy done."

Keu's silence was overall the most troublesome thing. Graff finished off his coffee, took the bolt and pocketed it. "Paperweight. Every paperpusher should have one. —Tell the construction boss I want to talk to him, in my office, right now."

"Ought to give him the thing at max v," Demas said.

"When we find the foreman who faked the parts count— I'd be willing." Graff headed for the door, tossed his cup in the collection bin.

Ben was back. Ben had been in the hall a while. Ben sat down with his chair close to the bed, put his hand on his shoulder.

"How're you doing, Dek?"

"All right."

"You were remembering, you know that? Pete and Elly? You remember that?"

Ben scared him. "I was dreaming. Sorry, Ben." If he was dreaming he could be in the Belt. Or the ship. But Ben shook at his shoulder and said,

"Dek, how did you get in the sim? What were you doing in there? I got to get out of here. I got twelve hours, Dek."

Sim chamber. Pods spinning around and around. Racket. Echoes. Everything tried to echo. And Ben said he had twelve hours. He didn't want Ben to leave. Ben came and Ben went, but as long as he knew there was a chance of Ben being there he knew what he was waking up to.

He said, "It's June 20th, isn't it? Isn't it, Ben?"

Ben took a fistful of hospital gown, under his chin, and said, "Dekker, remember what fucking happened. I got to be on that shuttle. It's my *life* at stake, you copy?"

He tried. Ben let him go, smoothed the covers, patted his

shoulder. Didn't ask him anything for a moment. Ben was upset and he earnestly tried to pull the sim chamber out of the dark for Ben. But it wasn't there.

Just that fireball. Second sun. They said it wasn't Wilhelmsen's fault. Maybe it wasn't. You died when you overran your limits.

"Target," he said. Ben said, "What?"

He said, "Target. Missed one. . . ."

CHAPTER

4

THE hearing was set up in A 109, not the biggest of the classrooms—dressed up with tables and a couple of UDC guards with sidearms—to do what, Graff asked himself bitterly, shoot down anybody who'd tell the truth out of turn?

Limited seating, they called it. No public access. That meant the workmen and the mechanics that worked for the EC, the vendors and the man who sold meat pies on 3-deck were barred, and those of them with security clearances still had to pass metal detectors. It meant that any military personnel showed if the committee knew they existed, and sent them passes: that meant ranking officers and the few like himself whose names were on the duty list the hour of the disaster. But there were passes issued for aides and for official representatives of the several services. And that meant the Fleet had Saito and Demas.

And the Shepherd trainees had Mitch and Jamil. They'd taken off the jewelry, taken off the earrings—couldn't hide Jamil's tattoos, but Jamil's single strip of black hair was braided tight against his scalp, and both of them were as regulation as the Shepherds could manage.

There were the various heads of department, maintenance chiefs, the ones who had security clearances. There was a big carrier schematic on one screen, others showing details of the docking ports. And an undetailed model on the table. Just the flat saucer shape. Manta shape, the blue-skyers called it. He'd seen a picture of the sea-dwelling creature and he saw why. Thin in one aspect to present minimum profile to fire or to high-v dust when it needed, broad and flat to accommodate the engines and the crew, and to lie snug against a carrier's frame.

Black painted model. The real thing was grayer, reflective ceramic. But they didn't advertise the coating. Thirty crew aboard when, please God, they got past the initial trials, thirty crew, mostly techs, mostly working for the longscanner. Core crew was four. The essential stations. The command personnel. The ones whose interfaces were with the active ship controls and the ones they had to risk in the tests.

The carrier dropped into a star-system and launched the riders—trusting that realspace ships, launched like missiles, with more firepower than ability to maneuver at v, could do their job and make a carrier's presence-pattern a far, far more diffuse element for an enemy's longscan computers.

And trusting the human mind could keep going for four hours on intermittent hyperfocus at that v with no shields, only a constantly changing VR HUD display and a fire-power adequate to take out what threatened it—if reactions were still hair-triggered after that length of time immersed in virtual space; if human beings still had consistent right reactions to a dopplered infostream of threat and non-threat and every missile launched and potentially launched. A longscan of a fractional c firefight looked like a plaid of intersecting probabilities, overlaid cones or tri-dee fans depending on your traveling viewpoint; and you overran conventional radar, even orders from your carrier: all you had was calc, com, and emissions.

Put an Artificial Intelligence above the human in the decision loop? Use a trained pilot for no more than resource to his own Adaptive Assist systems, with no power to override? Like hell. Sir.

He took a seat next to Demas and Saito, he cast a look down the row at Mitch and Jamil, and let the corner of his mouth tighten, surreptitious acknowledgment of their effort at diplomacy.

The committee filed in. Over fifty, Saito had said, and all male. Not quite. But the balance of the genders was certainly tilted. There were a handful of anxious execs from the designers and military contractors, from Bauerkraftwerke, who had designed the rider frame and some of the hardware; Lendler Corp, simulator software; Intellitron, which produced the longscan for both carriers and riders; Terme Aerospatiale, which did the Hellburner engines; and Staatentek, responsible for integrative targeting systems, computers and insystem communications. All of which could be pertinent. Lendler and Intellitron and Terme Aerospatiale were all Earth Company, but God only knew what side they were on. They'd doubtless been talking up the military examiners since last night: there'd been a UDC briefing.

"That's Bonner," Saito whispered, indicating a white-haired shave-headed UDC officer. Gen. Patrick Bonner, Graff understood. Tanzer's direct CO. Ultimate head over R&D, not a friend. And what was he saying to an EC contractor, both of them smiling and laughing like old friends?

People got to their seats. Bonner gave a speech, long and winding, a tactic, Graff thought, designed to stultify the opposition. Or perhaps his own troops. Not here to fix blame, Bonner said. Here to determine what happened and what caused it.

Introductions. Graff found himself focusing on the walls, on the topographic details of Bonner's receding hairline, the repeating pattern in the soundproofing, on the nervous fingers of the rep from Bauerkraftwerke, which tapped out a quiet rhythm on the table.

Statement of positions: Bauerkraftwerke insisted there was no structural flaw, that its engineers had reconstructed the accident and there was nothing to do with failure of the frame or the engines. Terme Aerospatiale agreed. Lendler said its simulation software wasn't at fault. Staatentek, the patent holder of the local AI tetralogic, maintained that the random ordnance software, the communications, the targeting software, had not glitched. Nobody was at fault. Nothing was wrong.

But a redesign in favor of the tetralogic control couldn't be ruled out.

Bangs and thumps again. "Ben?" Dekker called out. Ben had said he would be there. But he waked up in a corridor, on a gurney, with restraints he didn't remember deserving. "Ben!"

A nurse patted his shoulder and said, "It's all right, your friend's just outside."

He hated it when the illusions started agreeing with him. He lay still then, listening to the rattle and clatter. Someone said, from over his head, "We're going to take you in now," and he didn't know where. He yelled, "Ben! Ben!" And somebody said, "Better sedate him."

"No," he yelled. "No." And promised them, "You don't need to."

"Are you going to be all right?" they asked him.

"Yeah," he said, and lay there getting his breath. But there was a whine of hydraulics and a clank, and they shoved him into a tube, telling him: "You have to stay absolutely still . . ."

Like a spinner tube, it was. Like back in the belt, in the ship. He lay still the way they told him, but it got harder and harder to breathe.

Flash of light. Like the sun. He heard a beeping sound that reminded him—that reminded him—

"Elly—Elly, Wilhelmsen, don't reorient, screw it, *screw it*, you're past—"

"He's panicking," someone said.

He screamed, at the top of his lungs, *"Wilhelmsen, you damned fool—"*

Fifteen-minute recess. Break for restrooms and the corridor and the hospitality table.

Mitch moved close enough to say, "They're dithering, sir."

Graff said, "Ease down. Not here."

"They're saying it can't be flown. That's a damn lie."

"Ease down, Mitch. Nothing we can do out here." He had Saito at his elbow. He could see Tanzer down the hall with Bonner, in hot and heavy discussion.

Demas came back from the phone in the office. Said: "A word in private."

Graff said, "Mitch. Be good," and took Saito with him, farther up the hall. "You get him?"

"Couldn't get hold of Pollard. Talked to Higgins. The neurosurgeon wanted to run another brain scan. Higgins and Evans agreed. Dekker went off the edge, he's under sedation. Higgins says he remembers the accident. Nothing further. He may never be able to remember how he got in that pod."

"Damn."

"You've got to tell it plain, Helm."

"Break it wide open? We don't know what the captain wants. We don't know and if it were safe to use FleetCom he would."

Saito said, "It can't be worse. At this point I'd advise going past protocol. Worst we can do is alienate Bonner and a few handpicked legislators who came out here with him. This is a set-up. But it has records. The contractors are here defending their systems. And there may be a few line-straddlers in the senatorial party."

That was a point. Bonner was already alienated. This was

likely a breakaway group of legislators Bonner favored putting in here to hear what Tanzer put together—but the fact that they let him talk at all was either a try at getting something incriminating out of him; or maybe, maybe there were members of the group that wanted more than one view.

"God only knows what we're dealing with. No Pollard, no Dekker. It's a small hand we're playing. All right. I'll tell Mitch. Wraps are off."

Past lunch and beyond, and Ben paced the waiting room. He'd read all the damned articles available to the reader, he'd become grudgingly informed in the latest in microbiologic engineering, the pros and cons of seasonally adjusted light/dark cycles and temperature in station environments, the ethics of psychological intervention, and the consequences of weather adjustment in the hurricane season to the North American continent, not to mention five posture checks for low-g workers. He'd occupied himself making changes in a program he had stored on his personal card, he'd been four times at least to Dekker's room to see if he was out from under sedation—he'd lost count. You could hear the clangor and rattle of lunch trays being collected—they had a damned lot of hurt and sick people in here, people that had let a welder slip or gotten in the way of a robot loader arm, one guy who'd taken a godawful number of volts closing a hydraulic switch—he heard the gossip in the corridors coming and going, he was saturated with hospital gossip on who was missing what and how the guy with peritonitis was doing today and what was the condition of the limb reattachment in 109?

While the orderlies were having lunch.

Another trip out to Dekker's room. Can't wake him, Higgins said. We've gotten the blood pressure down now. But he's tired. He's just tired—

"I've got a shuttle pulling out tonight—tell the lieutenant I've done everything I can do. I want to see him. I've got to get out of here."

Higgins said, "He's involved in a hearing this afternoon. I don't know if I can reach him. I've left two messages with his office."

"The hell! Doctor, my luggage is still lost, I'm out of money for the damn vending machines—I never got a cafeteria authorization and I'm sick of potato chips—I never asked to come here, Dekker and I never were friends, dammit, I don't know why I'm his keeper!"

Higgins lent him five. Which wasn't the answer he wanted, but it was lunch, at least, and he wasn't going to offend Higgins by turning it down. Supper, he wasn't even going to think about.

Tanzer's turn with the mike. Nobody from the Fleet on the panel and no chance, Graff thought, of doing anything about that, except refusing to allow Fleet personnel to testify and trying to make an issue of it—but he was in a Position on that too, being one of the people on the list to testify; and he hoped the sweat didn't show.

Demas' advice, Saito's, Armsmaster Thieu's, for that matter, who might be called, was unanimous, and that it agreed with his only confirmed that if he was wrong and if he screwed this, the Fleet had to push him out the lock as a peace offering. That was one thing. He understood that kind of assignment.

But the thought that he could screw things beyond recall, offend the wrong senator, say something the media could get hold of and kill the riderships or bring the Fleet under UDC control—either of which would kill any hope of preventing the whole Beyond being sucked into Union's widening influence—that was the possibility that had his hands sweating and his mind chasing random imaginations throughout Tanzer's performance: he kept thinking, I've got to counter that; and, I've got to get that across to the committee, and, God, they're not going to ask me the right questions.

No way Bonner's going to let me answer those questions. The general's no fool. There's something he's got planned, some grenade planted and ticking, only where is it? With Tanzer?

Tanzer was saying: "It's the task of this facility to evaluate prototype systems and to take them to the design limits. The essential step before we risk human life is advanced, exacting interactive assist simulation. The second step is automated performance testing. And again, the simulations are revised and refined, and procedures and checklists developed in hours of Control Integration Trials, a process with which many of our distinguished panel are intimately familiar. They are also aware that in the world of high-velocity craft we are exceeding human capacities to cope with the infostream. We've overrun human reaction time. We've long since overrun conventional radar. Hence the neural net AA, which adapts and shapes itself threefold, for the pilot's past performance, enemy's past, pilot's current behaviors—and the longscan technique that extrapolates and displays an object's probability. We've developed dopplered communications and communications techniques to receive information faster than human senses can sort it, computer assemblies to second-guess the pilot on multiple tasks. The faster we go, the more the pilot becomes an integral component of the systems that filter information via his senses and the Adaptive Assists into the ship's controls. Right now the human is the highest vote in the Hellburner's neural network; but we've long been asking the question at what point the sophistication of the computers to provide the information and the speed and power of the ship to react may finally exceed the engineering limits of the creator— that is, at what point of demand on human capacity to react to data, do we conceive a technically perfect and humanly unflyable machine?"

The questioner, Bonner, said, "Have we done that, in your opinion?"

Tanzer said, "Yes. In my opinion, yes."

"Go on."

"The EC militia came here with a design within the

capabilities of the shipbuilding industry, and within the skills of its own pilots to operate. And the design for a companion ship they *claimed* could use off-the-shelf hardware and software—"

Damn him, Graff thought.

"—and serve as a high-velocity weapons platform. It was not, of course, operable as designed. The fleet insists that the unpredictability of human decisions without a tetralogic AI dominating the pilot-neural net interlink is essential to high-v combat. And we have six men in hospital and seventeen dead in the realworld discovery process."

Hell.

"We're putting crews into a ship that is in effect a high-v multilogic missile, with the sole advantage that the equipment is theoretically recoverable."

There had been dead silence in the room. There was a small muttering now. Don't blow, don't blow, Graff wished Mitch and Jamil. We get our turn.

The gavel came down.

Tanzer went on: "A pilot with twenty years' experience and no faults in the sims ran the course successfully for three hours, forty-six minutes and 17.4 seconds. The accident, which you've seen repeatedly, took place within seven tenths of a second. In the 17th second Wilhelmsen missed one random ordnance target on the approach and reoriented to catch it on the retreat, which he did. At this point telemetry leaves us to guess what passed through his mind— perhaps the recollection he was entering the probability fan of a target in his path. Pulse and respiration has increased markedly over the previous ten minutes. The armscomper and the co-pilot simultaneously indicated alarm as the maneuver started. The armscomper fired off-profile as required and missed. In the next .7 of a second the pilot's telemetry recorded three muscle twitches in conflicting directions causing the craft to undergo successive shocks, and one extreme reaction which caused the pilot and the crew to lose consciousness and sent the ship into a tumble.

"Possibly—Dr. Helmond Weiss will provide more specifics in his testimony—but possibly prolonged hyperception to a microfocused event like the double miss caused a spatial confusion. . . ."

Pens on TranSlates took rapid notes. Graff kept his notes in his head. And said to himself, on the memory of his own system entries: Wilhelmsen panicked.

"Seven tenths of a second," Tanzer said, "from first mistake to the ship entering a fatal motion. 4.8 seconds later it clipped a targeting buoy at .5 light. There is no recoverable wreckage. Our analysis of events rests entirely on telemetry—in which, ironically, the speed makes the microgaps significant data fallouts."

"Meaning the instruments couldn't send fast enough."

"Meaning our data-gathering had two phases: an infosift rapid transmission and a more detailed concurrent total transmission that was running 28 minutes behind the condensed report. Machines can't transmit that fast. More important, human neurons don't fire that fast. We're using human brains to improve a missile's kill rate at a sustained rate of decision that exceeds human limits. Meaning we can't think that fast that long. We've tried an Assisted handoff to a human co-pilot and it's not practical. The psychological stress is actually increased by the trade, and performance is critically reduced. Either we put an unexcepted AI override on the observed physical responses that preceded the incident, or we go back to design and put that ship under a tetralogic AI with the pilot at the interface—as the heart, not the head, of the affair; or, unacceptably, we outright admit that we don't give a damn for human life, and we breed human beings to do that job and tape-train the fear and humanity out of them, the way they do in Union space. There are no other choices."

Down the corridor to the vending machines, a cheese sandwich and a soft drink. Cheese was edible. The fish wasn't even to mention. It had something green scattered through it. Ben sat down, unwrapped the sandwich, tore the indestructible packaging on the chips and sipped his drink.

A guy came in, put chits in the machine. God, he didn't want a couple of orderlies discussing kidney function during his sandwich. . . .

But he caught the haircut and the uniform, took a second look, and found the shave-job staring back at him with sudden sharp attention.

"Pollard?"

The face almost rang bells, but he couldn't place it. The haircut, pure rab, didn't agree with the blue fatigues that said military. Civ docker, he thought. Then he thought: Dekker. Shepherd. And had a sudden notion in what packet of memory that face belonged.

"Mason?" he asked.

"Yeah!" the guy said, hands full. "Word is you're here for Dekker, damn! How is he?"

"Like shit." He indicated the place opposite him at the table and Mason brought his sandwich and his drink over and sat down. Ben asked, "What are you in for?"

"Therapy." Mason wiggled the fingers of his right hand. "Gym floor jumped up and got me. —Dekker's still bad, huh? He *say* anything?"

"Thinks he's in the fuckin' Belt most of the time." Ben took a bite of cheese sandwich, thought about that shuttle leaving at mainday end, and how there wasn't another til next week, wondered if there was a shortcut to the memory Graff wanted, and said, "Keeps asking for Bird and Cory Salazar. What in hell happened to him? *Anybody* know?"

Mason pulled a long face. "Just they pulled him out of a sim-pod bloody and beat all to hell. But we'd lay odds—" Mason looked at him about chest-high and stopped talking in mid-sentence. Mason filled his mouth with sandwich instead.

"—lay odds, what?"

Mason looked at him narrowly while he took time to chew the bite and wash it down with soft drink. "Nothing."

"What, nothing? What's that look mean?"

"You here as a friend of Dekker's? Or officially?

"Look, I'm a programmer, not a psych. I was minding my own business on Sol One. FSO hauled my ass out here because Dekker named me next-of-kin. Lt. Graff hands me his personals, doesn't tell me shit else, asks me find out what happened to him, and that's where I am, trying to find out why he's lying there seeing ET's and angels, so I can get back to Sol One before my posting's gone. What's that look mean?"

Mason said slowly, "You're not here on Tanzer's orders."

"I don't know Tanzer. The FSO jerked me over on a hush-up and hurry. *Humanitarian* leave, on account of Dekker wanted me. What's the UDC got to do with it?"

"Uniform you're wearing isn't exactly popular in some quarters."

"So what are we? Union spies? Not that I heard."

"Say Dekker wouldn't be lying in that bed except for the UDC CO here."

Ben took a look at the door. Nobody around. Nobody listening, unless they routinely bugged the vending machines. "Mason. This is Ben Pollard. Ben who was Morrie Bird's partner. Ben whose ass your ship saved once upon a while. You seriously mind to tell me what the hell's going on and why Dekker rates all this shiz?"

Mason swallowed a bit of sandwich and sat there looking at him and thinking about it. "Say it's a real pressured environment."

"Yeah?"

"The UDC doesn't *like* Belters. You must be the exception."

Belters who might be old, exiled rab, Ben thought, Shepherds who looked like Mason—that haircut wouldn't get a security clearance from the UDC, but he didn't say so. He said, carefully, "There's some feeling, yeah, but I never ran into it. Went into TI, computer stuff—in no pain until they snatched me here. What's this about Dekker and the CO?"

"Tanzer's run the R&D for the UDC insystem stuff since Adam was an Earther, he's got his System, and his friends in high places, til the Fleet signed us in to fly for them. The UDC wanted to do the test and documentation through their facility—all right, they had the set-up and the sims and the knowledge of the suppliers and the technical resources; which is how R&D's got their hands on the ships and put their guys in the seats, because the U friggin' DC is *trying* to get the Fleet demoted to a UDC command."

"I've heard that. Mazian's all over the news trying to get funds. The opposition wants it with strings."

"You've seen the big ships. But the secondary stuff the Fleet's building—top secret stuff, fast. UDC's never flown anything this hot. Design screw-ups, spec screw-ups, materials failures. They cut the budget which means they go to the drawing-board again and make changes—no mind it costs another 150 million for a study and an 80 mil legislative session that could've made up the difference—no, that's fine, that's going in the damn senators' pockets and feeding the contractors. We had one glitch-up with a pump that wasn't up to specs, we got another because security's so damn tight the company making a mate-up device can't talk to the company writing the software, you figure that?"

"Must be the programmer that did the EC security system."

"Listen." Mason's finger stabbed the water-ringed tabletop. "Right now they're six months behind schedule and talking about one damn more redesign on the controls. The UDC bitched and bitched about sim time, said Tanzer's 'boys' were the ones to do the test runs because they had the hours and the experience—you want to talk to *me* about hours? Shit, I'm twenty-seven, that's twenty fuckin' years I've lived on the *Hamilton,* and they give me 200 hours at nav? 200 fuckin' hours, you believe that? They won't log anything you ran up before you were *licensable* at your post. I was nav monkey when I was seven, I was running calc when I was ten, I was sitting relief on the edge of the

Well when I was twelve, and *then* they say they're counting only a quarter of the time our ships logged us—as a compromise because it was *civilian* hours? Ninety days a run, thirty heavy, and on call 24 fuckin' hours a day in Jupiter's lap for longer than these sim-jockeys would hold up, and they give me 200 hours? I was 2000 plus on my last run out from R2!''

"That's crazy."

"Yeah, but that's UDC rules. You only get hours for the time you're logged on. Who logs on? Who ever logs on? You do your fuckin' job, you're too busy to log on, with a load coming and the watch rousting you out of your bunk at 2100 to check you're where you think you are, because somebody thinks we got a positional problem, shit if I'm going to log on as officer of record and get my fuckin' *hours* for the UDC. Same shit they're pulling on the merchanters. You know why they don't count real hours on us? Because the UDC's got four pilots can claim real hours on a par with us, and last week they had five.''

"The guy with Dekker's crew?"

"Wilhelmsen." Mason leaned closer, said, "Listen, —''
And stopped as a nurse came in and carded a soft drink. The nurse left. Mason said, "We've got a lot of pressure. You got maybe four, five hours at a run. Virtual space display. Neural net Assist. Real sensory overload. Hyperfocus, nonstop. And you *don't* sub in some stranger in the last twelve hours before a run, you *don't* have bad feeling between the pilot and the techs, you don't plug in a guy with a whole different visualization system. You want to figure how much pressure Wilhelmsen was under to perform? Shit, he missed a target. He could've let it go. But he was too hot for that. He flipped back to get it, schitzed on where he was, and took three good guys with him. You know why Dekker's in here? Dekker—Dekker told Wilhelmsen's crew to their faces that *he* could have done it.''

"Shit."

"No kidding. Wilhelmsen's navigator took severe exception, there were words—"

"Before or after they sent Dekker to hospital?"

"Let me tell you about that, too. Yeah, Dekker was in shock. He was watching it in mission control. But he didn't need any hospital. They wanted him quiet. They wanted him not to say a thing in front of the senators and the VIPs they had swarming around the observation area."

"They."

"The UDC. Tanzer. They doped him down and let him out after they got the last of the VIPs on the shuttle out of here. And twelve hours later they haul Dekker out of the sim that's been running for six—"

Evans walked in. Stood there a moment, then said, "Lt. Pollard. Getting the local news?"

Ben remembered to breathe. And shoved back from the table. "We knew each other, back when. Old news. —Nice seeing you, Mason."

"Nice seeing you," Mason muttered, and got up himself, Ben didn't wait to see for what. He chucked his plastics in the bin and walked out, with a touch of the pulse rate and the cold sweats he'd used to feel in the Belt, when the Company cops were breathing damned close to them.

Infighting with the UDC? A major Fleet project going down the chute and the blue-sky UDC fighting to get its boys in the pilot seat and the Earth Company militia under its command?

He wished he were in Stockholm.

"Lt. Graff," Bonner said, and Graff got up from beside Demas, walked quietly to the table and swore to tell the truth.

"State your name, rank, citizenship, service and age," the clerk said.

"Jurgen Albrecht Graff, Fleet Lieutenant, EC Territories, ship merchanter *Polly d'Or*, assigned militia ship *Victoria*, under Captain Keu, currently Helm Two on the ECS8, uncommissioned, age thirty-eight."

Heads perusing documents, drowsing on hands, came up and looked at him with dawning close attention.

Gen. Bonner said, "Will you state your approximate actual age, for the record, lieutenant?"

Son of a bitch, Graff thought. "Actually, sir, I haven't calculated it since I was fifteen. But I was born in 2286, Common Reckoning, and the first EC president in my memory was Padriac Melton."

"Would you agree you're approximately early twenties, lieutenant, in terms of actual years?"

"I've no access to those records, sir. And it's not relevant to my experience."

"What is your logged experience?"

"Since I was posted to Helm—ten years, six hours a shift. . . ,"

"Logged hours, lieutenant."

"—conservatively, 18000 hours, since posting. Not counting apprenticeship. Not counting working during dock, which is never logged."

Bonner's face was a study in red. "*Logged* records, lieutenant. Answer the question as asked or be held in contempt."

"As far as I know, there are documents behind those hours, sir. The *Polly d'Or* is likely somewhere between Viking and Pell at the moment, and she maintains meticulous log records. *Victoria*'s whereabouts the Fleet commander could provide, if you'd care to query—"

"I doubt this committee has the patience, lieutenant. And let's state for the committee that your logged hours on Sol Two records are substantially less. Can we at least agree that you're not a senior officer, and you were in physical control of the carrier during the test run?"

"General." Saito's quiet voice from behind him, mild dismay registered on the faces of the panel. "Una Saito,

Com One, protocol officer on *Victoria*. —Lieutenant, as a matter of perspective, where were you born?''

Bonner said, ''Ms. Saito, whatever your rank may be, you're in contempt of this committee. Be seated before I have you ejected.''

Graff said, looking at all those frowning blue-sky faces, ''Actually, sir, if it's relevant, I was born on the sublighter *Gloriana*, on its last deep-space run.''

There was a murmur and a sudden quiet in the room. Graff sat there with his hands folded, not provoking a thing, no, and Bonner, give him credit, gave not a flicker.

''So you would maintain on that basis your experience is adequate to have managed the carrier on a critical test run.''

''I would maintain, sir, that I am qualified to take a starship through jump, an infinitely riskier operation.''

''You're qualified. Have you *done* it?''

''Yes, sir. I have. Once on initiation, eighteen times on hand-off on system entry.''

''Yourself. Alone.''

''Helm on *Victoria* is backed by 49 working stations, counting only those reporting in chain of command to Helm.''

''I'll reserve further questions. Senator Eriksson?''

''Thank you.'' This from the Joint Legislative Committee rep. ''Lt. Graff, Eriksson from the JLC technical division. Medical experts maintain that hyperfocus is not sustainable over the required hours of operation.''

''It's routine for us. If—''

''Let me finish my statement, please. Medical experts have stated that the ERP Index indicates mental confusion— stress was taking its toll. As a starship pilot you have systems which defend against impacts. You have an AI-assisted system of hand-offs. You have a computer interlock on systems to prevent accidents. Based on those facts, do you not think that similar systems are necessary on these ships?''

''Senator, all of those interlocks you describe do exist on

the rider, but let me say first that a starship's autopilot override is at a 2-second pilot crisis query in combat conditions, the rider's was set at 1 for the test, and that while the carrier does have effect shields, the size of the rider makes it possible to pass through fire zones in which the carrier's huge size makes such passage far riskier. The armscomp override isn't necessary, of course, because a rider's available acceleration isn't sufficient to overtake its own ordnance, but it does have a template of prohibited fire to prevent its ordnance hitting the carrier or passing through a habitation zone. The AI-driven autopilot did cut on when it detected a crisis condition in the pilot, which, as I said, was set at 1 second for this test. The AI queried the pilot—that's a painful, attention-getting jolt. It waited a human response—long, in the AI's terms, again, 1 second before it seized control. It was already tracking the situation on all its systems. It knew the moves that had caused the tumble. It knew the existence of the next target. It knew it was off course, but it had lost its navigation lock and was trying to reestablish that. The buoy's existence was masked for the test, but the AI realized it couldn't save the test: it entered another order to penetrate the virtual reality of the test to sample the real environment, accessed information concealed from the pilot and reckoned the position of the target buoy as potentially a concern, and correctly assigned it as a hazard of equal value but secondary imminence to the threat of the ship's high-v tumble. It reasoned that elimination of the target required the arms function, while evasion of the target required the engines, and that the motion exceeded critical demands of the targeting system. A subfunction was, from the instant the AI had engaged, already firing engines to reduce the tumble, and tracking other firepaths. It was doing all that, and attempting to locate itself and its own potential ordnance tracks relative to interdicted fire vectors—realspace friendly targets. Fire against the target was not set for its first sufficient window: the condensed telemetry of its calculations is a massive printout. The AI was still waiting for the window when its position and the target's became identical.''

Took a moment for the senator to figure what that meant. Then an angry frown. "So you're blaming an AI breakdown?''

"No, sir. Everything from the AI's viewpoint was coming optimal. A human with a clear head couldn't have outraced the AI in targeting calculations or in bringing the ship stable enough to get a window. A human might have skipped the math and discharged the chaff gun and the missiles in hope of destroying the object by sheer blind luck, but the AI had an absolute interdiction against certain vectors. It didn't even consider that it could violate that— that range safety could have taken care of the problem if it arose. Somebody decided that option shouldn't be in its memory, and this being a densely populated system maybe it shouldn't have been. But that ship was effectively lost from the moment the pilot reacted to his crew's apprehension. That communications problem was the direct *cause* of the accident—''

Bonner said, "Excuse me, senator. The lieutenant is speculating, now, far outside his expertise. May I remind him to confine himself to what he was in a position to witness or to obtain from records?''

He didn't look at Bonner. "A communications problem set up by a last-minute substitution of pilots.''

The committee hadn't heard that. No. Not all of them had, at least. And from Shepherds he knew were back there in the room, there was not a breath, not an outcry, just a general muttering, and he couldn't turn his head to see expressions.

The senator said: "What substitution, lieutenant?''

"The crew trained as a team. The Fleet pilot was replaced at the last moment by a UDC backup pilot the colonel lifted out of his own crew and subbed in on Fleet personnel. The Fleet captain in command objected in an immediate memo to Col. Tanzer's office—''

Bonner said, "Lieutenant, you're out of line. Confine yourself to factual answers."

"Sir. That is a fact upheld by ECS8 log records."

Somebody yelled from the back, "Do they show the Fleet laid those targets and set that random ordnance interval?" Several voices seconded, and somebody else yelled, "You're full of it, Jennings, you don't break an ops team! You never sub personnel! Tanzer killed those guys sure as a shot to the head!"

The gavel came down.

Somebody shouted, over the banging, "The Fleet set up the course. Check the records! The Fleet had orders to set the targets closer together to screw the test!"

And from nearer the front, as the MP's and Fleet Security moved in, "*Wilhelmsen* screwed the test—those targets were all right! He lost it, that's all!"

Bonner was on his feet shouting, "Clear the room. Clear the room. Sergeant!"

Institution green. Ben had seen green. Had eaten real lettuce, drunk lime (orange juice was better) and had real margaritas the way they could make them on Sol One, but he still wasn't sure why inner system liked that color that mimicked old *Trinidad*'s shower paneling, whether that shade was what Earth really favored. He sincerely hoped not. He honestly hoped not. But if Earth was that color wall to wall he'd take it over B Dock hospital corridors and vending machine suppers.

Dekker was still hyperbolic—swung on an intern, threatened the nurses, called the CO a psychopathic control junkie—

"How many fingers?" the intern had asked, holding up two, and Dekker had held up his own, singular—which was Dekker, all right, but it hadn't won him points. The intern had checked his pulse, said it was elevated—

Damned right it was elevated. "You're being a *fool*," Ben said, while they were waiting for the orderly with the trank. He grabbed Dekker by the arm and shook him, but

Dekker wasn't resisting. "You know that, Dek-boy? Use your head. Shit, get us *out* of this place!"

"Sorry," Dekker said listlessly, "sorry." And stared off into space until Ben shook him again and said, "You want to spend your life in here? You want a permanent home here?"

Dekker looked at him. But the orderly came in and gave him the shot. Dekker didn't fight it. And after the orderly went away Dekker just lay there and stared past him.

"Dek," Ben said, "count their fingers. Walk their damn line. *Remember* how you got in that damn sim. Maybe the lieutenant can get you out of here. Just play their game, that's all."

And Dekker said, while Dekker's eyes were glazing, "What's the use, Ben? What's the use anymore?"

That *wasn't* like Dekker. Wasn't like him at all. But Dekker was out then, or so far under as made no difference. They said people drugged out could hear you, and that under some kinds of trank maybe you didn't have the same resistance to suggestion: Ben squeezed Dekker's arm hard and whispered, right in his ear, "You're going to do what they say and get yourself out of here. Hear it?"

Dekker didn't give any sign he did. So it was out to the hall again, 1805h, and no likelihood Dekker was going to come around again this evening.

He might lie to the doctors, Ben thought, he might *tell* them Dekker had remembered, make something up—prime Dekker with it and hope Dekker had enough of his pieces screwed together to remember it. If he could figure out what they wanted to hear. *Say* it was Wilhelmsen's crew that attacked him, that was the signal he was picking up. That was what the Fleet wanted.

But not what the UDC wanted. And what the Fleet wanted wasn't any ticket to Stockholm, no.

Damn, damn, and damn.

Meanwhile Dekker got crazier, no knowing what drug they were filling him full of or what it was doing, and if he could get hold of Graff he'd tell him check the damn medication for side effects, it wasn't helping, it was making Dekker worse; he'd stopped trusting Higgins, and Evans hadn't been available since yesterday—

He'd seen this before, damn if he hadn't when an organization got ready to throw a man out with the garbage—some skuz in power had taken a position and bet his ass on it, and now the skuz in power had stopped wanting the truth, since it didn't agree with the positions he'd taken—

So you trashed the guy who knew what was going on; you pinned the blame on him as far as you could; you shunted out anybody who might be sympathetic—Evans' departure from the scene—and from where Ben Pollard was standing it didn't look as if Graff or the Fleet had any serious influence left in the hospital—not enough at least for Graff to get his ass in here and ask Dekker himself, which signal he should have picked up from the beginning if he'd had any antennae up.

Not enough to do a thing about the stuff they were shooting into Dekker, who, if the Fleet knew it, wasn't outstandingly sane to start with.

Triple damn.

"Good night," some nurse said to him. "G'night," Ben muttered, half looking around. Good night was what Earthers said to each other. Good night was where this guy had come from. The place of green and snow and rain. Tides and beaches.

He'd seen growing plants. Been into the herbarium on Sol One. Amazing sight. Guided tours, once a week. Keep to the walkway, don't pick the leaves. But the Guides demonstrated how some of them smelled. Flowers would take your head off. Leaves smelled strange. He wasn't sure he liked it. Grease and cold metal smelled one way, and that was home. This hadn't been, hadn't smelled quite edible, not quite offensive, not at all smell like anything he'd known. The ocean was what he wanted, not any damn woods full of stinking plants: snow that was water freezing, not methane, or the scary stuff you got when a seal was chancy.

Snow was the result of weather, which was the result of Coriolis forces, which he understood, and atmospheric rollover, which he theoretically understood—he thought about that, pushing the button for another damned cheese sandwich, he thought about a city that was like helldeck without an overhead, with the tides coming and going against its edges and snow happening—that was what he thought about for company on the walk home.

Didn't think about Dekker lying trank-dead in bed, or Dekker saying, What's the use, Ben? What's the use anymore—

When Dekker had hung on to life harder than any son of a bitch of his acquaintance. And when other sons of bitches were playing games with a defense system they called important—dammit, the services played games, with a war on? And the whole human race could find itself in a war zone if the Fleet *didn't* keep the mess out past the Oort Cloud?

The Earth Company was playing damn games again, that was what, in another of its corporate limbs, the friggin' Company and the UDC and the Fleet, that couldn't find his luggage, was politicking away as usual and throwing out a guy like Dekker who was sincerely crazy enough to want to fly a ship like that into combat.

He'd fought fools in administration before. And they were beatable, except there was such a supply of them.

He'd fought Systems before, and they were beatable, if you knew the numbers, or you could get at them. But damn, he'd tried to stay clean. Even with that EIDAT system, that begged for a finger or two in its works. Use the numbers he had to get to Graff?

Graff couldn't do anything or Graff would have done it. Possible even that Graff had screwed him from the start of this.

Get to Keu's office? Not damned easy. And no guarantee the Fleet even at that level could do anything.

Go to the UDC CO and screw Dekker by blowing his own service's hope of getting him back?

Walking the corridor to his so-called hospice quarters, he thought how if going to Tanzer would get him a pass out of here on the next shuttle, damned if it wasn't starting to look like a good idea. Screw Dekker? Dekker was already screwed. So what was one more, given he couldn't help the guy?

He held sandwich, chips, and drink in one arm, fished his card out of his pocket with his right hand and shoved it into the keyslot.

The message light was blinking on the phone, bright red in the dark. He elbowed the button on the room lights, shut the door the same way, and went to the nightstand to set his supper down

Found his luggage, maybe. He couldn't think of a call else he had in, unless Dekker'd taken a spell of something.

Couldn't be he'd broken anybody's neck. They had him too far out for that. Please God.

He plugged in his personal reader—never use a TI card in an unsecure device—and keyed up playback.

TECH/2 Benjamin J. Pollard
CTS/SS/UDC 28 BAT 2
CURRENTLOC: UDC SOL2B-HOS28
1719JUN20/24 SN P-235-9876/MLR 1923JUN20/24
TRANSFER TO: ACTIVE DUTY: UDC SYSTEMS TESTING
RANK: TECH2/UDC SOL2B-OPS/SCAN G-5: PILOT RATING C-3 WITH 200 EXPERIENCE HOURS LOGGED.
REPORT TO: 2-DECK 229, BARRACKS C: JUN21/24/0800h: ref/ CLASSIFIED: OUTSIDE COMMUNICATION SPECIFICALLY DENIED.

* * *

He sat down. He had that much presence of mind. He punched playback again with his thumb, and the same damned thing rolled past.

Transfer? Systems Testing? Pilot rating?

Shit!

The committee wanted another go. Immediately. The shuttle was two days on its way from Sol One, due in at maindawn, and, informed it wouldn't be held, senatorial demands notwithstanding, the committee decided to keep going through maindark, if that was what it took. You didn't snag a senator for a five-day to Sol Two—no famous restaurants, no cocktail lounges, no 'facilities' the way they legendarily existed downworld: the senators had important business to do, the senators wanted out and back to Sol One and down to Earth and their perks and their privileges, and they'd talk with the company reps over gin and tonic the whole way back.

Graff had hoped, for a while, after things went to hell, that some few members of the committee might want to ask *him* questions over gin and tonic, if they had the clout to ask him in for a go-over; or rec-hall coffee, if they had the clout just to get past Bonner. He'd kept his phone free. He'd hoped until he got the notification of the resumption of the sessions—the committee wanted a chance to review testimony and wanted certain individuals to 'stand by' a call.

Demas and Saito weren't on the list. Mitch and Jamil certainly weren't. No audience. No guarantee there would be any questions Bonner didn't set up. Graff sat there tapping a stylus on the desk and thinking about a fast call to Sol One via FleetCom; but that was still no use—if the captain hadn't noticed a shuttle-load of senators, contractor executives, and UDC brass headed to Sol Two's B Dock, there was no hope for them; and if the captain hadn't known something about the character and leanings of said senators and contractors and Gen. Patrick Bonner, Fleet Security was off its game. So the lieutenant was still left out of the lock without a line, and the lieutenant had to get his butt out there right now and give the senators what they asked as best he could.

So the lieutenant in question put his jacket on, straightened his collar, and opened the door.

"Mr. Graff."

Face to face with Tanzer.

"I'd like a word," Tanzer said as he stepped into the hall.

"About my testimony?" He *didn't* have an Optex, didn't own one and it wasn't legal for a private conversation; but he hoped Tanzer would worry.

Tanzer said, "Just a word of sanity."

A trap? A smear, if Tanzer was carrying a hidden Optex. He could refuse to talk; he could tell Tanzer go to hell; but he had to face Tanzer after the committee was long gone. "Yes, colonel?"

Tanzer said, quietly, "You could screw this whole project. You're a junior, you don't know what you're walking into. And you could lose the war—right here, right in this hearing. I'm advising you to answer the questions without comment—*no*, I'm not supposed to be talking to you, and no, I can't advise you about your testimony. By the book, I can't. But forget that business in the office. We both want that ship. We don't want it canceled. Do we? —Can we have a word inside your office?"

No, was his first thought. There were aides milling about down the hall. There were potential witnesses. But not knowing what Tanzer wanted to tell him could be a mistake too. Bugs, there weren't, inside. Not unless the UDC was technologically one up, and he didn't think so. He opened the door again, let Tanzer in and let the door shut.

Tanzer said, directly, "The companies aren't going to support finding a basic design flaw; that's money out of *their* pockets, do you understand me? That's not what we're going to push for."

Tanzer and a 4-star? Politicking with a Fleet j-g? What in

hell was going on at Sol One? ''I wasn't under the impression that *was* seriously at issue.''

''You don't understand me. Those companies don't want the blame. They're perfectly willing to put the accident off on the service. To call it mishandling—''

Oh-ho.

''A control redesign, existing technology—that, they'll go for. As long as it's *our* design change, out of our budget. You listen to me. This is critical. We've got some Peacenows kicking up a fuss—they want to grab that appropriation for their own programs. They're talking negotiation with Union. Partition of the trade zones. They've got some tame social scientists down in Bonn and Moscow talking isolation again.''

They'd talked it off and on for two hundred years. But Union was very interested in Earth's biology. *Very* interested.

''They won't get it.''

''They can dither this program into another five-year redesign with political deals. The Earth Company can end up deadlocked with the UN. We need the AI on top to let us get some successes with this ship—make it do-able, so we can go public as soon as possible. The thing can have another model, for God's sake, build the old design and lose ships to your heart's content, *after* we've got the first thirty out of the shipyards and trained pilots who know its characteristics. Prove your point and have your funerals, it'll be out of our hands, but let's get this ship online.''

''The effect will be training your pilots to pull it short—to worry when they're taking a necessary chance. Combat pilots can't have that mindset; and you *can't train* with that thing breathing down your neck.''

''You're not a psychiatrist, lieutenant.''

''I'm not an engineer, either, but I know the AI you've got won't accommodate it, you're talking about a very complicated software, a bigger black box, and that panel's already crowding armscomp, besides the psychological factors—''

"Cut one seat. One fewer tech. The tetralogic's worth it."

"That's ten fewer objects longscan can track, and that's one damned more contractor with an unproved software and another unproved interface to train to."

"That's *nothing* getting tracked if the ship doesn't get built, lieutenant, come down to the point. You're not going to get everything you want."

"If you want to cut a deal, you need to talk to the captain, I'm under his orders."

"What are his orders?"

"To keep that ship as is."

"Or lose it? You listen to me. You don't have to agree. Just don't raise objections."

"Talk to my captain. I can't change his orders."

Tanzer was red in the face. Keeping his voice very quiet. "We can't reach your captain."

"Why?"

"We don't know why. We *think* he's in committee meetings."

"Go to Mazian's office, colonel, I can't authorize a thing."

"We've been trying to reach *him*, lieutenant, and we've got your whole damned program about to destruct on us, out there—you'd better believe you're in a hot spot, and I wouldn't take you into confidence, you *or* your recruits, but we can't afford another shouting match for the committee. We're trying to save this program, we're not arguing the value of human hands-on at the controls: you know and I know there's no way Union's tape-trained clones are any match for real human beings—"

"They're not that easy a mark. Azi *still* aren't an AI with an interdict."

"They'll crack. They'll crack the same as anybody else. Their program's going to have the same limitations."

"They won't crack, colonel, they're completely dedicated

to what they're doing, that's what they're created for, for God's sake—''

"You listen to me, lieutenant. I was in charge of the program that put your *Victoria* out there and I don't need to be told by any wet-behind-the-ears what a human pilot is worth, but, dammit! you automate when you have to. You don't hold on to an idea til it kills you—which this is going to do if you screw up in there. You can lose the whole damned *war* in that hearing room, does that get through to you?''

"Colonel, in all respect to your experience—"

"You go on listening. Yes, we had to have a show, yes, I subbed Wilhelmsen. Your boy Dekker's got problems. Serious problems.'' Tanzer pulled a datacard from his breast pocket.

"What's that?''

"A copy of Dekker's personnel file. It's damned interesting reading.''

Damn, he thought. And hoped he kept anxiety off his face. It couldn't be Fleet records—unless there was a two-legged leak in the records system.

"Reckless proceeding and wrongful death.'' Tanzer pocketed the card again. "You want the reason I subbed him? There's a grieving mother out there that's been trying to get justice out of that boy of yours. Rape and murder—''

"Neither of which is true.''

"I had, if you want to know, lieutenant, specific orders to pull Dekker off that demo, because Dekker's legal troubles were going to surface again the minute his name hit the downworld media—and it would have.''

"On a classified test. He lost a partner out in the Belt. The incident isn't a secret in the Company. Far from it. Don't tell me you didn't know that, if you've got that record.''

"The name was going to surface, take my word for it. He's politically hot, too damned hot to represent this program— *that's* why I pulled him from that demo, lieutenant, and you had to ignore my warning. Stick to issues you're prepared to answer and leave Dekker the hell out of this. Cory Salazar. Does the name mean anything to you?"

"ASTEX politics murdered Salazar."

"Tell that to the mother. Tell that to the mama of the underage kid Dekker seduced out there."

"That wasn't the way it happened, colonel."

"You want to tell Salazar's mother that, —lieutenant? You want to tell that to a woman who's on the MarsCorp board? I couldn't put him in front of the media. I *had* to pull him off that team. You understand me? I'm trusting you right now, lieutenant, with a critical confidence, because, dammit, you've raised the issue in there and you'd better have the good sense to back off that point, waffle your way out of it and come into line if you want to keep your boy inside these walls. If he gets to be a media issue, he's dead. You understand that?"

"I understand Wilhelmsen died, I understand a whole crew *died* for a damned politicking decision—"

"You think I don't care, Lieutenant? Your boy Dekker's got a political problem *and* a mouth. And we've got a ship that kills crews and somebody's *mother* breathing down our necks, wanting your boy's head on a platter. You hear me? I didn't screw Dekker. Your captain put him in that position, I didn't. Damned right I pulled him from what was scheduled to go public, and damned right I shut him up before he got to the VIPs we had onstation."

"By shoving him into a pod unconscious?"

"No, damn you. I didn't."

Not lying, if he could rely on anything Tanzer said. Which he was far from sure of. "You told him *why* you pulled him?"

"Trust that mouth? No. And don't you. Hear me? He got into that pod on his own. Leave it at that. Attempted suicide. Who knows? I won't contest that finding. But you shut it down with that. I know he's popular with your recruits. I know you've got a problem. But let's use our heads on this and you quieten matters down and get *off* that issue.''

Damn and damn. Call the captain, was what he needed to do. But they *weren't* sure the UDC wasn't eavesdropping. And if Keu *was* currently caught up in committee at Sol—

Ask Tanzer if FleetCom was secure? Hell if.

''We'd better get in there,'' Tanzer said and opened the door and walked out.

Son of a bitch, Graff thought, what do I do? Demas is on board, Saito's on her way up there. . . .

He walked out, shut the door. Tanzer was down at the corner of the hall with Bonner, the two of them talking. He looked at his watch. One minute from late, the committee was about to convene. He could no-show, he could send Bonner word he was going to be late.

They could say any damned thing without hindrance then, finish the meeting without him in the time it would take to get FleetCom, let alone confer with the captain.

He'd faced fire with steadier nerves. He'd made jumpspeed decisions easier with a ship at stake. There was no assurance Tanzer had told him the truth, or even half of it. There was no assurance they had ever tried to get Keu, or Mazian, there was no assurance it was anything but a maneuver to silence him and ram something through, and there was not even absolute assurance they'd told the truth about political influence stalking Dekker, but if it was, God, somebody had found a damned sensitive button to push. If the Fleet didn't back Dekker, if the Fleet let Dekker take a grenade—the likes of Mitch and Jamil wouldn't stand still for it, there'd be bloodshed, no exaggeration at all, the Belters would take the UDC facilities apart first and work their way over to Fleet HQ. Betray them—and there was no trusting them, no relying on them, no guarantee the metal and the materials were going to go on arriving out of the Belt, and damned sure no crews to handle the ships.

Now he didn't know what Bonner was going to do in that hearing room. Or Tanzer. And he wasn't in a position to object—he felt he was heading into a trap, going in there at all, but he followed them in and sat down in a decimated gathering.

Not a friendly face in the room. Not a one.

Bonner called the session to order, Bonner talked about high feelings over the tragic accident, Bonner talked about the stress of a job that called on men to risk their lives, talked about God and country.

Blue-sky language. Blue-sky thinking. *Up* to an Earther didn't refer to phase fields, *war* was two districts on a plane surface in a dispute over territory, and the *United Nations* was a faction-ridden single-star-system organization trying to tell merchanter Families what their *borders* were: explain borders to them, first.

You had to see a planet through optics and think flat surface to imagine how *ground* looked. He hadn't laid eyes on a planet til he was half grown. He never had figured out the emotional context, except to compare it to *ship* or *station*, but there was something about being fixed in place next to permanent neighbors that sounded desperately unnatural. Which he supposed was prejudice on his side. Bonner talked about a righteous war. And *he* thought about ports and ships run by Cyteen's tape-trained humanity, with mindsets more alien than Earth's.

Bonner talked about human stress and interactive systems, while he thought about the Cluster off Cyteen, where startides warped space, and a ghosty malfunction on the boards you hoped to God was an artifact of that space, while a Union spotter was close to picking up your presence.

Bonner got Helmond Weiss on the mike to read the medical report. Telemetry again. More thorough than the post-mortem on the ship. Less printout. Four human beings hadn't output as much in their last minutes as that struggling AI had. Depressing thought.

Then the psych lads took the mike. "Were Wilhelmsen's last decisions rational?" the committee asked point-blank. And the psychs said, hauling up more charts and graphs,

"Increasing indecision," and talked about hyped senses, maintained that Wilhelmsen had gone on hyperfocus overload and lost track of actual time-flow—

... making decisions at such speed in such duration, it was pure misapprehension of the rate at which things were happening. No, you couldn't characterize it as panic. . . .

". . . evidence of physiological distress, shortness of breath, increase in REM and pulse rate activated a medical crisis warning with the AI—"

"The carrier's AI didn't have time to reach the rider?" a senator asked.

"And get the override query engaged and answered, no, there wasn't time."

Playback of the final moments on the tape. The co-pilot, Pete Fowler, the last words on the tape Fowler's, saying, *"Hold it, hold it—"*

That overlay the whole reorientation and firing incident, at those speeds. The panel had trouble grasping that. They spent five minutes arguing it, and maybe, Graff thought, still didn't realize the sequence of events, or that it was Fowler protesting the original reorientation.

You didn't have time to talk. Couldn't get a word out in some sequences, and not this one. Fowler shouldn't have spoken. Part of it was his fault. Shouldn't have spoken to a strange pilot, who didn't know his contexts, who very well knew they didn't altogether trust him.

The mike went to Tanzer. A few final questions, the committee said. And a senator asked the question:

"What was the name of the original pilot?"

"Dekker. Paul Dekker. Trainee."

"What was the reason for removing him from the mission?"

"Seniority. He was showing a little stress. Wilhelmsen was the more experienced."

Like hell.

"And the crew?"

"Senator, a crew should be capable of working with any officer. It was capable. There were no medical grounds there. The flaw is in the subordination of the neural net interface. It should be constant override with concurrent input from the pilot. The craft's small cross-section, its minimum profile, the enormous power it has to carry in its engines to achieve docking at highest v—all add up to sensitive controls and a very powerful response. . . ."

More minutiae. Keep my mouth shut or not? Graff asked himself. *Trust* Tanzer? Or follow orders?

Another senator: "Did the sims run the same duration as the actual mission?"

Not lately, Graff thought darkly, while Tanzer said, blithely, "Yes."

Then a senator said: "May I interject a question to Lt. Graff."

Bonner didn't like that. Bonner frowned, and said, "Lt. Graff, I remind you you're still under oath."

"Yes, sir."

The senator said, "Lt. Graff. You were at the controls of the carrier at the time of the accident. You were getting telemetry from the rider."

"Yes, sir."

"The medical officer on your bridge was recorded as saying Query out."

"That's correct."

"What does that mean?"

"It means she'd just asked the co-pilot to assess the pilot's condition and act. But the accident was already inevitable. Just not enough time."

Blinks from the senator, attempt to think through the math, maybe. "Was the carrier too far back for safety?"

"It was in a correct position for operations. No, sir."

"Was the target interval set too close? Was it an impossible shot?"

"No. It was a judgment shot. The armscomper doesn't physically fire all the ordnance, understand. He sets the priorities at the start of the run and adjusts them as the situation changes. A computer does the firing, with the pilot following the sequence provided by his co-pilot and the longscanner and armscomper. The pilot can violate the armscomper's priorities. He might have to. There are unplotteds out there, rocks, for instance. Or mines.''

"Did Wilhelmsen violate the priorities?''

"Technically, yes. But he had that choice.''

"Choice. At those speeds.''

"Yes, sir. He was in control until that point. He knew it was wrong, he glitched, and he was out. Cold.''

"Are you a psychiatrist, lieutenant?''

"No, sir, but I suggest you ask the medical officer. There was no panic until he heard his crew's alarm. That spooked him. Their telemetry reads alarm—first, sir. His move startled them and he dropped out of hype.''

"The lieutenant is speculating,'' Bonner said. "Lt. Graff, kindly keep to observed fact.''

"As a pilot, sir, I observed these plain facts in the medical testimony.''

"You're out of order, lieutenant.''

"One more question,'' the senator said. "You're saying, lieutenant, that the tetralogic has faults. Would it have made this mistake?''

"No, but it has other flaws.''

"Specifically?''

"Even a tetralogic is recognizable, to similar systems. Machine can counter machine. Human beings can make decisions these systems don't expect. Longscan works entirely on that principle.''

"Are you a computer tech?''

"I know the systems. I personally would not go into combat with a computer totally in charge.''

The senator leaned back, frowning. "Thank you, lieutenant.''

"May I make an observation?'' Tanzer asked, and got an indulgence and a nod from Bonner.

Tanzer said: "Let me say this is an example of the kind of mystical nonsense I've heard all too much of from this service. Whatever your religious preferences, divine intervention didn't happen here, Wilhelmsen didn't stay conscious long enough to apply the human advantage. Human beings can't defy physics; and the lieutenant sitting behind his carrier's effect shields can maintain that spacers are somehow evolved beyond earthly limitations and make their decisions by mysterious instincts that let them outperform a tetralogic, but in my studied and not unexpert opinion, there's been altogether too much emphasis in recruitment based on entry-level skills and certain kinds of experience—meaning a practical exclusion of anyone but Belters. The lieutenant talks about some mysterious unquantifiable mentality that can work at these velocities. But I'd like to say, and Dr. Weiss will back me on this, that there's more than button-pushing ability and reflexes that make a reliable military. There is, very importantly, attitude. There's been no background check into volunteers on this project . . .''

Dammit, he's going to do it—

''. . . in spite of the well-known unrest and the recent violence in the Belt. We have a service completely outside the authority of the UDC trying to exclude the majority of Sol System natives from holding a post on weapons platforms of enormous destructive potential, insisting we take *their word*—'' Tanzer's knuckles rapped the table. ''—that the policies and decisions of the UN, the world governments, and even Company policy will be respected and observed outside this system. It's imperative that these ships *not* remain under the control of a cadre selected by one man's opinion of their fitness for command, a man not in any way native to Earth or educated to Earth's values. The Fleet is pushing qualifications arbitrarily selected to exclude our own military in command positions, for what motive leaves me entirely uneasy, sirs.''

Some things a man couldn't hear and keep his mouth shut. ''General,'' Graff said. ''I'd like to make my own statement in answer to that.''

''This isn't a court of law, lieutenant. But you'll have

your say. In the meantime, the colonel has his. —Go on, colonel.''

Graff let go a breath and thought, I could walk out, now. But to what good? To what living good? I'm in it. The Captains can disavow what I say. They can still do that. But Tanzer wanted to cut a deal. Tanzer wanted me to agree on the redesign and what good is my agreement to them, what could it possibly influence if this committee's already in their pocket?

Tanzer said, "There are two reasons why I favor a tetralogic system. This ship is too important and too hazardous to civilian targets to turn over to personnel in whose selection our values have never been a criterion. I've been asked privately the reason for the substitution—''

My God, here it goes.

"In the recess I've also been asked the reason for the morale difficulties in this old and time-tried institution. Gentlemen, it lies in the assumption that these machines are flyable only by super-humans personally selected by Conrad Mazian and his hand-picked officers. Earth is being sold a complete bill of goods. Conrad Mazian wants absolute control of an armada Earth is sacrificing considerably to build. What's the difference—control of the human race by a remote group of dissidents—or by a merchanter cartel with a powerful lobby in the halls of the Earth Company administration? These ships and the carriers should be under UDC command and responsible to the citizens of the governments that fund them, not to a self-appointed committee of merchantmen with their own interests and their own priorities.''

Bang went the gavel. The growing murmur from the committee and the aides and witnesses ebbed down, and Tanzer went on:

"You've seen an unfortunate incident in this hearing room, resultant from what the Fleet calls discipline, beginning with the concept of command by committee and ending with the uniform variances that permit Belter enlistees to dress and act like miners on holiday. The carrier that is allegedly on operational alert at this moment for the protection of Earth itself doesn't even have its senior pilot at this facility, while Captain Keu is on an indefinite leave to Sol One. *Junior* lieutenant Graff insists he's qualified in an emergency—but his heads of station outrank him, a prime example of merchanter command order, and if he says decisions have to come at light speed, and he can't have an AI breathing down his neck, what does he say about a committee of senior officers calling the shots for him on the flight deck?''

He stood up. "I *object*, general."

"Sit down, lieutenant." The gavel banged. "Before I find you in contempt of this committee and have you arrested."

He sat. He was no good in the brig. The captain and the Number Ones needed to hear the rest of it. Accurately.

Tanzer said: "We need a disciplined system that can let us substitute a pilot, a tech, a scan operator, *anybody* in any crew, because this isn't the merchant trade we're running, ladies and gentlemen, it's war, in which there are bound to be casualties, and no single man is indispensable. There has to be a chain of command responsible to legitimate policies of the Defense Department, and in which there is absolutely no leeway for personalities too talented and too important to follow orders and do their job."

He couldn't stay quiet. "You mean downgrade the ship until cargo pushers can fly it!"

Bang went the gavel. "Lieutenant!"

Echoes in the core. High up in the mast sounds came faint as ghosts; not like R2 where half-refined ore shot through zero-cold, and thundered and rumbled like doom against the chamber walls. In this vast chamber sims whirled around the chamber on mag-levs and came like tame, dreadful flowers to the platforms, giving up or taking in their human cargoes—

You carded in before you launched. The pod's Adaptive Assists recognized you, input your values, and you input your tape for the sim you were running. You fastened the one belt that locked the others. But something was wrong. The pod started to move and he couldn't remember carding in, couldn't think through the mounting pain in his head and the force pinning him to the seat—

"Cory!" he yelled. Tried to yell. "Cory, hold on!"

But he couldn't reach the Abort. Couldn't see it, couldn't reach it, and the damn sim thought the belts were locked. "Mayday," he called over com, but it didn't answer. Someone had said he'd earned it. Maybe Ben. Ben would have. But he didn't think Ben would have done this to him . . .

"You're a damn screw-up!" someone yelled at him. "You screwed up my whole damn life, you son of a bitch! What'd I ever do to deserve you?"

Sounded like his mother. But his mother never grabbed him by the collar and hit him. That was Ben. Ben was the way out and he tried to listen to Ben, it was the only chart he had that made any sense now . . .

Ben said, "What day is it, damn you?" And he honestly tried to remember. Ben had told him he had to remember.

"I object vehemently," Graff said, calmly as he could, "to the colonel's characterization of myself, my captain, my crew and my service. I challenge the colonel's qualifications to manage this program, when he has had no deepspace experience, no flight time at those speeds, no experience of system transit at those speeds; and neither have any of the medics who've testified. This—" He clicked a datacard onto the table, and remembered with a cold chill the one Tanzer was carrying. "This is *my* personal medical record. I call that in evidence, on reaction times and general qualifications."

The gavel came down. "I'll thank you to reserve the theatrics, lieutenant. This committee is not impressed. You've asked to make a statement. Make it. I remind you you're under oath.''

''*Yes*, general. I call the general's attention to the fact that he did not so admonish the colonel. Can we assume it was an oversight?''

He expected the gavel. Instead Bonner leaned forward and said very quietly, ''The colonel knows he's under oath. Make your statement.''

''It's very brief. The colonel ordered me not to tell the truth to this committee.''

There was a moment of silence. Bonner hadn't expected that shot. He should have. Bonner said, then, ''Are you through, lieutenant?''

''No, sir.'' He thought of Dekker. And the bloodied sim-pod. And wondered if he would see another day in this place. ''I intend to answer the committee's questions. If it has any.''

A long silence, subjective time. Then a senator asked, ''You think you could have flown the rider?''

''If I were trained to do that, yes, ma'am.''

''You couldn't, say, step from the carrier into the ridership. Given the familiarity with the interfaces.''

''I've had years of training for the mass and the characteristics of a large ship. Cross-training could confuse me. Jump makes you quite muzzy. You're riding your gut reactions quite heavily in those first moments of entry. Certainly so in combat.''

Another: ''You think a training program can produce that kind of skill, here, in a matter of months.''

''No, sir. Not without background experience, I don't. That's why the Fleet didn't recruit from the local military. Test pilots like Wilhelmsen—he could have done it. I've no wish to downplay his ability. He was good. We'd have taken him in a moment if the UDC had wanted to release him. Or if he had wanted to go.''

''Are you doing the recruiting, now?'' Bonner asked. ''Or speaking for Captain Mazian?''

"I'm agreeing with the colonel, sir, based on my knowledge of Wilhelmsen's ability. But that ability can't be trained in the time we need; we need prior experience. We particularly need crews that can *feel* insystem space. The Shepherds and the miners and insystem haulers aren't trainees as the term implies; and they're not eighteen-year-old recruits who think a mass proximity situation is an exam problem."

"What *is* a mass proximity situation, lieutenant?"

God.

"A collision alert, sir." It was the least vivid description that leapt to his mind. He had no wish to offend the senator. The senator laughed, like a good politician, and leaned back.

Another asked, "Lieutenant?"

"Yes, sir."

"To *what* government do you hold loyalty?"

A handful of days ago he would have said something about historical ties, a center for the human species. But he didn't want to get into abstracts. Or create any apprehension of an outsider viewpoint. He looked the senator in the eyes and said quietly, "To Earth, sir."

But the answer appeared to take the man aback; and it struck him then for the first time that he was looking at Earth, at this table: a row of incomprehensible special interests. None of them could *see* Earth from the outside—the techs from subsidiaries of the Earth Company; the senators from the Pan-Asian Union and Europe. Bonner, from the Western Hemisphere. (Who first defined east and west? he wondered, hyperfocusing, momentarily as bereft of referents as they were, taking in everything. Politics of dividing oceans? And why not north and south—except the ice?)

The same senator asked, "And these recruits from the Belt? To whom are they loyal?"

Touchy question. A good many Belters were political exiles from Earth. He said, "I'm sure they'd tell you, individually, whatever their concept is. The human race, certainly. The one that nature evolved on this planet, not the one from labs on Cyteen."

"Loyalty to themselves, would you say?"

He quoted Bonner. "Isn't that the issue of the war, senator? Freedom of conscience?"

Silence from Bonner. Deathly silence.

"If this design goes AI," Graff continued quickly, wishing for Saito's eloquence, "so the enemy can predict it; or if some legislative compromise replaces our command with officers who don't know jumpspace tactics—we'll die, ship by ship. Then let the UDC hold the line with no carriers, no deepspace crews. Lose us and you won't have the merchanters. You won't have the far space stations. We're the ones that have risked everything carrying out your orders, trying to hold the human race together. What's on Cyteen isn't *like* us."

Bonner said, "Lieutenant, tell me, what do *you* care if Earth ceases to exist?"

He said, halfway into it before he remembered whose quote it was, " 'If Earth didn't exist, we'd have to create one.' "

Emory of Cyteen had said, a now-famous remark: "We all need to be from somewhere. We need a context for the genome. Lose that and we lose all common reference as a species."

But the committee didn't seem to recognize the source. Likely they couldn't recall the name of Cyteen's Councillor of Science—or conceive of the immense arrogance in that statement. Cyteen *was* terraforming, hand over fist. Ripping a world apart. Killing a native ecology, replacing it—and humanity—with its own chosen design. He'd seen the classified reports. And he wasn't sure Bonner had. Mazian was taking those records to the highest levels of the Company and the UN.

A senator said, "We're here to discuss technology. The fitness of a machine."

"The fitness of the men who fly it," Bonner said, "is also at issue."

The pod reoriented. Flesh met plastics. Dekker tried to defend himself, but something grabbed his collar, held him. Someone shook him, and said, "Straighten up, you damned fool, or I'll hit you again."

"Trying to," he told Ben's hazy image, and tasted blood in his mouth.

"Why in hell?" Ben asked him. "Why in hell'd you have to ask for me?"

"Dunno, dunno, Ben." Blood tasted awful. He tried to get his breath and Ben shoved him back against the pillows. Ben looked like hell.

Ben still had his fist wrapped in his collar. Ben gave him another shove. "I can't blame whoever shoved you in that simulator. You're a pain in the ass, you know that? You're a damned recurring pain in the ass!"

"Yeah," he said. He didn't want his lips to tremble, but they did, and tears stung his eyes. A long, long time he'd been alone. There'd been others, but they'd died, and Ben hadn't, Ben wouldn't, Ben was too hard to catch and Ben wouldn't get himself killed for anybody. He trusted Ben that way. Ben was too slippery for the sons of bitches.

Someone shadowed the doorway.

"Need to check his blood pressure, sir."

Somebody had said something about Have a nice trip. Someone who'd told him go to hell. . . .

He caught at the bed. Caught at Ben's arm as Ben started to get up and turn him over to the nurse. "No."

"Your blood pressure's getting up, Mr. Dekker."

"Screw it. —Ben, —"

"Lieutenant."

He swung his legs off the bed, made a try at getting up and the room went upside down. The nurse made a grab after him, he saw the blue uniform, and he elbowed it aside. He caught himself with a grip on the edge of the bed.

But Ben was gone. Ben had left him, and the nurse got a hand on his shoulder and his arm. "Just lie down, Mr. Dekker. Lie down. How'd he get in here, anyway? Visitors aren't supposed to be in here."

He didn't know either. But a lot of things happened here that shouldn't. And he hadn't been dreaming. Ben had been there. He had a cut inside his lip and a coppery taste in his mouth that proved it, no matter what the nurse said about visitors. He lay down and ran his tongue over that sore spot, thinking, through the shot and everything, Ben's here, Ben's here . . . and knowing it was Sol Two where Ben had found him: Ben hated him; but Ben had got here, Ben talked sense to him and didn't confuse him. Even if Ben wanted to beat hell out of him. He *liked* that about Ben—that for all Ben wanted to go on beating hell out of him, Ben hadn't. Ben had held on to him. Ben had shaken him and told him where rightside up was and told him to get there. Only advice he'd trusted in days. Only voice he'd wanted to come back to, since—

—since his crew died. Died in a fireball he wasn't in. Couldn't have been in, since he wasn't vapor.

Somebody'd said, later, Enjoy the ride, Dekker.

He couldn't remember who. Someone he'd known. But the voice had no color in his mind. No sound. And he couldn't recover it.

They said, shadows leaning over him, "Need to keep that blood pressure down, Mr. Dekker," and he said: "Screw all of you, I don't need your help," and kept his eyes shut.

Whine of mag-levs. You got that through the walls. There was light out there, but it didn't diffuse, despite the distances across the huge sim chamber, where a solitary pod was working. There was a safety stand-down in effect. Lendler Corp techs were doing an inspection on this shift, remoting the pod from the number two access. You could see the light on, far across the chamber.

Easy ways to get hurt out there. Pods pulled a lot of *g*'s, positive and negative. Graff touched the cold plastics of the dead panel, drifting in the zero *g*, antagonizing an already upset stomach, and watched the pod, figuring how hard a body could hit, repeatedly, during that gyrating course. Dekker was strong for his slight frame. Only thing that had saved him. God only knew how conscious he'd been, but enough he'd protected his head somehow. And his neck and his back and the rest of his bones. The meds who hadn't seen the inside of the pod had said the belts must have come loose. But the belts had been locked together under Dekker, deliberately to fool the safety interlocks, by somebody who hadn't left prints—unless it was the last man to use the pod, and that was Jamil, who hadn't a motive that he knew. Belts locked underneath Dekker—otherwise the pod wouldn't have moved. The MP's report had said, Suicide is not ruled out.

Suicide, to have a MarsCorp councillor on your case?

Suicide, to call Tanzer a bastard?

Don't let it get to you, Saito had said, when he'd called the carrier to tell them the hearing was over. Midge had hand-carried his report to the ship and a long transmission had gone out to the captain by now. Tanzer was going to rebound off the walls tomorrow.

But the report was at Sol One by now. So far as what he dared send the captain, the most urgent matter was one name, of everything related to the accident: Salazar. The rest was in Dekker's file. Beyond that, Keu needed to know how Bonner and Tanzer had run the hearing; needed to know how his Helm Two had answered the questions, right or wrong.

Helm Two had underestimated Tanzer, that was the fact, Tanzer had thrown him a last-minute set of choices in which his refusal to go against Keu's orders, and a lone lieutenant's blind run through a mine-field, Tanzer had said it, might just have lost the program tonight, lost the war for the whole human race, literally, right in that hearing room this evening—if somebody wiser and better at politics couldn't somehow take the pieces and put them together with more skill than he had mustered in front of that committee.

He was tired, God, he was tired, and he had had no business coming here. He wasn't doing entirely rational things now, he'd sent word with Midge where he was going and put com on alert, but he hadn't come to the Number Ones for aid and comfort and he was refusing to, knowing nothing they could tell him was of any use, since they didn't know any more than he did what was going on. He'd made some critical judgments left and right of the course he'd hoped to hold in the hearing and in his dealings with Tanzer, and he was avoiding their input til he'd mapped out the sequence and sense of those judgment calls, that was what he suddenly realized was pushing his buttons right now—he wanted to know the answers; and if he could shove Bonner and Tanzer into a move of some kind, even an assassination attempt, he'd know, all right; he'd have proof: more than that, the senators might have it, before they left here at maindawn: Explain that one, cover another attempted murder, Bonner, while the committee's still on station . . .

Otherwise, if Tanzer was only tracking him and more innocent than he judged, let Tanzer sweat what he was up to—looking for clues, maybe, trying to find something to prove Dekker's case, something politically explosive. Legal troubles in Dekker's past—it was all backgrounded, solved, just one of the connections Dekker had had and left when he left the Belt. He didn't go off Sol Two, he took no leaves, but there had been no particular reason for Dekker's name to rouse any anxieties in Defense—certainly no reason to fear him getting to the media. Dekker was allergic to cameras and microphones, Dekker certainly didn't want publicity bringing his name up again, any more than Defense did; and evidently there'd been a decision to take Hellburner public if the test succeeded. So someone high in the Defense Department had said pull him.

That being the case—the line certainly led to Salazar; and Salazar lived behind the EC security wall, the same EC that they were fighting for. That was a worry, and a real one, if the woman had penetrated security channels and found out *what* Dekker was working on, and where he was.

There was—top of the list regarding Dekker's injuries—Wilhelmsen's crew. Dekker hadn't been tactful. Dekker was, Pollard had said it, volatile. There was a lot of that in the crews they'd recruited—including the UDC test pilots. You could begin to wonder was it a pathology or a necessary qualification for this ship—or was it the result of ramming crews together in a handful of years, the few with the reflexes, the mental quickness—the top of the above-average in reaction time, who didn't, even on a family ship, necessarily understand slower processers, or understand that such slower minds vastly outnumbered them in the population? He'd told Tanzer, *You can't train what we need . . .* he hoped he'd gotten that across at least to one of the committee, but there was no knowing—he'd never excelled, himself, at figuring people: he'd certainly failed to realize how very savvy Tanzer could be in an argument.

He had his pocket com. The captain might send him word at any hour, please God, and give him specific instructions, either for a bare-ass spacewalk or a steady-on as he was bearing and he'd rather either right now than chasing might-have-beens in circles. After a jump you got a solid Yes, you'd survived it. But right now he could wonder whether the FSO was still operating on Sol One, or whether something might have gone wrong at levels so high the shockwave had yet to hit Sol Two. For all he knew the committee had *been* the shockwave of a UDC power grab and he'd just self-destructed in it.

Or why else hadn't they heard anything? Or why, according to the news that he had heard before he'd left the office, was Mazian still smiling his way from council to council in the European Union, and making no comment about the accident, except that a 'routine missile test' had had a problem.

The pod flashed by, unexpectedly, filling the viewport.

His heart jumped. He watched the pod whip across the far side and felt queasy after the visual shock. Dekker's pod had been running on the mission tape. Dekker had seen the accident. They'd treated him for shock, he'd gotten out of hospital and turned up here, at shift-change, in a pod repeating the exact accident set-up. On loop. Was there anything *in* that, but vindictiveness?

Higgins said only that Dekker had lucid moments. No recollection, most times no awareness even where he was. Cory Salazar had died out in the Belt. Dekker was back in that crack-up. Over and over and over.

Check-in records had listed no UDC personnel as in the area. The mission sims tape was checked out to Dekker—as mission commander, he'd had one in his possession. Dekker had been in hospital. One would have expected that that tape had been with his effects. Security should have collected it, with the tapes in all crews' possession, living and dead. But Library hadn't checked Dekker's in: Dekker was alive, and unable to respond to requests for the tape, Security said, they'd decided not to seek an order to get it from his effects—which would have had the Provost Marshal's staff going into Dekker's locker while Dekker was alive, a violation of policy in the absence of charges.

A hatch door crashed and echoed at the distant end of the access tube. The lift had just let someone in. The Lendler Corp techs, maybe, moving up to this bay. But the light was still on over there. And the pod was still running, the mag-levs whiting out anything but the loudest sounds.

Damn, he thought, Tanzer might be a fool after all. He might *have* his answer, all right: and if he and his didn't make the right moves now, he might *become* the answer. He'd gotten colder, standing here, and he had a sudden weak-kneed wish to be wrong about Tanzer—he hadn't thought through what he'd done in the hearing yet, he wasn't ready or willing to make gut-level choices in a physical confrontation. He closed his fist around the bolt in his pocket—he'd collected that from the desk; he drifted free and took out the pocket com he'd collected too. "D-g, this is 7-All, sim bay 2. QE, C-2-6, copy?"

"7-All, this is Snowball, C-2-6, on it, that's 03 to you, dammit, seal that door!"

Saito was on com. Saito must be lurking over Dan Washington's shoulder and the pocket com was wide open now and logging to files on the carrier. Saito wasn't as accepting of harebrained excursions as Dan was, Saito must have gotten uneasy, and, onto Helm Two's side excursion, was probably calling Demas in, besides having Security closer than he'd set them. But they would or wouldn't come in, depending on what Saito heard. Meanwhile he watched the hand-line quiver along the side of the lighted tube. Someone was on it, now, below the curve of the tube. Several someones, by the feel as he touched it.

First figure showed in the serpentine of lights, monkeying along the line. Not UDC. Their own. Flash of jewelry, light behind blond hair.

Friendly fire incoming, then. Not UDC: Mitch. He drew a breath, focused down off the adrenaline rush toward a different kind of self-protection, said to the com, "Snowball, easy on," before Security came in hard. More of them behind Mitch: Jamil, Almarshad . . . Pauli. A delegation. The Shepherds didn't have access to query over com. Saito was sure to give him hell; the Shepherds had tracked him, never mind Tanzer's 'boys' might have—it wasn't a good time he was having right now; and he hoped it wasn't a breaking problem that had brought them here. He couldn't take another.

He held his position as the Shepherds gathered in front of the open door, drifting hands-off on the short tether of their safety-clips, in the frosty-breathed chill and the low rhythmic hum of the mags. "Hear it was bloody," Mitch said.

"How did you hear? What's security worth in this place?"

Jamil shrugged, tugged at the line to maintain his orientation. "2-level bar. Aerospatiale guys with a few under their belts. Saying Bonner's pissed. Tanzer's pissed. Bonner told some female committee member it wasn't really important she understand the technicals of the accident, or the tetralogic, she should just recommend the system go AI.''

"Damn," he said, but Jamil was grinning.

"Happens Bonner mixed up his women *and* his Asians. Turned out *she's* Aerospatiale's number two engineer."

He had to be amused. He grinned. And he knew that via his open com, Bonner's little faux pas was flying through the carrier out there, for all it was worth. So the J-G wasn't the only one who could talk his way into trouble.

But that was one engineer and one company, with no part of its contract at issue: Aerospatiale was the engines, and they weren't in question.

The Belter trash, as they called themselves, wanted to know how it had gone. Correction, they knew how it had gone. He didn't know how they'd found him, didn't know what they expected him to say. He hadn't delivered. Not really. They couldn't think he had.

"What are you guys doing here?"

They didn't know how to answer, evidently: they didn't quite look him in the eye. But maybe he halfway understood what was in their minds—a feeling they'd been collectively screwed, the way the Belters would say. And that together was better than separate right now.

"How did you find me?"

Mitch said, "Phoned Fleet Security. *They* knew."

2-DECK 229 was a tacky little hallway in a tacky little facility that met you with a security-locked, plastic-protected bulletin board that said things like NO ALCOHOL IN QUARTERS and REMEMBER THE 24-HR RESTRICTIONS, along with SIM SCHEDULE and LOST CARD, DESPERATE, BILL H. SMITH.

Humanitarian transfer, hell. You couldn't shoot a Fleet officer. Wasn't legal. Couldn't even kill Dekker, who didn't know what was going on, who just looked at you and said, Yeah, Ben. All right, Ben. Like you could do anything you wanted to him, the worse had already happened.

Bloody *hell*.

He found Barracks C. He walked in, where a handful of guys with a vid-game looked up and got up and stared at him, a solid wall of hostility.

"Lost?" one of them asked.

"I'm fuckin' *assigned* here," he muttered, and got dismay and frowns.

"No such," one said, Belter accent thick and surly. "UDC shave-head? You got the wrong barracks, loo-tenant."

Fine. Great. He said, in deep Belter brogue, "Not my pick, mate, they do the numbers."

Wasn't what they expected out of a UDC mouth. Postures altered, faces did.

"You wouldn't be Pollard, would you?"

He'd hoped to get his assigned bunk, nothing more. But there was no good making enemies here. He said, grudgingly, "Yeah. Benjamin J.," and saw expressions go on changing for the positive. Not the reaction he generally got from people.

"Pollard." The head troublemaker came over. "Almarshad." A gesture to left and right, behind him. "Franklin and Pauli. What's the word on Dekker?"

Dekker didn't attract friends either, not among people who really knew him; and when a guy introduced himself the way Almarshad did you should worry about bombs. He shook Almarshad's offered hand, said, conservatively, "Not the best I've ever seen him," and watched reactions. *Looked* like they were friends of Dekker's. And it was true Dekker was a Cause in the Belt. A Name—among people who *didn't* know him. Not with Shepherds, much as he knew, and that was what this set looked to be—but it could be Dekker had found a niche in this classified hell.

Franklin asked,

"He say who hit him?"

Or these guys *could* be the committee that put Dekker in hospital, for all he knew.

He said, again carefully, "Bounced on his head too often. I don't know. *He* doesn't. —Friends of his, are you?"

Almarshad seemed to comprehend his reserve, then, frowned and said, "He's got no enemies in this barracks. You keeping that uniform?"

He hadn't many allegiances in his life. But, hell, the UDC fed you, gave you everything you could dream of, held out the promise of paradise, until Dekker helpfully dropped your name in the wrong classified ears—which landed you up to your ears in an interservice feud; and now some Shepherd-turned-bluecoat wanted to make an issue of your uniform? Hell, yes, you could take offense at being pushed. "Yeah, I'm keeping it. Far as I know."

"Shit," Pauli said with a roll of his eyes, and turned half away and back again with an outheld hand. "Tanzer give you your orders?"

"I don't know who gave me my orders. Captain over FSO *Keu* got me out here. The *Fleet* got me out here. Humanitarian leave. Now it's a fuckin' humanitarian *transfer,* I can't find my fuckin' baggage, I can't find my fuckin' bunk, I got no damn choice, here, mister! I'm supposed to be in Stockholm! I'd rather be in Stockholm, which I won't now! —I'm a security Priority *10,* and they got me in here for reasons I don't know, with a damn classified order I'm probably securitied high enough to read. But you don't question orders here, I'm certainly finding that out!"

A hand landed on his shoulder. Almarshad. "Easy. Easy. Pauli means to say welcome in. Tanzer's a problem, we know who you are, we know damn well you're not his boy."

"I don't fuckin' *know* Tanzer!"

"Better off," Franklin said under his breath. "Where've they got you? What room?"

"We got rooms." Thank God. "Said just—here."

"You're Dekker's, then. A-10. Demi-suites. If you count four bunks and a washroom."

Personally he didn't. But he'd been prepared for worse in the short term. He said, "Thanks," and took the pointed finger for his guide.

Hell if, he kept saying to himself. Hell if I'm going to stay here. Hell if this is going to be the rest of my life, —Mr. Graff, sir.

He'd flunked his Aptitudes for anything remotely approaching combat, deliberately and repeatedly: he couldn't pass basic without a waiver for unarmed combat on account of a way-high score in technical; he'd worked hard to clean the Belter accent out of his speech and to fit in with blue-skyers and here he was resurrecting it to deal with some sumbitch Shepherd who'd have walked over him without noticing, back in R2. Get into technical, get his security clearance—get connections and numbers, the same as he'd had in R2, that was his priority. His CO back in TI, Weiter—Weiter had connections, Weiter had let him make his rating in very fast order, and George Weiter had had the discriminating good sense to screw the regs, bust him past the basics and into levels where he could learn from where he was and get at those essential, top-level access numbers.

No guns, damned sure, nothing to do with guns. He'd made sure of that.

And here he was busted to a pilot trainee rating? It was crazed. It was absolutely insane. It was *going* to get fixed. Get to Weiter—somehow. Get to somebody up in HQ. In Stockholm. Fast.

He located A-10, at the corner of the hall, opened the door—

And found his lost luggage in the middle of the darkened room.

"Shit! Shit, shit, *shit!*"

The shuttle was in Servicing, the politicians, the engineers, the corporate execs and the general were tanking up in Departures, and now reality came due. Now it was back to dealing with Tanzer on a daily, post-hearing basis, and the Fleet's independence notwithstanding, when the UDC CO sent a See Me at 0800h, the Fleet Acting Commander had to show up.

"He's expecting you," the aide said. Graff said a terse Thank you, opened the door and walked into the fire zone.

"Lt. Graff," Tanzer said.

"Colonel," Graff said and stood there neither at ease nor at attention while Tanzer stared at him.

Tanzer rocked his chair back abruptly and said, "I expect cooperation."

"Yes, colonel."

" 'Yes, colonel,' what?"

"Whatever's good for the program, colonel."

"And what do you think that is, now, would you say?"

"Colonel, you know my opinion."

The chair banged level. "Damn your opinion! What are you trying to do to this program?"

"Trying not to lose a carrier, when its riders fail. I'll be in it. You won't, colonel."

"I won't, will I? I'm on the line here, you sonuvabitch."

"Not for the same stakes, colonel, forgive me."

"You son of *a* bitch."

After a sleep-short night that opening was extremely welcome. Tanzer was angry. Tanzer wasn't satisfied with what had gone down. That could be good news—if it wasn't the demise of the program Tanzer was foreseeing.

Tanzer said, with a curl of his lip, "Two more of your recruits are in from the Belt, I'm *sure* you'll be delighted with that. And Lendler Corp is recommending the Fleet change its security regulations with the sim tapes. And who in hell transferred Pollard into your command?"

"My command?"

"Your command, your captain's command, your navigator's command for all I know, who knows who's in charge in your office? You have a UDC trainee in your program, Mr. Graff, do you want to tell me just how that happened?"

He wasn't sure whether Tanzer was in his right mind. Or what in hell was going on. He said, "I don't know. I'll look into it."

"I'm already looking into it, I'm looking into it all the way to TI and Geneva. What do you say to *that*, Mr. Graff?"

"I don't know either, colonel. I'll find out."

Tanzer gave him a cold, silent stare. Then: "You find out and you come tell me. It's one of those things I like to keep up with, who's where on this station. Just a habit of mine. I think you can understand that. Hearing's over. I'd like to clear the record, just get everything back in appropriate boxes. I think you can understand that too, can't you, lieutenant?''

The passenger shuttle was going out, that was the maddening thing. But there was absolutely no question of Ben Pollard getting to it: it was ferrying the brass out from the hearing, the hearing was evidently over, Dekker hadn't remembered a thing he could take to Graff and get out of here, so evidently *that* wasn't his ticket out—and, dammit! he wanted to talk to Graff, wanted to ask Graff to his face what kind of a double-cross had caught him in this damned illicit transfer. But Graff had been 'unavailable' during the hearing, Graff's aides had only cared to ask if he had any report yet. Of course he'd had to say no; so Lt. Graff hadn't seen fit to return his calls yesterday; Lt. Graff wasn't in his office this morning—

While the transfer orders he'd gotten said, Outside contact specifically denied.

So what was Outside? Sol One FSO? Sol One UDC? —Graff's office?

In a moment of wild fantasy he thought of risking his clearance, his career and a term in the brig, getting to the Departure lounge by hook or by crook, snagging some UDC officer bound out of this station and protesting he'd been kidnapped: contact Weiter on Sol One.

But there were serious problems with that scenario. Abundant problems. Chief among which was not knowing what he was dealing with, or what Dekker was involved in, or how much of that hearing had involved Dekker specifically and how much had involved a program in trouble.

He didn't unpack. He'd just looked for a change of clothes—he'd been washing clothes in hospice laundry every day, wrapped in a hospice towel while they dried, thank God he'd had his shaving kit and two changes of shirts and underwear in his carry, but, God, he was glad to get his light station boots and his pullover, and find the textcards he'd packed—

And his personal computer, which thank God hadn't been damaged. They'd searched his luggage. They'd probably searched his computer files. Probably had to call in the station techs to read his to-do list, which now wasn't going to get done, if he couldn't get out of this. He entertained dark thoughts of finding a phone and using a handful of codes, but he didn't want the output directed to any terminal he owned. Or to his barracks. He figured all he'd better do with the phone was find out what was in his file right now, which would happen the minute he used his card.

All right. But we're *not* putting our only copy in, are we?

You couldn't copy a personal datacard. Copying was supposed to screw it. EIDAT said. Writing outside your personal memo area was supposed to screw it.

But EIDAT said a lot of things about security to its customers that didn't apply to its programmers: a few alterations to the 00 and the card would copy—if you had the Programming OS on the card, which wasn't supposed to fit in the MEM area. But if you got creative with the allocations it would. *Not* that he didn't trust the integrity of the UDC command here, *not* as if they just might have a watch on a Priority 10 right now that might notice him going out to the Exchange and buying a card with his remaining vending chits. But he could certainly sacrifice the chess gamecard—even in the paperless and police-controlled Belt, Customs had never quite apprehended gamecards and vidcards as write-capable media.

Yeah.

Quick sand-down of the gamecard edge on the nailfile he carried, a little application of clear nailpolish, available locally, at certain contact points—and you could write to it quite nicely. The cheerful, bright commercial label said it was a patented gamecard, a lot of worn-at-the-edges cards were out there that did show the critical contacts. EIDAT certainly didn't want to advertise the procedure even to the police, because people with access to EIDAT systems code didn't ever pirate gamecards. No. Of course not.

He stuck the datacard in the second drive and had his datacard copy in a nice secure place in quarters before he went out to the wall phone in the barracks main hall. He stuck his datacard into the slot. The write-function clicked. The new readout said CAF, MKT and MSFUNC. PRIORITY MS was blinking.

He keyed MS and the hash mark. It said, Report to Lt. Graff's office, 0900h.

And funny to say, when he tried to call over to Graff's office on a level 10, his level 10 authorization wouldn't work. Son of a bitch, he thought, smug, amused, *and* furious. He had to do it on a lowly level 3. They *had* fried his accesses. And he was illegal as hell now, with that other card as a holdout. Question was—*which* service had pulled his security clearance.

So Graff wanted to talk to him. And it was 0848 right now. He had about time to get his ass over to Graff's office, and find out such facts as Graff was willing to tell him about his transfer—

Which he was about to do when he caught sight of the two females lugging duffles into the barracks main hall— one dark-skinned, one light, one with a headful of metal-capped braids and one with a shave-strip of bright red curls.

My *God* . . .

He hung up. He had the presence of mind to take his card out of the slot. He stood there while two of the most unlikely recruits in the solar system came down the center aisle to the catcalls of the bystanders, saw them look right past him as if he was part of the landscape.

"Sal!" he called out. "Meg!" and saw two pairs of eyes fix on him, do a re-take of him and the uniform. Baggage hit the floor. The two best-looking women he'd ever slept with ran up, grabbed him, both, and kissed him breathless, one and the other.

Couldn't hurt a man's reputation. Whistles and howls from the gallery. He caught his breath, besieged with questions like what was he doing here, what was this about Dek, and how was he?

Questions without an easy answer. "What are *you* two doing here?" he asked, and got a stereo account: they'd gotten the word Dekker was in some kind of accident, they'd gotten word they were shipping a carrier out—

"God, that thing *moves*—" Sal said.

"So we rode it in and transferred over on the shuttle," Meg said. "And these damn MPs have got to stall us up with questions, shit! of-fi-cers and VIP's all over the place. —How's Dek, for God's sake, he got all his pieces?"

"Everything you'd be interested in. —You enlisted?" *That* didn't fit his expectations, didn't fit what he'd been reading in Dekker's letter file.

"They hail us down," Sal said, "in Jupiter's own lap, a carrier pulls up and says, Have you got Kady? And wants to talk to us. Wants to talk to Meg. And Meg talks to the Man, and we get this news Dek's in hospital—some kind of crack-up, they're saying, and they'd kindly give us a ride insystem—"

Shepherds began to ooze over. One said, "Well, well, look what pulled in. Hiya."

Meg looked. Sal did. Ben didn't know the face, but Sal struck an attitude and said, "Well, well, *look* at familiar faces—they let you in, Fly-by?"

Laughter from all about. Not a nickname Fly-by seemed to favor. "God, how'd *you* get past?" Belter accent, Shepherd flash. "I thought they had criteria."

"You skuz," Sal said, but it didn't have the edge of trouble. Sal put a hand on the skuz's shoulder, gave his arm a squeeze. "Jamil's a sumbitch, but he's an all right sumbitch. This is Ben Pollard."

"Got the whole team, but Morrie," another said. "Damn on!"

"Ben, where d' we sleep?" Meg asked. There were

immediately other offers. "Take you up later," Meg said.
"I got a date at the hospital, if I can get the pass they said I
had—"

"Get you to the room," Ben said, and, catching two
elbows, hauled them along to 10-A. Good-natured protest
followed from the rear, but it died, and a couple of guys,
Jamil included, overtook them at the door, set down the
baggage and made themselves absent. "Thanks," he said;
discretion was not dead here. "Thanks," Meg called back,
while he was opening the door. He put a hand on Sal's
back, got Meg's arm and got them inside, into privacy.

"What've we got?" Sal said. "Is my radar working, or
what?"

"It's working," he said. "We got a sumbitch in charge,
same damn sumbitch switched Dekker out and some guy in
on a test run and cracked up Dekker's crew, *Dek-baby*
thinks he's in the fuckin' Belt looking for Cory, and *I* got a
meeting with Floot Lieutenant J. Graff right on the hour."
He had a sudden idea, fished his temp hospital card out of
his uniform pocket, and held it up in front of Meg. "This is
a pass. You're me, just put it in the slot at the main desk,
won't trigger an alarm and in the remote chance they should
ask, tell 'em Graff sent you. Dekker's in room 114. They
pulled him out of a simulator beat to hell and concussed and
there's some chance he didn't climb in there on his own, by
what I can guess. Tell him straighten up. Tell him where he
is, tell him I said so, tell him I'm going to break his neck
next time I see him—*I've* got five minutes to make the
lieutenant's office. . . ."

"Somebody did it to him?" Meg asked.

"Hey. You know Dek. There's got to be a waiting list."
He recalled the atmosphere outside, and said, "We got to
talk. Fast. Sit. The lieutenant can wait five."

The sounds came and went. 2324. 2324. Dekker tried to
remember. He said it to himself to remember. And maybe
he was losing track of time, but it seemed to him breakfast

had come and gone and Ben hadn't come this morning. That upset him. Ben kept saying he couldn't stay, and maybe he'd just gone wherever Ben had to go to. He didn't even want to know where that was. He just wanted to go back into the dark if they'd let him alone, if there wasn't anybody going to come but doctors with tests and interns and if there was nothing to do but lie here and listen to the halls outside.

"Dek?" Female voice. "Dek?"

Voice he knew. Voice that shouldn't be here. So he was losing it. But if he was starting to hallucinate again maybe Ben wasn't gone. He came up out of the dark to see.

She was scarily real, Meg was, leaning over him. "How you doing?" she asked, and he said, "Dunno," because he didn't. She smelled real, she looked real, she sounded real. She asked him, "Anything wrong with the jaw?"

"No," he said, wondering why she asked, and Meg leaned down and kissed him the way she'd kissed him goodbye once, which caught him short of breath and half-smothered and no little dizzy as it went on, but if this was going to turn into one of those dreams, he didn't mind, he'd go out cold this way.

He got a breath, finally, he had Meg up close to his face, running a finger down his cheek, saying, "You been through some severely bad business, Dek. But it won't happen again. I'm here. Sal's here. Ben's here. We won't let the bastards get to you."

Good news. He really wanted to believe it. But he didn't let himself sink into the fantasy all the way. He only flirted with the idea, asking warily, "How'd you get here?"

She settled her hand on his, gave his fingers a squeeze. "They sent to me in the Belt, said, You got a friend in trouble, you want to come, and I said, Sure. Why not? I could do with a change."

So she wasn't leveling with him. That could only mean his subconscious couldn't think of an answer. Second question: "What about Sal?"

"Sal said she couldn't trust me on my own, said she'd keep me honest."

Her fingers on his felt warm and solid. She was in Shepherd civvies, she had this fondness for big earrings and he didn't remember the ones she was wearing. He wasn't artistic, he couldn't make up ones he didn't know, spiral and gold with some kind of anodized bar down the middle. He couldn't make up the blue eyeshadow and the pink. He wouldn't put those colors together with red hair. But it looked good. She did. And her really, truly being here was crazier than his thinking she was.

Third question. "Where's Ben this morning?"

"Ben's in the lieutenant's office. Ben's real pissed. Something about his security clearance and him supposed to be in Stockholm—didn't altogether make sense, but he was going to go complain. —What's this about you arguing with a simulator?"

Panic hit him. But he didn't know why he should be afraid of Meg. Or Ben. Or why there was a gap around his recollection of the sim room. Sounds. Mag hum and sudden motion. Ominous. Something had happened under that sound.

"There's been a hearing," Meg said, "senators all over the place. They're leaving. Ben asks if you'd like to tell them anything. Says if you could tell them how you got banged up it might be a good idea."

Senators. Mission control. Rows of instruments. Instruments on the sim panel, just the same.

"Shit," he breathed, feeling a cold sweat come on him. But it was all right, the memory was gone again. He willed his heart to slow down, stop fluttering like that: they filled him full of drugs if they caught his pulse up, and if they caught Meg here, Meg could be in trouble—Meg might not come back. People went out the door and you didn't know if—

— the Company'd let them back.

No. Not the Company. Tanzer. The UDC, that ran this place. . . . "Ben explained a skosh," Meg said, rab-speak, long time back, it seemed now. The Inner System had changed so, even in the few years he'd been to the Belt and back. "You don't got seriously to say: I know about the accident. But you got to get out of here, Dek, you got to get yourself straight. Ben said I should ask you the date."

"2324," he said, and found it suddenly worth a laugh, with what breath he could find. "2324." Meg didn't know why that message from Ben should be funny and he couldn't explain, he hadn't the coherency to explain, he kept seeing the readouts in the spex in front of him, green and red and gold, and, *dammit,* he could make it, he could've made it, but when he tried to imagine past that point the controls wouldn't work, weren't going to work again until he could get his hands on them and change those numbers. . . .

Meg shook his shoulder. "Heads up, Dek. First thing you got to do, you got to get straight. Ben said you didn't get into that pod on your own. That you should remember for him. He really needs that, Dek."

Sim room. Noise. And the memory just stopped. Got his pulse rate up again. "Can't. Can't get hold of it, Meg. Meg, —"

She leaned close and whispered in his ear, "You want to go back to barracks and you and me do a little rec-time? Mmmn?"

Offer like that—from Meg—could raise a corpse. Meg's touch on his cheek could. He thought about the barracks, had a sudden cold jolt, thinking of Meg there, and Ben and Sal; and not the faces he remembered. A whole puzzle-piece of his life just lifted out, gone, and another one clicked in, not the same shape, there were still dark spots—there'd been another puzzle-piece before that; but it was close, it was damned close. Pete and Elly and Falcone, they wouldn't have understood Meg. Wouldn't have gotten on with her, not easy. Might not get on with Sal or Ben. Cory either. He looked Meg in the eyes and remembered his blood pressure, realized he wasn't wearing the sensor.

Several things clicked into place. Where he was. How he

hadn't gotten his shot this morning, either. How he was clearer-headed now than he'd been since—

More panels. Instruments red-lighting. Alarms screaming. Inner ear going crazy.

"You all right, Dek?" Finger along his cheek. "You're white. You want me to call a doctor? Dek?"

He shook his head, suddenly sure of that. He sucked in a breath and got an elbow up under him, to see if his head was going to spin. Weak, God. Meg was trying to help him, saying he should lie down. But he didn't think so, he had a bad feeling about lying down and letting Meg call a doctor, they'd give him shots again and he'd go to sleep and go on sleeping—

He shoved up onto his hands, swung his feet over the edge. The room was tilting, felt like the pod, but he kept his eyes on the line where the wall met the floor. He sat there getting his breath and making the room stay steady.

"You sure you better not get back in that bed?"

He moved his arm. That shoulder had hurt. Didn't now, as much. He kept his eyes on that line and said, "Want to get up, Meg. Just give me a hand."

She did that. He didn't need it to lean on. He just needed it steady. Second reference point. He made it to his feet, risked a blink, then shut his eyes and stood there a moment. He opened them and took a step, with Meg's help. "Shot to hell," he muttered. "Too much zero *g*."

"Does that to you," Meg agreed. "Going back to it?"

"Inner ear's playing me tricks." Another step. A third. He took a breath, let go her hand and took a fourth.

"They ought to have had you walking. Especially a spacer. Especially you. What're the doctors worth in this place?"

A moment of vertigo. He got it back again. "Meg, how in hell'd you get here?" Months to get in from the Belt. They'd told her he was in trouble? Time threatened to unravel again. Except—

"Just caught a passing carrier. You got people real worried about you, Dek. Important people."

Carrier could make that passage in a handful of days. Better than that, the rumor was. And a carrier pulled Meg out of the Belt? Out of a berth she'd risked her neck to get? "Meg, make 'em send you back, don't get mixed up in this, I don't want you, I don't want you here—"

"Hell if, boy-doll. Anyway, I signed the papers. Going to make me an officer—"

"Oh, shit. Shit, Meg!" The room went spinning. He just stared at Meg's face for a reference point and kept his feet and knees from moving. "You were where you wanted."

"Yeah, well. It's not all al-tru-istic. —You want to sit down, Dek?"

"No." A shake of his head that risked his balance. "No. I'm all right. I need to stand up. They won't let me stand up. Have I got any clothes in that locker?"

Meg looked. He didn't dare track on her. She said, "No."

"Meg, I want you to go to the lieutenant. . . ."

"Graff?"

"Graff. I want you to go to him—" The place could be bugged. But there was nothing else to do. "I want you to tell him I need help. I don't trust what they're giving me. I want out of here."

"This then or now, Dek? Who's doing this?"

He tried a step and another one. His heart was pounding. Sounds came distant and strange. He walked as far as the door, opened it, and gambled his stability on a look at Meg. "You remember your way out of here?"

"Yeah."

"I'll walk you to the door. Five on ten I don't get that far. But you'll know, then, won't you?"

"Shit, Dek."

"Yeah." He took her arm. She grabbed his hand. "Let's walk, huh?"

* * *

"Aboujib," Graff said, and put out his hand for a non-reg handshake. Dark-skinned, exotic as they came to Inner System eyes, and by Ben Pollard's recommendation and the enlistment records, a Company-educated disciplinary wash-out who'd gotten another kind of rep among the Shepherds. Jamil had been by to give him a quick word. Pollard had shown up for his appointment with Aboujib in tow—one Meg Kady was 'visiting Dekker' on Pollard's pass ("It'll work in the lock," Pollard had said, with airy disregard of UDC security, but Pollard was *not* unconcerned, Pollard had just smiled, put a thoroughly stripped personal card on his desk and said, "I'm screwed, sir. Do you think you could just possibly get somebody to do something about this? *They* just put me in your command, sir, I'm UDC, and I'm mortally worried the colonel's going to want to talk to me.")

Hell in a handbasket. As the Earthers said. And here was the rest of Dekker's former crew, in on the Sol One shuttle without a word of explanation, warning, or advice what to do with them?

He wasn't highly pleased with the captain right now. Not pleased with Tanzer, not pleased with the situation, and not pleased to know one of the pair was loose in hospital on somebody else's Fleet pass.

But Jamil had been damned cheerful, saying, "We got us a couple of recruits, lieutenant. —Mitch is going to die."

It could give a man the feeling something was passing by him. And that things were careening out of control. "Welcome in, Aboujib. Scan-tech, is it?"

"Yessir." Aboujib had a solid grip, a steady eye, a distractingly quirky dimple beside a pretty mouth—and she was outside his crew and off limits, endit, right there. Not many women among the Shepherds and a consequent short-age of women in the program; and one of Dekker's former partners?

The captain had put Dekker's unit together again. That was what was happening. Keu wasn't saying a thing—so

FleetCom wasn't secure: the captain was just doing it, case by case: somebody had moved a *carrier* in from the Belt, for God's sake, or *Victoria* was back in-system: no other way to ferry Aboujib and Kady here since the accident.

Which could mean the captain hadn't been on Sol One for the last week; could mean Mazian had interrupted his diplomatic receptions to take a hand; or it might mean Keu had help: cooperative command in action—Col. Tanzer, *sir.*

He said, "Very glad to have you aboard, Aboujib. . . ." and the phone beeped. His calls were routing through the carrier's board and that wasn't to be ignored. He picked up the receiver, said, "Graff here," and heard:

"Lieutenant?" Thin voice. Strained. *"Dekker. Need some help, sir."*

"Shove it!" he heard in the background. Female voice. And something happened.

A hand came under Dekker's arm. Pulled. The nurse took hold of Meg's arm and lost that grip. Fast.

"You want those fingers, mister, you keep 'em the fuck *off my arm.*"

The nurse had hit an alarm, or something: a light was flashing. But Dekker knew where he was, he knew who was keeping his balance for him and he'd trust Meg in the black deep of space. He said, "Door, Meg. Now."

"He's not released," the nurse said. Other meds showed up. Higgins arrived at the desk, looked at Meg and said, "Who are *you?*"

"Ben Pollard right now," Meg said. "Ben's getting my pass straightened out."

"Get security," Higgins said to someone in the hall. "Lt. Dekker, they'll take you to your room."

"No such." He held his feet. "I'm going." Head was killing him. But standing was easier. "Where's my uniform?"

Security showed up, MPs, UDC. An MP grabbed for Meg, and next thing he knew he'd grabbed the MP—the guy looked at him, he looked at the guy with his fist doubled, but the MP with a fistful of his pajamas wasn't about to hit a hospital case. So he kept his hold on the MP, the MP kept his hold on him, and they stared at each other while the interns tried to drag him away. "You tell Tanzer fuck himself. Hear? —Meg? Get. Get out of here."

They told her, "You're under arrest. You're not going anywhere," and Meg said,

"Hell if. Spiel on, chelovek, a judge is going to hear every word of this. You seriously better not bruise him."

"Now wait a minute." Higgins pulled the MP off—tried to: he wasn't about to let go his only anchor, and Higgins was upset. "All right, all right, calm down. Everybody calm down. Lt. Dekker, let go of him."

Things were graying out. But he got a breath and held on, said, rationally, he hoped, "I'm walking out of here and I'm going back to my barracks."

Meg said, "Dek, calm down."

Her, he listened to. Kept his grip the way the MP held on to him and listened to Meg say, "He had a seriously bad time with Company doctors. Fed him full of prescription drugs, while he was spaced. You let him go. He'll be all right."

"I'm not a damn mental case, Meg."

Higgins said, smooth as silk, "We're not maintaining that. He's had concussion and broken bones. If you're a friend of his, persuade him back to bed."

"I've been in bed too damned long. Won't let me up, won't let me walk—"

"You've been to therapy, lieutenant. Don't you remember?"

Scared him. He *wasn't* sure. He didn't argue with what they might be able to prove. Or fake records for. He was afraid he was going to pass out, and end the argument that way. "I want my release. Now."

Higgins frowned, bit his lip. Finally, "I'll release you to your CO. Personally. If he wants you. Ms. —?"

"Kady. Magritte Kady. Meg, to whoever." She stuck out

her hand. Higgins looked confused and angry. "Higgins, is it?"

He ignored the hand. "Do you mind explaining who the hell you are and where you came from?"

"Manners," Dekker said. Still with his grip on the MP, he looked the man close in the eyes and said, "You want to let go? I want to let go."

Man wasn't amused. Man said, "Doctor?"

"Let him go."

Took a bit just to get his hand unclenched. The MP's uniform had a circle of sweaty wrinkles. The MP refused to straighten it. Man was cold and thin-lipped, and mad as hell. UDC was full of those types. He reached for Meg's hand and said, "Let's go."

"There are forms to fill out," Higgins said. "And a physical."

"Had one," he said, walking—he hoped Meg knew where the door was: he didn't. He halfway expected the MP was going to have his way after all. He remembered he was in pajamas when he saw the door. He didn't know any way back to the barracks but the Trans. Didn't know how he was going to stay conscious through that ride. Little bit of *g* it pulled would wipe him out.

But Meg steered him for a bench by the door and set him down. "You just stay there a minute. I'm going to go back there and call your CO. Isn't anybody coming near you. —Is your CO going to pull you out?"

"Yeah, yeah, I think he's already got somebody coming."

"Then I'll stand here and wait. If you're sure. —You going to be all right?"

"Yeah," he said. His teeth had started to chatter. He was barefoot. The pajamas weren't worth much. Meg took off her coat, put it around his shoulders, and made him hold on to it. She left him a moment and came back with a blanket, God knew how.

She said, "Higgins is severely pissed. He's on the phone.

But the nurse is all right. Nurse asked if you wanted a chair.''

Nurse was the one he'd hit. More than once. He shook his head, with some remorse for that—and regret for missing his chance at Higgins. Meg tucked the blanket around him, and under his bare feet, and sat down and offered him a warmer place to lean. They'd never been to bed together, had just been letter writers, at 830 million k remote from each other. They'd discovered they were attracted to each other too late to do anything about it, except that goodbye kiss. And now a hello one, a hug and a place to lean on, when he'd gotten to the absolute bottom of his strength. Meg never found him but what he was a mess. And here she was, he'd no idea how. She hadn't come straight with him. And maybe sitting here with her like this was all another hallucination. If he was hallucinating this time he didn't want to come back again, didn't want to fight them, didn't want to get even, didn't want to prove anything to anybody. Just sit, long as he could, long as he could hold himself awake.

Meg said, ''Well, well, *blue* uniforms, this time. That us?''

He focused stupidly on figures the other side of the glass. On one young, fair-haired . . . Graff, for God's sake. With Fleet Security.

He bit his lip til it hurt enough. He said, ''Don't let me fall, Meg,'' and stood up, letting go the blanket, as Graff came through the Perspex doors. ''Lt. Graff, sir.''

Graff looked at him, up and down, Graff frowned—you could never tell what Graff was thinking. Could have been of skinning him alive, for all he could read.

Meg said, ''They've been drugging him to the gills, sir. He never did do well with that.''

Graff said to the MPs, ''Take him to the ship.''

''Barracks,'' Dekker said, then was sorry he'd objected. He'd take anywhere but here. But he didn't know the ship.

He wanted somewhere he knew. He wanted people he knew, namely Meg, and Sal, and Ben.

"Just long enough for a check-up," Graff said. "I want you on record, Dekker. From the outside in. You behave yourself, hear? No nonsense."

"Yessir," he said. He let Security take hold of him, he sat down and they said they were going to borrow a chair; he heard Graff tell Meg Welcome in; and: "Hereafter, don't start a war. Wait for the UN to declare it."

"Yessir," Meg said. Which wasn't a word he ever recalled from Meg Kady. But Meg had enlisted. The fool. The absolute fool, if that was the price of Meg's ticket here. He felt tears in his eyes, thinking about that.

But damned if he could figure out how she'd managed it, all in all.

Time had gotten away from him again. It kept doing that. So maybe he was, the way Ben said, crazy.

CHAPTER

6

"WELCOME back," they said, "welcome back, Dek." Jamil and Trace, Pauli and Almarshad and Hap Vasquez—they intercepted him at the door when he was only calculating how much strength he had to get to his own quarters and fall into bed. Jamil warned the rest about grabbing hold of him, thank God, most of all thank God for Ben and Meg and Sal Aboujib showing up out of the depth of the room to rescue him from too much input too fast . . . he was tracking on too much: he knew and didn't know in any detail what he'd said to the guys or what they'd said to him, and for one dislocated moment he really thought Pete or Elly or Falcone was going to turn up in the barracks; they always had . . .

But they weren't going to do that ever again, dammit, end report, o-mega; he was here on this wave of time, and by a break of bad luck they weren't, and he was going to fall on his face if the guys didn't let him get to his quarters. He'd spent hours out in a null *g* sickbay, been prodded and probed and sampled and vid-taped from angles and in a condition he didn't want on the evening news, and his imagination until now had only extended to lying down in quiet, not running an emotional gauntlet of friends of dead friends— who could see how absolutely he'd been screwed over, dammit, when he should at least have gotten some of theirs back. He didn't know what had happened to him in hospital, not all of it; he didn't know what he'd admitted to, most of all couldn't remember what had put him there, and by that, he'd evidently let the lieutenant down, too, in some major way . . .

"Come on," Meg said, and he walked across a tilting, unstable floor, around a corner, down a short hall to a familiar door and a room that had been—images kept flashing on him out of a situation he didn't remember—cold and empty the last time he'd left it, clothes in the lockers nobody was going to use any more. . . .

Now it was alive with voices and faces out of a period of his life that never should have recrossed his track, except it was like a gravity well, things didn't fly straight, they kept coming around at you again and he didn't even know the center of mass. That should be a calculable thing. He should be able to solve that problem, with the data he had. . . .

"Get him in bed," Meg was saying, "he's severely spaced," and Ben said, "Damned fool had to walk it, where's his head anyway?"

Ben never minced words. He could cope with Ben far better than he could Sal Aboujib, who, after Ben had got him onto his bunk, pinned him with hands on either side of him, looked him in the face so close he was cross-eyed and said, "Oh, he's still pretty. Dek, sincerely *good* to see you. So good you're in one piece—"

"*Let* him alone. God!" Meg shoved Sal aside. "Man's severely had enough for a while. Go get his supper. Do you mind?"

Numb at this point. Completely numb. You hyped, and if things wouldn't calculate, what could you do but handle the things you could? He said, "Not reg."

Sal said, "Nyet. Lieutenant cleared it. Sandwich all right, Dek? Chips?"

"Yeah, I guess." Sandwich meant fish of some kind and that nauseated him. Then he thought of what he did want. What he'd wanted in his lucid moments in the hospital. "Hamburger and fries. —" And simultaneously remembered what happened to Belters who ventured the quick food in the cafeteria. "You watch the hamburgers, Sal. It's real stuff—"

"Dead animals," Ben said, and shuddered.

"Fish are animals," Meg declared.

"No, they're not."

The argument went completely surreal. The noise did. He was lying here and people promising to get him a hamburger were arguing Belter sensibilities, enzymes and whether fish were intelligent. "Milkshake," he said. But he was tired and he wanted to get under the sheets he was lying on, which took far too much effort. He just shut his eyes a moment and something warm settled over him. Blanket. And a weight pressed the mattress beside him and an arm arched over him.

He focused blearily on Meg. "Why in hell did you come here? You got no business here—"

"We'll talk about it later."

"We'll talk about it while there's still a chance, before you get into the security stuff—" The meds would say his blood pressure was getting up again. His eyes were blurry. He made the effort to lean on one arm, the one that hadn't been recently broken, and gathered all the detail of a face he'd never thought he'd see again. He'd wanted her once. He didn't know if he still did—didn't want to want her. Didn't know if he could take another dead friend. "Damn thing's a meatgrinder, Meg, the colonel's an ass—"

"Yeah, so Ben said. —Are you getting out? Seems to me you got a serious excuse here. Thinking about a Medical?"

His mind went blank on that. He couldn't see himself doing anything else. He couldn't see himself shoving freight around, going back to pusher work. But the future he'd had before the accident was black and void in front of him, just—not do-able now. For the last year he'd chased after being the first pilot to run that course. Making it. He'd believed that, even through the funerals of those who hadn't. And that wouldn't happen, couldn't happen, now, everybody was dead but him—

"You *want* to get out of the service?" Meg asked him.

He kept trying to look at that dark ahead. And finally he shook his head. No, he didn't want out. He didn't know what he was going to do, but he didn't want out of the Fleet—didn't know who might go with him next run, didn't know what they could pull together into a crew that wouldn't take another one apart—didn't want that. Maybe that was why he couldn't see where he was going. Crew was gone, they might well drop him back in training, let him shape up with Meg and Ben and Sal from the beginning up—granted Tanzer didn't kill the program.

Meanwhile some other crew would make that first run; and the second; and the third—he'd take the controls after someone else had flown the ship and it was documented and tame enough for the second line to try.

And maybe that was sanity. Forget his notions: maybe it wasn't what he'd trained for, wasn't what he'd wanted, but it was a way back into the cockpit, forget the naive confidence he'd had in his invincibility. He wasn't a kid any more. God hope he wasn't a fool any more, who had to have that number one status or kill himself and everyone with him.

He gave up the prop of his arm, fell back again and gathered the bedspread and pillow under his head. He looked in Meg's eyes and didn't see a woman who was young and mind-fried with love—just a friend, a sane, brave friend, who was older than he was, and whose reasons he didn't honestly know.

"Meg, I'm serious, don't want to offend you. Good to see you. Good you came. But if you've got any loophole

out of enlisting, any way in hell back to the berth you had,
you should go back. . . .''

"Five hundred-odd million k, I come for this man. What
about those letters you wrote? 'Getting along fine, a real
chance at something, the first thing in my life I know I want
to do—' ''

"That was bullshit. It's like anywhere else. We got a fool
in charge."

"Yeah, well, we dealt with fools before. Got no shortage
of 'em in the Belt. Some have even got seniority."

"They got plenty of it here. —Too damn many funerals,
Meg. I'm sick to death of funerals—''

"Death is, jeune rab. Better to burn than rot."

Plasma spreading against the dark. Whiteout on the cameras. He said, urgently, "Meg, go back where you've got a
life, for God's sake. You've got a berth—''

"—without shit worth of seniority."

"Well, you won't get any here. They won't count your
hours, just give you a flat 200. Spend your whole life out in
the Belt and that's all it's worth. They'll screw you any way
they can."

"Mmmnn. Yeah. Sal's seriously pissed about that—but
she's computers anyway. Straight quantifiable skills stuff. *I*
was an EC shuttle pilot, remember? Earth to orbit. LEO to
Sol One. You name it, I ran it, four years riding the gravity
slopes. And it's all in the EC's own infallible records. Here,
I *got* seniority."

"Shit," he said, cold inside, he didn't know why, except
Meg was hell to stop when she had an idea, and Tanzer was
a damned fool. It'd be like the UDC, to look at just that
record of Meg's hours and do something seriously stupid.
Like put a shuttle jock on the combat line. "Meg, you don't
know. We got innate stupidity here, serious innate stupidity.
The equipment's a real stress generator, you understand me?
They made the sims realtime to start, but the UDC guys
won't spend four, five hours in the sims, hell, no, we're too
short on sim-time for that, and we got guys too *experienced*

to need that, so what do we do? We pitch the sims down to be do-able. *Comfortable*. Spread the time around. You read that?'' His head ached. His voice was going. The capacity to care was. ''They're killing us. Take guys with reflexes to do the job, and then they fuck with the sims till you got no confidence in them. That's a killer, Meg, that's a damn killer, ship's so sensitive you can screw the thing if you twitch—''

''You fly it?''

A memory chased through his nerves, oxygen high and an adrenaline rush, hyperfocused—

''Yeah,'' he said, voice gone shaky with memory. ''Yeah. Mostly the sims. But twice in the ship.'' And he knew why he wasn't going to take a Medical. Better to burn, Meg had said. And he did that. He did burn.

Door opened. ''Mustard or ketchup?'' Sal's voice. ''Got one each way. . . .''

''Mustard,'' he said, grasping after mundane sanity. The smell ought to make him sicker than hell, the hospital food hadn't smelled of grease and he'd all but heaved eating it. But maybe it was the company: maybe it was the smell that conjured the cafeteria and the sounds and shoptalk over coffee: he suddenly wanted the burger. He took a real chance with his stomach and his head and hitched his shoulders around against the wall so he could sit up to eat, and handle the milkshake. A sugar hit, carbohydrates and salt, a guaranteed messhall greaseburger with dill pickles, chili sauce, tomatoes and mustard—

''How can you *eat* that?'' Ben asked. ''God!''

Meg said, ''Shut up, Ben,'' and took the ketchup burger herself.

Earth system, Meg had to be, then. Rab, rad, and, Meg had said it once, falling behind the wave of change on Earth: go out into the Belt and you stepped back a century at least—old equipment, a hodgepodge of antique fads and fashion—rab-rad gone to Shepherd flash and miner Attitude. But Meg was old genuine rab, he believed it, the rab they'd gunned down at the Company doors when he was a kid. So Meg had come home to hamburgers and ideas she was so far out of the current of, he hurt for her. And he was scared for her.

Damn right she was a pilot. The Fleet was raking up all the recruits they could beg or bribe away from the Shepherds, and they'd evidently made her an offer, given her her hours—a fool friend, an almost-lover near young enough to be her son, cracked up in hospital, needn't have been any part of it. Couldn't go by what Meg said. Couldn't. She had a lot of virtues, but strict accounts wasn't one of them. It was enough she'd come to the hospital to get him. It was enough she'd stand there and risk arrest and losing everything to get him out. Meg was like that. Might go, might stay. But if she stayed—

—if she stayed—

He got most of the hamburger down. He got down half the shake and half the fries. He sat there in a room with Ben and Sal talking about computers and the UDC, and Meg wolfing down the first hamburger she must have had in years, and looking not a bit changed—a few more lines around the eyes, maybe. And when he had to put the rest of his shake aside, he shut his eyes for just a moment and sat there, and thought about Cory. He thought about Bird, and the Belt. He thought he was there for the moment, but it wasn't a serious drift, just remembering. Safe.

Want to break his damn neck, Ben thought. Skuz ate the mess and went out cold, no wonder. Poor dead cow. Fish *weren't* intelligent. Thank you.

Sal leaned on his arm and whispered a thoroughly indecent proposal, which reminded him what he hadn't gotten in the last year, what with the course work and the computer time and all—a proposal that didn't make a man think all that clearly about the value of his life and the necessity of getting out of this hellhole . . .

"Yeah," he said thickly, directing thoughts to getting his

ass out of here *and* snagging Sal into the TI—and down to Stockholm. Sal was damned good. In several senses. "Yeah. —Meg, *hate* to leave you with the skuz there, —d' you mind sitting on him?"

"Any way he can make it," Meg said smugly. "Us freefallers are adaptable—how's yourself, Ben?"

He *was* out of practice. Polite society did that. He actually felt his face warm. "Hell, ask Sal in a while."

Sal hooked her arm in his and said, "Details later. Serious interpersonal relations. —You got a notion where, mate?"

"Whole damn room to ourselves," he said. And elbowed the door open.

Dek said, "You want to dispose that?" and handed Meg the remnant of the milkshake. She went to the bath to dump it and came back to find Dek on his feet rummaging a locker—his, she figured, and hoped he wasn't thinking of getting dressed. Her own back ached with the *g*-shift off the shuttle—she'd gotten soft, living on the *Hamilton*'s c-forced decks. It was the little muscles that hurt, the ones you used pulling your body around in freefall, a lot of them in unusual places, and she seriously didn't want to face the guys outside....

"You're not going to walk," she said; he ignored the question, lifted a stack of folders in the top of the locker and said, sounding upset, "The tape's gone."

"What tape?"

"Sim tape. I guess they took it back to library. Damn sure they've been through here."

"They?"

"MPs. Crash investigators. Whatever."

"They already had the hearing, Dek. VIPs left this morning."

He was looking white. He leaned one-handed against the locker frame and looked at nowhere. "I'm tracking, Meg."

Meaning quit treating him like a spacecase. Joli jeune

rab, face like a painted angel and a body language that said Screw *you*—in any sense you wanted to take it.

A lot like herself, truth was. But there had to come a moment in a lifetime when a person looked in the mirror and knew age had happened; and Dek was her mirror—that body and that face that carried all its worry-lines in muscle, not engraved permanently beside the mouth or around the eyes. Age had sneaked up on her; and Dek's mama wasn't older, she'd bet on it. So might be he didn't want any forty-year-old woman putting the push on him. With his looks he'd have his pick of anybody out there, and probably had had, all his life—probably had damned well enough of everybody who saw him wanting him, and no few laying uninvited hands on him—pretty guy had that problem no less than anybody else; maybe more, because *he* was supposed to like it.

So back off the kid, Magritte Kady, and shut the hell up—he's tired, he's probably sick to death of being hit on, probably thinking hard how to finesse a middle-aged woman out of his bed tonight; and not doing real well with the words, is he?

Dek didn't say anything. He wandered into the bath, ran water, came out again with his face and the front of his hair wet, and looked at her with eyes like a lost, battered kid's.

She said, "Nothing comes with the package. I came here to haul your ass out. Not laying claim to it by any right. Isn't as if I didn't get something—I got back to inner system, didn't I? So no debts. I owed you."

Disturbed him, that. She saw the frown. He said, "How's the arm?"

Half-thinking, she rotated the hand, lifted the arm. "Works."

"Reflexes?"

She shrugged, moved the thumb that was a little stiff. "Age is, jeune rab. It does hit us all."

"*You* aren't old, Meg."

Gallant jeune fils, too. She didn't let the face react. Just the gut felt pain. She told it shut up and laid out the truth.

"Still not saying I should have been at the controls, on my best day. You pulled our asses out of a bad one, Dek, you got what I never had: if you want me on your team, all right, I'll back you; or if you want me or Sal off it, you say that too, right now, plain as plain, because I owe it to Sal. I'm forty and counting, arm isn't what it used to be and it won't be again. Sal's young but she's got experience to collect. That's what you get. Can't lie to you. No good doing that. . . ."

He came closer. Looking into his face was a send-off; looking into his eyes was the deep dive, gravity well, painful as slow compression. His face went out of focus as he leaned and kissed her on the cheek—deeper hurt, that. But the jeune fils didn't, couldn't know. . . .

"Call it even," he said, then, "Paid is paid," —but his hands traveled down and behind her. Came a light kiss on the mouth that shook a forty-year-old's good sense. Another one that—

God.

"Don't *do* that," she said shakily, when she had a breath, and meant to crack some half-witted joke about their relative ages, but he said, "Bed, Meg," and pulled her down on the bunk with him.

Not real copacetic, no, the jeune fils had far more ideas than substance left, but clothes and covers went one way and the other, boots thumped out from under the sheets, and a bunk that wasn't designed for two meant real caution about putting an elbow into his sore spots. She did. But he said never mind, hell with the ribs, he didn't care, if he was hallucinating he didn't want to wake up, she could fly him to hell and gone, he'd take the trip—

Didn't care. That was the operative word, that was the danger word she was hearing from him—but she didn't know what to say on the instant but to punch him on the leg and say, "I'm damn well here, jeune rab. Shut up."

Struck him funny, somehow. Didn't recall as she'd ever seen him laugh like that, and there wasn't much healthy about it; but he sort of snuggled down then, hugging her close, said, "Anything you want, Meg, whatever you like," and started drifting out, little at a time.

Murmured, finally, "Cory, —" But she didn't take offense. Man'd busted his ass trying to save Cory Salazar, done everything for his partner a man could do and then some, and what would you want in a man—that he'd forget, now, and switch Cory off like a light?

Not any partner she'd ever give a damn for.

So she ruffled his hair, said, "Hush, it's Meg," and he said, with his eyes shut, "Meg, for God's sake get out, go back, don't get mixed up in this, dammit, you had a berth—"

"Yeah. They were going to make me senior captain. You got my knee pinned, you want to move over, Dek?"

Bed with Aboujib was a long, long experience. You didn't get away easy—tech-nique, Sal called it; and he didn't know—he was here, where the competition back at TI couldn't eavesdrop; and Sal wasn't a critic, Sal just took what was—Sal was all over you and kink as hell, maybe. You couldn't be ice with Sal, maybe that was why he was thinking suddenly, amid his attentions to Sal, that he *truly* didn't want Stockholm to see this side of Ben Pollard— that wasn't real sincerely in his right mind, feeling as he did for the moment that he'd actually missed R2's sleaze and neon, that he'd *missed* Mike Arczzo's synth-egg breakfasts and the noise of helldeck—

Stockholm was a VR image, Stockholm was special effects, there wasn't an Earth and you couldn't get to it, the Company only made it up to explain the universe—got its Earth-luxuries out of fancy tanks, it was all synth for all he knew, what the hell difference whether it was a cow or a tank culture, he wasn't going to eat what had blood running through it—hell, Earth was full of eetees no less than Pell, and what was Ben Pollard doing trying to fit in with people who ate hamburgers and ran a department that bought a damned EIDAT?

Ben Pollard was trying to stay alive and stay out of the war, that was what he'd been doing. Ben Pollard was back on helldeck, the bubble had burst, and what turned up but Sal Aboujib, the Fleet's own damnable *doing*, screw the bastard who was responsible for this—

Hell, when it came down to it, Dekker was *responsible* for it, it didn't matter the UDC and the Fleet had gotten their shot in, Dekker could reach out from the hereafter and screw his life up with one little touch, the way he'd screwed Cory Salazar's—way he'd screwed the program up—

Off chance that part wasn't his fault, but you didn't protect yourself by figuring a mess of this magnitude that Dekker just happened to be in the middle of—didn't have Dekker's fingerprints all over it. Wasn't that the guy necessarily did anything, he didn't have to do it, he just *was*. Like gravity and infall, things went wrong in his vicinity. . . .

Sal cut off his air, and lights went off a while. When he came down he was halfway tranquil, catching his breath, and said—it still bothered him: "You know, you could've written once."

Sal didn't answer that one right off. She came over on top of him and made a cage out of her elbows beside his head. Her braids hit him in the face. Her lips brushed his nose.

"That's no answer."

"Didn't figure you wanted one," Sal said.

Fair answer, one he hadn't thought of. Fact was, when he was trying to settle in with inner-system pets and sorting the threats from the bottom-enders he hadn't had but a few twinges of regret for helldeck—tried to clean the Belt out of his language, tried not to dream about it, just wanted to see those clean green numbers in his head, different life, Aboujib. Different aims. . . .

So he didn't answer that. He just said, "Here's seriously screwed. Dekker's involved. Thought you had better sense. Thought Meg had. I can understand her, maybe, got to be hell getting seniority out there, but *you're* Shepherd, you got the connections, you didn't have to dump and come—''

Sal slid down, slid over, rolled onto one elbow, all shadow, braid-clips a-wink in the dim light. Eyes eclipsed and looked at him again.

"Weren't treating her right, Ben. She took it. But, tell the truth, she wasn't seriously happy on the *Hamilton*."

"Personalities?"

Sal traced something with a long fingernail on the sheet between them. Second eclipse. And glanced up. "Could say. Guys put the push on her. Guys said—" Shift of the eyes toward the door and a lowered voice. "Said it was damned good she'd got shot, it put Dek at the controls. . . ."

"Shit."

Sal shrugged. "Probably true. She says it is. But that's the Attitude, you understand? She took the jokers. She took the shit. But they said she'd got an affinity for gravity wells, didn't want her flying in Jupiter's pull—big joke, right?"

Severely big joke. The idea of infalling a gravity well made him nervous as hell. Going down to Stockholm, if he got there, as happened, he intended to drink a lot of cocktails before the dive—because *he* was Shepherd—a Shepherd orphan, as happened, thank God he'd been on R2 when the ship went. But sometimes, on his worst nights, he dreamed of metal groaning, bolts fracturing, the sounds a ship would make when compression began—pop, and *bang* and metal shrieking—

Yeah, Shepherds made jokes. Shepherds defended the perks and prerogatives they got from the Company for flying where others couldn't. And Meg was insystemer, *inner* systemer, even blue-sky; and there on Sal's ticket. . . .

So Dekker got the credit with the Shepherds, for one hell of a flight; and Meg, who'd nearly got her arm blown off for the cause—got the shit: *Dekker* hadn't asked for a post with the Shepherds, that was the Attitudinal difference. . . .

"She wanted to come," Sal said. And gave a long breath. "Couldn't let her go alone."

"To find Dekker? She didn't effin' *know* him. She didn't—"

Pi-lut, he thought then. Meg was a pilot same as Dekker, didn't care about anything but to fly. And the Shepherds didn't want her at controls?

Double shit. But things the other side of the wall still didn't make sense in that light.

"So she's in *bed* with the guy?"

A movement of sheet, shrug of Sal's shoulders. Silence a moment. Then: "Hormones."

"What kind? That's the question."

"Like he's the best, you know what I mean? Beating him'd—I dunno, it'd prove a lot of things."

"God." He fell onto his back to think about that a tick.

"I mean," Sal said, "if even the Fleet had offered her back then what they'd offered Dekker—if they'd just *offered*, she'd have been gone. But she was lying in pieces and patches, as was—couldn't blame them, really, but it severely did hurt. . . ."

Up on his elbow again. He was hearing craziness he might have to fly with. "She's not any damn twenty-year-old, Sal, if you want to talk hormones, here, you got to have a whole different wiring. Reactions aren't there. They're not going to *be* there for any sane human, Sal, the guy's flat crazy, it seems to be a pre-rec on this ship—"

Silence a moment. Sal was all shadow and maybe anger, you couldn't know when you were talking to a cutout in the dark. Finally Sal said, with a definite edge to her voice, "She's not any twenty-year-old, but she was *damned good*, Ben, you weren't out there with us, you didn't see how she'd finesse a rock—and we got shit, Ben, the Company gave us *shit* assignments, because we were worse than freerunners, we were freerunner *lease* crew, and they were trying to run us broke, to crack the ship-owners, that was what they were up to. We never got one good draw from that 'random assignment procedure'—Meg had a record on Sol, Meg was on the Company's hit list because Meg was rab, Meg didn't dress by the codes, Meg didn't think by the codes, Meg wouldn't kiss ass and they screwed her, Ben, same as B.M. screwed her, same as the *Hamilton* screwed her— So here the damn Fleet comes in and says, By the way, will you come in and haul Dek out of his mess? —Didn't even say, You want to fly for us? Said, You want to come haul this chelovek out of his funk and we'll cover your record? That's all, that's all they promised, Ben. And she got this look—shit, what was I going to do? She'd stuck by me. Maybe it's time somebody went with her."

He'd never heard Sal talk that way—Sal with an attack of Obligations. But, shit-all, —

That thought led down a track he didn't want to take, something about old times, about what they'd had on helldeck, confidence that came of knowing the guy you were sharing a ship with wasn't out to screw you—whole damn universe might be out to do that, but your partner wouldn't, your partner had to have the same interests you did, and you just didn't cheat on him.

You just didn't cheat on him. . . .

He rolled out of bed, buck naked and cold in the draft from the vents, he walked over to the other bunk and leaned his arm against it, because if he stayed in that bed he was going to start thinking about Morrie, and he didn't like to do that, not in the middle of the dark.

So Sal was being a fool. So Meg thought she could get the years she'd lost back again and the system wouldn't screw them all.

Rustle from behind him. Movement. Arms came around him, and the chill myriad clips of Sal's braids rattled against his back.

"Cold out here, Ben."

"I want out of here, dammit, I'm not aptituded for combat. I got a place in Stockholm . . ."

Sal said, holding him tight, "What's Stockholm?"

CHAPTER

7

MAINDAWN and in the office early, trying, before the mainday rush hit, to make sense of the reports from the designers and the sims check. Graff took a slow sip of vending machine coffee, keyed the next page on the desktop reader. The report writer liked passives: 'will be effectuated,' 'will be seen to have incremented,' and especially convolutions: 'may have been cost-effective in the interim while result-negative in the longrange forecast—'

Graff keyed the dictionary for 'forecast.' It said something about 1) terrestrial weather patterns and, 2) prediction. The latter, he decided, but keyed it up; and found something, as he'd suspected, different than his own definition of 'prediction.' These were the people who designed the computers and the software that ran the sims, for God's sake, and they were giving him messages about Old Earth weather patterns and fortune-telling?

He tried to read these reports out of Tanzer's staff. He felt responsible in the captain's absence. He worried about

—146—

missing something. He worried about not understanding Tanzer face to face, and these were the only lessons in blue-sky usage on his regular reading list.

'Effectuated,' he could guess from particles. And he didn't have that small a vocabulary. He *didn't* use that many semicolons in his reports; he wondered was his style out of fashion; and he wished not for the first time that he'd had at least one of the seminal languages—given the proliferation of derived meanings, that was what Saito called the problem words, cognates; and metaphor. All of which meant a connection between 'forecast,' planetary weather, and the Lendler Corp techs who, between working on the sims and writing reports, danced a careful and convolute set of protocols between his office and Tanzer's—'effectuate,' hell. 'Obfuscate' and 'delegate' and 'reiterate,' but nothing *effectual* was going to happen with that investigation except Lendler Corp gathering evidence to protect itself against lawsuits from the next of kin.

Save them the trouble. Stick to Belters. Belters didn't sue Corporations, Belters didn't have the money or the connections to sue Corporations.

But come into *their* territory—

Lendler didn't want to do that. Didn't want to interview the Belters. Even when he had it set up.

The phone beeped. He hoped it was Saito coming on-line: he could use a linguist about now—and he could wish Legal Affairs hadn't left their office to a junior: the Fleet needed to enlist a motherworld lawyer, was what they needed, maybe two and three of them, since they never seemed unanimous— he'd had the UDC counsel on the line last night, talking about culpabilities and wanting releases from the next-ofs—

"*Lt. Graff?*" Young male voice. Familiar male voice. "*Col. Tanzer on the line.*"

He'd never been in the habit of swearing. But association with the Belters did suggest words. He kept it to: "Put him on, Trev."

Pop. "*Lt. Graff?*"

"Colonel?"

"I'm looking at the file on Paul Dekker. Just wondered if you had any last-minute additions, before we write our finish on this accident business."

"I'd appreciate that, colonel, as soon as we finish our own investigation."

"Dekker's been released from hospital, I understand, on your orders."

Possibility of recorders. Distinct possibility. "Released to Fleet medical care. His blood showed high levels of tranquilizer and pain medication. My medical staff says it was excessive. Far excessive. The word malpractice figured in the report."

A moment of silence. *"Blood samples taken after he was in your doctors' care, lieutenant. I'll inquire, but you'll excuse me if I choose to believe our own personnel. File a separate report if you like. Call the Surgeon General. It's completely of a pattern with the rest of your actions. But you may find some of those chickens coming home to roost very shortly."*

Another one for Saito. But the gist of it got through, quite clearly.

Tanzer said: *"The phone isn't the place for this discussion. I'll see you in my office in ten minutes. Or I'll file this report as is, without your inspection, and add your objection in my own words."*

Moment of silence from his side. A moment of temptation to damn Tanzer for a bastard, hang up, and call the captain on uncoded com. He might be a fool not to have done that: Tanzer made little moves, niggling away at issue after issue, day after day; *damn* the man, he could be recording the conversation right now. But caution won. Follow the forms. "I'm on my way," he said.

The sojers had this perverse habit called reveille, which meant after the com scared hell out of you and you hauled yourself bleary-eyed awake, you ran for the breakfast line before the eggs disappeared—Meg had gotten into that routine on the ship coming here, got a few days spoiled on the shuttle, and here she and Sal were again—standing in line, the only females in sight, with two guys who drew their own kind of attention.

Orientation, the lieutenant had told her, outside hospital. Keep him busy. Push him, but not too hard. Don't let him off by himself.

Which meant they were a kind of bodyguard, she supposed. Against what, she wasn't sure—against Dek's own state of mind, high on the list: too much death, Sal put it, for anybody to tolerate. Everybody he'd gotten really close to, except Ben and her, had died; he'd watched it happen every damned time; and last night he was telling her to try to de-enlist, get out of his life?

Only convinced her how seriously she meant to follow the lieutenant's orders and keep a tag on him.

So Dek was supposed to show them around, get them acquainted with the classrooms and the VR labs and the library, get their own cards picked up. *Lab* schedule, soon as they could get settled, hell and away different than *she'd* learned flying, but that was the way they did it in the Fleet: Dek said you took a pill and they hooked you up to a tape and they fed the basics of the boards into you by VR display like programming some damned machine—

"Confuses you at first," Dekker was telling them, in the breakfast line, the other side of Ben. "Reactions cross what you know, you face it the next day and you don't remember learning something new—your hands know. They use it just to teach you the boards. The brain takes a while to get used to it—a while to know it knows. Handful of people can't take the pills. But it's rare."

She listened. She tried to imagine it.

"They're experimenting with that stuff over at TI," Ben said. "Hell if they're going to mess with *my* head. I'm a Priority 10. Programmer. Security clearance. Damn chaff, that's what's going on, it's that screwed-up EIDAT they're using—drop me in here and *my* level isn't in the B Dock system, oh, no, all it knows is pi-luts and dock monkeys, so I got to be one or the other, right? Right.'' Dollop of synth eggs onto Ben's plate. "So it lets some damn keypusher screw with my assignment. Does somebody over at Sol wonder where I am? Not yet. Personnel isn't supposed to think, oh, no, *they* trust the EIDAT. I got a post waiting for me, God hope it's still waiting. —What the hell *is* that stuff?''

"Grits," Dek said.

"Was it alive?''

"It wasn't alive." Dek slid his tray to the end of the line and drew his coffee.

"You want me to carry that?" Meg asked.

"I'm *fine*," Dek said, and stuck his card in the slot. "That's present and accounted for. Laser scans the bottom of the containers, figures your calories and your allotments—dietician's worse than—hell." Reader's read-line was blinking.

"You have a message," the checkout robot said, as if Dek couldn't read.

"'Scuse." Dek carried his tray over to a corner table, quiet spot, Meg was glad to note, following him, while Ben waited for Sal to check through—a skosh too many Shepherd eyes in this place for her personal comfort, all picking up every move they made. Hi, Dek, they'd say soberly, sounding friendly enough. Giving her and Sal the eye, that was a natural—women being severely scarce here; and sort of glossing Ben.

But the UDC boys looked at Ben and looked at them and heads sort of leaned together at tables, she could see it going on all over that other corner of the hall, thick with UDC uniforms.

Dek set his tray down. "I'll check that message blinker. Probably your stuff. Hope it's your stuff."

As Sal and Ben showed up with their trays and set them down.

"What's he doing?" Ben asked with a glance over his

shoulder. "You don't ask what a message is before breakfast, you never ask what a message is before breakfast—"

"Thinks it could be our accesses." Meg set her tray down and cast a glance at Dek over by the phone, a skosh anxious, she couldn't even tell why, except Dek had had this edge in his voice: he was On about something, she read it in his stance and his moves, and she hadn't been able to read all the codes that had popped up. She said, still on her feet, "Ben? You capish the code on that blinker?"

"Accesses stuff," Ben said, sitting down.

"Uh-oh," Sal said.

Understatement. Serious understatement. Dek hit the phone with his open hand. "Scuze," Meg said, and went that direction.

Dek snatched out his card, and ricocheted into her path. "What is?" she asked, catching at his arm. "Dek?"

"They clipped me, Tanzer's fuckin' *clipped* me, the son of a bitch." Dek shoved her and she didn't know whether to hang on or not—her hand stung as he blazed past her. But that didn't matter. Dek going for the door like a crazy man—that seriously mattered. Dek knocking into guys inbound—

Mitch, for God's sake—

Dek got past. Hot on his track she hit the same obstacle, who didn't give way a second time. Neither did the other guys. "Kady," Mitch said, not friendly. "I heard they'd gotten desperate."

"I got a seriously upset partner—out of my *way*, dammit!"

"So what's with Dekker?"

"Something about getting clipped."

"Shit!" Mitch said, and: "Pauli," to the big guy behind him, Shepherd from the hall yesterday. She remembered. "Haul his ass back here. Fast."

"What's going on?" Sal asked as she and Ben showed up with a handful of other curious.

"Dekker's been clipped," Mitch said. "Just calm down, we're going to see what the lieutenant says about this."

Hell if she understood 'clipped,' she didn't know Pauli from trouble, she knew Mitch too damn well, but Mitch's outrage at least sounded to be on Dek's side and stopping Dek seemed to be a priority on their side too. Pauli-whoever took out in the direction Dek had gone, and she went with, at a fast walk.

First corner showed an empty hall; but Pauli broke into a jog for a side corridor as if he knew where he was going, she caught up, and spotted Dek, all right, traveling at a fair clip himself.

"Dek!" she called out; and he stopped, took a damn-you stance and stared at them cold as cold.

All right. *That* was the surly young sumbitch she knew. She panted, "You got friends, chelovek, capish? Slow down. Deal with people."

Dek looked half poised to walk off. Pauli said, "Is it true? They pulled you?"

"Yeah." Dek's mouth didn't look to be working real well, he clearly didn't want to talk; but about that time Ben and Sal showed up with some of the other Shepherds from the messhall, Ben with:

"What's going on? —Dekker, are you being a spook?"

"Ben," Meg exclaimed. Sal said the same. But Dek made a disgusted wave of his hand and managed to unlock his jaw.

"Nothing's wrong, nothing's the hell wrong. Sorry I got you here. Sorry I got you into this."

A sane woman had to get things off personals. Fast. "Ben, Sal, this is Pauli, friend of Mitch's; Pauli: Ben Pollard, Sal Aboujib. Say how-do, and somebody answer a straight question, f' God's sake. What's going on here?"

"The damn UDC," Dek said, "that's what's going on. Tanzer's just tossed me out of the program."

"He can't do that," Pauli said. "Screw him. He can't do that."

Somebody else said, "No way, Dek." And another one:

"Mitch is on his way to talk to the lieutenant right now. No way that's going to stick."

Dek wasn't highly verbal. He was white, and sweating. Sal said, quietly, with her arm in Dek's: "You want to go back to the room, Dek?"

Ben said: "Screw it, he's got a breakfast sitting back there, we all got breakfast back there, if nobody's grabbed it."

Leave it to Ben. Sal had a crazy man halfway turned around and stopped from strangling the colonel and Ben wanted his effin' breakfast. Dek was looking at Ben like he was some eetee dropped by for directions.

"You mind?" Ben asked him impatiently.

"Yeah. All right," Dek muttered. And went with him.

God, both of them were spooks.

"I'm looking at Dekker's record," Tanzer said, tapping a card on his desk, "right here: the medical report and his disciplinary record—including his violent behavior here in hospital, his defiance of regulations in the sims—"

"His behavior, colonel, was thoroughly reasonable, considering the level of drugs in his system. Drugs with possible negative psychological impact considering his history—which is in that file. That from *my* medical experts. He has grounds for malpractice."

"This is the accident report." Tanzer shoved a paper form across the desk at him. "Sign it or don't, as you please. I'll spare you the detail. I'm *not* calling the hospital records into question, I'm *not* charging him with flagrant violations of security with that tape, I'm *not* charging him for disregard of safety regulations. I *am* concluding there was no other person involved in the sims accident but Ens. Dekker."

He kept every vestige of emotion from his face. "How are you proposing he got into that pod?"

"I'm supposing he got in there the ordinary way, lieutenant, the same as any fool can climb in there. He just happened to be on trank. These are the records of his admission—he was flying before he got in there.''

''Was put in there.''

''He was in illegal possession of a tape that should have been back in library—''

''He had license to possess that tape, colonel. He'd been in hospital, he'd just been released, in condition *your* medics knew when they let him out with a prescription drug in his system—''

''Whatever drugs were in his system, he put there, before he decided to go on a sim ride.''

''Pardon me if I don't rely on those doctors' word, colonel, or their records.''

''Rely on whatever you like. I'll tell you one thing: Dekker's barred from the sims.''

''He's going in there on my orders, colonel.''

''Check your rules, lieutenant. The sim facility and its accesses are under UDC direction.''

''You restrict one of my people from the sims, colonel, and the case is going clear to the Defense Department.''

''Then you better start the papers moving, lieutenant, because he's barred. And if you give a *damn* for your program you won't file—that's my unsolicited advice, because you don't want him in public. Take my word for it you don't want him in public. But until I get cooperation out of your office, you don't get cooperation out of mine.''

''Do I understand this as blackmail? Is that what you want? My signature, and Dekker's back in?''

''I wouldn't put it that way. But let's say it might signal a salutary change of attitude.''

''No deal. *No* deal, colonel. And you can stand by for FleetCom to be in use in fifteen minutes.''

''Good. About time you woke up your upper echelons. Tell them they've got a problem with Dekker. A serious problem.''

* * *

Trays were still sitting. They came into the messhall and guys stopped and stared in that distant way people had when they were trying to spy on somebody else's trouble. Talk stopped, mostly, and started again, and Dek didn't look at anybody, didn't talk to anybody, just sat down at his place at table and put the straw in his orange juice.

Ben gave her a tight-jawed look. Table was still all theirs. Pauli and the guys had gone off toward the breakfast line, but they hadn't made it: they'd gotten snagged, talking to guys over by the wall, all Shepherd. There were UDC guys on the fringes—tables were either UDC or they were Shepherd, Meg marked that suddenly: there wasn't another mixed table in the whole damned hall.

She didn't like the quiet. Didn't like the feeling around them. Dek was having his eggs. Ben was having toast. Sal gave her a look that said she was right, everybody else was crazy but them.

Young woman, blond hair in a shave-strip, came up, set her tray down, said, "You mind, Dek?"

Dek shrugged. That one sat down. "Trace," the interloper said, looking her way, and offered her hand across the tray as a dark-skinned Shepherd kid took the seat next to Sal: "Almarshad. Friends of friends."

Pauli sat down, him with no tray, and said, "It's us Tanzer's after. —Pollard, you mind to answer whose side you're on?"

Hell of a question, Meg thought. She watched Ben frown and think, then say, with a cold sweet smile on his face: "Hell, I'm not in Tanzer's command. I'm Security-cleared. I'm Computer Technical, out of TI. I'm due somewhere else, and if I get there, frying Tanzer's ass'd be ever so little effort. So why doesn't somebody get me out of here?"

"Hear you were a good numbers man," Pauli said.

The frown came back. "Damned good," Ben said. Ben wasn't lying. "But I'm not flying with him. I'm not flying with you guys. I'm not friggin' going *near* combat..."

"Small chance you'll have in my company," Dek said

under his breath. "If they get this mess cleared, it'll just be one more thing they find. Dammit, Pete and Elly—what in *hell* is it with me that—"

Pauli's hand came down on Dek's wrist and shut him up. Thank God, Meg thought. She didn't know the danger spots here, but her personal radar was getting back severe oncomings.

Hadn't even gotten back to the office before he had a hail from behind and a "Lieutenant, we've got to talk to you—"

No doubt what it was before Mitch and Benavides overtook him. Graff said, "Dekker's banned from the sims, is that what this is about?"

"Tanzer's doing?" Mitch asked—and didn't ask was it his.

"*Col.* Tanzer," he reminded them. "In the office, Mitch. Let's keep it out of the corridors—"

"It's in the corridors, sir, it's all over the messhall. The UdamnDC doesn't care where it drops its—"

"Mitch. In the office."

"Yessir," Mitch said meekly; and the delegation trailed him down the corridor and around the corner to his own door. He could hear the phone beeping before he even got the door open. He got to his desk, picked up the handset.

"Graff here."

Saito's voice. "*J-G, we have a problem. Paul Dekker's been restricted.*"

"I'm aware, I assure you. Word to the captain. FleetCom. Stat. Code but don't scramble. Tell the captain we'd urgently like to hear from him."

"*Aye.*"

He hung up. He looked at Mitch. "Where is Dekker right now?"

"Messhall," Mitch said. "Granted Pauli and Kady could catch him."

"Catch him."

"He wasn't damned happy, and he was headed spinward."

"You catch him. You sit on him if you've got any concern about this program."

Quiet from the other side. Then: "We enlisted. We signed your contract. We've got plenty of concern about this program, lieutenant, we're damned worried about this program, —we're damned worried about a lot of things."

"First time I've asked this, Mitchell. Follow orders. Blind. Just do it."

Mitch looked at him a long time. So did the others. Finally Mitch said,

"We'll follow orders. —But what the hell are they *doing*, lieutenant? D' you hear from the captain? Do we know anything? What's happening at Sol?"

"You want it flat on the table—I don't know what the situation is, I don't know whether the captain's tied up in the hearings or what. I'm asking you, I *need* you to go back to your labs, follow your orders, show up for sims—get everybody back to routine. Like nothing's going on. Like nothing's ever gone on."

Long silence then. Long silence. And finally Mitch broke contact.

"Yeah," Mitch said. "You got it. You got it. But Dek's damned upset."

"Tell Dekker my door's open, I know what happened and I'm on it. May take a bit. But he's going back in there."

Opened his mouth on that one. If you made a promise like that to these men, you'd better plan to keep it.

Like dropping into system, he thought; sometimes you had to call one fast. He thought it over two and three times, the way you didn't have time to reflect on a high-*v* decision— but the fallout from this one was scattered all though the future, and he didn't know whether he was right to promise a showdown—for one man.

Damned if not, he decided. You could count casualties by the shipload—in an engagement. But if it was your own service taking aim—damned right one man mattered.

Whole roomful of tranked-out fools sitting at consoles, making unison reaches after switches, unison keystrokes, as far as Ben could tell. "Damn *spacecases*," he said, with a severe case of the willies. Deepteach, they called it, VR with drugs and specific behaviors involved; and hearing about it wasn't seeing thirty, forty people all sitting there with patches on their arms and faces and elsewhere and in private places, for all he knew: forty grown people making identical rapid moves like the parts of some factory machine. "Talk about Unionside clones. . . ."

"Just basic stuff," Dekker said. They were in the observation room, looking out through Spex that reflected their disturbed faces—disturbed, in his case, and Meg's and Sal's. Dekker, professional space-out, tried to tell them it was just norm.

"Spooky," was Sal's word too. "Seriously spooky."

Ben asked uneasily, "They do computer work that way?"

"Basic functions," Dekker said. "Basic stuff. For all I know, they do: armscomp, longscan—'motor skills,' they call it. They teach the boards that way. Some of the sims are like that, when there's one right answer to a problem. Anything you can set up like that—they can cut a tape. It's real while you're seeing it. Damned real. But you move right. You do it over and over till you always jump right."

Wasn't the answer he wanted to hear. He said, "*I'm* not taking any damn pill. I'm already right. Righter than any guy this halfass staff has got, I'll tell you. You let them muck with your head?"

"Just for the boards," Dekker said, and cut the lights as they left. "Just to set the reactions. 'Direct Neural Input,' they call it. You do the polish in sims, and you do that awake—at least you're supposed to . . ."

Two years he'd known the guy and he realized he'd never actually heard Dekker's sense of humor. He decided that was a joke. A damned bad one.

Meg asked, "So what if it sets a bias that's not *right*, once upon some time?"

"You aren't the only one to worry about that. Yeah. It's a question."

"So what are they doing? Set us up to jump on the average we're right?"

"That's part of what they call 'documentation'—meaning there's nobody who's flown the ship."

"Nobody?" Sal asked; and Ben nearly managed unison.

"Docking trials, yeah. They got that part. Straight runs. Milk and cookies. Rotate and reorient. Do it in your sleep. But *not* with armscomp working. You got enough problem with system junk."

"Like a damn beam-push through the Belt."

"You got it. At that *v* it's a lot like that. Only where we're going—there *aren't* any two-hundred-year-old system charts. You get stuff off the system buoy when you drop into a known system, where there's regular traffic, but out at the jump points, there's chaff you just don't know's there. And maybe stuff somebody meant to dump—ship-killers, scan-invisible stuff, you don't know."

"Shit." Cold chill went down Ben's back. "These guys ever *made* a run with Mama shoving you?"

"A lot of these guys have done it—if you mean the combat jocks. Yeah. That's what it's like. And we just run ahead and blow the sumbitches they dump out of the carrier's path."

"You're kidding."

"That's what she does."

"That's the damn stupidest thing I ever heard!"

"That's why they like us Belter types. Shipkillers and rocks—no difference. Same gut feeling for how rocks move— same thing that makes a good numbers man or keeps a Shepherd out of the Well, that's what they want."

"Hell if, Dekker, hell *if*! Not *this* Belt miner!"

"You a good miner?" Dekker had the nerve to ask.

"A live one! On account of I never *let* MamBitch boost us like a missile—except once. In which you figured, you son of a —"

Meg said, "Hell, Ben, they *give* you guns. . . ."

"Yeah, and it won't work—that's what they're doing in

there, they're brainwashing those poor sods, they brainwashed *him*, for God's sake, blow rocks out of the way, hell! They got *that* on those tapes?"

"Not yet," Dekker said, just as quiet and sober as if he was sane. "But they'd like to. Get the reactions right on *one run*, so they can bottle it and feed it into the techs—word is, that's what they want to do, ultimately. Get one crew that can do it. And they'll teach the others. Hundreds of others."

"God," Sal said, and hooked a thumb back at the human factory. "Like *that*?"

Dekker shrugged. "That's what they think."

"That's what they think," Ben muttered. The human race was shooting at each other. Dekker said Union was building riderships, too—

"I thought the other *side* was where they wired you to a machine and taught you to like getting blown to hell. Not here. Not on *this* side, no *way*, Dek-boy. What the hell are we fighting for? That's Union stuff in there!"

"They developed it, what I hear."

"God."

" 'Not yet,' " Meg quipped.

"Damn funny, Meg."

Ben looked at Dekker, looked at Meg and at Sal, with this sudden sinking feeling—this moment of dislocation, that said he was surrounded by crazies, including the woman he went to bed with; including every hotshot Shepherd tight-ass in this whole establishment, *and* the CO, *and* the lieutenant.

"What's it do to your reflexes?" Meg said.

Dekker said, "Screws 'em to hell. Scares shit out of you. Like I said at breakfast. Hands move, you don't know why, you threw a switch, you don't know why. Moves are right. But you got to convince yourself they are. You can't doubt."

"Any chance it came around on this Wilhelmsen?"

Dekker didn't answer that for a second or so. Ben wasn't

sure about keeping his breakfast. "Yeah," Dekker said. "But that's the one thing you never better think. You *never* think about it. Not in the sims. Especially in the real thing—"

Dekker's voice wandered off. He stood there with his hand on a door switch and looked off somewhere, just stood there a breath or two—then drew a larger breath and said, "Worst enemy you've got—asking whether your moves are right. You just can't doubt—"

"Yeah," Ben said, with the sudden intense feeling they had to get him out of this hallway before a guard saw him or something. "Yeah, right. Why don't we go tour somewhere else? Like what there is to *do* on this station?"

Dekker looked at him like he'd never thought of such a thing. "Don't know that there is. This isn't One."

"What I've seen, it isn't even R2. What do you do for *life* in this can? Play the vending machines?"

"Not much time for social life," Dekker said faintly. Which reminded him there hadn't been outstanding much in TI, either. Even attached to Sol One, where there was plenty.

"Not much where we've been," Meg said. "Either."

They walked down the hall in this place full of labs where human beings learned to twitch like rats, to guide ships that moved too fast to think about, and you couldn't help thinking that helldeck on R2, for all R2's faults, had been the good old days. . . .

"So what *do* you want to do, Dek-boy? I mean, granted we all get our wants, —what's yours?"

Scariest question he'd ever asked Dekker. And Dekker took a while thinking about it, he guessed, Meg sort of leaning up against Dekker, one visible hand on his arm— where the other one was might have something to do with his concentration. . . .

But Dekker said, real quiet, "I want to be the one cuts that tape. I want to be the one that does it, Ben."

He wished he hadn't asked. Sincerely wished he hadn't

asked. Sincerely wished Meg would put her hand somewhere to disrupt the boy's concentration and shake him out
of his spook notions.

"There a chance?" Meg asked, quiet too; and he thought,
God, it's in the water, they got to put it in the water—

Dekker didn't answer that one right off. "If they let me
back in the sims, there is . . ." And a few beats later. "But
I'm not doing it with you, Meg. I can't do it with you."

Silence from Meg. Then: "Yeah."

"I don't mean that." Dekker stopped cold, took Meg by
the shoulders and made her look at him. "I mean I don't
want to. I can't work with you. . . ."

Meg didn't look real happy. Meg was about as white and
as tight-lipped as he'd ever seen her. Meg shoved his hands
off. "You got a problem, mister? You got a *problem* with
me not being good enough, that's one thing, you got a
problem about setting me on any damn shelf to look at—
that's another. You say I'm shit at the boards, that's all
right, that's your damned opinion, let's see how the Aptitudes come out. I'll find a team and I'll fly with somebody,
we'll sleep together sometimes, *fine*. Or I'll wash out of
here. But you don't set me on any damn shelf!"

After which Meg walked off alone down the hall, sound
of boots on the decking, head down. Not happy. Hell, Ben
thought, with a view of Dekker's back, Dekker just standing
there. Sal was with him—he wondered that Sal didn't go
with Meg; he was still wondering when Dekker lit out after
Meg, walking fast and wobbling a little.

"You make sense out of either one of 'em?" he asked
Sal.

"Yeah," Sal said. "Both."

Surprised him. Most things came down to Belter and
Inner-systemer. So maybe this was something he just wasn't
tracking. He asked, for his own self-preservation: "Yeah? I
know why *he's* following. I don't know why she's pissed."

Sal said, "Told you last night."

"He didn't say she couldn't fly. He said—"

"He said not with him. Not on his ship. She'll beat his ass. That's what he's asking for."

Talking was going on down the hall, near the exit. Looked hot and heavy.

Sal said, "She'll pass those Aptitudes. You never seen Meg mad."

He thought he had. Maybe not, on the other hand. Meg was still lighting into Dekker—boy was a day out of hospital, shaky on his feet, and he didn't look as if he was holding his own down there.

Then Dekker must've said something, because Meg eased off a little.

Probably it was Yes. Probably. Meg was still standing there. Meg and Dekker walked off together toward the security door, so he figured they'd better catch up.

The other side of the door, Meg said, "We got it worked out."

Ben said, "Not fair, man's not up to this." Dekker looked as if he wanted holding on his feet, as was. But Dekker said,

"Going to try for that tape, Ben. You want to test in?"

He threw a shocked look back at the doors, where roomfuls of walking dead were flying nonexistent ships. "To *that?* No way in hell. Non-com-ba-*tant*, do you read? No *way* the UDC is risking my talent in a damn missile. I'll test for data entry before I do that—"

"What's Stockholm got?" Sal asked. "They say *Pell's* got a helldeck puts Sol to shame. Got eetees and everything."

"Yeah?" He was unmoved. "I've seen pictures. Can't be that good in bed."

"Got real biostuffs, just like Earth. There's Pell, there's Mariner Station—"

"Yeah, there's Cyteen going to blow us to hell or turn us into robots. Don't need to go to Cyteen—our own service is trying to do it to us . . ."

Seriously gave him the willies, that did. Get into his mind and teach him which keys to push, would it?

A programmer didn't need any damned help like that.

* * *

No answer, no answer, and no answer. Graff was beyond worrying. He was getting damned mad. And there was no place to trust but the carrier's bridge, *with* the security systems engaged—but workmen had been everywhere, the UDC had very adept personnel as capable of screwing up a system as their own techs were of unscrewing it—and it was always a question, even here, who was one up on whom. "I *know* the captain knows about Dekker," he said to Saito and Demas and Thieu—age-marked faces all; and the only reassurance he had. "Pollard, Aboujib, Kady all shipped in here—you'd think if he *is* moving them, they'd be couriering something, a message, two words from the captain—"

"Possibly," Saito said, over the rim of her coffee cup, "he feared some shift of loyalty. Dekker is the keypoint. None of them have met in over a year. Friends and lovers fall out. And Pollard is UDC."

"They came. Dekker's leavetaking with Kady was— passionate to say the least. Pollard joined him here. Protocol says none of this is significant?"

"They're not merchanter. That's not what's forming here."

Puzzles, at the depth of things. Silence from the captain, when a word would have come profoundly welcome. He looked at Demas, he looked at Armsmaster Thieu, he looked at Saito. Com One. If *Victoria* spoke officially, it was Saito's voice. If the Fleet spoke to Union or to blue-skyers, it was Saito, who made a study of words, and customs, and foreign exactitudes—and psychologies and expectations.

"What *is* forming?"

Saito shrugged. "That's the question, isn't it? I only point out—you can't take our social structure as the end point of their evolution. Blue-skyers and Belters alike— their loyalties are immensely complex. Ship and Family don't occur here. Only the basis for them. Difficult to say what they'd become."

"Prehistory," Demas murmured.

"Prejudice?" Saito asked softly.

"Not prejudice: just there's no bridge between the cultures. The change was total. Their institutions are seminal to ours. But they don't *need* kinships, they don't *need* to function in that context. Their ancestors did. We've pulled our resource out of the cultural matrix—"

"Matrices. Wallingsfordian matrices."

God, they were off on one of their arguments, splitting theoretical hairs. Demas was a hobbyist, and the carrier's bulletin board had a growing collection of Demas' and Saito's observations on insystem cultures. He hadn't come shipside for Wallingsfordians versus Kilmer or Emory.

"Saito. *Is* the captain setting up something you know about?"

A very opaque stare. "I'd tell you."

"Unless you had other orders. *Has* the captain been in contact with you? Am I being set up?"

A moment more that Saito looked at him and never a flinch. "Of course not."

CHAPTER

8

H ARD day?'' Villanueva asked, at the dessert bar.

"Could say." The one claim you could make for Earth's vicinity was more varieties of sweet and spice than a man could run through in a year. And Graff personally intended to try during his tenure here—a tenure in which combat was beginning to look preferable. "What's this one?" he asked of the line worker, but Villy said, "Raisin cake. Allspice, cinnamon, sugar, nutmeg—"

"You have it down." Graff was fencing. He was sure Villy wasn't here entirely for the dessert. He didn't want the lecture. He didn't want the inquiry. He was, however, amazed at Villy's culinary expertise.

Villy shrugged. "You guys always ask. —How's Dekker doing?"

"All right till the colonel clipped him." He weighed asking. He couldn't stand the suspense. "Did he send you?"

Hesitation. "Could say that."

"What's he after?"

"He's saying put the boy back into lower levels. Use Mitchell's crew, use me and mine. He says he takes your point, no command substitutions, no crew subs until we get this thing operating."

"Why doesn't he make his own offers?"

"Seems us pi-luts talk better to each other, at least where it concerns capabilities. You want the truth—I suggested he lay off the substitutions."

"Wish you could have done that earlier."

Villanueva gave him a look back. "Truth is, I did."

Graff picked up his tray and tracked Villy to the tables in the officers' mess, said, "Do you mind?" and sat down opposite him before he had an answer.

"Be my guest," Villy said.

There had to be looks from other tables, assessing their expressions, the length of their converse. Graff said, urgently, "It's no deal, Villy. I can't. Your colonel's got *no* right to pull him—"

Do him credit, Villy didn't even try to defend the technicality. "Mitchell's crew and mine. No subs. When Dekker passes the medicals and the reaction tests—ask the colonel then. He'll put him back on. Just wait till the boy quiets. For his own sake. For the program's."

"Whose medicals? Yours or ours?"

Villy evidently hadn't considered that point. "I'll talk to the colonel. Maybe we can arrange something. We *can't* afford another set-back. You know it and I know it. We've got to pull this thing together before we lose it."

"I'm willing. But I want the heat *off* Dekker's tail. The kid's had enough."

"No argument here."

A bite of cake. Time to reflect. "Captain Villy, —do you personally *know* what happened in the pod access?"

Villy didn't answer that one straightaway either. "If I knew it was us I wouldn't say. If I didn't know anything, I wouldn't have an answer. What does that tell you?"

"You dance well."

Villy laughed, not with much humor. Tapped the table with his finger. "We got the senatorials and the techs out of here. We've got the program back in our hands. We're *not* going to get another design. That's the word."

First *he'd* heard. Had they won one? "No redesign?"

"That's the whisper going down the line. Heard it from the Old Man. We don't get the AI. Rumor is, we're going for another run in the sims, try to build a stricter no-do into the pilot, not the machine."

Graff leaned back, heart thumping. Took a breath. He couldn't tell whether Villanueva was happy with that situation or not. "So what's your opinion?"

"Go with it. That's what I'm saying. Your best. And ours. We try to set the tape, best we can. Then we fly with it. —You won it, J-G. Enjoy it."

The nickname was traveling. And he wasn't sure he'd won anything: he'd gotten extremely wary of concessions from Tanzer's office. But Villy said:

"We're not happy with the situation—I don't trust your tape-teaching, and that's evidently what they're leaning on, heavier and heavier. I don't *like* the damn system, I still don't think drugging down and walking through any situation is any cure for some kid hitting his personal wall—we can't guarantee your reflexes, or mine, are going to be in every guy that's ever going to run through this program."

Old argument. Graff said softly, delicately, "That's why we're getting them where we're getting them." But he didn't say, And we'll fill out the primary pilot list outside Sol System. You didn't say that. On the captain's orders you didn't. Earth didn't want to know that.

No.

"Listen," Villy said, "you know and I know we're reaching the bottom of the barrel. People don't go out to be miners and Shepherds because they're upstanding citizens. They're ex-rab, they're asocials . . . These two girls you got in—both of them have records . . ."

The rab was some kind of Emigration movement. Prospace. Anti-Company. It had turned violent, ten years ago, big blow-up, company police had panicked, opened fire on a crowd . . .

"Dekker has a record," he reminded Villy. "He's also popular in the Belt. The Company system out there was crooked. He beat it. You know what the UDC's setting up, making his life difficult? It's certainly not the best PR move the UDC could make. And Kady and Aboujib were part of Dekker's crew out there, such as survived—another pilot and a numbers man, as the Belters call it: good ones, for what the record shows."

Villy made a wry expression, took a sip of coffee. "Maybe. We'll see—once the boy's back in the sims. Personally, I hope he makes it. He's a son of a bitch, but Chad didn't dislike him."

"Wasn't any animosity on either side, that I know. Dekker got along with Wilhelmsen."

A pause. "J-G, off the record—between you and me: do you really buy it that Chad's crew dumped him in that pod?"

"I don't buy it that Dekker went crazy when he saw the ship blow. Not till the MPs tried to make him leave mission control, get him away from the senators and the VIPs. After that, no, he wasn't highly reasonable. Would you be? So he said something that wasn't politic—people *do* that. Other people don't necessarily try to kill them in cold blood. *No*, I'm not accusing the crew. I find it almost as unlikely as Dekker doing it to himself. You've got to understand, Villy: this kid spent a couple of months in the dark, in a tumble, in the Belt—*bad* accident. He couldn't get the ship back under control. This isn't a guy who's going to suicide *that* way, of all the ways he could pick. And no Belter's going to do that to him. Not the way they did it. So you tell me what happened."

Villy thought about that one, thought about it very seriously, by all he could tell. Then: "Let me tell you about Chad's crew. They're professionals, Rob's got a father he's supporting, guy got caught in a tractor accident, insurance won't pay anything but basics; Kesslan and Deke are real close with Rob—they're not going to risk it, for one thing, even if they were that mad, which I don't think they were. I think they understood Dekker's outburst. Might not have liked it, but understood it. Murder just doesn't add.''

Made some sense—granted the father had no means of support; which he personally didn't know—nor understand, inside Earth's maze of cultures and governments, any more than he understood the motives and the angers that bred in the motherwell.

"Won't say," Villy added, "that there aren't some others Dekker could've touched off. But *don't* try to tell me it was Chad's crew."

"I respect your judgment." Mostly, that was the truth. "But what do we do? Dekker doesn't deserve what's happened. His crew didn't deserve what happened. Wilhelmsen—didn't deserve what happened. Let me tell you, in that hearing, I never tried to suggest that Wilhelmsen was primarily at fault, because I never believed it. He was good. It was *exactly* what I said: that substitution killed him and it killed the rest of them."

Villy was listening, at least. Maybe it was something in the coffee. Reason seemed possible of a sudden and he hammered it home. "It's not possible, it's not the way things *work* at light speed, Villy, it can't be, you can't treat people like that. An ops team is a living organism. You don't split it and expect it to perform with anything like efficiency."

Long silence. A sip of coffee. "We've changed the damn specs so often it's a wonder anything mates with anything. The mechanics are overworked, they can't *do* the maintenance in the manufacturers' specs, on the schedule they're being handed, with the staff they've got. That's the *next* disaster waiting to happen and nobody wants to listen to them. We've got a program in trouble.''

"We've got a human race in trouble, Villy. I've *been*

there, I've *seen* what we're fighting—I don't want that future for the species, I don't happen to think that social designers can remake the model we've got—''

But when you thought about it, just trying to talk to Villy—you began asking yourself—*Haven't we, haven't we, already? Hasn't distance, and hasn't time?*

Like to take you outside the well, like to open your eyes, Captain Villy, and let you feel it when you drop out and in. They'd never get you back here again. . . .

Because the part of Villanueva there was to like, came alive when he was talking about his job. You saw that sometimes in his face.

"You have no attachment," Villanueva said, "no feeling for being *from* this planet."

"I've met what isn't," Graff said.

Interest from Villy. Quirk of a brow. "What are they like?"

"They're them. We're us. Sociable fellows. They don't fight wars."

"So why are you in this one?" Villanueva asked. "Earth didn't ask for this—not our business, a plane clear to hell and gone away from us. Earth Company brought us this thing. The old bottom line. They rooked us into it. Rooked you in too? Or what made you enlist?"

Good question. Complicated question. "Our ship's routes. The ship I was born to. *Polly d'Or.* Didn't ask for trouble, but they tried to cut us out, wanted to regulate where we came and went—retaliation for the Earth Company's visas. Economics on one scale. Our ship on the other."

Villy still looked confused, still didn't get it.

"We'd lose everything. The Fleet's what keeps those routes open. Only thing that does. They can't enforce their embargo."

"Hell and away from us."

"Now. Not forever. Lucky you have us. It'll come here— eventually it'll come here."

"Not everybody believes that."

"Nobody outside this system doubts it. You'll deal with Cyteen—on your terms. Or on theirs. Their technology. You want your personality type changed? They can do it. You want your planet re-engineered? They can do that. They *are* doing it—but we can't get close enough to find out what. We don't get into that system anymore."

"We."

"The merchanters they don't own."

"You ever been down to a planet?"

He shook his head.

"Ever thought about it?"

"No."

"What are you afraid of?"

The question bothered him. He was in a mood right now. Maybe it was Tanzer. Maybe it was because he'd never really thought about it.

"Maybe all those people. Maybe being at the bottom of the well, knowing I can't get myself out of it."

Villanueva frowned, said, finally, "I grew up under blue sky. But if they get me down there I can't get out either. Trying to retire me to the damn HQ. I want this ship to fly. It'll be the last one I work on. I want this one to fly. That's my reason."

"We got a few slots, Captain Villy."

A glance, a laugh. "Old guy like me?"

"Time's slower out there. Remember I'm in my forties."

Villanueva pushed back from the table, leaned back in the chair. "Damn you, you're trying to seduce me."

He felt a tight smile stretch his mouth. "We're the only game there is. You don't want to die in the well. Take you out, Captain Villy. Don't let them send you down. . . ."

"Damn you."

"Think on it."

Villy set his elbows on the table. "About the Dekker business—"

He *was* merchanter—before he was militia, before he was

Fleet. And you did try to get it screwed down tight, whenever you talked deal.

"Dekker's back in the program."

"Marginally back in the program. Contingent on the medicals."

"Our medicals."

"Coffee could use a warm-up. Yours?"

Rec hall, the term was, but it was the same messhall, they just pulled the wall back and opened up the game nook next door: dinner started at 1800h, canteen and a bar opened at 2000h if you could keep your eyes open that late, which Dekker didn't think he could, even if it was one of the rare shifts his duty card wouldn't show a No Alcohol Allowed. He was walked out, talked out—"Get the man a sandwich and shove him in bed," was Meg's advice; and he was in no mind to argue with it.

There were a few empty tables left in the middle. They drew their drinks. "Stake out a table," Dekker advised them. "Nobody'll take it if your drinks are sitting."

Ben was in the lead; Ben stopped and hesitated over the choice of seats in front of them. "They got a rule where you sit or what?" Ben asked, with a motion of his cup forward. Dekker looked, numbly twigged to what was so ordinary a sight it didn't even register: all UDC at the one end of the hall, from the serving line; all Fleet at the other.

"This end," he said.

"There some rule?" Ben repeated.

"They just do." Sounded stupid, once you tried to justify it. "Not much in common." But you didn't sit at the other end. Just didn't.

"Plus ça change, rab." Sal gave a shake of her metal-capped braids, set down her drink and pulled back a chair. "You sit, Dek. We'll do. What shall we get? Cheese san? Goulash? Veg-stew?" Fast line or the slow one, was what it amounted to.

"Dunno." He hadn't known how sore he was till he felt a

chair under him, and now suddenly everything ached. The walking tour of the facility was a long walk, and bones ached, shoulders ached, head ached—he said, ''Chips and a chicken salad—automat, if you don't mind.'' Do them credit, the cooks kept the stuff as fresh as you could get on the line; or the rapid turnaround did. Something light sounded good, and come to think of it, sleep began to. He wasn't up for a long evening. In any sense. He hoped Meg wouldn't take offense.

They'd done all the check-ins, gotten Meg and Sal scheduled for Aptitudes tomorrow—Ben had outright refused to sign up, declaring they could damned well get his Aptitudes from the UDC, or court-martial him for failure to show for tests: not an outright show of temper with the examiners, no, just a perfectly level insistence they look up his Security clearance, Ben said; turn up his assignment to Stockholm... Benjamin Pollard wasn't taking any Fleet Aptitudes until they showed him his old ones or put him in court.

Damned mess, he reflected, sorry for Ben, truly sorry for what had seemed to a pain-hazed mind his only rescue. Ben's talk about court-martial upset him. Ben's situation did. And all the lieutenant would say, when he had in fact gotten a phone call through to him, was: We'll work with that. Let me talk to the examiners, all right?

He ground at his eyes with the heels of his hands, listened to the dull buzz of conversation and rattling plates over the monotone of the vid, and wondered if there was anything unthought of he could do, any pull he personally had left to use, to get Ben back where he belonged—as much as that, if there was anything he could do to send Meg and Sal back home—no matter that Meg really *wanted* her chance at the program. He'd been on an emotional rollercoaster since this morning, he'd been ready to go back to routine and they'd stopped him; they'd told him the lieutenant was fighting that, and he'd been ready to come from the bottom again—

til, God, Meg hit him with the business about flying either with him or against him.

He didn't want her killed, he didn't want to lose anybody else—he didn't want to be responsible for any life he cared about. He kept seeing that fireball when he shut his eyes; in the crowd-noise, he kept hearing the static on Cory's channel, in the tumbling and the dark—because Meg's threat had made it imminent, and real.

The hall seemed cold this evening. Somebody had been messing with the temperature controls, or the memories brought back the constant chill of the Belt. He sat there rebreathing his own breath behind his hands, knowing (Ben had a blunt, right way of putting it) knowing he was being a spook, knowing he hadn't any right to shove Meg around, or tell her anything—no more than he'd had any right to take Ben's name in vain or ask for Meg and Sal to come here—he supposed he *must* have asked for Meg, too, since they were here, even if he couldn't figure why the Fleet had gone to that kind of trouble—

Except the captain had wanted him to testify in that hearing Ben had told him about, the one it was too late to testify in, even if he could remember—which he couldn't.

So he'd let the captain down, he'd let the lieutenant down—in what cause he didn't know; he only knew he'd disrupted three lives.

So Meg *hadn't* been happy where she'd been, so the *Hamilton* wouldn't let her right to the top of the pilot's list: you didn't get into that chair just walking aboard, Meg had to have known that, Meg must have known what to expect, coming in on a working crew with its own seniorities and its own way of doing things . . .

So you took a little hell. So you stuck it out. Everybody took hell. He hadn't been all that good at keeping his head down and taking it, but, God, he'd started a police record when he was thirteen: he'd been a stupid kid—and Meg had done a stupid thing or two, run contraband, something like that, that had busted her from the Earth shuttle to the Belt;

but he and Meg were both older, now, Meg ought to know better and do better—he'd made it in the Belt; so had Meg—so she had to have damn-all better sense than she was using—

"You all right?" Meg asked. They were back with the sandwiches. He took a drink of the cola, wished he hadn't gotten an iced drink.

"Yeah," he said, chilled. He took his sandwich and unwrapped it while they sat down with their trays. Something on the vid about the hearings. 'Missile test,' they called it. That was Hellburner's cover story. They talked about hearings adjourning on Sol One. . . . He wished they'd change the channel. Watch the stupid rerun movies. Had to be better. The message net had to be better.

"What else do we need?" Meg was asking. "What about these tests tomorrow? Is there anything we can do to prep ourselves?"

"Nothing but a lot of sleep. Relax. They put you through anything on the carrier? They did, me."

"Didn't see a damned soul on the carrier, except at mealtimes. We played gin most of the way."

"Nice guys," Sal sighed, "and the reg-u-lations said we couldn't touch 'em."

That got a frown out of Ben. And Sal's elbow in Ben's ribs.

Meg said, "So what *do* we do? What's it like?"

"They hook you up to a machine, like medical tests, eye tests, response tests, hand-eye, that sort of thing."

"Hurt?" Sal asked.

"Yeah, some."

"You going to study up?" Sal asked Ben.

"I'm telling you, I'm not taking them. I'm not showing. *Let* them court-martial me, it's exactly what I want."

"Ben, —"

Guys stopped by the table. C-Barracks. Techs. Mason, among them, nudged his shoulder with his tray. "Dek," Mason said. "How you doing?"

"All right," he said, "pretty tired."

"Good to see you. Real good to see you...."

"Pop-u-lar," Ben said when Mason and his guys had moved on. "Just can't figure how. All these people get to know you and they haven't broken your neck."

"Ben," Sal said, defending him. But it didn't sting, couldn't even say why, just—it didn't. Ben didn't ask for help, Ben didn't ask for anything—Cory had been a lot like that. Ben was going to fight his way out of this mess on his own, and that was at least one piece of karma he wouldn't have to worry about.

"Best—" he started to say. And caught a name on the vid, sounded like Dekker. He picked up *Sol Station*, and... *lodging a complaint—*

"Ms. Dekker, what specifically are you alleging?"

God. It *was*. She looked—

"Dek?" Meg asked, and turned around to look where he was looking, at the vid, at a woman in a crowd of reporters. Blond hair was faded. Face was lined. She didn't look good, she didn't look at all good...

Something about MarsCorp, something about threats, an investigation into phone calls... Some organization backing a suit—

Sal said: "What's going on?" and Meg: "Shhh."

He couldn't track on it. Didn't make sense. Something about losing her job, some civil rights organization launching a lawsuit in her name—

"It's his mother," Ben said; he said, "Shut up, dammit, I can't hear—" But he could see the background, see the MarsCorp logo, he knew *that* one—MarsCorp offices on Sol Station, police, reporters, some guy who said he was a lawyer—something about her son—

Picture jumped, tore up. The local station cut in with the channel 2 program information crawl—but he wasn't finished yet, wasn't damned finished yet...

"They cut it off!" He shoved the chair around to get up, get to a phone, saw the shadow of the tray and the sense of balance wasn't there. He staggered, hit it, food went everywhere, cup bounced—"Shit!" He was flat off his balance, elbowed the guy trying to hold his feet, guy grabbed at him and he didn't want a fight, he just wanted the phone. "Get out of my way!"

"You son of a bitch!" The guy had his arm. Ben and Meg and Sal grabbed for him, Ben saying something about Let him go, the man's upset; but the guy wasn't letting him go, the guy swung him and he grabbed for a handhold on the UDC uniform, about the time there were a whole lot of other chairs clearing, and Fleet was all around them. A high voice yelled, "You damn fools, stop it—"

Wasn't any stopping it. The UDC guy hit him, and he hit the guy with everything he had, figuring it was the only blow he was going to get in—couldn't hear anything, with guys coming over the tables, guys pushing and shoving and punches flying past his head—he didn't want to be here, he *wanted* the damned phone, *wanted* the truth out of the station, that was all—

Lights were flashing on and off, shouting filled his ears, fist rattled his skull and gray and red shot across his vision as arms came around him and hauled him out of it.

He wasn't breathing real well, couldn't half see: he yelled after Meg and Sal in the melee, couldn't tell who he was hitting when he tried to break free—

"Dekker!" That was the lieutenant. So he was in deeper shit; but more imminently of a sudden, he had his wind cut off as they bent him over a table. Something cold clicked shut around his wrists. That scared him: he'd felt *that* before . . . and it got through to his brain that the guys holding him were the cops, and Graff's voice made him understand that help was here, the fight was over, and the lieutenant wanted him to stand still. He tried to; which meant they got the other wrist, locked the cuff on, and at least pulled him back off the table so he could get a breath . . .

"The guy shoved him." Meg's voice rang out loud and

clear. "Wasn't Dek's fault, he was just trying to get up—it was an *emergency*, f' God's sake. This ass wanted to argue right of way!"

Guys started shouting all around, one side calling the other the liars.

"Clear back!" Voice he knew but couldn't place. His nose was running and he sniffed. Couldn't say anything, just tried to breathe past the stuffy nose and the clog in his throat.

"What happened here?" the Voice asked he blinked the haze mostly clear and saw a lot of MPs, a lot of angry guys standing along the wall with more MPs and soldiers. What Happened Here? drew shouting from all around, Meg and Sal profane and high-pitched in the middle of it, how the guy'd bumped him, how his *mother* was in some kind of trouble on the news . . .

Had to talk about his *mother*, God, he didn't want an audience, didn't want to talk about his mother in front of everybody. He tried to look elsewhere, and meanwhile the lieutenant was saying they'd better move this out of here, *he'd* take him in custody—

Please God. Anywhere, fast.

The other voice said: "I think we'd both better get this moved out of here," and he made out the blurry face now for Captain Villy, with a knot of UDC MPs and a whole lot of trouble. They were holding Meg, and Sal, and Ben, among a dozen mixed others. "Move 'em," Villy said, and there were Fleet Security uniforms among the lot. He started to argue for Meg and Sal and Ben; but: "Dekker," Graff said sharply, and said, "Do it."

He did it. He kept his head down and walked where they wanted him to, he heard Graff at the top of his lungs chewing out the rest of the guys in the messhall and Villanueva doing the same, telling them they were all damned fools, telling them how they were on the same team—

Yeah, he thought. Yeah. Tell 'em that, lieutenant.

Himself, he didn't want to think what was going on back at Sol Station, didn't want to think what he'd just done back there in the messhall; he kept his mouth shut all the way to the MP post, and inside; him, and Ben and a whole crowd of their guys and the UDC arrestees; but when they tried to take Meg and Sal into the back rooms:

"I want *Fleet* Security—laissez, laissez, you sumbitch —ow!"

And Sal screamed how she was going to file complaints for rape and brutality. . . .

The MPs got real anxious then. "Where's Cathy?" one asked, and a guy got on the phone and started trying to scare up a female officer, while Meg argued with them about holding on to him, "Dammit, let him go, he's just out of hospital, for God's sake—man got up and bumped a tray, his mother was on the news—"

God. "Meg, shut *up*. It doesn't matter!"

"That sumbitch shoved you!"

At which the sumbitch with the custard all over him started yelling at Meg, somebody shoved, Sal started yelling, and he couldn't do anything, he was cuffed, same as Ben was, same as the UDC guy was, except they'd made the mistake of not doing that with Meg and Sal.

"Meg," he yelled, "*Meg!*"

They got rough with Meg, they got rough with Sal, he kicked a guy where he saw a prime exposed target and they shoved him up against the wall, grabbed him by the hair and by the collar and shoved him into a chair.

"She didn't *do* anything," he said, but nobody was listening to him. He said, "None of them *did* anything. . . ."

They got Meg and Sal out of the room. Ben and the other guy, too, and left one guy to stand and watch him. He was dizzy, the adrenaline still had his head going around, and his nose dripped a widening circle on his shirt. He tried to sniff it back, breathing alternate with that disgusting sensation; and in his head kept replaying as much as he'd heard on the vid about what was going on with his mother. . . .

A lawsuit, for God's sake—but she wasn't anybody to show up on vid, with lawyers from—what the hell organization was it?

The Civil Liberty Association? He didn't know who they were, but she'd looked like hell, hair stringing around her ears, makeup a mess. He kept seeing her blinking at the strong lights and looking lost and angry. He *knew* that look. She'd worn it the last time she'd bailed him out of juvenile court.

. . . I don't need any more trouble, she'd written him. *Stop sending me money. I don't want any more ties to you. I don't want any more letters. . . .*

He had never taken leave back to Sol One: there was a serious question, Legal Affairs had warned him from the beginning of his enlistment, whether once he came onto Sol Station where lawyers could get to him with papers, he could escape a civil process being served or whether the Fleet could prevent him being arrested. The Fleet had put him behind a security wall only because having him on trial wouldn't *sit* well with the Belt, where they mined the steel; and the EC cooperated because letting Cory Salazar's case get to the media would raise questions about a whole long laundry list of things about ASTEX and MarsCorp the Earth Company itself didn't want washed in public. Anything to keep him out of court—

Because damned right there was a connection between his mother and MarsCorp, it was *him*, it was Cory Salazar's *mother*, who'd wanted to have a daughter, had one solo and tried to run that daughter's life and now her afterlife as a personal vendetta against the pusher-jock who'd romanced her collegiate offspring out of her hands.

Hell if that was the way it had been. Cory had dreamed of starships, Cory'd hated her mother's laid-out course—college to a MarsCorp guaranteed success track—so much that Cory couldn't run fast enough or far enough to escape it. Maybe starships had only been a kid's romantic answer—but Cory had come to the Belt because she'd thought she could double and triple her money freerunning—she'd lured *him* along for a pilot, and they'd nearly done it, until Cory ran head-on into the corrupt System her mama had wanted her to sit at the top of—and it killed her.

That was the bloody truth. *That* was the thing Alyce Salazar wouldn't see. He'd wanted to tell her so: he'd imagined how he'd say it if he got the chance, maybe talk to her sanely, maybe just grab her and shake some sense into mama, so she'd do something about the system that had killed Cory.

But Legal Affairs had nixed any such move, said plainly, Don't communicate with her. Don't attempt to communicate with her. And made it an order.

So now Alyce Salazar had communicated with his mother: he knew that was the case, because his mother wasn't dedicated to finding trouble, his mother was the absolute champion of Never get involved . . .

The side door opened. A team of medics came in, with: "Let's have a look at you," so he sat where they wanted and let them look at his eyes with lights, and into his ears, and his mouth. They got the nosebleed stopped, at least, then said they'd better have him down in the clinic for a thorough go-over.

"No," he objected, suddenly panicked. "There's nothing wrong with me."

But they took him anyway.

Aboujib, assault with a weapon, incitement
Basrami, assault
Bissell, assault
Blumgarten, assault, assault on an officer
Brown, assault with a weapon
Cannon, assault, incitement
Dekker, instigation of riot, assault
Franklin, assault with a weapon
Hardesty, assault
Hasseini, assault, verbal abuse of an officer

Jacoby, assault with a weapon
Kady, assault, assault on an officer
Keever, assault, destruction of government property
Mason, assault
Mitchell, assault, assault on an officer
Pauli, assault, incitement
Pollard, assault with a weapon
Rasmussen, verbal abuse; (hospital)
Schwartz, assault
Simmons, assault
Vasquez, assault; (hospital)
Zeeman, aggravated assault

Graff read the list, handed it to Petrie, the junior out of Legal Affairs. "I want interviews, any way you can get them. Record everything. I want them now, I want any releases you can get, I want them an hour ago. And I want condition, instigator and perpetrator on our hospital cases."

"Yessir." Petrie put the list in his case. The temper must be showing. Petrie didn't stop for questions of his own. The door shut.

Demas, resting against the counter, said, "Doesn't seem there was anything premeditated: the channel 3 news boss recognized a correspondence of names on the Sol One news feed, suddenly realized it was sensitive, and jerked the report off the air—*bad* decision. Dekker happened to be in the messhall, the vid happened to be channel 3. Charlie Tyson happened to be behind him with a tray; Dekker jumped up—bang into the tray. Tyson blew up, Dekker blew, the whole messhall blew."

"I want a tape of that news broadcast, I want to know what's going on with Dekker's mother, I want to know what she's involved in."

"You want it in capsule now?" Demas asked. "I've got the essentials."

"Go."

"Dekker's mother got fired two days ago. She was a

maintenance worker—electrician—for SolCorp. The maintenance office claimed incompetence—the record is apparently inaccessible—she claimed she was a victim of MarsCorp pressure inside the EC, claimed Salazar's agents had been harassing her on the phone. She showed up in front of the MarsCorp office with lawyers and reporters, MarsCorp called Security, and a MarsCorp spokesman went on camera to charge Ms. Dekker with sabotage and threatening phone calls—apparently Ms. Dekker had been doing some work inside the MarsCorp sector and got some phone numbers, by what Ms. Salazar charges. Ms. Dekker claims they've been harassing her—calls on her off watch, that kind of thing. Ms. Dekker's got some civil rights organization on her side, they're charging Ms. Salazar used pressure to get Ms. Dekker's job on personal grounds. End report."

"Harassing phone calls. Is Ms. Salazar *on* One?"

"She was eight days ago, at the time Ms. Dekker claims she got two of the calls. She's in London at the moment. Ms. Dekker claims she asked for a trace on the calls. The station office claims there was no such request and says their records *show* no calls to Ms. Dekker's residence." Demas folded his arms. "Ask how sophisticated Ms. Salazar's employees might be."

"I take it there are ways to evade those records."

"Abundant methods—limited only by the sophistication of the operator and the equipment. This is a woman who maintains apartments in *two* space stations and a couple of world capitals, on two separate planets. I would not match a station electrician against her technical resources."

"We've been sleeping through this one. I need a structural chart of MarsCorp and the EC. With names and kinships." Damn, the Security chief was—where else?—with the captain. "Can we get that through our own channels?"

"We can try. It's going to be a maze. Kinships, I'm not sure are going to be systematized anywhere. They're illegal, remember—where it regards government contracts. Personal friendships are illegal."

"Are animosities?"

A humorless laugh. "Unfortunately there's no such rule. Among those cards on your desk is the Alyce Salazar file such as we have it—with Saito's compliments. Some of the information may be in there. It's going to take Legal Affairs to—"

"—unravel the MarsCorp connections?"

Demas nodded. "If they can."

"Meanwhile there's the next shuttle to One. I want somebody on it. I want somebody to go personally to the captain's office—if there still is an office—and *get* a report to him we're sure isn't intercepted. And I want some message back here that isn't wearing a UDC uniform or Belter chain and claiming they don't know a thing. I should have done it when Pollard came in here."

Demas looked thoughtful. "I'll look up the schedule."

"Due in at 0900h on the 27th, out at 2030h the 29th, we've got a service hold for scheduled maintenance. They're claiming it's booked full outbound. There's always some contractor holding seats. If we've got any pull—get one."

He'd gotten used to being handled like a piece of meat. He'd gotten used to cameras and doctors and cops. They made a vid record of the new skin on his shoulder and the finger-marks on his arm. They asked him who'd hit him, he just shook his head, didn't even have to come out of his haze to talk to them. They took samples of his hair, his skin, his blood, and whatever fluid they could wring out of his body; "Pulse rate just won't go down," one of them said. "That's on his hospital records."

"What do you *expect*?" he asked, only time he'd opened his mouth except for a tongue depressor, and one of them said he should calm down.

"Yeah," he said. His stomach was upset from the poking around they were doing. He tried to go on timing out, just go away and blind himself with the lights and not to let his heart flutter, the way it felt it was doing. Couldn't think about anything if you wanted to fake out the meds. Think of—

—Sol One. His mother's apartment. But that was no good. His mother was in trouble, thanks to him . . .

—*Way Out*. But that ship was dead. Like Cory.

Think of stupid stuff. Name the moons of Saturn. Jupiter had used to work, but he'd learned that real estate too intimately.

Docking fire sequence for a miner ship. Range and rate of closing.

Finally one said, "Name's Parton. Fleet Medical. How are you doing, Lt. Dekker?"

Fleet. He said, "The lieutenant agree with this?"

"The lieutenant doesn't agree with fighting."

So he was in trouble. With everybody. He slid a glance over to the wall, where he didn't have to look at Parton or get in an argument, and wondered distractedly if he could get a word out of the news channel if he could just get permission to make a phone call. . . .

But the medic, Parton, was talking with the other medics— said, of the blood pressure, "Yeah, he does that. Doesn't like hospitals. Doesn't like UDC medics, if you want the plain truth. . . ."

Not real fond of any meds right now, —sir. Can I get up?

But he didn't ask that, he didn't think it was smart to ask, at this point. He got an elbow under him—they had him lying on a table freezing his ass off, and he only wanted to relieve the ache in his back. But a hand landed on his shoulder: it had a UDC uniform cuff. MP. He lay back and stared at the lights and froze in silence until the Fleet medic came back and stood over him.

"Lieutenant's orders: you go where you're told to go, you don't argue, you don't say anything about the incident to anybody but our legal staff, you understand?"

He said, burning with embarrassment, "Something about my mother on the news, can anybody for God's sake find out what happened to my mother?"

"Lieutenant's aware of that. He's making inquiries."

"What about the other guys? Pollard and Kady and Aboujib—"

"They're fine."

"They arrest them too?"

"Riot and assault." Parton looked across him, over his head. "Lieutenant wants him *with* his unit. The three he named."

"Kady and Aboujib are women."

"They're his unit, sergeant."

Long silence. Then: "I'll have to ask the major."

Age-old answer. Dekker shut his eyes. Figured they'd be a while asking and getting no. "It's protecting me from Kady you better worry about," he told them. Bad joke. Nobody was laughing. He wasn't amused either. Meg had a record of some kind. Meg had just gotten it cleared, got a chance to fly again. Ben had his assignment in Stockholm. . . .

His mother used to say, *You damned kid, everything you touch break—*

You messed up my whole life, you self-centered little brat—why can't you do right, why can't you once in your life do something right, *you damned screw-up?*

Long time he lay there freezing, with a knot in his gut, replaying that newscast for the information he could get out of it, telling himself they couldn't prove anything on his mother, she'd at least got some kind of lawyer, so she wasn't without help—

He'd got a little money ahead, he'd saved it out of his pay, he wasn't spending anything. He'd tried to give it to her before, for what he'd cost her, but she hadn't wanted it. Maybe he could get Ben to send it to her. Maybe she'd take it from Ben—she was going to need funds fast, if she wasn't drawing pay, she never got that far ahead of the bills, and even if she had free legal help, it wouldn't pay for food . . .

"Word is, he can't go in a cell with the women," the MP said. "Regulations. We can put him with Pollard. . . ."

He didn't argue. Parton only said he'd report that refusal to the lieutenant.

Parton left. The UDC medics got him up. The MPs locked a bracelet on his wrist that they said he wasn't to mess with, and took him out and down the hall to the cells.

Guys from his barracks yelled out, along the way, "Hey, Dek!" and he looked numbly to the side. Mason and Chiv were there. Pauli. Hardesty. And across the aisle—a guy he didn't know, familiar face, who looked murder at him. So he didn't look. He walked where they wanted him, they took the cuffs off when he'd gotten to Ben's cell and they opened the door and put him in.

Ben gave him a sullen look. He didn't figure Ben wanted to start a fight in front of the MPs. So he got over in the corner, there being just a double bunk and a toilet, and Ben sitting on the bunk: he sank down on the floor with his back to the corner, feeling the bruises and feeling the silence from the bunk.

MPs stood there a moment more looking at him. He had the fanciful notion that after they left Ben was going to get up and come over and kill him. But he didn't truly think so. Hit him—yeah. He expected that. He even wanted it. Anything to stop him thinking about the mess he'd made.

The MPs went away.

Ben said, "The place is probably bugged."

Which meant Ben wouldn't kill him—not in front of any cameras. He sat there with his knees drawn up to his chest so tight he couldn't move and felt numb.

"You going to sit there?"

He didn't know what else to do. Didn't care about climbing up to the top bunk. He was comfortable enough where he was—comfortable as he was going to get.

"You sure got a way of finding it, you know that?"

"Yeah," he said. It cost to say, "Sorry, Ben," but he did it, past the knot in his throat. He hadn't said it often enough, maybe, over the years, and a lot of the people he should have said it to—it was too late to tell.

Ben didn't say anything for a while. Finally: "You break anything?"

"No." He wasn't sure about the ribs, and the lately-broken arm and the shoulder ached like hell, but the meds hadn't taped anything, or sent him back to hospital, so probably not. He just generally hurt.

"Son of a bitch," Ben muttered. Ben might hit him after all. Ben's chances of getting out of here and back to his security clearance had sunk, maybe, as low as they could go. Ben had nothing to lose.

Ben muttered, "Get out of the damn corner. You look like hell."

He made a tentative move of his legs. But he was wedged in. Couldn't do it without more effort than he wanted to spend. So he shook his head, just wanted to be left in peace a while. Didn't want an argument . . . or he just wanted this one to play itself out and come to some distracting conclusion.

"Damn." Ben got up, came over and grabbed him up by one wrist and the other, turned him back to the bunk and shoved him onto it.

Bang went his head against the wall. He just rested where he'd hit and stared at Ben, Ben with this thoughtful expression he couldn't figure out. Mad, he expected. But he didn't want to deal with complexities or have Ben trying to con him. And Ben's frown didn't look as angry as Ben should. "You sick? You want the meds?"

"I've had 'em." He curled into the corner where the bunk met the wall, tucked up and tried to project a thorough Leave me alone.

Ben sat down, put a hand on his ankle and shook him. "You all right?"

"Yeah." He jerked his leg, Ben moved his hand, and he sat there with his arms across his gut, because he felt the pieces coming apart, the one reliable guy he knew was after him in a way that didn't mean Ben had just gone friendly—oh, no, Ben had just changed the rules; Ben was after something, maybe his neck, maybe just after using him to get what he wanted: Belters were like that, that were born there. You could partner with them. You could deal with them. But you didn't ever take for granted they thought the way you did.

"Your mama's in some kind of trouble, is she?"

"Her trouble."

Ben said, "Sounds to me like Salazar."

They'd gotten altogether too friendly one watch, on the ship, on the trip out from the Belt. Their lives had been changing. Late one night he'd told Ben a lot of things he wished now he hadn't. Early as the next wakeup, he'd known it was a mistake. "Leave it the hell alone, Ben. It's not your business."

"Not my business. You *are* a son of a bitch, you know that, Dekker?"

"Yeah," he said. "I've been told."

"Listen, Dekker, —"

"I said let it ride!"

"What *else* does your mama have to do with MarsCorp?"

"She fixes the damn circuits, all over Sol One. She's an electrician—they don't ask her politics or her religion before they send her into an office—maybe she screwed up a job—"

"MarsCorp? Come *on*, Dekker."

"MarsCorp, the Vatican for all I know, I don't know what she's into, I don't know what's going on, they cut the damn news off, weren't you listening?"

"Dekker, —I want you to say nice things to the cops, I want you to use your head, I want you to say I'm sorry to the nice UDC guys and yessir to the colonel and don't the hell get us in any more heat, you understand me?"

"Yeah," he said. Simple demands, he could cope with. He got his back into the corner and his knees tucked up out of Ben's convenient reach. Didn't like guys touching him. He was sure Ben didn't mean it any way but Pay Attention, but he didn't like it. "It's my fault. The whole damn thing's my fault, I got that loud and clear, all right? I'm sorry you got involved.''

Ben hit his foot. Another Pay Attention. ''Dek-boy, you are in deep shit here, have you noticed that? Stop thinking about your mama, *you* have got enough shit to occupy your time. I do not want you to screw up in front of the lieutenant, I do not want you to mouth off to the MPs, I do not want you to get us in deeper than we are. You copy that? Now, for all those watching, we are going to agree there is involved in this a Name that they won't want in court, no more than they did when they the hell raked you into the Service and gave *me* my slot at TI. That Name is, let us agree, Salazar. So we are not going to court martial, we are not going to see any outside lawyers, we are behind the thickest fuckin' security wall in the inner system, and I think it would be a most severely good idea not to antagonize the Fleet at this point, since the UDC is for some whimsical reason not all that happy with you. Do you follow?''

Jaw wasn't working all that well. He nodded. He couldn't stop thinking about his mother. He couldn't help thinking how a lot of people would be alive if he'd never existed and how people connected to him might have better lives now if he was dead and Salazar didn't have anybody to go after.

Ben said it right—Salazar couldn't get a message to him through ordinary channels, so she sent one on the news. I'm here. I'm still waiting. I'll get what you care about until I can get you. . . .

He didn't track on everything Ben said—but that, *that*, he understood. He wanted to get to a phone. He *wanted* permission from someone to get a call out.

Which was exactly what Salazar wanted. So he couldn't do that. *Couldn't*, dammit. Not without thinking more clearly than he was right now. . . .

Let her have him, maybe, do something so the Fleet would throw him out and all the Belter and Shepherd types who'd protected him wouldn't want to, wouldn't give a damn if he went to trial. . . .

Then, if they ever let him testify, he could tell mama Salazar to her face she'd killed her own kid. Only revenge Cory would ever have—unless you counted a few execs out of jobs. But they'd find others. The Company always found a place for the fools. Ben said so. And he believed it. They just promoted them sideways, somewhere they hadn't a rep—yet. The Company took care of its own.

"Severe mess," Sal said with a shake of her braids. Meg concurred with that.

"Sloppy place," she said, looking around at a scarred, dirty cell. "The tank over at One is ever so nicer." She felt a draft from a torn coat sleeve, and leaned her back against the wall, one leg tucked. They weren't in prison coveralls. The Es-tab-lish-ment was still trying to figure what to do with them, she supposed, on grounds of her previous experience with such places. "D' you s'pose the lieutenant has got a plan, or what-all?"

"I sincerely do hope," Sal said. Sal had an eye trying to swell shut. A cut lip. Sal did not look happy with her situation. Sal looked, in fact, intensely scared, now the adrenaline rush was gone and they were sitting in a cell with a riot charge over their heads.

"It was a set-up," Meg said. "Don't you smell set-up? I never saw a room blow so fast. Just a skosh peculiar, they let Dek out and they run him back in, and *us* so seriously important and all? *We're* the ones they shagged a carrier to get here. Are they going to forget us? Nyet. Non."

Sal was still frowning. "Amnesia's been known. Strikes people in office, most often. I hear they got no vaccine."

"Faith, Aboujib. *Believe* in justice."

Sal snorted. Almost laughed.

"I believe, Kady, I *believe* we are in un beau de fuck-up here. . . ."

Truth was, she was scared too. But scared didn't profit

you anything when it came to judges and courts, and she'd said it to Sal—the Fleet hadn't gone to all this trouble to invite them to a messhall brawl.

"I believe in they hauled our asses a long, long way to haul Dek in out of the dark. *That* is a truly remarkable al-truism, Aboujib."

"Des bugs."

"Bien certain they would. Bien certain someone's playing games. Dekker's mama lost her job. Does this rate news? Does this rate the peace movement lawyers giving interviews in front of the MarsCorp logo? Nyet. But there it was."

"You think somebody made it up? Faked it?"

"Nyet. *Peace* movement, Aboujib. *Peace* movement is involved. Does not the antenna go up? Does not an old rab ask herself why and what if?"

There was a spark of interest in Sal's dark eye. The one that showed. Sal didn't say a thing, but: "Rab is. The Corp is. Amen."

"That chelovek in the suit, that lawyer? That's a plastic. You mark."

"Why's he with Dekker's mama?"

Scary to think on. Truly scary. Sal looked at her, Sal as Belter as they came, and Shepherd; and how did you say the motherwell's mind in Sal's terms?

"Think of helldeck. Think of all those preachers, them that want to save your soul. And they each got a different way."

Another snort. "Crazies."

"On Earth they got their right. That's why they got it still on helldeck. On Earth you got a right to say and do. So they say and do. On Earth you can say a straight-line rock won't hit you. And maybe it won't. It might be too heavy. Might fall. You understand?"

A straight-line rock was one thing to a Belter. Fall was a contradiction in terms. You didn't have rocks on station, where things *fell*. And *fall* didn't go straight-line. Thoughts and puzzlement chased through Sal's expression, and rated a frown.

"What I said. Crazy."

"A rock might fall on its own before it hit you. You got to know its size to know."

"Why'd it move?"

"Because some crazy threw it at you. Bare-handed. But it might fall first."

"So. On station, natürlich."

"In the motherwell, *everything*'s like that. Gravity and friction are always in the numbers. Not a lot of blue-skyers can figure those numbers. Things just happen because they happen and sometimes they don't happen and you don't know why, so you were lucky or you weren't. You don't know. Very few can comp it. Ask a peacer what the answer is. He'll tell you it's not war. Ask him how you'll get no war. He'll say don't make one. Half the time it works. You got, however, to convert the other side to this idea. Ask a peacer how to make peace. He'll say, Don't fight. Half the time that works too."

"Guy was going to beat hell out of Dek."

"Yeah, well, this rab did have such a thought. And I sincerely wasn't going to sit and watch it."

"So why're the peacers paying for a lawyer for Dekker's mama?"

"Peace on Earth's like that rock. You got to calc things you don't, in space. You got to ask, primarily, *whose* peace, whose way, how long? But Earthers don't, generally. Blue-sky's used to not calcing all the factors."

"Trez sloppy," Sal said.

"The Corps don't *like* you to calc all the numbers. Neither do the helldeck preachers. Listen all you like, you sojer-boys with the bugs. You sleep down with the Corp, you get up with fleas. How good's *your* addition?"

"There is no excuse," Tanzer said, "there is *no* mitigating circumstance except your personal decision to release

Dekker from hospital without psychiatric evaluation, without appropriate procedures. The man's a fuse, lieutenant. *You* knew that. Or don't you read your personnel reports?''

Graff didn't ask how Tanzer had. He said, patiently, standing in front of Tanzer's desk: "Dekker didn't do anything. He got up in a hurry and bumped a man he didn't even know. . . .''

"This is a finger you want on the trigger of the most sophisticated weapons system ever devised? Can't navigate from a chair in the messhall? Is that his problem?''

"Your news service released a story without a next-of notice. Was that deliberate?''

"Is it a death situation? I think not. Your boy can't tolerate a little stress? What in *hell* is he doing in this program? He blows and your whole side of the messhall comes out of the seats—''

"Your man did the grabbing and the shoving. Don't try that one. It was simultaneous. There are too many witnesses.''

"Your *witnesses* were all in the middle of it. Your latest recruits were instigators. Is that what you call leadership? Is that what you call a cooperative relationship? Damned right, I don't put all the blame on Dekker, *I* don't blame the boy you dragged out of hospital and put into a high voltage situation, *I* blame the officer who made that boy a cause, which is damned well what you've done with your attitude and, for all I know, your direct statements to your command. You piled the pressure on that boy, you put those women in the middle of it, you set him up to draw fire—he was guaranteed to blow the first time he got *any* load more than he had. So his *mama* lost her job, damned right his mama lost her job—she was calling MarsCorp board members at two in the morning, *threatening* phone calls, you read me? She's a spacecase—like mother, like son, if you want my opinion. It's congenital!''

"You have no basis for any such conclusion.''

"Haven't I? I'm telling you right now, right here, he's never getting back in a cockpit and you aren't giving any more orders in a UDC premise, not in the messhall, not the offices, not the classrooms, not the corridors or the hospital. Try *that* one, lieutenant. Take *that* one to your captain and see what he has to say."

He had *no* instructions how to play that one. He wasn't a lawyer. He didn't know whether Tanzer could legally do that. He wasn't in charge of policy. He didn't know whether he should use Fleet Security to guarantee access. It was down to that. The phone rang—thank God for two extra seconds to think while Tanzer jabbed a button and growled an irritable, "I'm not to be disturbed."

"*Sir,*" the secretary said, on intercom, "*your line.*"

Unusual. Tanzer picked up the phone to listen in private and his expression smoothed out and went completely grim.

"When?" Tanzer asked; and: "Any other information?" And, "Find out, dammit, however you have to."

After which Tanzer hung up, glowered at him and said, "Get yourself and your crew up onto the carrier. Right now."

"Incoming?" A strike at Sol? Union missiles?

Tanzer's fist slammed the desk. "Get your ass out of this office, lieutenant, and get it the hell up to the carrier where you're *supposed* to be competent!"

Incoming was no time to stand arguing, and arguing with Tanzer was no way to get information through the carrier's systems; but if it was Union action there was no way he was going to make the carrier's deck before criticality. "Phone," he said, and reached for the one on the desk. The colonel made to stop him, and he held on to it with: "Dammit, they need a go-order. —Carrier-com," he told Tanzer's secretary. "Fast," —after which the secretary muttered something and he heard the lighter, fainter sound of Fleet relays. "This is Graff," he said the instant he had a click-in. "Status."

"*J-G,*" Saito's voice came back faintly. "*You're on a UDC line.*"

"Yes." Short and fast. "Colonel's office." It *wasn't* an

incoming—he knew that in the first heartbeat of Saito's remark about his whereabouts and he knew in that same second that UDC was a codeword on its own. Saito said, calmly: *"Stand by,"* and the phone popped and went to com-noise.

"This is FleetCom Command. ECS4 ETA at Sol Two 2 hours 3 minutes. Command of Sol Two facilities has passed to Fleet Command. UDC personnel are being—"

The message went offline. Went on again. *Somebody* in the outer office had a nervous finger.

"—with Fleet personnel. This message will repeat on demand. Key FleetCom 48. Endit."

He looked at Tanzer, who *didn't* know. Who was worried, clearly. And mad. Tanzer's secretary said, in his ear: *"Lt. Graff, this is Lt. Andrews. The colonel has an urgent message. Would you turn over the phone?"*

"For you," he said, and passed the handset to Tanzer. Stood there watching Tanzer's face go from red to white.

Number 4 carrier was incoming from Sol One, *not* at cap, but as much as they meant anyone's optics to see at this stage. The captain?

"Get a confirm on that," Tanzer said to whoever was on the line.

Tanzer wasn't looking at him. He could ease things or complicate matters—here in this office. He could end up with what had happened in the messhall played out on dockside—at gunpoint, if he and Tanzer both wanted to be fools. He put on his blankest, most proper expression—was very quiet when Tanzer finally hung up and looked at him.

"I trust our messages were similar," he said, with—he hoped—not a flicker of offense. "May I suggest, sir, we present this to personnel in a quiet, positive manner. I'd suggest a joint communiqué."

Tanzer didn't say anything for a moment. Then, with a palpable effort: "I'd suggest we keep this quiet until we can sort it out."

"Colonel, I appreciate the difficulties involved. FleetCom

is handling approach and docking. In the meanwhile my command has its own set of procedures, primarily involving dock access at this point. I'd suggest we move your security into a secondary position and move ours into supervision of debarcation facilities."

"I've no authorization to do that. You'll *wait*, you'll bloody wait!"

"I'll wait," he said, trying to add up in his head what all the Alpha and Beta Points on this station were, and what he could do to secure records without creating an incident he was virtually certain FleetCommand didn't want. "On the other hand, that carrier will dock in a little less than two hours, by which time I have to have a secure perimeter, colonel, that's mandatory under our procedures."

They'd done it at Mariner, they'd done it at Pell, and he had no doubt, now, that it was his mandate to secure that area here, as quietly and peacefully as possible. It was only now sinking in that a transfer of command *had* happened, but how it had happened, he had no idea. The thought even occurred to him that it might be a lie—a final, extravagant lie—that maybe things had gone critical—on Earth or at the front, and they were pulling what they had, while they had it. That was what the whisper had been, always, that there might not *be* the time they needed to build the riderships or the full number of carriers; and then they could take their choice—let the Fleet die, let Earth fall, and lose themselves in space or in the motherwell, anonymous and helpless; or run with what they had, and gather the marines and the trainees they knew would be targets . . .

And run and spend their lives running—

Danger-sense had cut in, for whatever reason: his brain was suddenly doing what it did when hyperfocus was coming up, no reason, except Saito's evasion yesterday, and the colonel's being caught completely by surprise. If negotiations had been underway—it was a shock to Tanzer, or Tanzer acted in a way that didn't make sense.

So he took a quiet leave, out through the anxious secretary's office—he stopped to say, "Andrews, for your own sake, *don't* spread anything you may have heard,"—and saw nervousness pass to estimation and fear.

Into the corridors, then—feeling the air currents, sampling the ambient. No panic in the clericals, nothing evident. The carrier had left Sol, presumably with notice to insystem defenses—then word had flashed via FleetCom, and presumably a UDC message from some quarter had chased that transmission to the colonel. Maybe Saito and Demas hadn't known what was about to happen.

Or maybe they had. Maybe they always had.

He walked quietly to his office, he checked in on FleetCom and asked Saito again: "Snowball, this is 7-All, status."

"7-All, that's LongJohn, we've got a Code Six."

Stand down but stand by. And LongJohn wasn't any of their crew. LongJohn was Jean-Baptiste Baudree, *Carina.* Mazian's Com Two. "That's a copy," he said; thinking: *Damn.* What's *he* doing here? It's not the captain, then. What aren't they saying? "Status," he insisted; and got the information he next most wanted:

"7-All, that's Jack."

Edmund Porey?

Lieutenant Edmund Porey?

He hung up and, with a pang of real regret, stopped trusting Saito and Demas.

CHAPTER

9

t. J-G Jurgen Albrecht Graff
SB/Admin
2152h JUN24/23; FGO-5-9

Command of Sol B has been transferred to
FleetOps. You are hereby ordered to render all
appropriate assistance, including securing of files and
records, under direction of Comdr. Edmund Porey. . . .

Commander. The hell!

And Jean-Baptiste? *Mazian's* second-senior?

Thoughts ran down very scattered tracks since that message. Thoughts needed to, on an operational level: Tanzer was only marginally cooperative, communicating through his secretary, BaseCom was a steady stream of query and scant reply from the UDC at Sol One—one assumed: a great deal of it was going in code one assumed FleetCom couldn't breach.

Tanzer had been blindsided, that seemed evident. And maybe FleetOps had had to keep the junior officer in the far dark to carry it off, but it was evident, at least as best he could put matters together, that the business with the committee and the general had been a flanking action—try to stir up some chaff, maybe throw a rock into the Sol One hearings. Who knew?

Certainly not the junior lieutenant. Possibly the Number Ones had. Certainly the captain had—and kept silent in spite of his repeated queries, which Saito of *course* had sent, the way he'd ordered Saito to do . . .

Damn and damn.

The deception shook him. You relied on a crew, you dumped all your personal chaff and trusted, that was what it came down to. You assumed, in throwing open everything you had, that you had some kind of reciprocity. Never mind the gray hair he didn't have. The *Fleet* could decide he was expendable. The *Fleet* could use him any way it had to. But they put you in charge, you made what you thought were rational decisions and if the people who were supposed to be carrying out your orders weren't doing that, you trusted they'd at least trust you enough to tell you—before you assumed you had a power you didn't, and put yourself and them into a no-win.

You did the best you could in a touchy situation and they promoted *Edmund Porey* two ranks in the last year?

God, what did the man do? The Captains had to know Porey. *Had* to. Were they blind?

But Nav Two on *Carina* had a good head for Strategic Operations—Porey was back and forth to the Belt, Porey was ferry-captain on the carriers as they moved in for finish, which made him currently one of the most experienced with the ships, and Porey was probably working tight-in with Outsystem and Insystem Surveillance: that had to be where he got the merits. Clever man. *Clever* man, Edmund Porey was, and, clearly now, command-track, which he himself would never be: hyperfocus and macrofocus weren't the same thing—not by a system diameter they weren't.

So Porey had the stuff. Clear now how desperately they needed a mind of Porey's essential qualities.

Clear now whose command he just might end up serving Helm for. The captain hadn't trusted him. So they brought Porey in over his head?

He didn't want to think about that. Instead, he arranged his priorities and issued his orders, *trusting* they were getting through. It gave him the same surreal feeling he'd had writing his will, for the handful of personal possessions he did own—that past the time those instructions were carried out, his personal existence was going to be very much different.

He had ordered the records secured. That first. There were a lot of extremely upset UDC security personnel on the loose. There had very nearly been an armed stand-off. The UDC ordered erasure on certain files, he was quite certain. He was equally certain he had been too late to prevent that, during the time of the stand-off and queries flying back and forth between his office and Tanzer's—he was sure UDC security had done exactly what they should have done, and that he had not been able to prevent it (although outside of going hand to hand with UDC personnel and cutting through a lock he didn't know what he could have done) would be written down for a failure on his part.

He had not let them throw the database into confusion. That was a plus. He had not lost the library tapes. That also.

He had ordered personnel in detention transferred; he had taken hospital and testing records under Fleet protection. He might order the release of detainees, but the disposition of those cases as a policy issue was not within his administrative discretion. He did not *like* the new commander. He, however, did not personally approve of creating administrative messes, which, counting his administrative style and Porey's, might be the worse for the difference. He advised the UDC officers that all facilities *were* passing under Fleet administrative command, and personally phoned the UDC provost marshal and UDC Legal Affairs to be certain that all legal proceedings were frozen exactly where they were: no sense letting anything pass into record that need not.

Demas called, to say that the carrier was braking, directly after ceasing acceleration. Demas said that there was a contingent of marines aboard needing gravitied accommodations.

"I copy that. What's the head count?"

"Two thousand."

That was a carrier's full troop complement. They wanted miracles. He called Tanzer, he listened to the shouting, he calmly requested invention, and ordered an emergency galley set up in an idle SolCorp module, ordered its power-up, ordered an Intellitron communications center linked in as FleetCom relay for the marine officers, ordered the Fleet gym given over to troop exercise, the Fleet exercise schedule combined with the UDC, on alternate days; located every class-4 storage can in Sol-2, shifted all class-4 storage to low-*g* and ordered station ops to consolidate the remainder and clear section D-2 for set-up as habitation. Sol-2 civil Ops bitched and moaned about access-critical supplies.

"I assure you," he said coldly and courteously, "I appreciate the difficulty. But human beings have priority over galley supplies . . . That is a problem. I suggest than you move your dispenser equipment to 3-deck to handle it. There *are* bottles and carts available . . . —Then get them from maintenance, or we'll order them. I'm sure you can solve that. . . ."

Meanwhile, the thin nervous voice of approach control tracked the carrier's braking, in a tone that said approach control wasn't used to these velocities. Inner system wasn't a place merchanters ever moved at anything like that *v*. Merchanters drifted into the mothersystem at a sedate, mind-numbing leisure, sir, while bored techs and mechanics did whatever repair they'd had on backlist— days and days of it, because the mothersystem with all its traffic had regulations, and a starship, which necessarily violated standard lanes, made mothersystem lawyers very anxious. The

mothersystem was a dirty system. The mothersystem had a
lot of critical real estate, the mothersystem had never
accurately figured the astronomical chances of collision, and
the Earth Company had made astronomically irritating regulations. Which they now saw Exceptioned. That was the
word for it. Exceptioned, for military ships under courier or
combat conditions.

The ECS4 wasn't even at hard stretch. But station was
anxious. If braking utterly failed (astronomically unlikely)
that carrier would pass, probably, fifty meters in the clear.
But tell them that in the corridors, where the rumor was,
Security informed him, that the carrier was aimed straight at
them.

Porey, the bastard, might shave that to 25 meters, only
because he hated Earth system. But Porey never said that in
outside hearing.

Porey had other traits. But leave those aside. Porey was a
strategist and a good one, and that, apparently, was the
priority here. Not whether Edmund Porey gave a *damn*
about the command he'd been given. Not whether he had
any business commanding here, over these particular mindsets.

The Shepherds were *his* crews, dammit, down to the last
two women the captain or someone had finagled in here.

Fingers hesitated over a keypad.

The captain. Or someone. *Anyone* in Sol System must
have known more than he had. What in *hell* was going on?

He had a call from Mitch Mitchell on the wait list. He
returned it only to ask, "Where are you?"

"*Sir?*" Mitch asked. "*What's going on? What's—*"

He said, "Where are you?"

Mitch said, "*Your office in two minutes.*"

"You don't read, Mitch. Where?"

"*Coffee machine in one.*"

Not that long to work a carrier into dock, not the way
they'd learned it in the Beyond, especially when it was a
tube link and a straight grapple to a mast. The carrier used

its own docking crew—marines, who simply moved the regular staff aside. More and more of them. A familiar face or two: Graff recognized them, if he couldn't place them. *Carina* dockers. Mazian's own crew. A lot of these must be.

Lynch, the sergeant-major identified himself, close-clipped, gray-haired, with no ship patch on his khaki and gray uniform, but Graff recalled the face. He returned the salute, took the report and signed it for transmission of station Secure condition.

More of them were coming off the lift. "Sgt.-major," he said, with a misgiving nod in that direction. "We've had a delicate situation. Kindly don't antagonize the UDC personnel. We've got a cooperation going that should make your job easier."

"The commander said take the posts. We take 'em, sir."

He frowned at the sergeant-major. Darkly. Kept his hands locked behind him, so the white knuckles didn't show. "You also have to live here, Sgt.-major. Possibly for a long while. *Kindly* don't disturb the transition we have in progress. That also is an order."

A colder face. A moment of silence. Estimation, maybe. "Yes, sir," Lynch said. *Carina* man for certain. Dangerous man. Close to Mazian. Lynch moved off, shouted orders to a corporal.

Steps rang in unison. Breath steamed in the air in front of the lift. Marines were headed for the communications offices, the administrative offices, the lifesupport facilities, simultaneously.

The lift let out again. Armored Security and a scowling, close-clipped black man in a blue dress jacket.

Graff stood his ground and made his own bet whether Porey would salute or put out a hand.

It was the hand. Graff took it and said, "Commander."

"Lieutenant. Good to see you." He might have been remarking on the ambient temperature. "I take it the report is in our banks."

"It should be. I take it you heard about the interservice incident. We have personnel in the brig . . ."

"The colonel's office," Porey said, shortly, and motioned him curtly to come along.

Quiet in the cell block, deathly quiet for a while. Then someone yelled: "Hey, Pauli."

"Yeah?"

"You know that five you owe me?"

"Yeah?"

"Cancel it. You got that sumbitch."

"That sumbitch is in here!" another voice yelled. "That sumbitch is going to whip you good, Basrami!"

"Yeah, you got a big chance of doing that, Charlie-boy. How was dessert?"

"Your guy can't navigate an aisle! What's he good for, him and his fe-male pi-luts? Couple of Belter whores, what I hear—"

Dekker stood at the bars, white-knuckled, Ben could see it from where he sat. From down the aisle Meg's high, clear voice. "You a pi-lut, cher, or a mouth?"

"You come in here to save Dekker's ass? Bed's what you're for, honey. It's where you better stay."

Ben winced. Meg's voice:

"Fuck yourself, Charlie-boy, but don't fuck with me. What are you, a tech or a pilot?"

"Pilot, baby, and you better stay to rock-picking. You're out of your league."

Chorus of derision from one side of the cell-block. Shouts from the other. Dekker hit the cross-bar with his fist, muscle standing hard in his jaw, and from down the row, Meg shouted:

"You got a bet, Charlie-boy."

Wasn't any way she wouldn't take a challenge like that. Her and Sal. Ben felt his gut in a knot, saw Dekker lean his head against the bars, not saying anything, that was the danger signal in Dekker. And somebody down the row yelled,

"Hey, Dekker! You hearing this?"

Shouting over the top of it. Dekker had to answer, *had* to, way the rules worked, and Ben held his breath and crawled off the bunk, not sure what he was going to do if Dekker blew.

"Dekker? You hear?"

Man couldn't talk. Ben added those numbers fast, yelled out: "He's ignoring you, mouth! You're boring."

"Funny he had a lot to say when Chad bought it! That right, Dekker? That right?"

Ben shoved his arm, not hard. Dekker was frozen. Hard as ice. Staring into nothing. Other guys were yelling. Something hit the middle of the aisle and rattled to a stop. And Dekker looked like a guy hit in the gut, wasn't saying anything, wasn't defending himself, was letting others do it. Another shove wasn't going to push him into thinking. God only knew what it might do. He had the look of a man on the edge of cracking and Ben didn't know what to do with him, he didn't know how to answer the catcalls and the shouting that was going on, he hoped to hell for the MPs to come in and break it up. Wasn't any more from Meg. He could hear Sal's voice in the middle of it, but he had a desperate feeling he was in a cell with half a problem and Sal had the other half . . .

"Hey, Custard Charlie," somebody yelled. "You want to run the sims full hours? Take you on."

That was a hit. Belters tagged you and you stayed tagged until you burned it off—and then it could come back years later.

"Take you on, take Dekker and his women on, any day, any day—what about it, Dekker? You got a voice, pretty-boy? Where's your ladies?"

'Ladies' included one UDC shave-head in the mix, Ben figured, but he wasn't going to get into it, wasn't his business, wasn't going to win a thing.

But Dekker came alive then, shouting, "We got enough of that Attitude, mister, we got too damn many *dead* with that Attitude. I *liked* Chad, you hear me, you son of a bitch? I liked him all right, it was your own CO set him up." Dekker's voice cracked. He wasn't doing highly well right now, but at least the jaw had come unwired. He hit his fist on the bars, turned around and said to the ceiling or the walls, Ben didn't think it was to him, "God, they're making me crazy—they're trying to make me crazy."

Wouldn't touch that line, Ben told himself, and held his breath, just stood out of the way while Dekker walked the length of the cell and back.

"Hey, Dekker," another voice yelled. "You son of a bitch, was that your mama on the news?"

Shit. Dekker was at the bars and that knot was back in his jaw. "You want to discuss it? Is that Sook?"

"No way," another voice yelled out. "Sook's not guilty. That was J. Bob."

Catcalls went one way and the other. Shouting racketed up and down the hall, until starting with the far end, it got suddenly quiet. Quiet traveled. Ben leaned against the bars and tried to see what was going on, and all he could make out was UDC uniforms and MPs.

"That's better," someone said. "*Keep* it quiet. Fleet personnel are being released—"

A cheer went up.

"—to Fleet Security, for your own officers to sort out. You'll file outside, you'll give the officers your full name, your serial number, your rank, in that order. You'll be checked out and checked off . . ."

"Where do *I* go?" Ben muttered, suddenly with the notion he didn't necessarily want to go into a pool of UDC detainees with a grudge. "Shit, where do *I* go?"

"You go with me," Dekker said. "You're in our barracks, you go with me."

Doors had started opening. You could hear the clicks and the guys moving out.

Their door clicked. Dekker shoved it and they both walked out. Walked down the hall toward the MPs and it was only UDC guys left in the cells on the right, staring at them. They're not going to let me out, Ben kept thinking, they're not going to let me out of here . . .

"Wrong flock, aren't you?" an MP asked him; but the other said, "That's all right, that's Pollard."

It wasn't highly all right. Hell if it was. He was all but shaking when they got through the doors and out of the cell block, into the outer hall where sure enough, a couple of Fleet Security officers were waiting with a checklist. "Dekker," Dekker muttered, "Paul F . . ." and didn't get further than that before the senior officer said,

"Dekker, go with the man. —You Pollard?"

Ben nodded. Saw one of the Security officers motion Dekker toward another set of doors, saw Dekker look at him and had this panicked sudden notion that if he let Dekker off alone *something* stupid was bound to happen—Keu and the lieutenant had tagged him with Dekker, and the only way to ensure Dekker didn't drag him into worse trouble was to stay with him. "Excuse me," he said, "but I have orders to keep an eye on him—*lieutenant*'s orders . . ." Highest card he knew.

But the guy said, "You have the *commander*'s orders to go to your barracks and stay put until further notice. The lieutenant's not in command now. Comdr. Porey is."

He must have done a take. He felt his heart stop and start. "*Commander* Porey?"

"Follow orders, mister. This whole station's under the commander's orders. The UDC's command's been set aside."

He wasn't the only one in the area now. Mason and Pauli had shown up under escort. "Hot damn," Mason said.

But Ben thought, with a sinking feeling, Oh, my God. . . .

Graff was extremely glad he didn't have to hear what happened inside what had, until an hour ago, been his office. Occasional words came through the closed door, while he stood outside in the hall with Tanzer's aide Andrews, neither of them looking at each other, with MPs and Fleet Security at their respective ends of the corridor.

It was not a happy situation. He didn't like Tanzer. But he felt only discomfort in seeing the man finally walk out of the office white-lipped and red-faced. Tanzer swept up Andrews and walked back the way he had come, with, as Graff understood Porey's intentions, *no* transfer out of here, no resignation accepted, and a hardcopy of an order from Geneva that in effect put Edmund Porey in charge of Tanzer's office and Tanzer's program.

He still didn't know how it had happened, or what might have shifted in the halls of power, as the captain would put it. He hadn't talked to Demas or Saito in any informality, hadn't exchanged anything with them but ops messages as they coordinated internal security with the marine details and Porey's own Fleet Security force.

And not a word even yet from the captain. Which might be because he didn't rate one in their list of priorities. But which left him wondering again—what wasn't perhaps wise to wonder.

Since Porey had issued no request for him, since Andrews and Tanzer were gone, he walked down to the intersection of corridors and to the messhall, only observing the temper of things. There were very few out and about, but Security, and aides.

Tone down the dress, he'd advised Mitch. Between you and me; but pass it on—things are going to shift. Minimum flash. Minimum noise for the next few days. Observe this man before you make *any* push at him. Do you read me? I'm not supposed to be telling you this. If it gets out that I did, it will be to my damage. Do you understand me?

Longest solemn silence he'd ever gotten out of Mitch. Then Mitch had tried to ask him specifics—who is this guy? What in hell—excuse me, lieutenant, —but what in hell's going on with the program?

Apparently, he'd thought to himself, politics of a very

disturbing bent. But he'd said to Mitch, I don't know yet. It's a wait-see. For all of us.

He went to the messhall, as the most likely place to find anyone out of pocket, anyone who had missed the barracks order, or thought he was the universal exception—an attitude more likely with Belters than with UDC or merchanters, and he was resolved none of his trainees was going to get swept up by Security—

None of his had *met* Porey's idea of Security. None of his own Security people got nervous at a joke. Ease off, they'd say. That's enough. They'd call the Belter in question by name or nickname, like as not, and get a generally good-natured compliance—

Not now. Not with these men, not with Lynch. He didn't know where they'd pulled this particular batch of marines in from, but they didn't have the look of basic training—Fleet Command had pulled something in from the initial set-up squads, he'd bet on it, though he'd have to get into Fleet Records to find out, but these weren't eighteen-year-olds, they weren't green and they sized up an officer they didn't know before they even thought about following his orders. . . .

Merchanters, maybe. But serving as line troops—when the Fleet needed every skilled spacer they could recruit? His stomach was upset. He carded a soft drink out of the machine and spotted a pair of marines at the administrative entrance, the galley office. What did they think, the cooks were going to take the cutlery to the corridors?

Exactly why those guards were standing there. Damned right. Tell it to Porey that the guys weren't going to go for the knives. Tell it to Lynch. A sight too much real combat readiness and overreaction in the ambient, thank you. A sight too much readiness in these troopers for any feeling that things were safe or under control.

"J-G."

Demas. Behind him. He took a breath and a drink, and disconnected expression from his face before he turned around. "We're on standby," he said, disapproving Demas' leaving the ship unofficered, before he so much as realized they weren't the primary ship at station any longer; Demas said, "LongJohn's on. We've got a while."

He nodded, tried to think of somewhere pressing to go, or something he had else to do, rather than discuss the situation with Nav One.

"You all right, Helm?"

As if he were a child. Or a friend.

"I'm tired," he said, which might cover his mood; but it sounded too much like a whimper. He didn't like that. He didn't like Demas conning him. He said, point-blank: "How much of this did you know?"

Demas' face went very sober, very quickly. It took a moment before he said, "Not who."

He hadn't expected honesty. He hadn't expected *that* answer. So Demas wasn't happy with the new CO either. And Demas was indisputably the captain's man. That came clear of a sudden.

He asked, under the noise of the heat pumps, "When did this get arranged?" and watched Demas avoid his eyes. Or look anxiously toward the marines—who might have Security audio, he realized that of a sudden. Damn, he wasn't *thinking* in terms of hostile action, it was their own damned *side*, for God's sake. But Demas was clearly thinking about it.

And Demas was the captain's man.

Demas said, in a low, low voice, "The Company pulled every string it had, in every congress on the planet. You want to go out to the ship, J-G?"

Of a sudden he had a totally paranoid notion, that Demas and Saito might be reeling him in for good, getting him where he couldn't get into trouble—where he couldn't *cause* trouble. Arrest? he asked himself. —Have I done that badly—or been that completely a fool?

"*Hear this,*" the com said suddenly. "*This station and all station facilities, civilian and military, have passed under Fleet Tactical Operations, by action of the Joint Legislative*

Committee. Military command has been transferred as of 1400h this date to the ranking Fleet Officer.

"Let me introduce myself. I am Comdr. Edmund Porey. I am not pursuing the interservice incident that marred the station's record this afternoon. I am releasing all personnel from detention with a reprimand for conduct unbecoming . . ."

The glove first.

". . . but let me serve notice that that is the only amnesty I will ever issue in this command. There are no excuses for failure and there is no award for half-right. If you want to kill yourselves, use a gun, not a multibillion-dollar machine. If you want to fight hand to hand, we can ship you where you can do that. And if you want to meet hell, gentlemen, break one of my rules and you will find it in my office.

"Senior officers of both services meet at 2100 hours in Briefing Room A. This facility is back on full schedules as of 0100 hours in the upcoming watch. Your officers will brief you at that time. Expect to do catch-up. If there are problems with this, report them through chain of command. This concludes the announcement."

He looked at Demas, saw misgiving. Saw worry.

He thought about that request to go up to the ship, and said, "Nav, I *understand* these people. I've worked with them. You understand? I don't want any mistake here."

Demas looked at him a long moment—frowned, maybe reading him, maybe thinking over his options, under whatever orders he had, from the captain, from—God only knew.

"J-G, —" Demas started to say. But there were the guards, who might well be miked. Demas put a hand on his arm, urged him toward the door, toward the corridor, and there wasn't an office to go back to, unless he could get one through Porey's staff. Demas' hand stayed on his arm. He had a half-drunk cup in his other hand. He finished it, shoved it in the nearest receptacle as they passed.

Demas said, in a low voice, "Helm, be careful." Squeezed his arm til fingers bit to the bone. "Too much to lose here."

"The Shepherds'll blow. One of them's going to end up his example. If you want to lose the program, Nav—"

"Too much to lose," Demas repeated; and a man would be a fool to ignore that cryptic a warning. He let go a breath, walked with less resistance, but no more cheerfully; and after a moment Demas dropped his hand and trusted his arrestee to walk beside him.

"Ens. Dekker," the man said, letting him into Graff's office. But it wasn't Graff at the desk. It was Porey, for God's sake—with a commander's insignia. Didn't know how Porey was here, didn't know why it wasn't Graff standing there, but it was Fleet, it was brass and he saluted it, lacking other cues. He'd dealt with Porey before, had had a two-minute interview with the man on the carrier coming out from the Belt and he didn't forget the feeling Porey had given him then; didn't find it different now. Like he was somehow interesting to a man whose attention you just didn't want.

"Ens. Dekker," Porey said, with his flat, dark stare. "How are you?"

"Fine, sir."

"That's good." Somehow nothing could register *good* in that deep, bone-reaching voice. "Hear you had a run-in with the sims."

"Yes, sir."

Long silence then, while Porey looked him up and down, with a skin-crawling slowness a man couldn't be comfortable with. Then: "Bother you?"

"I'm not anybody's target, sir."

"And you lost your crew."

"Yes, sir."

"Hear they were good. Hear Wilhelmsen was."

"Yes, sir."

"So what are you?"

Nerves recently shaken, shook. He didn't know what the answer was, now. He said, "I want to fly. Sir."

"What are you, Dekker?"

"Good. Sir."

"You're going back in that chair. Hear me? You're going to go back in and you're going to forget what happened here. You want to fly?"

"Yes, sir."

"Then you do that. You take that crew we've put together for you and you get back in that sim and you *do* it, do you hear me?"

He wasn't thinking clearly. Nobody he'd ever been in a room with gave him the claustrophobic feeling Porey did. He wanted this interview over. He wanted out of this office . . . he wasn't up to this.

"Do you hear me, Dekker?"

"Yes, sir," he said.

"Then you go do that. I want results. You say you're the best. Then *do* it. Do you hear me?"

"Yes, sir," he said.

"You're dismissed."

"Yes, sir," he said again, and then remembered Meg; and Ben; and Sal. "But with another *crew*, sir, than the one I've been given . . ."

"The Fleet's assembled the crew you have at cost and expense, Ens. Dekker. We're told they're good. We'll see it proved or we'll see it disproved—in the field."

"They're not ready, sir." He shoved himself forward, leaned on the desk and stared Porey in the face. "They haven't had the year I've had, they're not up to this, they haven't flown in a year at least. . . ."

Porey said, "That's what the sims are for."

"What are you after, a body count?"

People didn't talk to Porey that way. He saw the slight surprise in Porey's eyes, and something else, something that chilled him before Porey said,

"I'm after whatever you've got. As much as you've got.

Or you die. And your crew dies. That's understood, isn't it? We're Test Systems here. And you test the systems. Do you want them to live? Then you don't question me, you *do* it, mister. Do you have that?''

''It's not reasonable!''

''I'm not a reasonable man.'' Porey's eyes kept their hold. ''I never have been. I never take second best. Have you got it, Ens. Dekker? Or are you talk, and no show?''

He trembled. No human being had ever made him do that, but he shook and he knew Porey could tell it.

''We give you everything you ask for, Dekker. Now you *do* what you say you can do, you pull the Hellburner out. You *do* it. Don't give me excuses. I don't hear them. Am I ever going to hear your excuses?''

''No, sir.''

''You're meat, til you prove otherwise. Prove it. Or die. I don't personally care, Dekker.''

He couldn't get his breath. He couldn't think, he wanted to strangle Porey so bad. He choked on it. Finally: ''Yes, sir. I copy that clear. Am I dismissed, —sir? Because you fucking *need* me, don't you, *sir*?''

Porey kept staring at him. Looked him up and down. Said, ''Aren't you the *bitch*, Dekker?'' and finally made a backhanded move that meant Get out. Dismissed.

He took it, saluted, turned and walked out, oxygen-short, still on an adrenaline burn, and shaking, while he was still remembering Porey from the ship, remembering that Graff had said even then: Don't get close to him.

Then he hadn't been able to figure whether Graff had meant that literally or figuratively, but he had a sinking feeling he'd just made a move that amused Porey—in the sense of defying Porey's expectations. That was an intelligent man—maybe the most intelligent man he'd ever met; maybe too intelligent to mind who lived and who died. He believed what Porey had said—he believed lives didn't matter in there, lives didn't matter in this station at the moment, law didn't matter...

Guards fell in with him, the same that had brought him there. He hadn't even any notion where they were taking him, but they escorted him to the main corridor and told him go to barracks, everybody was confined to barracks.

Deserted corridor. Deserted conference rooms. Guards posted line of sight along the curvature. The vacancy of the corridors was surreal. The echoes of his own steps racketed crazily in his ears. The downside of the adrenaline surge left him dizzy and chilled.

Another several turns, more empty corridors. Guards at the barracks section door asked for his ID. "Dekker," he said, and pulled his card from his pocket, turned it over numbly, all the rush chilled out of him. "Off duty. Just out of detention."

The soldier guards said go through. He went, through the corridor into a barracks main-room crowded with people he knew, people he liked, guys who grabbed his arm and wished him well. He thought,

If you only knew what I've done to you . . . . . .

And almost lost everything when Meg got through the crowd and flung her arms around him. Cheers and catcalls from the company, egging her on for a kiss he didn't shy away from, but all at once he was leaning on Meg, not certain which way was up. Dark was around him, that hazed back to light and the faces—

You all right? someone asked him, and he tried to say he was. Guy belongs in bed, somebody else said, but he said no, and they shoved him at a chair and told him the galley was sending food to barracks and in the meanwhile things had to be better, they were under *Fleet* control, they were trying to straighten out the duty roster and figure who was on what tomorrow . . .

Meg hauled a chair up facing his, grabbed his hands and made him look at her.

"Dek. You tracking, cher?"

"Yeah," he said. He wanted a phone, he wanted—he didn't know now whether he could cope with the news station or his mother. He kept hearing echoes, like the sim room. Someone saying, *Enjoy the ride, Dekker.* But the voice never had any tone. It drowned in the echoes.

He kept seeing the accident sequence on the tape. Not threatening, just a problem. He kept thinking about his mother, the apartment, the dock at R2. He kept seeing mission control, and a silent fireball. And the dizzy prospect down the core, all lines gone to a vanishing point. Fire pattern in the sims. Intersecting colors. Green lines. Track, and firepoints. He shook his head and took account of the room again, guys he ought to love, if he had it left. But maybe he was like Porey. Maybe he didn't have it, or never had had. More comfortable not to have it. More comfortable to love the patterns more than people. Patterns didn't die. They just evaporated. People went with so much more violence . . .

"God, he's spaced. Get him on his feet."

"We're going to *fly* with this moonbeam?" Arm came around him, hauled him to his feet, and he didn't resist it. "I tell you, I should've been in Stockholm, should've got my transfer—I *hate* this shit." Friends here. People he trusted. People he'd betrayed in there with Porey, because he'd been a damned fool.

"Man's got to eat."

"Somebody ought to call the meds."

"*No* meds." He'd had enough. He walked. He got to his room. He hit the bed.

"Didn't search the room," he thought he heard Meg say. "Didn't mess up the drawers, I mean, these MPs are politer than Company cops."

"Peut-et' they're just neater," Sal said; and Ben:

"There wasn't a search."

"How do you?" Sal started to ask. And said: "Silly question. Trez dim of me."

Electronics and flash-scan assured privacy, even against fiber and remotes. Security swore so. Graff could feel secure in this cubbyhole next the carrier's bridge, if he could trust present company.

Ask Demas and Saito who they belonged to? They'd say—Captain Keu. Of course. Saito would say it without a flicker. One preferred to hope and reason that was the case, rather than ask a pointless question.

"Tanzer's actually dispatched a resignation," Saito said, apropos of the situation within the station, "but it came back negative out of Geneva. That means the UDC wants him where he is. Which could be show of opposition: they could replace him three days from now. Or they want him where he is because he knows where the records are and what's in them, which could be useful to them here. They lost a big one. Forces inside the JLC lost a big one."

"We *didn't* know," Demas put in, doubtless reading minds, "when it would shift. That it might—one hoped."

He considered a question, shot a sidelong glance at Demas and asked pointblank: "And Porey? Where does he fit?"

Demas broke eye contact, just momentarily. Saito's face was absolutely informationless.

Saito said, then, "Porey is highly successful."

"At *what*?" Anger betrayed him into that bluntness, anger and the memory of dealing with them differently. "At covering his trail, evidently." If they were Porey's or about to be, he was laying a firetrack in his own path, he knew he was, but he had his personal limit of tolerance. And he disturbed them. Even Saito flinched, looked down, saying:

"Some things are excused, as long as the results are evident. Some patterns of behavior simply do not come through in social context. . . ."

"Other things," Demas said with unexpected harshness, "are blindly ignored. The captain is head of Strategic Operations. The captain is *too valuable* to assign back to Hellburner, so says the EC. Porey is available. He could be promoted into qualification. *That* is what happened, J-G, plain and simple."

He looked at Demas, saw fire-flags left and right of this conversation and knew he could self-destruct here. He took a chance on them—a last chance. "Who wanted him? Who?"

"—promoted him? Who *does* promote by executive order these days?"

Mazian. Who *wasn't* the best of the militia captains: Keu was; or Kreshov, maybe. But Mazian was the promoter, Mazian was the one who could smile his way through corporate and legislative doorways, Mazian could say things the way they needed to be said . . .

"The Earth Company," Saito said, "has SolCorp, LunaCorp, ASTEX, all space-based entities. But it also has its hands deep into the whole EuroTrust industrial complex—Bauerkraftwerke, Staatentek . . . the list is extensive—that have very good reasons to want extension of their facilities outside the reach of pressure groups and watch committees—meaning, into space. Those Earth-based companies give the EC an enormous influence inside the Joint Legislative Committee. The citizen pressure groups are enormously naive, usually single-issue. They think they move events. But in general the JLC is riddled with influence-trading, purchase decisions made on relationships, not quality. . . ."

"Ancient terrestrial lifeform," Demas said. "Dinosaur. Vast body. Little brain. It flourished in an age of abundant food supply."

"I've heard the word," Graff said.

"Not to overwhelm you with local history," Saito said, "but the UDC is a composite creature that never did function well. The Earth Company created us to oppose Cyteen's secession; but it never imagined a splinter colony could raise a population base of Union's size and it never imagined the light barrier would fall so quickly."

"More," Demas said, "it didn't understand the ship-building capacity of an enemy with no social debt. Ships cost Union nothing but sunlight, ultimately. Do you want more facilities? Create more workers."

"But now the EC understands," Saito said, "at least enough to frighten them. The special interests understand enough to see their interests are threatened. Now everybody wants to manage the crisis. Everybody wants to safeguard their power base. Everybody believes there's fault, but it's most certainly someone else's. The free-traders are making headway."

"Union-run merchanters," Graff muttered. "Long *we'd* last. And they'd be nothing to Union but a supply source. Cyteen manage Earth? There'd be short patience."

"Possibly they'd founder of bewilderment. —But that *is* the truth, J-G: the Company brought us here because Earth doesn't *believe* in star-travelers unless it sees us: and its own problems absorb its attention. The EC needed the demonstrable presence, the face and the voice to make the outside real to these people. And whether they've believed their own myth, or simply view Mazian as manageable—he's gotten far more important than we planned."

He was listening to sedition. To conspiracy. The captains had sent Mazian downworld, they'd chosen their spokesman—who excelled mostly at salving over wounded egos, at getting the captains to make unified decisions. It was merchanter command structure: Mazian was only the Fleet's Com One. . . .

"They're putting him in single command," Demas said.

"God." He didn't believe it. He couldn't believe it. But Demas went on:

"The EC stamps his personnel choices as a matter of course. Yes, he does the things that have to be done. But he's not following the rules we laid down."

"Hellburner has all but foundered," Saito said, "on citizen groups that *fear* the EC, who've insisted the UDC do what it doesn't have the personnel to do—"

"They've run us out of time," Demas said. "So now, *now* the EC steps in and gets us the power to do something—but it's Mazian they give it to. The captain's still sitting at

Sol One with a mess on his hands, the whole UDC administrative system suddenly shoved inside our operations, but—''

"We begged him," Saito said, "to break with Mazian, to repudiate his personnel assignments, catch the commercial back here and take command of the carrier, the *hell* with Mazian's reputation with the EC.''

His heart was beating faster and faster. He was sure what he was hearing, and surmised what must have been passing, God, on FleetCom—

"But the captain won't do it," Demas said, "won't expose dissent among the captains. Not now, he says: with Earth, appearances and public belief are everything. If we don't get the riders and the rest of the carriers funded in this legislative session, we're back to the spooks and the rimrunners.''

He was still reeling from the first shock. Nerves wanted to hype and he tried to hold it. "What in *hell* did the captain want me to do here? Was I supposed to foul it up so badly he'd have to take it over? —Or is Porey what I won us?''

"That rump session of the committee wasn't supposed to come here," Saito said. "You handled it as well as it could have been handled. You were sincere. You were indignant. You were the epitome of the Fleet's integrity and professionalism. You didn't know anything to the contrary.''

"So now we've got Mazian's hand-picked command here? Mazian's put *Edmund Porey* over a program that's already self-destructing? Have you worked with this man? I *have*. I was in the Belt with him.''

"We're extremely concerned," Demas said. "We're concerned about those carriers out in the Belt, and at Mars, that have yet to have officers assigned. Yes, they'll bring in our people. But fifteen of the captains will be UDC. That was the deal that was cut.''

His stomach turned over. A second time. "You're serious.''

"That is the deal. Fifteen of the carriers—with Earth-born command.''

"Who do they have?''

Saito made a ripple of her fingers. "They'll have a selection process. Earth believes in processes."

"That's fifteen dead ships—first *time* they take them past Viking."

"J-G, this is the crash course on truth in this venue. Mazian projects well. As a strategist he's even competent. But thank God for the Keus and the Kreshovs. They'll keep us alive. They may even keep Mazian alive."

"I've got a—" —kid on the verge of insanity, he was about to protest, when he recalled he didn't *have* anything, he didn't *have* a command, so far as he knew. "Dekker's not going to work well with Porey. Dekker's the best we've got. *Mitch* is not going to work well with Porey. He's the next. We're going to lose this program."

"No, we're not," Demas said. "Porey's in command of the program. Porey's put *you* in charge of personnel."

"*Me?* Where did you hear this?"

"Say it went through channels."

"Did he do the picking? Or was my selection—"

"Compromise. Though in Mazian's view I think you're to keep us in line," Saito said. "Technically, we equal his rank. But we're not command personnel. We're not designated as such, by the captain. Consequently the captain can recall us at will and Porey can't take us under his command—or get us assigned to that carrier. I'm afraid that isn't *your* case."

"We're concerned for that," Saito said. "But there's nothing we can do, but advise, where our perspective is of use."

He was glad he'd not had time for supper. He thought he might lose it, if that were the case.

"All personnel?"

"All flight and technical associated with the program. Tanzer's still there, of course, but he's promoted sideways, still in charge of R&D, but Hellburner's being lifted out of R&D—"

"Into *what*?"

"Fleet Ops. The parts manufacturers and the yards are being given a go-ahead, on a promise of funds tied to test success. They're pushing this ship for production, we're funded for one carrier's full complement, but no further; and the plain fact is, we're out of time. Latest projection is—we're going to see the first carrier-rider system in the field in six, seven months. Theirs or ours. Naturally we have our preference."

"What in hell are they asking me to do with these people?"

"Mazian sets the priorities. Porey carries them out. You keep the crews sane."

"You mean I promise them *anything*. Have I got a shred of authority to carry it out?"

For the second time, Demas evaded eye contact. "I'd say it's more than we can do. But, no, in effect, you don't."

"Is he asleep?" Ben asked quietly—made a trip to the bathroom while Sal was drowsing and stopped for a look-see. Dekker looked skuzzed, thoroughly, face down in the pillows. Meg was using his reader, scanning through Dekker's manuals—there was a lot of study going on in the barracks, over cold dead hamburgers and breaded fish. The smell out there could gag you. And the atmosphere was crazed. Guys *glad* they were going to fly this thing—the pilots and the lunatic lead techs who made up the core crew.

He should have counted, he told himself. He'd been a numbers man. He should have added it—and panicked when the number of him and Dekker and Meg and Sal tallied four, same as the other core crew units out there.

"He's out," Meg said. "Cold. Thank God. Man's seriously needing his sleep."

He came and sank down on the edge of the other bunk, said, ever so quietly, "You like this guy?"

Meg shrugged. You never got unequivocal out of her or Sal. But she was here. She'd risked her neck and her license for him. Partner, yeah. But Meg didn't do things for one reason, or even two. A solid part of it was in that datacard, was in the way Meg looked right now, sharp and serious and On as he'd ever seen her.

He didn't say what he'd sat down to say: Flunk that damn test. He slid a glance at Dekker and back and said, "You know, you better carry a pocket wrench."

Any Belter knew what a wrench was for, on helldeck. Meg's mouth quirked.

"The CO's crazy," he said very quietly. "I flew out here with that guy."

"So did we."

"*That* where they got him? Belt garrison?"

She shook her head. Whispered, "That carrier came in from deep. We dunno where. All the time we were on there, we saw crew, never but once saw him."

"What'd you think?"

Meg frowned. "Didn't like the signals."

He said, under his breath, "We got a serious warning. Don't know what that guy's problem is, but it is. We saw him far more than once. Just watching us. The body language. He wants his space, he wants yours. Smiles and laughs but he doesn't smile, you know what I mean? He watched Dek real close. Dek didn't like him."

"Grounds?"

"Just that." He didn't think the place was bugged. Events hadn't proven it and it was too egocentric to think Porey's security had made a straight line to their quarters. But he got uneasy with the topic. He said, "Helldeck radar, maybe. Guys you'd insist do the EVA, if it was the two of you in a miner can, you know what I mean?"

Meg got real dead grim. "Ask Sal about that kind." And then bit her lip like she'd said too much of Sal's business. "Yeah. Same signals. You ever ship with Sammy Wynn?"

Awful thought. Guy with some serious personality faults, that wouldn't get better on a long, lonely haul. "I wouldn't share a bar table with Sammy Wynn. Whatever happened to him?"

"Spaced by now, I hope." She stopped and looked aside as Dekker turned over and buried his head in a pillow. Time to go, Ben decided, before they woke Ens. Moonbeam. He stood up, stood still til he knew Dekker wasn't going to wake up.

"You going to take the Aptitudes?" Meg asked him.

Sore spot, that. "Yeah," he admitted. And went back into the room with Sal. He had signed the assignment roster out there. He hadn't intended to tell them. But what had happened here, with the UDC CO busted out of command, himself being caught behind a Fleet Security wall . . . he didn't give a real thought to a transfer right now. He could test into something administrative. Damned sure the Fleet wouldn't want him going back under the UDC curtain with what he'd witnessed here, if by any means they could finagle hanging on to him—and it certainly looked as if they had the clout. He *didn't* have the instincts or the nerves for combat, he'd proved that before, and that was bound to show. Drugged you down, they did, even for the basic test. Hooked you up to a machine and read your responses and your answers. You couldn't fake this one. They said.

He passed the door back into his room, sat down on the bed carefully, so as not to wake Sal. Low light, scatter of braids on the pillows, innocent-as-a-babe profile with parted lips, slight snub nose—dammit, the conniving kid was his partner, he *liked* being with her, he'd found a piece of himself clicked back into place when she'd come walking into the barracks—and being without her again was a dreary thought. He earnestly, honestly liked Sal; *and* Meg; which he'd never said about anybody but Morrie Bird; and God help him, he could even get acclimated to Dekker, or just plain nerve-dead.

Fact was, skuz as this whole place was, somehow the echo and the racket and the coming and going in the barracks fit him like an old sock—fact was, he *liked* the racket and the activity and the accent he'd grown up with echoing off the bulkheads. Pressure here was from fools higher-up, different than TI's carpeted, high-voltage corridors, where competition was cutthroat and constant.

But this wasn't any damn mining run this group was prepping for. At TI your highest chance of fatal injury was sticking your finger in a power socket or ODing on caffeine. Here—

God, they weren't even sure the damn ship would *work*. Rumor out in the hall was that they were going max *v* with the program and they still hadn't proved any crew could run it once—let alone fly it in combat.

That was crazy. And he wasn't—even if insanity got the rest of them.

Sal—go out there and turn herself into a missile? Sal and Meg end up in a fireball? Hell if, if he could stop it. But he didn't know how to; couldn't stop Meg, damn the woman, if Dekker couldn't. And if Meg went, Sal went, and if Sal went—

Oh, hell, he was *not* a fool. There were women in Stockholm. There'd be a way to get down there, even through Fleet Command—if he just got Aptituded into strategic technical.

Stockholm women wouldn't ask stupid questions like What's the Belt? They'd have university degrees and stand and watch the tide come in and the snow fall and . . . think it was all damned ordinary.

Hell. Bloody *hell* with women. *Dekker* was saner. At least Dekker knew what he wanted.

I *nsert card please,"* the neutral voice said. The phone clicked. Dekker held the receiver and waited. And waited. Meg and Ben and Sal were in Testing. His day didn't start until 1015, when he had an appointment with Evaluations. Which meant he could go to the gym to try to settle his breakfast and his nerves; or try a phone call, see if he could get a personal call through to Sol One, on FleetCom, in spite of the security crackdown.

"Ens. Dekker." Human voice this time. *"Is this an official call?"*

"I'm trying to call my mother." He *hated* to sound like a strayed six-year-old. *Mother* always felt strange to him. Mama he'd long outgrown, though it came naturally to Belter ears. "It's a next-of. There was something on the news. —Look, can you put me through to Lt. Graff? He knows the situation."

"—I'm not being obstructionist, Ens. Dekker. I'm aware of your situation, but I am required to get an authorization for personal calls."

God, everyone in the solar system knew his business. "Yeah, well, can you *do* anything, FleetCom? The lieutenant's not outstanding easy to find this morning."

"I'll page him."

"Everybody's paged him," Dekker muttered. "I'll card in every little bit, I'm going down to gym 3A."

"I'm sorry. The gym is now off limits to Fleet personnel. Use the one on 3-deck, section 2."

"How do I get my clothes out of the locker in 1A?"

"Check with the office on 3-deck."

Everything was on its ear. "Thanks," he said glumly, and went four sections and took a lift in—it was about as much exercise as he wanted, just walking it. But one thing he'd learned in his tour in the Belt, if you could crawl to the gym, you crawled there and worked out; and if you got the spooks or the nerves—you went there and burned the chill off, you didn't let your mind go in loops—never let that start, not when you worked in cold, dark places, with things that went bang all too commonly.

The office there had his gym clothes, everything in sacks with old locker numbers. They had his name on the gym records. They had lockers already assigned to him and his crew. . . .

He hadn't had a run of things that worked in weeks. It gave him a moment of ridiculous cheerfulness. He had the whole gym to himself for the hour, everybody else being in sims or in special briefings—he wasn't fondly looking forward to his own session with the meds upcoming. Warm up the sore spots and go in there with the adrenaline burned out of him, was the plan—lunch on carbohydrates and go into Evaluation at 1300 warmed-up and hyped, and blow hell out of their damn tests . . . he could do it. The doctors had kept him flat on his back too long, he'd dropped five kilos on the hospital food, and Custard Charlie Tyson had gotten a couple of good hits in, but he could do it if he could get the chill out of his bones.

Light workout with the hand weights raised a sweat.

Coordination was shot. That *wasn't* good. He leaned on his knees a moment, trying to get his wind back and the rubbery feeling out of his arms, getting madder and madder at the meds, at the UDC, at the Fleet that had busted Graff over to a desk job and put in a bastard with an Attitude—

Temper wasn't helpful. Demas would say that. Calm down, Dekker. Use your head. Adrenaline's for speed, not stomach acid.

Yeah. But it didn't help when the knees wanted to cave in, when you had serious worries about three fools who'd gotten themselves into a Situation for his sake, and had a CO who'd flat *warned* him he didn't give a damn for their survival—

Stomach acid, hell, he wanted to beat the shit out of Porey, that was why he was shivering. And if he did that, with all the esoteric consequences of people he knew and didn't know, it wouldn't stop bastards from being bastards, and wouldn't get Porey out of here, he'd only make it worse.

He didn't want to be in this situation. He didn't want to be anybody anyone else relied on for anything: he was schitz as hell. He was crazy. Ben knew it. He didn't see why Fleet Command couldn't see it. He didn't know why he'd ever been made an issue, or put where they'd put him, except the Shepherds had needed somebody crazier than they were to press their differences with the insystemers— and people who wouldn't have given a damn about him back in the Belt, found a use for him here. He wasn't Paul Dekker to them: he was this to one group and that to another and nobody really knew shit about him. . . .

Hi, Dek, good to see you, Dek, how you doing? He couldn't stand it any more—because Ben was right, they didn't know him, didn't know he was a screw-up, a damn dumb pusher-jock who didn't think before he opened his mouth. Only value he had to anyone, the fact that his nerves jumped faster than average. Only thing he was good at, that ship—*that* was all that had mattered to him; Pete and Elly

and Falcone had had themselves, and they'd gone together—
the Fleet had thrown them together, they'd tested high, that
was all. And they were good and they'd worked together,
but he was burned out this morning, he didn't even know
whether he'd ever felt anything with them but comfort, and
that was cheap—

He didn't know why Ben had decided to take the damn
test this morning. Ben had skuzzed out on him. If Ben had
held out, Ben might have persuaded Sal and Sal *might* have
reasoned with Meg—

Like hell. *He* hadn't seduced Meg out here. At least Meg
and Sal weren't his fault. The ship had done that. Some
lying bastard in the Fleet had done that, who'd told Meg
they'd give her a chance—

Yeah. A chance. Thanks.

Drug made you seriously spaced. You had sensor spots
patched all over you, in places that made a body most
emphatically wonder if it was procedure or the femme tech
having a few loose circuits of her own—

"Do it where?" she remembered asking. But the examiner, that was a guy, nice-looking grayheaded man, asked
her to match up all these shapes and holes—God, she hadn't
done this one in years. "I'm not good at this," she said. "I
don't *fly* little cubes."

Neither did he, he said. At least he had a sense of humor.
So she ran the test and she tracked on discrimination stuff
that flashed on screens, they moved her to another station
and belted her in and the computer spun her around and
around—easy piece, nothing hard at all. Til the floor dropped
out from under her and *then* the thing went through its
paces.

Wanted you to draw a straight line? Right.

Wanted you to get up and walk one?

Yeah. Maybe.

Sit in the spin chair again. Wait for the light and press the
button while the chair spins?

Siren blast. Right before the light flash.

Dirty trick, sumbitch. Dirty trick. Flash again. Flash, flash. Pause. Flash.

Hold the yoke and the toggles, make the VR lines meet? This was a good one. Hadn't done this one before. . . .

Weight escaped his balance and bounced. Dekker ended up on one knee, caught a breath and waited for the room to stop spinning before he went to pick it up and rack it and lock it in. Good show he was going to make for the meds in an hour. He drew long breaths, sat down and felt after the towel to mop his face.

Stars came out of a vast dark. Lights on the panel glowed with information. . . .

It was in his head, the same as, in the Belt, you got to seeing rocks in your sleep, not rocks as they existed in the deep dark, but the way they were in the charts, the courses they ran, falling sunward, faster and faster, and then more and more slowly outward—

He wiped the sweat that stung his eyes. He heard somebody come in, challenged at the office for numbers and names. "Yeah," he heard someone say, far away and a door shut . . .

Echo. Door opening and closing. He'd seen a shape. He'd talked to someone. But he couldn't remember to whom. He chased the memory. But the voice that came back lacked all tone:

Just checking. Do what you were doing. . . .

Who in *hell* would he take that answer from?

Piece of nonsense. He *could* screw this test. They wanted him to discriminate a damn lot of advancing lines and dots? Easier if the sensors didn't itch.

He muttered, "Quick way to solve this. Who programmed this?"

Examiner said, "Don't talk."

"This is a piece of *shit,* major. Begging pardon." Zap. "Damn arcade game."

"Watch that one."

"This is fuckin' *armscomp!* I'm not testing for this—" Zap.

"You're not damn bad, lieutenant . . . But you're not real modest, either."

"I'm damned *good*. But I'm not killing things."

"You have a moral objection?"

He put hands and eyes on autopilot and left them to search for screen-generated threats. At definable intervals. Random number generator in the virtuals, for God's sake. "I got a moral objection. I got a moral objection to getting shot at."

"Exactly what we're looking for."

He thought about that reasoning. He thought about screwing the test, while he was zapping stupid dots. Faster now. "Screw it, you severely got a pattern in here."

"I've been telling them that."

"Tell you something." Zap. "I'm supposed to be in Stockholm. Somebody skuzzed my records." Zap. "Matched me up with the lunatic." Zap. Zap-zap-zap. "Oh, hell."

"See? Not all a pattern. You missed that one. Getting cocky, were you?"

Faster now. "Son of a bitch," he said.

"You have two hands, two keysets. Brain can do both operations. Hands can. How good are you?"

"Damned moonbeam partner of mine," he muttered. "You give me programming. I'm telling you—anywhere else is a waste—" Zap. "I don't want combat. —I *know* what this mother's doing—"

Zap/zap/zap—.

Hand on the other pad. Interrupt to Command level and invoke the chaos o/i off the internal generators. Obsolete as a security device, but certainly an improvement on *this* antique.

Resume. Let them figure that one. Let their *techs* come in and patch it if they didn't like it.

"Where did you get that code?"

"Telepathy," he said. "Sir. I told you. I *belong* in Stockholm."

Watch the lights, track the dot, do you have any blurring of vision, Mr. Dekker?

Have you had any headaches?

Stand here, stand there, look at the light, bend over, Mr. Dekker . . .

He escaped with a grudging Release on his card and an admonition to take his mineral supplements, got to a phone outside the med station and put the card in to check the readout for messages. Lunch, he thought, might bring people to check their messages. Might get a phone call, however muzzy, from Meg, telling him how she was doing.

None from Graff; none from Meg or Ben or Sal. No authorizations. Just a reminder of his appointment in Evaluations.

And a note from the gym that he hadn't carded in his preferred time slot and was he interested in team volleyball?

Hell.

Marine guards at every intersection. Corridors everywhere had a decided chill. God, there were even guards in the messhall. . . .

He started in, saw Mitch and Pauli and the guys at the tables and they saw him.

Upset him. He couldn't say why. He walked by for politeness' sake—"Sit down," they said, offering him a chair. But he couldn't face lunch of a sudden, in this place—too many faces in the room, too many people trying to be friendly who didn't know all that was going on with him, and the guards and the UDC watching him from the other end of the room. He muttered, "No, I'm on medicals right now, just time for a soft drink, thanks."

"Got anything back on the tests?"

Wasn't a thing stirred in C-barracks but what everybody was in it. "No. Not yet." He patted the back of Mitch's chair and made his escape to the rec-area foyer, where he could card a soft drink and a granola bar that tasted like cardboard and hit his stomach like lead.

They probably were talking about him back there. And he couldn't talk to them, couldn't deal with them until he knew what he was, whether he was going to clear the tests himself, whether his partners were passing theirs—he wasn't anyone, until he knew who he was working with, what he was, where he'd be, what they'd assign him to—

Fly again, yeah. Porey would see to that. Front of the line-up. Or the bottom— at Porey's discretion. He'd opened his damned mouth, he'd forgotten for a critical second he had partners who could be in danger from what he did or promised—

Couple of UDC guys came over and carded a candy bar. Names were Price and McCain. Techs. They hardly even looked at him, but he was sweating. He kept thinking, If I'd kept my mouth shut, if I'd done what the colonel wanted, if I'd only once ducked my head and played the game—

Tray banged somewhere. The room felt cold. His mother had said, Paul, what is it with you? Why do you always end up in the middle of it?

He wished to God he knew that. He wished to God he could go over there with the other guys and sit down and be what they wanted him to be, but he couldn't even tell them what he'd done or what he was waiting to find out—

Please God, they'd Aptitude somewhere down the list, somewhere out of immediate usefulness, and he could go maybe to Chad's crew, patch things up with them, he couldn't think of a match-up else he could make that might have a chance. He should have offered *that* to Porey, Porey wasn't crazy—he didn't want to lose another ship, for God's sake: Porey probably would have called it a good idea— good for morale, pull the program together. UDC *and* Fleet.

He should still propose that to Porey—talk to Chad's guys himself in advance, if he could get them to talk to him . . .

God, why couldn't he think about people? He was all right with machines, all right with anything that reacted in just one way when you touched it—he could understand that. He just—

—couldn't figure how to stop himself before he said things. When he opened his mouth it was wrong, when he didn't say anything it was wrong, he never got it figured out, some people just understood him and most didn't, and the ones that did were always in trouble because of the ones that didn't. Sum of his life, that. Evaluations said he was smart. So why couldn't he get that right? Like go in there and apologize to Porey and take what he had coming?

Because when he walked up against a guy like that something went snap inside, he went hyper and he *couldn't* think, that was the whole damn problem—

So calm down, don't do that?

It was why the Fleet had recruited him, it was what they trained him to do, split-second, hyped and half crazy, and they wouldn't understand he didn't come with an off switch . . .

Except maybe Graff understood. But Graff wasn't answering pages today. . .

Damn him.

A little hyped. They said, You can relax now. But there wasn't any sleep. Just the boards, alive with lights. Hands knew where to go and went there. Hell of a way to teach. But they said, "This is a sim tape. Familiarization. It won't prioritize for you. Just give you the handedness of the boards. . . ."

"Got it, yeah. No trouble."

"Don't fight the sims, Kady. You want to bring that pulse down."

"Yeah. I'm not fighting it." Happy as hell. God. I *want* this thing, don't want to screw it up—God, I don't want to screw it—

"Calm."

"Yeah, yeah." So *don't* get excited, Kady, don't go after it, ride with it, just float and enjoy it—

"Lot better, lot better, Kady. How're you doing?"

She laughed. Laughed like an idiot.

"You all right there? You know what you're doing?"

Her hands were reaching. She wasn't doing it. But she didn't object. The sequence made complete sense. "Jawohl, mate, piece of easy, there."

Clumsy direction, then. Her hand shook. "Shit!"

Boards went dark. Direction stopped. She grabbed for the B-panel and the fuse conditions, and the examiner said, "Abort, abort, it's all right."

"What did I do?" Her heart was going half light. The drug made her light-headed and she hated the sensation.

"Tape error. Not yours. Relax."

Made her mad. They had no right to screw up. But you didn't get mad while you were at the boards, you paid attention. All attention. Save mad for later.

"Ms. Kady." New voice. "That was a system abort. Don't worry about it. You can stand down."

"Thank you." Cold and calm. Same as you did when something went seriously wrong. She flipped the board-standby switch. Habit. Fool, she thought. It was a toy-board anyway.

"Thank you." Another delay. "You can get up. Go to the room with the red light showing. You are in .9 gravity."

"I think I can remember that," she muttered.

"Some don't."

"Thanks." Anger was the immediate reaction. She was embarrassed to beg; but, putting her foot off the platform: "Do I get another try on that abort?"

A hesitation. Somebody had blanked a mike. Then: "How are you feeling?"

"Good enough for another try." Self-disgust. "If I can get one."

"Get back in the chair, then."

Thank God. She was all but shaking. And damped that down. Fast.

"Pulse is up, Ms. Kady."

"Yeah. Re-start."

"Hyped as hell," came a mutter from the earplug. Faint. Then at normal volume: "The yoke is an automated assist. It *is* changing its responses. Do you perceive that?"

"Yeah." Absolute relief. They hadn't told her the sim could do that. "But I got my own numbers. Let's shorten this. What are you, IMAT?"

"IMAT or CSET. A or B, select your format, input your actual license level."

"No problem." She took B, ran her numbers in, hoping she remembered them, hoping she was still that sharp, and watched the readout for response profiles. "Shit! Excuse." 12.489 sudden *g*'s on a tenth of the yoke range. She cut it back, re-calced in her head, thinking she could have a seriously pissed examiner if she dithered too long, but dammit, she needed the fine control on that hairline correction in the sims and you had to have it wide enough if they threw you an emergency. *Hell* of a thrust this sim was set for—different than shuttle controls by a long way...

Forgot to ask if time counted. Too late to spare a neuron. You did it right, that was all, you did it real, hell with them...set the controls to your own touch and take the time it took, they should have effin' *said* if there were criticalities not on the instruments—it was a new kind of adaptive assist, *piece* of nice, this was....All kinds of interlocks and analyses it could give you. Mining in the Belt, you adapted your jerry-built and most egregiously not AI ship by whittling a new part out of plastic, and what you saw on your boards was a whole lot of hard-to-read instruments, not an integrated 360° V-HUD with the course plot and attitudes marked in glowing lines. *This* thing was trying to find out your preferences, arguing with you when its preconceptions thought it knew you. But it would listen.

—Damn it, machine, soyez douce, don't get cheek with

me . . . used one of these things ten plus years ago, she had, but, God, that had been an antique, against this piece . . .

"All right." She calmed her breathing rate. Panel lights lit. Scopes lit. "Go!"

Numbers hemorrhaged.

"God!"

"Nothing yet?" Dekker asked the desk on his mid-test break; and the secretary in Testing said, "No, sir. No result yet."

"Are they out yet? Have they left?"

"I don't think so, sir."

He tried FleetCom. He had a new comtech and had to explain everything again. "I just want to know if the lieutenant's ever checked in."

"He's in a meeting," FleetCom said.

"Has he gotten his messages?"

"I think he has. Excuse me. . . ."

On hold again, when all he wanted to do was hang up; and he didn't want to offend FleetCom by doing that before the tech got back to him. He wished he hadn't called. Five-minute break from his own Evaluations, it was 1456 by the clock, the granola bar and soft drink were wearing extremely thin, and he was regretting it. *If* he could get off the phone, he could get down the hall to the vending machines.

No word on his partners. Aptitudes was a four-hour session. You could take a little longer coming out from under the trank if you reacted. . . .

God, he didn't know what to—

"Ens. Dekker? Sorry to keep you waiting. I did get hold of the lieutenant. He says see him in his office at 1400. That's 21a, Admin."

"I'm in Evaluations til 1700. I'm in the middle of tests—"

"Excuse me. . . ."

Hell!

He put a hand over his eyes, he leaned against the counter and waited. Looked pleadingly at the secretary across the desk, then. "Do they *ever* take this long on Aptitudes?"

"I don't know, sir. I've only worked here for four..."

"Ens. Dekker? I'm sorry. ... the lieutenant says he can't talk at 1700, he's got another meeting."

"Will he clear a phone call for me to One? That's all I want."

"I think he wants to talk to you about that."

Shit. "Look—" He shut out the light and the secretary's presence with the palm of his hand. Tried to think. But he kept seeing fireballs. Hearing that door clank. "Is that all he wants? The phone call? Or does he want—look, can *I* talk to him online? Two minutes."

"He's in a meeting, sir. Just a moment."

He was late by now, by two minutes. You weren't late in Evaluations. You didn't antagonize the examiners. Who were UDC to begin with.

"The lieutenant says he needs to talk to you. He says at 2200."

"2200." Graff didn't plan to sleep, maybe. "Right. Thanks. Yeah. I'll be there."

"My partners aren't out of Test *yet*," Dekker said. "They went in at 0600. It's 2202 and Testing doesn't answer questions. ..."

"They're all right," Graff said, quietly, from the other side of the desk. "I can tell you that much."

"So *what* do you know?"

"That they're being very thorough."

"They're not reacting to the drug or anything—"

"No. They're all right. I did check."

It wasn't regulation. He wasn't convinced. He wasn't at all convinced.

Graff said: "On the other matter—"

"I just want to call my mother. Make sure she's all

right." He kept his frustration to himself. He didn't want to push Graff. He was running short of friendlies in Admin.

Graff said, "I got your message. I understand. There's a good possibility her phone calls are being monitored by the police. Possibly by someone less official."

"Who?"

"All we know," Graff said, "is the same thing you saw in the news. We're investigating. I could wish this lawyer weren't involved—personally. Is your mother a member, a contributor—of that organization?"

"I don't know. I don't think so. Are you asking me her politics?"

"You don't have to answer that."

"She hasn't got any politics that I know of. She didn't when I lived there. I don't think she would change."

"She was never politically active. Never expressed any opinions, for or against the government, or the Earth Company?"

Bit by bit the line of questioning made him uneasy. It wasn't like Graff—at least as he knew Graff—to probe after private information. He didn't think it was necessarily Graff's idea—and that meant whoever was investigating. So he offered a bit of his own reasons: "I was rab when I was a kid, the clothes, the haircut—Kady says I was a stupid plastic, and I guess I was; but I thought I was real. I used the words. My mother—got hot about it, said politics was all the same, didn't matter what party, all crooked, she didn't want any part of it—told me I was a fool for getting involved. They'd shot these people down on Earth. I think—"

—Meg was there, he almost said. But that was more than Graff needed to hear—if a deep spacer cared about the Company, the Earthers trying to emigrate . . .

"Think what?" Graff asked.

He couldn't remember his thread for a moment. He shrugged. "Doesn't matter. She's just not the kind. Works a full shift, mostly over, if you want extras you have to do that—and that was all she wanted. A nice place. Maybe a station share. Security. That kind of thing. You wouldn't get her involved in anything."

"You know the Civil Liberty Association?"

"No, sir. I never heard of them."

"They're the ones funding your mother's lawyer. They're headquartered in Munich. They support lawsuits in certain causes, that's mostly what they do. Their board of advisers has some of the same associations as the Sun Party, the Peace Front, the Karl Leiden Foundation—the Party of Man—"

He shook his head. "I don't know anything about them. I doubt she does."

"They're Earth-based Internationals: of several related groups, only the Civil Liberty Association and the Human Research Foundation maintain offices off Earth. They apparently do each other's business. So I understand. I'm no expert in terrestrial affairs. But I thought you should know, this organization does have political overtones that aren't friendly to the program or to the Fleet."

"What do you want me to do?"

"I only thought you should be aware of the situation."

Deeper and deeper. He thought of saying, I'm in no position to restrain her from anything. I can't do your politics for you. But it was all on their side and nothing on hers. And probably the lieutenant didn't want a blunt question, but it wouldn't be his first offense this week. "So hasn't the Fleet got strings it might pull?"

"Possibly."

"So what do you want me to say to her?"

"Nothing. Nothing on that score. I just want you to be aware of these things."

Why? In case of what, for God's sake?

"Do you still want to call her?" Graff shifted a glance toward the phone on his desk.

He had never believed of himself that he was smart, no matter what Evaluations told him—if he was smart, he wouldn't be here now, put on the spot to make an excruciatingly personal phone call in front of a man he'd thought he trusted, whose motives he didn't now entirely understand.

And, God, he didn't want to talk to her . . . he was fast losing his nerve.

"Do you want to do that?"

"Yes, sir," he said, before all of it evaporated. "If you can get me through."

Graff took up the handset and punched in. "FleetCom. Route this through our system, FSO, Sol One. —Number there?"

"97 . . . 2849. Dekker, Ingrid. Routing can find her." 2210 mainday and she ought to be home. She didn't have a nightlife—at least she hadn't had, when he'd been living at home.

"Takes a bit," Graff said, and gave him the handset. "It's going through, now."

He held it to his ear. Listened to the clicks and the tones. His heart was beating fast. What in hell was he going to say? Hello, mother?

Click. Click-click. Beep.

"There's a noise on the line."

"A beep?"

He nodded.

"Somebody's got it monitored. FleetCom's picking that up."

Hell. It was going through. He listened for the pick-up. But the answering service came on instead. *Ms. Dekker is out at the moment. Kindly leave your name and number. . . .*

You'd know. "Mother. Mother, this is Paul. I'm sorry to hear about the trouble you're having. . . ." It was hard to talk coherently to a machine, hard to think with that steady beep that meant the police or somebody else was listening. "I don't know if I can help, but if you just want to talk, I'm here. I'd like to talk to you. I'd like to help—" He wondered if he should mention money. But while he was thinking, it clicked off and connections broke, all the way back along the route, leaving him the sound of static.

"She wasn't home," he said, and gave the handset back. "I left a message on the machine."

"Anything that comes through—you *will* get. I promise you."

"Thank you." They'd taught him to say thank you. Please. Yes, sir. No, sir. Stand straight. Answer what you're asked. They'd told him he wouldn't fly if he didn't. His mother hadn't had that advantage in dealing with him. He didn't remember he'd ever said Yes, ma'am or Please or whatever boys were supposed to answer to their mothers. Fuck you, he'd said once, in a fit of temper, the week she'd bailed him out of juvenile court, and she'd slapped his face.

He'd not hit her. Thank God, he'd held it back, he hadn't hit her. Only respect he'd ever shown her, that last year . . . and if they shipped him out from here—the only respect he might ever have a chance to show, except that phone call.

"Forgive me," the lieutenant said. "I have to ask this—in your judgment, is it possible—is it remotely possible she did make threats against MarsCorp?"

Ingrid Dekker wasn't a walkover. She wasn't going to stand and take it—not without handing it back. "If they threatened her. But she wouldn't—wouldn't just take it into her head to do that, no, I don't believe that." I have to ask this . . .

At whose orders . . . sir. . . .

"Are you close to your mother—still?"

God. He didn't want to discuss it. But the lieutenant had been on his side, Graff if anybody was still his lifeline. He didn't want to put his mother in a bad light. She was the one in trouble and she needed all the credit she could get. He said, looking at a spot on the front of Graff's desk: "I was a pain in the ass, sir. She said if I went to the Belt I didn't need to come back. I—was sincerely a pain in the ass, sir. I was eighteen. I was in with a rough crowd. —I was stupid."

Graff didn't say anything to that, except: "Have you corresponded with her?"

"No, sir." He stared fixedly at that spot on the desk, wondering if they might search his room and bleed his datacard for it, next use he made. Maybe they already had. "Not recently. —I've got about four, five k I'd like to send over to her account. If I could do that. She's not working, she's going to need the money."

"I'll talk to Legal. See what the procedures are. —As I said, we're going to be looking into the case. If there are strings to be pulled, maybe we can pull them."

"I appreciate that, sir."

"Are you ready to get back to work?"

"Yes, sir."

Graff keyed something on the deskcomp. Glanced at it. "I don't know if they can get your friends back to quarters this watch. But you're their unit commander, you have access there on any shift, if you want to check up on them."

Not back to quarters? Not in this watch? His heart did a tic and a speed-up. He looked at Graff, met a level, I-can't-tell-you kind of stare.

"What are they *doing?*" he asked Graff. "They're in there for Aptitudes—it's a four-hour test, for God's sake . . ."

"You have access there."

"I've *been* over there. They wouldn't tell me a damn thing!"

Graff had never been one to hold back information, not under Keu, and not under his own administration. Now . . .

"I suggest you go over there," Graff said. "That's all I can say."

Didn't *like* the damned drugs. Didn't effin' *like* the floating feeling. Told you stuff you didn't want to hear. Told you you'd effin die if you screwed it . . . and Ben didn't want to die, he sincerely didn't want to die . . .

"Fire!"

His heart took a jump, he felt neg *g*, he went spinning away—you should feel blood pooling in your head and your feet and he didn't, didn't feel anything right except cold breeze on his face and his lungs getting air again—

He could see light. Felt somebody holding his sleeve. He was flat on his back in g and *Dekker* was holding on to him, saying, "It's all right, it's all right, Ben—"

Wasn't who he wanted to wake up in the arms of. He stared at Dekker, with his heartbeat still thumping away like explosions, and recalled they were surrounded by dots all but six of which were trying to kill him—

—except he was in bed and Dekker wasn't flying the ship.

He took slow assessment of this fact. He took a look around the ceiling of a disgustingly barren room, recalled signing his name, and them telling him Sal was in, and him talking to the tech and screwing with the sim, because he'd been mad as hell and wanting to get court-martialed and wanting to go to bed with Sal Aboujib if he had to get shot at to do it—only viewed backwards, as he had to see it now, that sequence didn't highly make sense.

Neither did Dekker sitting on his bedside. He'd come here to sit with Dekker. He wasn't in the hospital. He was in the sims lab and Dekker, with this scared look on his face, was holding him by the wrist.

"Ben."

"Yeah?" He began to think he'd better wake up.

"Ben. You all right?"

Dekker asking really worried him.

"Don't agitate him," somebody else said. "You know the rules."

"Trying to give him a heart attack, what's the damn hurry?"

There wasn't any answer. Dekker took hold of his hand. Said, "Shit . . ."

Dekker holding his hand? He'd really rather not. Unless he was dying. He didn't feel like he was dying. He stared at Dekker, made his fingers bend and his hand draw back and decided in this moment of clarity that he wanted his foot on the floor.

"Ben. Ben, —don't do that."

Froze right there. Face down in the bend of Dekker's arm. And couldn't think how to get out of that situation.

"Skuzzed," Dekker said. Light came back. Dekker swore at nothing in particular. That was all right. Saved him the bother.

"Aboujib did pass," he wanted to know.

"Yeah."

"Meg?"

"Yeah. I got three of you. Same condition." With which Dekker got up and stalked out.

That was Dekker, all right. Boy had a lousy temper.

"Shit!" he heard from the hall.

2345h and all Dekker wanted was his own bed, didn't want to talk to anybody, just skuzzed through the door into a darkened barracks, went straight to his quarters around the corner and down the corridor, and got undressed on autopilot—wasn't even thinking clearly when he heard the stir outside. A knock came at his door and he stared at it and blinked.

Second knock. He thought, What in hell? and opened it, on Mitch and Pauli and Trace and God-only who else the shadows behind them were.

"Want to talk to you," Mitch said, and Dekker leaned his forearm on the doorframe and reasoned that even if he could talk them into leaving him alone now, it was too late, the adrenaline he thought he'd run out of was up again, sleep was gone, leaving just caffeine-ragged nerves and a body shaking with chill and exhaustion. Didn't have a shred of embarrassment left, Trace there and all—he just said hoarsely, "What?"

"The rest of your guys didn't come in?"

"No."

"Dek. What's going on?"

"I don't know what's going on, I don't know any more than the rest of you guys." Struck him then, though, that a lot of the aforesaid guys had risen to his defense in the messhall, a couple of them had gone to hospital and a lot of them had suffered serious inconvenience on his account—so they had some right to knock on his door in the middle of his sleep and want a piece of his hide.

Mitch asked: "Is it true they're going to bust your guys right into active? They're going to put Pollard and Kady and Aboujib straight in?"

Wasn't hiding any damn thing around here. He'd been trying to get the same admission out of Testing and he couldn't do it, *or* find out who the order came from that had shoved his crew straight out of Aptitudes into the board-sims—he stared at Mitch a beat or two, muttered, "Something like."

"'Something like.' They're going to take Kady's hours for legit?"

"Mitch, I don't know what they're taking for anything, nobody's told *me* a damn thing, I don't know what your source is, but it's more than I know..."

"So where are they right now?"

"In the labs sleeping it off. They started in at 0600 and they got through somewhere around 2200, that's all I know, except they're Aptituded in, that's the only official word I have on anything." He got short. His temper was on the edge. But he hadn't reassured anybody. And maybe they'd heard something: he hadn't been in the rumor mill all day, he'd been chasing around in places rumors didn't get to— back and forth between offices and Evaluations. And rumor was evidently saying for fact what he suspected and couldn't get the labs or the techs to admit to....

Shove them up into Mission Ready, with him?

God, Porey wouldn't do that. Porey'd said himself that he

wouldn't lose another ship: the Fleet couldn't afford it. They weren't going to do that. . . . They *couldn't* do that. . . .

"Rumor is," Jamil said, "the Fleet thinks your guys have the stuff, so they're just going to go with them, put them right in on the pods—"

"They can't do that," Dekker said. It came out a thin, helpless kind of voice. "No way. They haven't got ships to throw away on a notion like that—"

"Rumor is," Mitch said, "they were running some kind of new tape off Pete and the guys during the mission, rumor is the Fleet thinks they can take that tape and sub it for the whole damn training sequence—"

Legs nearly went out from under him.

"Seems," Jamil said, "they wanted crew that hadn't been *biased* by all this prior training—"

"Shit, no. . . ." He couldn't feel anything below the gut. He got a couple of breaths and managed to stay on his feet. "This is shit, guys, I don't know where you got this, but this is shit. No way are they going to do that . . ."

Trace said, "First we got Tanzer, now we got a guy thinks he can program us like computers?"

"*Where'd* you hear this stuff?"

"In the slightly off chance," Mitch said, "that we're dealing with bugs, we decline to answer that in specific. But we thought you'd like to know."

"Shit—" He wasn't doing too well with words. His teeth started chattering. "I got to talk to the lieutenant. . . ."

"It's Porey we have to make a dent in."

"Good luck with that," Trace said.

"We can not show up tomorrow. The whole lot of us."

Dekker shook his head, made a wave of his hand, suddenly struggling to get control of his jaw. "N-no. This is a m-man m-makes ex-examples. Trust me that I kn-know."

"God, the man's freezing," Trace said. "Get him a sheet or something."

"I kn-know what I'm t-talking about. You don't pull a st-strike—he'll p-pick one of you—" Pauli got past him into his room. But he kept looking at Mitch. "Guy's a control freak. I m-met him. F-flew out here with him..." A blanket settled around him. He made a stiff, half-successful grab after it. But it did nothing for his chill. He let Pauli pull him back toward the bunk, while Mitch said, "You guys go on. Let's get his door shut...."

Mitch stayed, and Pauli did, and Jamil and Trace. Dekker sat down on the bed, tucked the blanket around him. Mitch said: "The man's making an example, all right —he's going to kill you, you understand that? High team gets the next run. That's us or that's you, Dek. You can kill yourself in sims, if one of those girls screws up."

"They aren't damn b-bad..."

"Listen, *Pollard* may know what he's doing, Pollard had a background, but they hauled these girls in here for no other reason than they were with you in the action out there and they're somewhat famous in the Bell. They've got *no* place in the program, Fleet's listening to helldeck gossip, *no* solid background in hours—"

"They survived."

"Yeah, they survived whoring their way around helldeck. That's what they did for a living, Dekker, I don't know if you heard, but that's the plain truth."

He didn't believe he'd heard that. That was how it got as far as it did. "Screw *you*, Mitch, you keep your opinions to yourself."

"All right, all right, they're friends of yours, I'm sorry. But you came in there new. You ask Pollard where these girls got their credit. With him, with Morrie, with any ship they ever handled... no bad karma for it, but they didn't make their keep with the runs they made—"

"You stow it, Mitch. I *worked* with them."

"You never flew with them. Never knew shit what they could do, and now because they were with you, they got a rep the Fleet takes for granted—"

"They *passed* the Aptitudes, Mitch, the examiners shoved

them right into the board sims, you're telling me any of *us* sailed through into the sims?''

"Hey. Maybe their brain-tape works. Maybe you *can* program human beings to act just like a robot—just like the damn AI they tried to hang over our heads. They don't build one, they make *us* one. But what happens under fire, Dek? What happens when the answer isn't in any damn *tape*, and those girls don't know it? That's when it's going to make a difference. . . .''

"Meg's the coolest head under fire I ever saw. Meg saved our *asses* on R2, and *you* weren't there, Mitch, *you* couldn't get to us, if you want me to bring that up—"

"Well, you can thank God she caught a bullet, because if Meg Kady had been flying, she might have taken out the *Hamilton*. Don't blind yourself, Dek. She was a second-rate miner jock who got caught running contraband—she's got a helldeck rep and now they're going to hype her and Aboujib and Pollard on some tekkie tape and put you head to head with us. I don't want to see you crack up. I don't want to see those girls hurt. I don't have a personal grudge against them, I just have a real gut reaction when I see somebody running totally on rep and getting somebody else fuckin' *killed*, Dek, and sending this program down the out-chute.''

"Maybe we'll see," he said, set his jaw and looked elsewhere, because he didn't have anything left to say on the subject and he was too tired and too shaken to punch Mitch out. There were things he could say, like firstly, Where were you, Mitch, when we were depending on you? But he didn't honestly know that answer, he'd been too charitable to ask; and he didn't want a war with Mitch.

Mitch is a mouth, he told himself, Mitch was born with an Attitude—he wouldn't deal with *me*, except I'm the competition, and he has to take me seriously. It's Shepherd, that's all it is—Meg's insystemer and she's flash and they don't like her style, that's the problem—

Jamil said, "Dek, you have to protect yourself. I don't personally know whether Kady and Aboujib have got it, I think Pollard probably does, but not the way they need to have it now. The examiners didn't bust them through into the sims because they're good, they busted them through because they were *told* to, that's the truth, Dek, and we're worried, we're worried for you, we're worried for your crew, we're worried for the reason that we signed up for this program in the first place, because we're in the center of some serious games, here—we got congresses playing games with a ship we could fly if they'd get the hell off our backs and quit screwing with the way we work—"

"We don't want to see you killed," Mitch said. "We don't want to see anybody else killed. You better find out what's going on. You better find out what your crew's capable of—before you put your lives on the line out there, that's what I'm saying. The lieutenant hasn't got any power to do anything about anything right now. But he might tell you the truth and he might listen. And he might pass what he knows to the captain—who is the *only* authority we can think of who might pull the plug on this damned tape—"

"It's what they use Unionside," Trace said. "That's where they got the tech. They don't even know what they're doing with it, that's my guess, they just got it, they can't come up with a fix on the program, and now they're going to try this, they're going to make *you* the guinea pigs. You've got to lay back, Dek. Lay back and lay out and don't *try* to take those guys realtime . . ."

Mitch took Jamil's arm, hauled him to the door. Trace lingered, just stood there, the only female in the group, with, he suddenly uncharitably surmised, other intentions than argument.

"Go on," he said, "out."

"Dek, I know they're friends of yours, that's what—"

"Trace. Get the hell out. Now. And turn out the lights."

She turned out the lights. She left. He fell back on the wreckage of the bedclothes and felt the cold hit his chest and stomach—thought about getting up and putting the bed back in order, but he didn't, right now, have the fortitude.

He just rolled over in the blanket and tried to fall unconscious, if sleep was out of reach; but images rolled over and
over like riot behind his eyes, the argument with Meg about
her flying, Graff sitting there and telling him Get over to
Testing, Porey saying, You're meat, until you prove
otherwise. . . . But the sequencing of events didn't make
sense. They'd *brought* Meg and Sal here to wake him up,
they'd had to start from the Belt directly after the accident,
directly after he ended up in hospital—they'd brought Ben
from closer in and Ben had gotten here faster, that was all,
but they must have started at the same time.

They'd had the hearing, Graff had said, and they'd
wanted him to testify. But he hadn't. And still Porey had
come in to take the program over. And they had tapes.
Tapes they'd made off Pete and Elly and Falcone on the
mission, leading up to the wreck—

Union tech, then, the same deep-drug tech that they'd
sworn once they could beat—but the ship wasn't up to specs
and the program was screwed and they had to keep their
funding going, *had* to keep getting the ships built—

So the Fleet had seized control and they had to have
another pony show? They swore to somebody they'd get the
program turned around and to do that they had to hold out
some brand new tekkie trick that was going to win the war
so they could get the money?

They wanted to try out the tech on *unbiased* crew—and
for that, they hauled in Meg and Sal clear from the Belt,
pulled in Edmund Porey *and* a carrier, blasted away from
Sol Station like a bat out of hell an hour after the riot in the
messhall landed him and half the program in the brig?

Then Porey had wanted to talk to *him,* personally, when
he hadn't, that he knew, talked to Mitch, or any of the other
recruits in any private interview?

Porey knew him—personally, at least insofar as they'd
met during his trip out from the Belt in the first place; Porey
had ferried him out from the Belt—it wasn't impossible that
Porey had had his hand on his career long before this . . . maybe

even suggested him for the program when they enlisted him: he had no idea, but Porey had been in a position to have done that. Maybe *that* was why the interview in the office, that had gone so badly; maybe Porey was justifiably angry that he'd been in the center of controversy, when Porey had brought him here specifically to keep him out of media attention, because of the Salazar mess—

Then his mother, devoutly noninvolved, got fired—and went after MarsCorp; and peacer groups showed up with lawyers to back her suit?

He lay shivering in his bed, thinking, Why? on the frenetic edge of exhausted sleep. Everything looped back, as if he was the gravity well nothing could escape. . . .

There were so many things that didn't make sense. There were so many pieces of his life being gathered up and shaken—everything that went wrong from here to Pell seemed to have his name on it, in bright bold caps. Paul F. Dekker.

A guy couldn't have that kind of luck, no way in *hell* one stupid miner-jock could just chance to be where carriers moved and officers intervened—

And Graff just happened to care so much he went to all the trouble to collect his friends to rescue him?

Like hell. Like hell, lieutenant, sir.

"What was I going to say to him?" Graff asked. "Ask these people and they might give you what you want, but dammit, you don't deal with them like that."

Demas said, in his null-*g* unmonitored sanctuary in the heart of the carrier, "Nothing you can do, J-G. No way to stop it even if you'd known in advance. This was decided at much higher levels."

"Did you know? *What* do you know?"

Demas shook his head. "I don't and I didn't. I would guess there was consultation. I would hope there was consultation of more than Porey with his own captain, but knowing what Mazian decides these days, I have some trepidation on that account. But who knows? Tape-tech works for Union.''

''Not at the *cost*,'' Graff said, and looked left at a sound that in no wise belonged in this place. ''Saito, —''

''Medicinal,'' Saito said. The bottle Saito had just uncapped broke five regulations Graff could think of immediately: it was glass, it was private property in an ops area storage, it was liquid, it was alcoholic and it probably hadn't passed local customs.

It was, however, null-stopped, and Saito sailed it his direction. ''You're not on call. Jean-Baptiste is on the line, we're still on stand-down. You need your sleep and your morality won't let you. So join the rest of us and turn it in.''

''So where do you do that? Fleet HQ? There must be a waiting line. It seems a damned busy traffic this year.''

''There's nothing we can do. No help to the boy, ruining yourself. If we were attacked this instant you're worthless. Best you know it beyond a doubt.''

He took a sip and made a face at the sting; and in the midst of his indignation, realized flavors still evolving on his tongue, an unfolding sensory sequence, the way Earthly flavors tended to do—nothing simple. Nothing exactly quantifiable. From instant to instant he liked and loathed the taste. He found it significant that the sensory overload could reach even through his present mood to say it was rich, it was expensive, it was—if you could synthesize it—only one of endless variations on which a whole trade flourished— from a gravity well in which Conrad Mazian had been sunk for weeks.

''This place *corrupts*,'' he murmured. ''It's the motherwell of corruption. When did we forget what we came here to prevent?''

''Take another, J-G. Edmund Porey is in charge of the people in charge of the tape. He brought the tape, he brought the applications techs. They're officially *Carina* crew.''

"What are we fighting to keep away from? What in *hell* are we fighting to keep out of Sol System?"

Demas caught the bottle that drifted from his hands, took a sip and sent it on to Saito, third leg of their drift-skewed triangle. Demas said, "I earnestly recommend sleep, J-G. Perhaps a night of thorough debauch—we might manage that. There's absolutely nothing else we can do."

"We can help the boy. We can at least do something about his next-of's situation."

"Technically Ingrid Dekker is not, you know, next-of. Pollard is. Dekker explicitly took her out of that status . . ."

"For her safety. *He* knows the situation. That's why he didn't call on her."

Saito frowned, cradled the bottle in her arms. "I've been over and over the Dekker file. There is a remote possibility someone at Sol One leaked the story about Dekker's accident. The information was at Sol One via FleetCom and one can never assume there was no leak. One hopes not. But it's remotely possible she might have found out, and she may have learned about Salazar's proceedings against her son. She might have taken action of her own—but there is that last, troubling letter from the mother to Dekker—in his file. . . ."

"In which she tells him not to communicate? But he disregarded it."

"He doesn't know we monitor these things."

"He should suspect. —You think she may have attacked MarsCorp, in revenge for her son?"

"Difficult. Difficult case. Neither Cory Salazar nor Dekker had a father of record—not an uncommon situation for Mars, much less so for Sol One. Sol's still very tied to the motherwell. In all senses. Ingrid Dekker had a son. Had she named a father, tests would have established paternity. That man would have had financial and legal liability—under local law."

"Possibility she didn't know?"

"Possibility she didn't know or didn't want to say. It

would extend legal rights to the child. She took full financial responsibility. She had the child—again, her choice.''

Graff frowned, revising attitudes. He had no idea who his own father was, but his mother had had a cheerful account of possibilities, all from one ship—who had not the least liability in the matter: not for him and not for his cousins of the same stopover. Who might even be half-sibs, but who cared?

Earth certainly did.

''Mother,'' said Saito, ''has nothing to do with ship-loyalty. Not in the least. Unitary family. He grew up in a two- or three-room apartment alone with one woman. No sibs, no cousins, no other kin—not an abnormal situation. Not the local ideal either.''

Claustrophobic, what he could feel about it. He watched Saito take a drink and sail the bottle back to him.

''Dekker did not get on well in school,'' Saito said. ''Fell in with a group of young anti-socials—read, quasi-rab—and got caught vandalizing station lifesupport—a series of smokebomb incidents, as happened. One might assume it was their idea of political statement.''

''A very stupid one.'' He had read the file, though not with Saito's interpretation. Sabotaging one's own lifesupport hardly qualified as intelligence—and Dekker was far brighter than that. Or should have been.

''He got very little education. It's all classroom theory, there. Very little hands-on. Dekker doesn't learn by lecture. His episode with the court nearly had his mother fired and deported, for a minor out of control—''

On a merchanter ship, it would have had the youngster scheduled for a station-drop and a go-over by psychs. Possibly with mother or cousin in tow, but not absolutely. There was no use for such a case aboard—

But Dekker was not insane. Quite remarkably sane, considering his upbringing. Graff took a sip and frowned, passing it on to Demas.

''She spent her personal bank account on lawyers and

bond for the boy's behavior," Saito said. "She enrolled him in vocational training. Electronics, her own profession. He ducked out of that and got a position pushing freight. Lied about his age. Made very little money, but he was out of trouble. He went back to school—probably found out he needed the math for a license—and apparently became an upstanding citizen, though by this time he was in remedial in all his subjects. . . ."

"One brush with the rab. And no other troubles," he said, "until the Belt."

"Until he absconded with Alyce Salazar's daughter—with whom he'd been a correspondent since his return to school."

"Mmmn," said Demas, "the miraculous reform."

"And no record there," Saito said, "until Cory's death. A model citizen. Solvent—"

"On Ms. Salazar's money."

"But solvent. A hard worker. He had been on Sol before he left. Had, one suspects, a habit of pushing himself beyond the legal limits on his license. . . ."

"Certainly a talent," Graff murmured, thinking . . . "Why did no one at Sol ever Aptitude him?"

"With that score in social responsibility, I don't think anyone ever thought of tracking him for ops."

"A mortal waste."

"Earth has a million more who want the slot. They can afford human waste."

"Dekker's a statistical anomaly."

"Especially in that population. But they didn't recognize the profile. Sports or trouble, that was their analysis. And he was off the team very quickly. He wasn't physically adept, of course. And temper didn't serve him well. You do not frustrate that lad. But you know that."

Morbidly interesting, Graff thought, to know what a profile like his own might have meant—in the motherwell. "Pressure on the genome."

Demas muttered: "Emory? Or Wallingsford?"

And Saito: "Don't we fight this war for that distinction?"

"Who knows why we fight? Because we stayed by the Company? But what's the Company? Not wise, nor representative of the motherwell. Nothing I've met tells me that answer." Demas passed the bottle again, to Saito.

Graff asked, "Can we help his mother? We've civilians working in FSO. Maybe she could be employed there."

"There's that peacer contact. She certainly won't pass our security clearance with that attachment."

The bottle came back to him.

"Because she's naive and desperate, she's a security risk? She wouldn't have access to the FSO lunch schedule."

Saito said: "Being Dekker's kin and outside our wall is a security risk. And there's the vid. The Dekker affair may have died out of the media—but watch them remember it now. Command will be extremely reluctant to solidify that association. The peacer connection—"

"Our employing her could be an interesting embarrassment to their side."

"And there's the claim of harassing Salazar."

A most uncomfortable thought occurred to him. "You don't think Salazar could have hired Ms. Dekker's lawyer, to control *both* sides of the lawsuit?"

"Not legal, of course—to pay both sides' legal help. That much is true even in Sol System."

"Possible, though. Isn't it? Their system of exchange makes a private transaction hard to trace."

"Oh, it's even possible the peacer groups see Salazar as a way to their objectives; possible that the money is flowing to this conflict from the peace and the defense committees. Mars is relatively leftist, relatively isolationist. They see their interests remote from the EC as a whole. Pursue some of these groups deeply enough and you come out the door of their opposition."

"Moebius finance," Demas said. "These groups survive on fund-raising. Particularly their executives and staff. How could these people survive without each other?"

Completely paranoid.

"The enemy of my enemy," Demas said, and took the bottle up, "threatens both our livelihoods. And of course the Fleet is innocent in this game. Earth's parliaments and congresses understand Mazian. Mazian gains command of R&D. Of Sol Two. God, one wonders what traded hands."

Graff thought privately, and dared not say, even to them: Our integrity. Our command. Mazian was going to fill the captaincies with his choices—

Porey among the first.

Fingers felt all right. Wasn't sure about the ownership of the hand, though. Schitzy experience, that was. Meg held her eye from blinking with one set of fingers and tried to apply the pencil without blinding herself—Dek had been kind enough to make a supplies run from the quarters to the lab dorm, only thing she'd asked of him last night: Get our makeup, God, we got to look like hell—

"Dek was a skosh bizzed last night," she said to Sal, who was putting earrings in, stealing a bit of mirror past her shoulder. "Don't you think?"

"Man's doing all right."

"You?"

You had to catch Sal like that, blindside. Sal met her eyes in the mirror, wide-open.

"So, Aboujib?"

Sal said, scowling, "Scared as I hoped to be, give me a damn field of Where-is-its? and a: Some of these things are rocks, Aboujib, and some of these things are missiles? I never memmed a field faster in my damned life—"

"Pass?"

"Hey. I didn't have a heart attack. —Kady, I got seriously to talk to you about your sojer lessons. They're severely *real*, these sumbitches."

She would have turned around. But mirrors was the best place to catch Sal. "Truth, Aboujib. You want to go back to the *Hamilton?*"

She saw the hesitation. The little nip of a lower lip. "Without?"

And had this moment with her heart up in her throat. She'd passed, dammit, they'd told her. Finally got a chance at a ship and a guy she got on with, and, dammitall, here was Sal pulling in the other direction, she saw it plain.

And it was a lot of hours with Sal, a lot of bad times and a lot of good, but on the other hand there was Dek—there was Dek, who—God. . . .

Sal's frown had gone. The lower lip rolled out in a rueful sulk. "I dunno, Kady, I dunno how you talk me into these things."

"Aboujib, come serious. You want to be back there."

"I tell you what. I want, I seriously want, a little damn couple finesses on that simulation. They got no mem-check, there's not a damn interset macro in there—maybe they been getting this thing from *Shepherd* types. Ought to ask a freerunner about rocks, Kady, ought to ask us how not to go boom in a fire-track—"

"I'm not asking that."

"Well, I'm not the hell going back to the *Hamilton*. Leave you here with the guys?" Frivolous. Deliberate. The mask was back and Aboujib's long eyes were half-lidded. "*I* lay you bets, Kady." Flick of a nail against a large earring. "Ben didn't flunk that mama. Not our Ben. Scare hell out of him the way they did me—and they get a class A per-for-mance. So with this child. Miner nerves, here. Don't tell *me* fire-track. They're saying I got to set up the positionals? Somebody else is going to have his finger on the fire-button? Shit-all. I want the *guns,* Kady."

"Effin' right I passed, Dek-boy. No question I'd pass if I wanted to. Ap-ti-tuded, hell, they put me in *armscomp,* are you satisfied?"

Dekker wasn't. He sincerely didn't want that. He watched Ben shaving in this dormitory the labs afforded their test subjects and kept his chilled hands in his pockets.

"Sorry doesn't cover it. I know. But—"

Ben looked around at him. "You're worried, Dek-boy. Tell me why you're worried."

He wasn't sure he ought to say that either—since Ben didn't know; since self-doubt was the deadliest creature you could take into the program. The program was full of egos. Ben's was fairly healthy.

"So what's the matter?" Ben prodded him.

He had to say something—because somebody would, back in barracks. "Say the Fleet has that new program—say they came up with this tape stuff . . ."

"You mean what they gave us wasn't reg?"

He was supposed to be a fast thinker. He wasn't doing well this morning. Mute as a rock, he was.

"Look, Moonbeam, what in hell are they up to? Gives a guy a real uneasy feeling, that look of yours, and you're the lousiest liar I know of."

"It's supposed to work, that's all I know."

Ben gave him a long, suspicious stare.

"All I know," Dekker said; and Ben said,

"Hell if. What's going on?"

"Nothing," he said. "Nothing but they want results. Fast. And the heat's on my tail. But it doesn't get to you guys. It doesn't."

"Yeah? They put you in command, did they, of the whole friggin' Fleet?"

"No. Porey said it. They don't want to lose another ship. And I swear to you, —I won't lose another crew."

CHAPTER

12

GLOWING lines converged. Dekker blinked sweat and the simulator manufactured an uncharted rock on split second Imminent for the carrier.

Missed the bastard and redirect to take it out on the fly—

Got it, got the beta target before the bloodflow caught up with his knees.

Targets coming.

Carrier showed up on the scope. That was the priority— your carrier showed and you got the come-home, and you were done, far as you could clear it a path, granted you could get through the effect shield without glitching.

Soft and smooth—you got the slight buffet as you came through the shield, momentary LOS of everything on the boards and you had to know its v, the extent of those shields, how close you were going to be when you came through the envelope—damned close, *damned* close.

Touch. Slight mismatch. Within tolerance. Probe caught.

Mate.

Power down.

Good run, solid run. Not flashy, except that UO and making that shot. He could cut the sim, meltdown and unbelt, he'd earned it *and* a hot shower. Fine control when you'd been hyped was hell, and switch-off was the co-pilot's job, if there'd been a co-pilot this sim—he wouldn't lose points on that. But he was a fussy sumbitch. He set his switches. He set every effin' one.

Damn, it felt good. Felt solid.

Home again.

He shifted his legs as the pod opened and he could unbelt and drift out. Breath frosted, while sweat still ran under the flightsuit.

Take *that* in your stats, Tanzer.

Card game went on, Ben and Sal running up favor points on Almarshad's and Mitch's guys, and the spectators drifted down there. "Hey, Dek," came back, but Dekker tried to ignore it and concentrate on his math and his set-targets for tomorrow's run.

Conversation floating back from the table said, "It's one thing in sims. Live fire's going to be something else."

"You just hit 'em," Ben said, and took a card. "Dots is dots."

"No way," Wilson said. "Ask Wilhelmsen."

"They don't have to," Mitch said, and a chill ran through Dekker's bones. He was thinking what to say to shut that up when Meg said, acidly, "Dunno a thing about Pete Fowler, mister. Nice guy, I s'pose, and I highly 'preciate his help, but he's not the one does the thinking."

"Still not live fire, Kady."

"Ease off," Dekker said, and shoved his chair back.

"Hey," Mitch said. "No offense."

"Doesn't bother me," Meg said, and dealt out cards. "Testosterone's not the only asset going. Shepherds seriously got to rethink that."

"Meg," Sal said.

"Hey. I'm easy."

"You been easy, Kady."

Meg pursed her lips. "You a virgin, Mitch? I swear I don't know."

"Hold it, hold it," Ben said.

"The program's making a serious mistake," Mitch said, "putting you girls in here. Tape can't give you the wiring, Kady, there's a *reason* they never pulled women in on this program—"

"Yeah," Meg said acidly. "Look at the scores, Mitch."

"Meg," Dekker said.

"Tape off a real *pi-lut*, Kady."

That tore it. "Mitch," Dekker said.

"No, no," Meg said coolly, "not a problem, Dek. Man's just upset."

"Bitch."

"Yo," Sal said. "You want to match score and score, Mitchell?"

"Just hold it," Dekker said into the rising mutter from Mitch's crew and Almarshad's. "We don't need this."

"We don't need any damn *tape*," Mitch said, "and we *damn* sure don't need any tape off any women. *Reactions* aren't there. You're never going to see a female pilot on this ship, Kady, you don't see 'em in the carriers, you don't see 'em in the riders, and you're never going to. You'll crack under fire, you're going to screw this whole damned program, on a rep you didn't earn."

Meg said, with a riffle of cards, "Cher, you got a truly basic misconception, there. Ship's aren't shes, they're hes— you got to make love to them the right way, got to keep 'em collected so you *both* get there . . ."

Laugh from some of the guys, thank God. Wasn't funny at the table. Mitch was pissed. Mitch was being a son of a bloody bitch, was what he was being, hurt feelings, and a mouth that made you want to knock him sideways.

But Mitch gathered up the cards Meg dealt. "You're in over your head, Kady."

"Cher, I had a shuttle go dead once, lost a motor on lift, landed in the Seychelles, and *that* was a bitch. I haven't sweated since."

"Bullshit."

"Yeah. Tell me yours."

Mitch glowered a moment, then laid down a card and said, "Well-divers are fools."

"You got that," Meg said. "I resigned it."

"Didn't resign it," Sal said. "They threw you out."

"Huh. I was getting tired of it. Too much same stuff. You seen Luna once, you've seen it. Big damn rock."

"Smug bitch," Mitch said, in better humor. Dekker eased back and found himself shaking, he was so wound up. But Meg wasn't. Cold as ice, or she hadn't any nerves between her hands and her head. Couldn't tell she might want to knife Mitch Mitchell—

But he'd lay odds Mitch knew.

"Damn, damn. You got a rhythm in this thing."

See those programs, see how that infodump selected for the human operator, and how it prioritied—*that*, that was a serious question. They'd had a problem like that in TI, putting a human into the supercomputer neural-net, without letting it take over infoselection. This one sampled the human needs as well as the environment and it wasn't doing all it could. The data behind it was flatline. He pushed it, and it gave him the same input.

"You're not supposed to critique it, Pollard. Just stick to the manuals."

"Screw the—begging your pardon. But I *worked* on something like this. Staatentek program or independent?"

"Classified."

He bit his lip. Didn't raise the question of his clearance.

"Just a minute, Pollard."

Just a minute was all right. He sat and stared at the screen that offered such interesting prospects: infodrop for the human decision and infocompression for the computer. Reality sampling against a chaos screen in a system Morrie Bird's prize numbers man found achingly familiar, after a stint in TI's securitied halls. . . .

Screw supply systems modeling, this thing talked to him with a familiar voice.

This isn't sim software, he thought. Main program's elegant. *This* is real, isn't it? Ignore the cheesy recorded randoms, son of a bitch—the system under this is a piece of work—

He said, to the air, "Staatentek didn't do this, did they?"

No answer for a minute. Then a different voice: "Pollard. Leave the programs alone."

"You can *feel* the randoms. I didn't have to look for them."

A pause. "That's very good, Pollard. What would you suggest we do about it?"

Obvious answer. To the obvious question. The Belt. The numbers. The charts. The *feeling* you got for the system— the way the rocks moved. Real rocks, with the Well perturbing what the Sun ruled. . . .

. . . Shakespeare; and Bird . . .

Ben, leave the damn charts—

"Pollard? What would you do?"

"I'm sure you have," he said. "Use Sol."

"Or Pell. Or Viking. You haven't met Tripoint, Pollard. Would you like to see Tripoint? That one's an excellent example. . . ."

Balls hit and rebounded on the table. Ben walked around the other end, considering his next shot, gave a twitch of his shoulders, estimated an angle, and took careful aim with the cue.

"Mmmn," Sal said. Ben was sure it was Sal's voice behind him. Muscles were absolutely limp this evening. He was a little off his game—give or take a year's hiatus. Dekker, the skuz, had had practice. Keep the run going. He didn't want the cue in Dekker's hands, not from what he'd seen.

Two in succession. It was rec hall, bar in the middle—a lot of UDC guys on Permission down there, drowning their sorrows. Fleet at this end, some of them too. And a scatter of marine guards—more khaki around the corridors than Ben personally found comfortable, thank you.

Real wringer of a sim this afternoon, he'd earned a beer, dammit, but they had him up again tomorrow, same with all of them.

Opened his big mouth and they'd reset the sim, all right.

Dots and more dots, in a space where the effin' familiar *sun* didn't exist . . .

Spooky situation. Wanted to feel it out and you were busy tracking damn dots.

Gentle shot. Balls rebounded. "Come on, come on—"

"Ouch," Sal said.

Shit.

Dekker drew a breath. Armscomper *wasn't* the opponent you'd choose in this game. Pilot versus armscomper got bets down, never mind he'd had practice. Ben swore you didn't have time to take at TI.

Hell if. Ben had learned it somewhere, helldeck, maybe. And a Belter didn't show you any mercy. You damn sure didn't want to let him get the cuc back.

He saw his shot. Lined it up. Bets were down. Favor points. Military didn't let you play with money. And nobody had any.

Click and drop. Sighs from half the spectators. Muted cheers from the rest.

Second shot. Ball dropped, balls rearranged the pattern. He was sore when he bent to survey the situation, but it was a good kind of soreness, kind you got from a hard run. Never had realized there was good pain and bad. He'd felt the other kind. Too damn much.

Click.

"Right on, Dek!"

Meg and Sal had bets on opposite sides.

He grinned, took aim.

Click. Perfect bank.

Sudden disturbance, then, in the ambient. Dekker felt it, looked up as everybody else was looking, at a handful of

UDC guys who'd showed up at the table. Marines were in motion, starting to move between.

Rob Childers. Kesslan and Deke. Chad's crew. A marine said, "Let's not have any trouble. Get on back there."

Rob said, "Dek."

He felt a sudden queasiness in the approach. A sense of confrontation. The marines weren't pushing. They weren't letting the UDC crew closer, either, and there was starting to be noise, other UDC guys moving in.

"Wait a minute," Almarshad protested, thank God somebody on their side had the sense to say something, offer a hand to object to force; and he had to move, himself, had to do something in the split second.

He dropped the cue to his left hand, took a nonbelligerent stance.

"Dek," Rob said and held out his hand.

Put him entirely on the spot. Marines didn't move, didn't know who was who or what was happening here, he scoped that—scoped the moment and the move and the necessity to do something before they all ended up in the brig.

"Rob," he said, and went quietly past a confused marine and took the offered hand, looked Rob in the face and wondered if Rob *was* the one who'd tried to kill him, or if Rob knew who had. He took Kesslan's hand, and Deke's. The music system was grinding out a muted, bass-heavy beat, that had the silence all to itself.

"Too much gone on," Rob said. "Both sides."

He had to say something. He took that inspiration, said, "Yeah. Has," and couldn't find anything else to say.

"Let you get back to your game," Rob said.

"Yeah. All right." He stood there while the room sorted itself out again, Rob and the rest of them going back to their side. He never managed to say the right thing. He didn't know what he could have said. He felt a hand on his arm—Meg, pulling him back to the table, while Franklin muttered, "Shit all."

"They do it?" Mason asked him under his breath.

He gave it a desperate thought, trying to believe they were innocent. But he remembered getting hit, remembered the pod access, and couldn't be analytical about the dark, and the pain of broken bones, and the toneless voice that said, in the back of his memory, Enjoy the ride, Dekker.

Tape going into the slot. The voice said, Let me—

Let me, what?

Wasn't anybody but the pilot handled the mission tape. Didn't make sense.

He didn't answer Mason. He got down and lined up his shot again, determined. Made it. There was a sigh of relief. He was relieved too. Was all he asked, for his pride's sake. Didn't want to show how rattled he was. He focused down and made a run of three, before a ball trembled on the verge of a drop. And didn't.

"All *right*," Ben said, out of a sigh and a stillness. Ben sounded less than satisfied. Everything seemed paler, colder, he didn't know why. He stood by Meg and Sal, arms folded, and watched Ben make a straight run.

UDC MPs looked in on the situation. You could hear the music over the voices. When things were normal, you couldn't.

He wanted a drink, but regs didn't let him have one. He thought of desperate means to get one, but if they caught you at it, you were screwed. He didn't want a session with Porey. Didn't.

Bets got finalized. He'd bet himself, as happened, so had Ben; and Sal could collect. But something passed between Meg and Sal, and Meg took his arm and said Sal was taking a wait-ticket—

"You better get to bed," Meg said, and he'd have paid off, he wouldn't have minded, he was halfway numb at the moment—her change in arrangements made him think maybe he was better with Sal, who wouldn't pry—Sal and he never had gotten into each other's reasons for anything.

But Meg had set up what she evidently thought was a rescue, and he gave himself up and went off with her.

She was upbeat, cheerful, talking about the game, not a single question who that had been or why—must have gotten her information on her own, because Meg didn't favor ignorance, depend on it: she got him to bed, was willing to go slow if he'd had the inclination: he didn't; and wrapped herself around him after and snuggled down to keep him warm, about the time Ben and Sal came trooping through.

"Shhh," Meg hissed, and they were immediately quiet, quiet coming and going to the bathroom—the front room had its drawbacks; but he was on the edge of falling asleep, suddenly exhausted.

Glad he'd made some sort of peace, he decided. Even if their move had put him on the spot and forced what he wasn't ready for.

Likely they weren't the ones who'd ambushed him. He hadn't been sure of that when he'd taken Rob's hand; and even if he was somewhat sure now, he couldn't come to peace with it, couldn't forgive them, could he, if there was nothing to forgive in the first place, if they were innocent and it was somebody else he saw every day in the corridors, ate with in the mess hall. Maybe whoever had put him in hospital had been in the crowd getting a further kick out of his confusion.

He'd lost an argument or two when he was a kid—he'd lived through the chaff he had to take, he'd faced the guys again—they'd been two years older: he'd lived in fear and gotten hell beaten out of him a couple of times by the same guys before he'd made them believe they were going to take so much damage doing it they didn't want to keep on his case—not the ideal outcome he'd have wanted, but at least he could believe he'd settled it, at least he'd made a point on them and at least they didn't give him any more trouble.

But out there in front of everybody, they'd put him directly on the spot, damn them—yeah, he could have acted the touchy son of a bitch Ben said he was, told them go to hell and had the program in a mess and the lieutenant ready to kill him. He'd had an attack of responsibility, he decided finally. Mature judgment or something. His mother had sworn he'd never live that long.

But it didn't solve his own problem. Just theirs. He was still walking around not knowing, still a target for another try, God only when, or on what provocation. In the meanwhile he knew those he'd trust with his life, and those he just didn't know. In the meantime somebody was off scot free and probably laughing about it.

"You all right, cher?" Meg stirred beside him, massaged a shoulder. He realized the tension he had, then, probably as comfortable as a rock to be next to.

"Yeah." He tried to relax. "Cold."

Meg put a warm arm over his back. "Roll over, jeunc fils. No questions. Do. We got sims in the morning. Big day. Relax."

Couldn't understand why she put up with him. Couldn't understand why Ben did, except Sal was with Meg. He wished he could do better than he did, wished he could say they weren't in a mess of his making. But it was. And they were. And Meg somehow didn't care he was a fool.

The rec hall was quiet. It was a Question whether to acknowledge what had happened or ignore it; but the former, Graff decided—word having drifted his way via Fleet Security via Sgt.-major Lynch. Probably word had drifted to Porey too and no orders had come. But it was Personnel's business to take a tour, while the alterday galley staff was cleaning up. Music was still going. Most of the participants were back in barracks, hopefully.

"Quiet here?" he asked a marine on watch.

"Quiet, sir."

"Any feeling of trouble?"

"No, sir. Not lately. Real quiet, sir."

He made no approach toward the last few celebrants—a few UDC, a few Fleet personnel, a little the worse for drink, at opposite ends of the hall. He wasn't there on a disciplinary. But he meant to be seen. His being there said command levels had heard, command levels were aware.

Dekker hadn't blown it, by all he'd heard. He didn't know where the idea had started. He didn't know that it had done any good, but at least it had done no demonstrable harm.

Someone walked in at his back, walked up beside him.

"Tables still standing," Villy said.

"Noted that."

"Hope it lasts," Villy said. "Difficult time."

Villy had never said anything about the change in command. Like having your ship taken out of your hands, Graff thought, like watching it happen on, Villy had said, the last big project he'd ever work on.

What did you say? What, in the gulf between his reality and Villy's, did one find to say?

"Good they did that," he said. "I hope it takes."

B IG empty section of the mast—you'd know where
you were blindfolded, null g with the crashes of
locks and loaders and the hum of the core machinery, noises that made the blood rush with memories
of flights past and anticipation of another, no helping it.
Meg took a breath of cold, oil-touched air, a breath that had
the flightsuit pressing close, snug as a hardened skin, and
hauled with one hand to get a rightside up view of what Dek
had to show them, screen with a live camera image from,
she guessed, optics far out along the mast.

Big, shadow-shape of the carrier—wouldn't all fit in the
picture—with spots on its hull picked it out in patchwork
detail, all gray, and huge—

And on the hull near the bow, a flat, sleek shape clung,
shining in the floods.

"That's it?" Ben asked.

"That's it," Dek said. "Her. Whatever you want to call
it. They built three prototypes. That's the third. That's the
one that's make or break for us. Crew of thirty, when we

prove it out. Four can manage her—in a clean course, with set targets. Most of her mass is ordnance, ablation edge, and engine load. You've had the briefings.''

Meg stood by Sal's side and got a shiver down the back that had nothing to do with the cold here. Beautiful machine, she was thinking; Sal said, Brut job, and meant the same thing, in a moment, it sounded as-if, of pure gut-deep lust. Wasn't any miner-can, that wicked, shimmery shape.

And most imminently, in the sim chamber behind the clear observation port, the pods, one in operation, a mag-lev rush around the chamber walls, deafening as the wall beside them carried the vibration.

"Damn," she breathed. But you wouldn't hear it.

"The pods you see moving," Dek said, over the fading thunder, "that's the tame part. That rush is the dock and undock. They can take those pods more positive or neg g's than your gut's going to like. But that's not the dangerous part. That pod, there, the still one—" He pointed at one floating motionless, away from the walls. "That's the real hellride. Could be at ¾ light, what you know from inside. That's the one they mop the seats on. That's the one can put you in hospital—unstable as hell in that mode—screw it and you'll pull a real sudden change."

"Thanks," Ben said. "I like to hear that, damn, I like to hear that."

Meg said, "Going to be all right. No problems. Hear?"

But Dek looked up at that pod in a way she kept seeing after he'd turned away and told them it was up the lines to the pod access—like an addict looking at his addiction, and a guy scared as hell.

"Take you on the ride of your life," was the way he put it.

"Now wait a minute," Ben said. But Dek took out on the handlines and Sal snagged Ben's arm with: "Now, cher, if we don't keep with Dek and Meg here, they'll assign us some sheer fool pi-lut we don't know the hell who . . . Do you want to go boom on a rock? No. Not. So soyez gentle and don't distract the jeune fils."

"No," Graff said, "no, colonel, I *don't* know—I've got a meeting with him . . ."

"He's got no right," was the burden of Tanzer's phone call. Which didn't over all help Graff's headache. Neither did the prospect of dealing with *Comdr.* Porey face to face.

"I'll pose him the question," he told Tanzer. Couldn't honestly blame the colonel this morning—discovering that his carefully constructed sims schedule was in revision, that Villanueva's team had been opted straight off test systems into the priority sims schedule and three others of the test systems crews had been bumped off the sims schedule entirely, in favor of Dekker and three raw recruits, who'd been given access-on-demand, on any shift.

The officer in charge of Personnel ought to know what was happening. One would logically think so.

The officer in charge of Personnel hung up the receiver, put on his coat and took his hangover headache down the corridor to the CO's office.

Marine guards let him in. Porey was all smiling, smooth congeniality.

"Jurgen," it was. And an offered hand as Porey got up from his desk. One had to take it or declare war. "I've been going through the reports. Excellent job you've done, getting us settled into station. I don't find a thing I'd change. Sit down, sit down . . ."

"Thank you," Graff said, and sat, wondering whose name those actions had gone out under in the report to FleetCommand—wonder, hell, he *knew* what games Porey was playing, with the reports, with his smiling good grace: Porey's aides never knew what they'd meet when they walked into his office, the smiling bastard or the shouting, desk-pounding sumbitch, but either one would knife you. It was, knowing your career could hinge on Porey's approval, damned easy for a staffer to start twitching to Porey's cues.

He could see it working in *Carina* junior crew out there, in the marine guard—he could see it going on all around him, suggesting that it might be wise for him to play Porey's game too; suggesting that this man, clearly on his way to a captaincy, and certainly in Mazian's good graces, could be a valuable contact . . .

Except that he'd seen this game going on since they were both junior lieutenants, and he felt the urge to puke.

He said, with a fixed smile, "Edmund, do you think your staff could possibly give Personnel any sims schedule changes a day in advance? Tanzer is *not* happy. I could have minimized the disturbance."

"Didn't that come to you?" Porey was all amazement.

"No, it didn't come to me. I had to hear it from Tanzer. I *don't* like dealing with the UDC when I don't know what's going on. It makes me feel like a fool. And I don't *like* that, Edmund, I truly don't."

Satire on Porey's own style wasn't what Porey was used to meeting. Porey had a thinking frown as he sat down, guarded amusement at the edges of his mouth: everything for effect, most especially the expressions on his face. Peel Porey layer by layer and you never got to center.

"Matters of policy," Porey said, rotating a paperweight in his fingers, "are handled in this office. Tanzer has no power that you don't give him. If you choose to coddle him, that's your decision. Not mine." The paperweight stopped moving. "The assignment of personnel and priorities, however, is mine. Relations with the UDC—use your talents at diplomacy. I'm sure you're up to it."

Distraction and a shot across the bow. "By the Procedures, Personnel involves health and welfare, neither of which works when my office has no say in reassignments or systems changes." Attack on his own. "In consideration of which, I want a briefing on the tape-learning procedures from the techs that came in with you. I don't have time to read science reports."

"Jurgen, my staff hasn't time to handle delicate egos, Tanzer's or yours."

"Or three hundred fifty-six Shepherds who've been rooked out of their seniority, lied to by the UDC, shafted by the legislature and killed out there on the course because nobody's ever damn listened to them. Edmund, we have tempers at critical overload here, and a blow-up isn't going to look any better on your record than it looks on Tanzer's. If you want a riot, these are the ones that will do it. They're not kids, they've had too many fools in command over them here and in the Belt to trust anybody now on credit. They don't reject authority: they're looking for it, they *want* it—but don't expect them to follow orders til they know the ultimate source is sane."

Porey didn't say anything for a moment. He wasn't stupid and he cared about his own survival. That was one thing you could believe in.

Porey said softly, "You're an honest man, Jurgen. How do you plan to get out of Earth system alive?"

"By keeping my CO from making mistakes."

Long, cold stare. A slow smile. "You don't have any resentment, do you, for my being installed here?"

"I'm not command track. I never pretended to be."

Still the stare. "You think I'm pretending?"

"I don't think you're pretending anything. I *know* you."

Feed the fantasy—and the anxiety. Porey didn't like to be known, but he liked to be respected. The man did have an ego. A parsec wide. Porey smiled slowly, in a way that almost touched the eyes. "Good. A vote of confidence from you, I appreciate, Jurgen. I truly do."

Odd chill of unease as the pod cruised up to the access. Thump of the pressure seals. Hydraulics as it opened and offered its dark, screen-lit interior. Ordinary sounds. Shadows moved on the white plastic of the control console as Dekker put the tape in and he felt an irrational urge to look behind him, as if his crew wouldn't be there.

No damned reason to get nerves. But it had been Pete on the line beside him, all the times before. It wasn't now. It wasn't Elly, it wasn't Falcone. It was Meg, on Pete's tape, and Ben and Sal—they belonged here. He made himself believe that, stop remembering what had been . . .

For no reason, a piece of the puzzle snapped in, unbidden. Null-g. Shadows on the console. He felt the blow at the base of his skull. He knew where he had been—at the entry. Knew where they'd been. Shadows. Two of them . . .

Dammit. Not the time to be woolgathering. He looked back at Ben—Ben looked scared, but Ben looked On, tracking wide and fast on the pod, taking in everything, the same as Meg and Sal. All business—the way they were when the jokes stopped and they were thinking and absorbing. He gave them the lecture tour, the buttons on the console, the read-out window, the authorizations procedure— "Card and tape in the slot for a check-out. It reads your ID, takes your personal numbers and sets, and double-checks the tape for authorizations. Ready?"

"Are you serious?" Ben said. Then: "Yeah. Yeah. Go."

He caught the handholds on either side of the entry, angled his feet for inside and eeled into his station. "Sal," he called back, over the hum of a passing pod, caught her by the arm as she sailed into the dark, shadow against the lights, a glitter of braids tied into a cluster, for safety's sake. He aimed her for the far side of the four-wide cockpit. "Ben." Same as Ben came feet-first through the hatch, for the seat between him and Sal. Meg came last, for the seat between him and the hatch, settled in. Green-lit gold on plain stud earrings. Green dyed her side-shaved profile, green turned her red curls black. Ringed fingers found the belts and buckled in, eyes glowed wide and busy in the light of the screens, assessing the instruments.

He drew his own belt over—he waked reaching for them at night, with a recurring nightmare of drifting free. Suit braces powered up as he plugged in, and the helmet cut off side vision. It was deep-field V-HUD now. Switches on, power up. "Comfortable?"

"Yeah," from Meg. "As possible," from Ben.

Belts were tight. Second tug, to be sure. Orientation run. Starting over, primer stuff—only he wasn't the neo this run. There was something surreal in the moment, in the familiar lights, in the ordinary sounds of the pod, the dark masquerading as routine. They were On. Anxious. Wanting to be right. But he kept expecting other voices.

"This thing got any differences?" Meg asked, last-minute.

He shoved the tape into the console, pushed LOAD. "One. See that yellow ABORT, upper left? Doesn't exist on the real boards. It'll stop the pod—if you don't get a response from me, or if you detect anyone in trouble, you hit that. Takes you right back to the bay."

"Cher," came Meg's low voice, "you just do. I got confidence in us."

"More 'n I got," Ben muttered. "Hold it, hold it. I'm not set yet."

"Response check, thing doesn't glitch, but be sure. Boards are all in test mode."

Passengers was all they were required to be; but that wasn't Meg's style, wasn't Ben's or Sal's either. He tried his own boards, set his arms in the supports, heard Meg's voice saying, "I got it, right on." Ben muttering, "Don't screw it, Dek-boy. Yeah, I'm on, on, go."

Sal's, saying, "Hit it, Dek."

Dark, flash of lights—

He kicked the thumb switch on his keys. Readout glowed green against the dark. Finger moves on opposite hands, the undock sequence switch.

Bang! of grapples. Mag-levs and human voices mixed—a 6 *g* shove butt-first for ten eternal seconds to a sustained straight-at-the-spine shove at +9 *g*.

Green lines wove fast and faster . . . the pod was alive and the tons of thrust were mag-lev sim, but it was all in his hands, responsive to a breath, a stray thought, a moment's doubt—where he was, when he was, who he was with—

He didn't want to do this.

Serious panic, a flash on instruments in chaos—

Then. Not now. Now was now. Not a time to lose track, God, no—

Focus down. Focus wide. Attention to the moving lines, that's all—

"Politics," Porey said, "pure politics. Let me explain it to you. Fifteen of the fifty carriers have to be UDC—that's the deal we cut, and that's what we have to do. The accident *gave* us Hellburner, and that tape's going to *give* us the program. The parliaments on Earth want *responsible* individuals in policy positions—read: no captains will violate policy laid down by the JLC. And this won't change in the field."

Graff stared at Porey. He thought he'd heard the depth of foolishness out of Earth.

Porey made a small, sarcastic shrug. "They have our assurances. And if the news services should call your office, Jurgen, and since you're over Personnel, they might, the answer you give is: No, of *course* these ships are launched at carrier command discretion, with specific targets. No, they will never be deep-launched, with less specific orders. That tactic won't work."

"You mean I lie."

"I mean the Joint Legislative Committee's expert analysts say not. The changing situation over time—read: the commanders of individual ships making decisions without communicating with each other—would make chaos of strategic operations. So it can't be done. End report. The JLC analysts say it's not appropriate use of the riders. The legislators don't *like* what these ships can do, combined with the—irregular character—of the crews we've picked to handle them. These crews are, historically, trouble Earth got rid of. Earth's strategic planners are obsessed by the difficulty they've discovered of conveying their orders to ships in the Beyond—they've apparently just realized the time lag. They can't phone Pell from here and order policy about—"

"They've always known that."

"The ordinary citizen hasn't. The average businessman *can* get a voice link to Mars now. Or the Belt—if he wants one."

Lag-com was a skill, a schitzy kind of proceeding, talking to a voice that went on down its own train of logic with no regard to your event-lagged self. That was one of the reasons senior Com and psych were virtually synonymous. And Earth hadn't realized until now you couldn't talk to a launched rider—or a star carrier? He refused to believe it.

"Lag-com has finally penetrated the civil user market," Porey said, "since *we* increased the pace of insystem traffic. Earthers are used to being told the antenna's gone LOS, used to being told Marslink is out of reach for the next few months, used to shipments enroute for years and months— supply the market counts but can't touch. Their ship-borne infowave was so slow as to be paralytic, before we started military operations insystem. The last two years have upset that notion—this, from the captain. So if anyone asks you—of *course* we're going to have a strong mother-system component in FleetCommand. Of course riderships will never make command decisions. We're going to loop couriers back to Earth constantly."

"Mazian's *promised* this?"

"The same as they promised us. —Jurgen, you have far too literal a mind. This is a game. They play it with their constituents. The legislature's technical advisers are under influences—corporate, economic, political . . . but you've met that. They certainly won't deviate from party line. Where does the funding for their studies come from, anyway?"

Lights flared, green numbers bled past in the dark. Do the run in his sleep, Dekker kept telling himself, piece of easy.

But it didn't stop the heart from pounding, didn't stop hands and body from reacting to the situation on-screen—you didn't brake the reactions, you didn't ever, just presented the targets to your inert armscomp, accepted Ben was going to miss most of the time and tried not to let that expectation ever click into the relays in your brain.

"Screw that," he heard Ben mutter, and all of a sudden got input on his aux screens, targets lit, armscomp prioritizing.

Chaff, he determined. Then targets flashed and started disappearing. Longscan was coming from a living hand, not the robot inputs. He heard "Shit!" from Ben and saw the scan image shift, tracking fire. Meg's gold data-sift to his highside HUD was making sudden marginal sense. Not like Pete. . . . Not the same. . . . "Doing all right, doing all right," he muttered, "just—" Heart jumped. Hands reacted. Sim did—

He stopped the bobble before his vision cleared. Guys weren't talking, someone had yelped, short and sharp, but the dots that meant conscious were still lit, data was still coming up on the screens, fire was still happening, longscan shaping up. Had three scared guys in the seats. Next four shots were misses. His fault. He'd pulled a panic, lost it—had no time now to be thinking about it—targets—
dammittohell!—

"The UDC," Porey said, rocking back his chair, "believes in a good many myths. We don't disabuse them. And, yes, this room is secure."

"What else haven't we said? What *else* hasn't filtered out here? Or is this a longstanding piece of information?"

"The ECS4," Porey said, "is fully outfitted. *Fully* outfitted. We're operational, and we have a com system they can't penetrate. To our knowledge—they haven't even detected its operation. Installation on the ECS8—is waiting a shipment. Communications between you and FSO have been, I understand, infrequent. That situation is going to improve."

"When?"

"Estimate—two months, three."

"Until then? Edmund, —I want to know. Who pulled Kady and Aboujib out of the Belt? Who opted Pollard in? Where did this damned new system come in?"

"Exact origin of those orders?" Porey asked with a shrug. "I'm sure at some high level." Meaning Keu or Mazian, which said no more than he knew. "But the reason for pulling them in—plainly, they were Dekker's crew, we know things now about Hellburner we didn't know. We've adjusted the training tape to reflect that, we've chosen a crew with a top pilot to start with a—tragically—clean slate. It's the best combination we can come up with."

"Not to rush into schedule. Dekker's just out of hospital. Look at his psychological record, for God's sake. You're putting an outrageous load on this crew."

"I leave that to the medics. They cleared him. He's in."

"Cleared him with how much pressure from command?"

"What are you suggesting?"

"That there's too damned much rush on this. That Dekker's not ready to go into schedule."

Porey leaned back in the chair, frowning. "You expressed a curiosity about the tape system. Have you ever *had* deep-tape, Jurgen?"

"No." Emphatically. It occurred to him at the moment that Porey could order that even in his case. And he didn't like the thought.

"Ordinary DNI tape isn't so different from deepteach. Less detailed, in general. But the real difference is the class of drugs. Deepteach trank suppresses certain types of brain activity. Eliminates the tendency to cross-reference with past experience. General knowledge is still an asset. Specific training isn't. Hostility to the process certainly isn't. The other trainees have both handicaps. They've been trained otherwise and they won't trust a tape telling them different-ly. But this crew knows nothing else. They have general knowledge. They're not afraid of it. So their judgment can override the tape.''

"Theoretically."

Another shrug. "So the technicians assure us: that with no trained response to overcome—they can do it and not panic. We cut a new tape from what succeeds—and bootstrap the others."

"You bring this *tape* business in," Graff said, "you slip it on a novice crew without an explanation—then you want to shove off Belt miner reactions on Shepherd crews that've risked their necks for a year training for these boards? What do I say to these people? What's the official word? Because the rumor's out, Edmund, they didn't take that long to put two and two together."

Porey looked at him long and coldly from the other side of what had been his desk. "Tanzer's complaining. You're complaining. Everybody's bitching. Nobody in this facility wants to take this program to implementation. I have other orders, Jurgen. If crews die—they'll die in the sims. We do not lose another ship on display. We haven't, as happens, another ship we can lose."

"We haven't another core crew we can lose, either. Where are you going to get recruits if you kill our best with this damned tape? Draft them out of Earth's pool? Persuade the Luna-Sol cargo runners to try what killed the Shepherds?"

"Maybe you don't have enough confidence in your recruits."

"I have every confidence in them. I also know they've never been cut free to do what they know—not once. They're a separate culture from Earth, separate from Mars, separate even from the Belt. The UDC regulated them and played power games with their assignments and their schedules. The JLC changed the specs and cut back the design. These crews *thought* when the Fleet came in here that somebody was finally on their side. So what do I tell them when they ask about this tape? That we took it off the last spectacular fatalities? That's going to give them a hell of a lot of confidence."

"Dekker should trust it. The tape did come from his crew. And he certainly knows the crew we've given him."

"The crew we've given him never worked ops together. They were *financial* partners. Everyone seems to have forgotten that!"

"Dekker's confident."

"Confident, hell! Dekker's numb. He's taken the chaff that's come down from the UDC, his crew's dead, somebody tried to kill him, he's got a personal problem with a MarsCorp board member, which is why the UDC pulled him from that demo in the first place, on somebody's orders I still haven't heard accounted for. You put him into the next mission and what guarantees you won't get the same communiqué Tanzer got: Pull Dekker, keep him out of the media, take him out of the crew that's trained for that run—and then what will you do? Fold like Tanzer did? Or tell the EC go to hell?"

Cold stare. Finally Porey said, "I'm aware of Dekker's problem."

"Is that all? You're *aware?* —Do you realize his mother and the peace party lawyers are all over the news right now? The case is active again. Do you think that's coincidence? Salazar doesn't care what she brings down."

"I'm aware of Alyce Salazar."

"So are you going to pull Dekker? Or are you using him as test fodder? Doesn't matter if he cracks up in the sims, it solves a problem—is *that* it?"

"You have a personal attachment to this boy—is that your problem?"

No re-position. Straight through. Straight through. He got a breath and tried to tell himself it was all right, it was only a sim. A last target.

Miss. Sal said, "Damn," and: "Sorry, Ben."

"Yeah, yeah," Ben said.

"Dekker." Sim chief's voice. You didn't hear them break

in like that, they didn't remind you they existed unless you were totally, utterly screwed. *"Dekker. What's the trouble?"*

Pod was in neutral now. They wouldn't abort you cold—a shift like that messed with your head. But nothing further was going to happen in the sim. Virtual space was running, green lines floating in front of his eyes, but without threat. His heart was going like a hammer. Breaths came in gasps.

"Muscle spasm."

He lied to the sim chief. Chief was going to order them in, no question. New crew—he could well glitch *their* reactions— He'd never, never gotten called down over com. Never gotten a stand-down like this.

"Going to order a return. Your crew all right?"

"Crew's fine." He didn't get any contradiction over com.

"You want to push the button?"

Abort was quicker. Abort would auto them to dock. His nerves wanted that.

"I'll go manual. No abort." Hell if he was going to come in like a panicked neo. He got his breathing calmed. He lined them up, minute by excruciating minute. He brought it as far as basics. "Meg," he said then, "take it in. Dock it, straight push now. Can you do that?"

"Got it," Meg said. "Take a breath, Dek."

Three more minutes in. Dock was basic—now. Lesson one. Punch the button. Mind the closing *v*. They'd killed one man and a prototype module getting that to work realtime, before Staatentek admitted they had a problem.

Whole damned program was built on funerals . . .

"Doing all right, Meg."

He unclenched stiff fingers. Watched the numbers run, steady, easy decline in distance: lock talked to lock and the pod did its own adjustments.

Bang into the grapples. System rest.

A damned pod, not the ship, but he was having trouble breathing as the hatch opened, to Meg's shutdown—

"Shit!"

His heart jumped. "Easy, easy," he told her, as she made

a frantic reach at the board. "Lock's autoed, not your fault, not your fault, it's automatic on this level."

"Not used to these damn luxuries." Breath hissed between her teeth. "Got it, thanks."

No word out of Ben. Ben wasn't happy. Sal wasn't. He could feel it out of that corner. He thought about saying Don't mind it, but that wasn't the case, you damned well had to mind a screw-up like this, and they did. He thought about telling them some of those were his fault, but that wasn't what they needed to set into their reactions either. He just kept his mouth shut, got the tape, grabbed the handholds and followed Meg out the hatch.

Caught Meg's attention, quick concerned look. He shied away from it, hooked onto the handline and heard Ben and Sal exit behind him. He logged the tape out on the console, teeth clenched against the bitter cold.

"Cher," Meg said, gently, hovering at his shoulder, trying for a look at him or from him, he wasn't sure and he wasn't coping with that right now.

"We'll get it," Sal said. "Sorry, Dek."

They were trying to apologize to *him*. Hell.

He started to shiver. Maybe they could see it. Maybe they were realizing how incredibly badly he'd screwed that move—or would figure it once their nerves settled. He didn't know how much to tell them, didn't want to act like an ass, but he couldn't put his thoughts together—he just grabbed onto the handline and headed off down the tube, not fast, but first, so he didn't have to see their faces.

He heard Ben say, "Damn temper of his. Break his neck, I'd like to."

"Hey," Meg said, then, "we screwed up, all right? We screwed it, we screwed him up, he's got a right."

He wanted to tell Meg no; and he wanted to believe that was the answer; but he couldn't. He handed off at the lift, waited for them.

Sal said, "Dek, we'll get it. Trez bitch, that machine. But we'll get it, no problem."

"Yeah." First word he'd been able to get out. He punched the lift for exit level, snatched back a shaking hand toward his pocket.

Meg was looking at him, they all were, and he didn't want to meet their eyes. He stared at the lift controls instead, watched the buttons light, listened to the quiet around him, just the lift thumping on the pressure seals.

"So?" Tanzer asked, on the phone; *"Does this mean a runaround or does it mean you've found an answer to my question?"*

"There is an answer, colonel. Negative. The orders come from outside this base. We can*not* change policy."

"Policy, is it? Policy? Is that what we call it now, when nobody at this base can answer questions? What do you know, lieutenant? Anything?"

Graff censored what he knew, and what he thought, and said quietly, "I repeat, I've relayed your objections. They've been rejected. That's the answer I have to convey, colonel, I'm sorry."

"Damn you," Tanzer said, and hung up.

He hung up. He sat for a long few moments with his hands folded in front of his lips and tried to think reasonably. No, he could not call the captain. FleetCom went through Porey now. No, he would not go running to his crew—and maybe that was pride and maybe it was distrust of his own reasoning at the moment. He was *not* command track. He was *not* in charge of policy. He was *not* in authority over this base, *not* in authority over strategy, and *not* in the decision loop that included the captain, who somehow, in some degree, had to know what was going on here—at least so far as Demas and Saito had said: they'd warned Keu, they'd pleaded with him, and Keu—had refused to rein Mazian back, had *let* Mazian make his promises and his assignments.

So what was there to say? The captain had refused to disapprove Porey's command. The captain had refused Demas, refused Saito . . . who was he, to move Keu to do anything? Perhaps the captain was more farsighted, or more objective, or better informed.

Or more indifferent.

Porey was aware of Dekker's problem? And Porey shoved Dekker and a novice crew toward mission prep?

Bloody damned *hell*!

"You blew it," Porey said.

"Yessir," Dekker said on a breath. "No excuses."

" 'No excuses.' I told you I wouldn't hear excuses, and I wouldn't hear 'sorry.' You're the pilot, you had the say, if you weren't ready you had no mortal *business* taking them in there."

"Yessir."

Porey's hand came down on the desk. He jumped.

"Nerves, Mr. Dekker. What are you going to do about it?"

"Get my head straight, sir."

Second blow of Porey's hand. *"You're a damned expensive failure, you know that?"*

You didn't argue with Porey. The lieutenant had warned him. But too damned many people had told him that.

"I'm not a failure, sir."

"Was that a success? Was taking trainees into that sim and screwing them up a *success*?"

"No, sir."

"Nothing's the matter with you physically. The meds found nothing wrong with you. It's in your *head*, Dekker. What did you claim after Wilhelmsen cracked up? That you *knew* better? Do you still know better?"

"Yessir."

"Can you do the run he did?"

"Yessir."

"You're no use to me screwed up, you are no damned use, mister. I've got other crews. I've got other pilots. And let me tell you, if you don't straighten yourself out damned fast, we've got one more way to salvage you. We've got one more tape we can use, *which* I haven't, because you said *you* were better, because the techs said untrained personnel were better on tape, but if you're no other good to anyone, Dekker, then we might just as well put you right down in that lab and input what *might* improve your performance. You know what I'm talking about?''

He guessed. He managed to say, ''Yessir.''

''I'll make a promise to you, Dekker. You've got one week. I'm not restricting you, you can do any damned thing you want, I don't give a damn for the regulations, for the schedule, for whatever you want to do. You've got carte blanche for one week. But if you don't pull those sim scores right back where you were before your 'accident,' then we put you into lab, input *Wilhelmsen's* tape into your head, and see if it improves your performance. You understand that?''

''Yessir.''

''Are you clear on that?''

''Yessir.''

''Then get the hell out of here and *do it,* Dekker, while the labs try to straighten out the damage you've done to your crew. I don't want to see your face right now. I don't know if I want to see it again.''

CHAPTER

14

S EQ. 285t-III. Dekker, Paul F. Authorized.

He waited, clinging to the line, felt like a fool inputting the card and checking the tape serial number on the display for the second time, but the cold feeling in the pit of his stomach refused to go away, and nothing seemed right, or sure enough.

Couldn't *remember* if he'd done it. Things he'd done weren't registering. He was thinking on things other than here and now and the number didn't damn matter. There wasn't a training tape he couldn't handle.

Come apart on an orientation run, for God's sake? Their input couldn't have overridden his displays if he hadn't let it, and they were apologizing to him for screwing up? If he was glitching on their input, he could have spared a hand to shut them out. He could have let go the damned yoke and recovered it at leisure. The number one sim was a walk down the dock if you didn't seize up like a fool—

Muscle spasm. Point zero five second bobble—not wide

enough to invoke the braces or trigger an abort on a sleeper run like that; and he'd spaced on it—in that five-hundredth second, he'd been in the Belt, he'd been back at Sol, he'd been with Pete and the guys and lost with Cory—God only where his head had been but he hadn't known his next move. He'd blanked on it, without reason, without warning.

Pod drifted up, opened for him. He grasped the handholds and slid into the dark inside—respiration rate coming up. Sweat starting. He could feel it on his face, feel it crawling under the flightsuit as he prepped the boards. Belts, confirm. Power up, confirm. Single occupant, tape 23b, Dekker, P, all confirm.

He adjusted the helmet. The dark and the glowing lights held a surreal familiarity. It was no time. It was every time.

Some drugs came back on you, wasn't that the case?

But the guys weren't with him now. If he screwed it he screwed it by himself. Wasn't going to let them do to him what they'd done to Meg and Ben and Sal, wasn't going to take that damned tape—

No.

"Dekker."

Sim chief again.

"Dekker, you want to stand down for an hour?"

Didn't like their telemetry. Picking up his heartbeat.

"No. I'm all right."

"Dekker."

Series of breaths. "Porey's orders. Free ticket. I'm all right, let it go."

Seemed like forever that light stayed red.

They had guys over in hospital that couldn't walk straight, that never would fly again . . .

Had guys in the mental ward . . .

Sim chief was probably checking with Porey's office.

Calm the breathing down.

Light went from red to green.

Punch it in.

GO!

* * *

"Dek," it was, "how'd the run go?" and "Dek, you all right?"

He winced, shrugged, said, Fine, working on it.

And stopped the lift on three-deck, made it as far as the nearest restroom and threw up non-stop.

From Meg, back in barracks, a shake at his shoulder: "Dek, cher. Wake up. Mess call. You coming? You'd better come."

He hauled himself out of half-sleep and off the bunk, wobbled into the bathroom to pop an antacid—the meds didn't restrict those, thank God—and to scrub normal color into his face. He walked out again to go with Meg, navigated ordinary space, trying not to see the glowing lines and dark, not to hear the mags or feel the destabilizing jolts of thrust.

Familiar walls, posters, game tables, drift of guys out to the hall. Ben and Sal gave them a: Come on, you're late, and he wondered suddenly where this hall was, or why he should stay in it, when there were so many other like places he could be —spaced, he told himself, sane people didn't ask themselves questions like that, sane people didn't see the dark in the light . . .

"Hey, Dek, you all right?"

Mason. "Yeah. Thanks."

Hand on his shoulder. Guys passed them in the hall.

"He all right?" Sal asked.

"Yeah," he said. Somehow he kept walking as far as the messhall, couldn't face the line. "I'm just after coffee, all right? I'm not hungry."

They objected, Meg said she was getting him a hamburger and fries, and the sumbitch meds and dieticians would log it to her, the way they did every sneeze in this place, maybe screw up her medical records. He waved the offer off, went over to the coffee machine and carded in.

Nothing made sense to him. Everything was fractured. He was making mistakes. He'd glitched the target calls right and left this morning.

It *had* been this morning. It had to have been this morning . . . but he'd run it so many times . . .

He walked back toward the tables, stood out of the traffic and muttered answers to people who talked to him, not registering it, not caring. People came and went. He remembered the coffee in his hand and drank it. Eventually Meg and Sal came out of the line, so did Ben, and gathered him up.

Meg had the extra hamburger. "You're eating," she said. "You want the meds coming after you?"

He didn't. He took it, unwrapped it, and Ben hit him in the ribs. "Pay attention, Dek-boy."

"Huh?"

"Huh," Ben echoed. "Salt. Pass the salt. God. You are a case today."

"Thinking," he said.

Ben gave him a look, a shrug in his direction. "He's thinking. I don't think I've ever seen that before."

"Ben," Meg said.

"Dekker. Pass the damn salt."

"Shit!" *Wasn't* approved com, the sojer-lads got upset, but *she* was upset, so what?

"It's all right, it's all right," the examiner said. "You're doing fine, Kady."

"Tell me fine, I screwed my dock . . ."

You couldn't flap the voice. "It gets harder, Kady. That's the object. Let's not get overconfident, shall we?"

"Overconfident, my—" She was shaking like a leaf.

Different voice. Deep as bone. "You shoved a screen in over your pilot's priority. Did your pilot authorize that?"

Hell, she wasn't in a mood for games. She thought she *knew* that voice. It *wasn't* the examiner.

"Kady?"

"Had to know," she muttered. Hell, she was right, she'd done the right thing.

"Not regulation, Kady."

Screw the regs, she'd say. But she did know the voice. There weren't two like it.

"Yessir," she said meekly, to no-face and no-voice. Dark, that was all. Just the few yellow lights on the V-HUD and the boards, system stand-down.

"You think you can make a call like that, Kady?"

Shit. "Yessir."

Silence then. A long silence. She waited to be told she was an ass and an incompetent. She flexed her hands, expecting God only—they sometimes started sim on you without warning.

Then the examiner's quiet voice said—she wasn't even sure now it was alive—

"Let's go on that again, Kady."

She couldn't stand it. "Was I right?"

"Your judgment was correct, Kady."

"Ms. Dekker, do you have proof of your allegations?"

"Talk to my lawyer."

"Is it true your son is in a top secret Fleet project?"

"I don't know where he is. He doesn't write and I don't give a damn."

"How do you feel about Ms. Salazar's allegations—"

More and more of it. A Paris newsservice ran a clip on Paul Dekker that went back into juvenile court records and the other services pounced on it with enigmatic references to 'an outstanding warrant for his arrest' and his 'work inside a top-secret Fleet installation.'

Graff punched the button to stop the tape, stared at the blank screen while Demas hovered. FSO had sent their answer: Regarding your 198-92, Negative. Meaning they'd turned up nothing they cared to say on the case—at least nothing they trusted to FleetCom—or him.

"Influence-trading," Demas said. "Scandals of the rich. Young lovers. Salazar and her money against the peacers. The public's fascinated."

The Fleet didn't need this. He didn't. Dekker certainly

didn't. A bomb threat involving Salazar's plane, the peacers denying responsibility, the European Police Agency finding a confidential report in the hands of the news services. Rode the news reports outside Sol Two almost as hot and heavy as the Amsterdam Tunnel collapse.

While Demas and Saito only said, Hold on, Helm. Hold on. *Don't* make a problem, the captain doesn't need a problem.

"I honestly," Demas said, "don't think Dekker needs to see this particular broadcast, regardless of any promises."

"She's never called him. Never returned the call."

"Lawyers may have advised against. I'd advise against. Personally, J-G."

"I knew you would."

"So you didn't ask."

"I don't know Earth. Now I wonder if I even know Dekker. He's never asked me, either—whether there was word."

Light and dark. The AI substituted its interlink for crew, he was *fine* till the randoms popped up, till he saw the wicket he had to make and the pod reacted—bobble and reposition, reposition, reposition—

Fuckin' *hell*!

Screwed it, screwed it—screwed that one—redlight—

You're hit. Keep going. Don't think about it.

Chest hurt, knees hurt, right arm was numb. Damn hour and five sim and he was falling apart—

Made five. Lost one.

Randoms again. Five minutes down. God, a chaff round. . . .

Blinked sweat. Tasted it. *Hate* the damn randoms, hate the bastards, hate the Company, dammit—

Overcorrection. Muscles were tired, starting to spasm, God, where was the end of this run?

Couldn't hold it. HUD was out, the place was black and blacker—

* * *

"Dek, Dek, wake up," from the other side of the door and Ben, with the territory behind his eyes all full of red and gold and green lines and red and yellow dots, hoped Meg would just put a pillow over the sumbitch's face. Beside him, Sal moved faintly.

"Dek!"

"Shit," Sal moaned, and elbowed him in a muzzy catch after balance.

"Dek? Come out of it."

"Son of a bitch," Ben muttered, felt a knee drop into the cold air outside the covers and set a foot on the floor, hauled himself to his feet and banged into the chair by the bed.

"Ben?" Sal murmured, but the blow to the hip did it. He shoved the door open into the dark next door and snarled, "Dekker!"

Dekker made a sound, Meg gave a sharp grunt above a crack of flesh and bone meeting. The son of a bitch had got her.

"Dekker!" He shoved past a smooth female body to get a shove of his own in, got a grip and held it. "Dekker, dammit, you want to take a cold walk?"

Same as he'd yelled at Dekker on the ship, when Dekker got crazy. He had one hand planted against a heaving, sweating chest, right about the throat, and Meg had cleared back, gotten to the light switch. He couldn't see anything but a blur, and he didn't let up the pressure—if Dekker moved to hit him Dekker was going to be counting stars, he had his mind made up to that. Dekker was gasping for breath—eyes open now.

"Spooks again," Meg panted.

"I'll say it's spooks, this is the damn spook! I dunno why you sleep with him."

The inside door opened and Sal came in at the periphery of his vision. He heard Meg saying, "It's all right, it's just surface," and kept his own hold on the lunatic, who still looked spaced and shocky. Dekker's heart was going hard, felt like detonations under his hand. Dekker's eyes had lost their glaze, started tracking around him.

Drifted back again, looked halfway cognizant.

"Let up," Dekker said.

He thought about that. He thought about Meg saying for the last damn week Dekker was just confused, and Sal saying back off and give him some space. While Dekker kept a sim schedule the other crews were talking about. He gave Dekker a shove in the chest. Hard.

"Let up, hell. I'll solve your problem, I'll break your neck for you. You hit Meg, you skuz, you know that?" Dekker didn't say anything, so he asked, for Dekker's benefit, "You all right, Meg?"

"Yeah."

"Hell of a bruise coming," Sal muttered.

Dekker set his jaw again, didn't exactly say go to hell, but that was the look he gave, along with the impression he might not be in control of his voice right now. When Dekker shut up, you either kept a grip on him or you got out of his way. So he kept his hand where it was, asked, civilly, "You still talking to him, Meg?"

"Wasn't his fault, Ben." Mistake. Meg sounded shaky herself, Meg had evidently gotten clipped worse than he thought, and that wobbly tone upset Dekker, he saw that. Dekker quit looking like a fight, just stared at the ceiling, gone moist-eyed and lock-jawed.

Great.

He gave Dekker another shove, risking explosion. "You want to, maybe, get a grip on it, Dek-boy? Or you want to schitz some more?"

Dekker made a move for his wrist, not fast, just brushing him off. He let Dekker have his way, stood back and let Dekker sit up with his head down against his knees a moment, to wipe the embarrassment off his face.

"You know," he said, pressing that advantage, "you do got a serious problem, Dek. You busted Meg who's trying to help you, the meds are bitching you're pushing it too damned hard—you seriously got to get your head working, Dek-boy, and we got to have a talk. Meg, Sal, you want to leave him with me a minute?"

Dekker looked away, at the wall. Sal shoved Meg out of the room and Dekker didn't look happy with the arrangement, didn't look at him when the door shut, just sat in bed and stared elsewhere.

Towel on a chair. Ben got it and wrapped it around himself—wasn't freezing his ass off, wasn't matching physique with pretty-boy, either—wouldn't effin' be here arguing with him, except he was supposed to go back into pod-sims with a guy who couldn't figure out what time it was.

"Just drop it," Dekker said.

"Drop it, huh? Drop it? Wake me up in the Middle Of, and I should drop it? We're getting back in that pod at 0900, I'm not seriously inclined to drop it!"

Dekker leapt up off the bed and shoved him. "Just fuck off! Fuck off, Ben, all right? —I'm resigning."

Took a second for that to make sense. Didn't look as if Dekker was going to shove him twice, didn't look as if Dekker was anything but serious. Resign from the Fleet? You couldn't. From the program? Moonbeam had cold feet of a sudden?

Serious problem here, damned serious problem, from a guy who had dragged him into this so deep he couldn't see out, whose neck he had every moral right to break already; Dekker was piling the reasons higher, except Dekker wasn't exactly copacetic enough for a fight at the moment, and there were two women in the other room, primarily Meg, but Sal, too, who would take severe exception to his murdering the skuz.

"Resigning," he echoed Dekker.

Dekker leaned an elbow against the wall, wiped his shave-job mop out of his eyes and muttered, "Before the sim. First thing I can get anybody on mainday."

"When did this notion take you?"

Dekker's jaw locked again, visibly. Knot of muscle. Nowhere stare. But you waited and it would unlock, sometimes in ways you didn't want, but he waited. Dekker took a second swipe at his hair, and stood with his hand on the back of his neck.

"I haven't got it, Ben, that's all. I'm schitzing out."

"Yeah?" He wasn't eager to climb into that pod with a lunatic, he didn't know why in hell he had this urge to pull Dekker out of his funk and assure he was going to have to do that—it was instinct kept him here, to hold the seams of the partnership together, maybe, what they had right now being better than the hellish situation they *could* have. "Schitz I'm used to. You want to explain this new idea?"

"Doesn't need explaining. I can't cut it anymore. Can't do it."

"Nice of you."

"Yeah."

"Dekker, you are the absolute *nicest* son of a bitch I ever met, God, what do we do to deserve how nice you are? We are stuck in this fool's outfit, they're feeding us this damn experimental tape on account of they got it off your crew and *you* skuz out on us. Do you think they're going to give up on the investment they got in us? —No, they're going to put us out on the line with some only skosh saner fool and take stats on how long we take to make a fireball! Thanks, thanks ever-so for the big favor, Dek, and mercy for the vote of confidence, but you got to excuse us if we don't all break into party, here."

"I'm sorry." Dekker turned his back on him, leaned a second against the bathroom door, then went in and shut the door.

"Dekker, —"

Didn't like that sudden cut-off. Didn't like that, I'm sorry, out of the son of a bitch. There weren't locks on the doors. Not in this place. So he hauled the door open.

Dekker was bent over the sink. Mirror-Dekker looked up,

white as death, with a haggard expression that scared hell out of him.

"You contemplating anything stupid, Moonbeam?"

"What time is it, Ben? You know what time it is?"

"You know what the hell time it is."

"Not all the time, Ben, not all the fuckin' time I don't know what time it is, all right? I'm losing it!"

"You never knew where it was in the first place."

"It's not funny, Ben. It's not damn funny. Let me the hell alone, all right?"

Hell if. He grabbed Dekker by the elbow and steered him out of the closet of a bathroom, Dekker balked in the doorway and Ben slammed him hard against the doorframe. "Listen, Moonbeam, you don't need to know where the hell you are, that's Meg's department. You don't need to wonder what's coming, that's Sal's. You don't need to know a damn thing but where the targets are and get *me* a window, you hear me? Time doesn't mean shit to you, it doesn't ever have to mean shit, you just fuckin' do your job and leave ours to us, you hear me?"

Door opened. It was the marincs or it was Meg to Dekker's rescue. But Dekker wasn't fighting the hold he had, Dekker was backed against the bathroom doorframe with a kind of consternation on his face, as if he'd just heard something sane for once.

"Ben, back off him."

"Yeah, yeah, he's all yours, I got no designs on him." He let Dekker go and Dekker just stood there, while Sal grabbed his arm and said, "Benjie, cher, venez, venez douce."

Hell of a mouse Meg had on her cheek. Meg was wearing a towel around the waist and not a stitch else when she put her arms around Dekker's neck and said something in his ear, Come to bed, probably—but he wasn't sure that was what Dekker needed right now, Dekker needed somebody to bounce his head off the wall a couple more times, if it wouldn't wake the neighbors.

"Cher. Come on."

Sal tugged at him. He went back to their room, Sal trying to finesse him into bed. Ordinarily nothing could have distracted him from that offer. But he was thinking in too tight a loop, about Dekker, the sim upcoming, and the chance of a screw-up. He sat down on the edge of the bed. Sal massaged his back, then put her arms around his neck, rested against his shoulders.

"Meg'll handle him," Sal said.

"Meg should take a good look at him. Sal, we got a problem. Major. He says he's quitting."

"Quitting!"

"You want to lay bets they'll let him? No. Nyet. No way in hell. We got ourselves one schitz pilot. I got nightmares. He's got 'em. He's been pushing himself like a crazy man—"

"Put Meg in?"

"I think we better consider it. I think Meg better consider it—at least on the one tomorrow. I don't know if they'll stand for it. But that's our best current idea, if we're going to get in there with him."

Sal gave an unaccustomed shiver. "They give us that damned tape. Hell, I'm used to thinking, Ben. I'm used to making up my own damn mind. I can't. I don't know that I am. It's a screw-up, soldiers no different than the corp-rats, you get the feeling on a screw-up."

"You're doing all right."

"The scores are all right. But I still never know, Ben, I don't get anything solid about what I'm doing, I don't ever get that feeling."

He didn't either. He hauled Sal around in front of him, held on to her, Sal being warm and the room not.

Sal held on to him. He buried his face in Sal's braids and tangled his fingers in the metal clips. "Dunno, Sal, I dunno. I've done everything I know. Meg should screw him silly, if he wasn't so skuzzed."

"Won't cure everything, cher."

"Makes a start, doesn't it?"

"He's a partner," Sal said.

"Yeah. Moonbeam that he is."

"Soldier-boys aren't going to listen to him or us."

"Dek-boy's on total overload. I've seen this guy not at his best and this is it. He's not stupid. Lot of tracks in that brain—that's his problem. All he has to do is follow one and he's in deep space so far you need a line to bring him back. But none of them pay off. His crew's dead, he's still hurting, not a damn word out of his mama, Porey's on his back, we're in deep shit, and he's not thinking, he's just pushing at the only track he's got. The only one that'll move. Don't give this boy *time* as a dimension. He's just fine—as long as it's *now*."

"Yeah. Yeah. I copy that. What do they say, hyperfocus and macrofocus?"

"And dammit, you don't let this boy make executive decisions. Paper rank's got nothing to do with this. It's who *can*. Effin' same as the merchanters."

"Meg?"

He hesitated over that. Didn't have to think, though. "Meg's Meg. Meg's the ops macrofocus. The Aptitudes pegged her exactly right. Meg always knows where she is. Knows two jumps ahead. Dek's the here and now, not sure what's coming. No. I'm the exec."

Silence a moment. Maybe he'd made Sal mad. But it was the truth.

"So how do we tell *them*?" Sal asked.

"Sal, —you want to switch seats tomorrow morning?"

She sat back and looked him in the face, shocked. "God, you're serious. They'd throw us in the brig."

"Is that new? No, listen, we can do it: same boards, different buttons. You got eight different pieces of ordnance, that's the biggest piece of information to track on. I can diagram it for you. Inputs, you got two, one from Meg if you got time to sight-see, one from longscan, which you know what that looks like . . ."

"Ben. What *are* you up to?"

"Surviving this damn thing." A long, shaky breath. Going against military regs wasn't at all like scamming the Company. But it did start coming together, now that he was thinking about the pieces. "Because I want the damn comp. Because, screw 'em, it's what I *do*. Because I think that ET sumbitch in there effin' knows we're in the wrong spots and it doesn't feel right to him and it's killing him. I don't know this crew that died, but I can bet you, one of them was the number one in this unit, no matter who they had listed. That guy died and they bring us in and put Dekker in charge? No way."

"What's that make me, mister know-all? Why in *hell* did they Aptitude me longscan and you the guns?"

He'd spent a lot of time thinking on that. He reached up and laced his fingers with Sal's. "Because you want 'em too much, because you *enjoy* blowing things up. —Because that's *not* what the tests want on that board."

She let go. "Where'd you get that shit?"

"Hey. Helldeck psych. Cred a kilo. And I know what the profiles are. I'm from TI. TI *writes* these tests. They got this Command Profiles manual, lays out exactly what qualifications they want in fire-positions and everything else. Enjoying it'd scare them shitless. We're *not* inner system. You got to *lie* to the tests, Sal, you got to psych what they want us to be and you got to be that on those tests—*only* way you get along."

"Meg—Meg is doing all right with this stuff. Tape doesn't bother her."

"Meg's an inner systemer, isn't she? She knows how to tell them exactly what they want to hear. Meg's doing what she wants. We're *not*."

"So what do we do? Is Aptitudes going to listen, when they *made* the rules?"

"Lieutenant might." If Graff could do anything. If it wasn't too late. He was scared even thinking about what occurred to him. But running into a rock was scarier than that. And that was likely. A lot of scary things were likely. Like a crack-up tomorrow morning. Stiff neck for a week after Dekker's twitch at the controls.

"Should we go talk to him?"

"No. Not direct." He eased Sal off his lap, went and got a bent wire out of a crack in the desk drawer.

"What—?" Sal started to ask, and shut up fast. She watched in silence as he bent down and fished his spare card out of a joint in the paneling.

He put it in the reader, typed an access, typed a message, and said, "'Scuse, Sal. Taking a walk."

Sal didn't say a thing. He opened the door, went out through Dekker's and Meg's blanketed, dark privacy—towel and all.

"Ben?" Dekker asked.

"'S all right," he said, "forgot something."

He slipped out to the corridor, around to the main room of the barracks, and around to the phones.

Linked in. Accessed the station's EIDAT on system level. With a card with a very illegal bit of nailpolish on its edge.

"What in hell?" Dekker asked when he came through again.

"Hey," Meg said. "Easy."

He got through the door and Sal didn't ask a single question, not while he folded up, not while he put the card away in its hiding spot behind the panel joint. You grew up in ASTEX territory, you learned about bugs and you developed a fairly sure sense when you might be a target for special monitoring. He didn't honestly think so. But he took precautions and hoped to hell the bugs, if they existed, weren't optics.

Most of all he hoped the lieutenant was one of the good guys, because the lieutenant was no fool: the lieutenant knew enough to figure who around here could get into the system and drop an unsigned message in his file. They didn't *have* TI techs above a 7A in this place. He'd checked that, already.

CHAPTER

15

SHOUTING in Porey's office again. Dekker sat on the bench outside, between a couple of marine guards, and stared at the opposite wall, acutely aware of the traffic in the main corridor, people stealing glances in this direction—you got a feeling for notoriety, and disaster, and you knew when you'd achieved it. Wake up to a stand-down and a see-me from Graff, who had nothing to tell him, except that somehow the Aptitudes in his unit were skewed, that they wanted to see Ben and Sal back in Testing, and Graff was due in a meeting with Porey, immediately. Which left him here, in the hall, listening to war going on in the office, and he hoped it didn't aim at Graff. Mutiny in the Shepherd ranks, if that was the case—Graff was the *only* point of reason in their lives since the disaster of the last test; and personally, he wanted to kill Porey. They told him he was supposed to go fight rebels from a planet clear to hell and gone away from Earth and right now the targets he most wanted were Comdr. Edmund Porey and whoever had screwed up Ben and Sal, if that was what had happened.

Something crashed, inside the office. He tried not to twitch, found his hands locked, white-knuckled. The guards exchanged looks, dead expressionless.

Marines weren't anxious to go in there either.

Weights rang back down into the pad, and Meg collapsed on her back on the bench, nerve-dead. Patterns still danced behind her eyelids, but the adrenaline was gone, it was only phosphenes.

Message came from the lieutenant, and Dek had been outright shaking when he'd read it. *Bad* shakes. Thank *God* Ben had done—whatever Ben had done. Sal was close-mouthed on it—but she had the idea it involved last night, phones, and messages Dek would have highly disapproved.

Weights banged, close to her head. Her eyelids flew open. *Mitch* was standing over her. Hell of a start, even if he was decorative: the son of a bitch. *She* had as little to do with Mitch as possible. Ben and Sal had gotten called in to Testing. Dek . . .

"What's this about Dekker getting scrubbed?"

Mitch wasn't alone. The other traffic in the gym wasn't casual. A delegation gathered around—Pauli, Franklin, Wilson, Basrami, Shepherds, all of them on her case; Shit, she thought, and sat up, looking for a way to shut this action down. "Maybe you better ask the lieutenant. I dunno."

"Word is there was a fight last night."

Double shit. Damned thin walls. "Wasn't any fight. A discussion. That's our business."

Pauli said, "Discussion that scrubs a crew?"

Basrami said, "Word is, the lieutenant gave him a mandatory stand-down. The lieutenant's been climbing all over Testing. Saito's still there, with Porey's com chief. Now the lieutenant's talking with Porey and Dek's hanging outside with the guards. Doesn't look arrested, but he doesn't look happy."

More information than she'd had. The grapevine in this place was efficient except in her vicinity.

Mitch asked, "So what's going on, Kady?"

"All I know," she said, "we got the stand-down before we got to breakfast. They wanted Ben, they wanted Sal in Testing, they wanted Dekker in Porey's office. They didn't want me, so I came here to blow it off."

"Come off it, Kady."

"It's the truth! I don't know a damned thing except Dek's been severely pushing it. Could be a medical stand-down—I hope to hell it's a medical. Porey's been on his back. He hasn't said, but *we* screwed a sim, he talked to Porey, and he's run hard since. You want to tell *me*?"

Silence from the guys. Then Mitch said, "They giving any of this special tape to him?"

Nasty question. "Not that I hear. I don't think so. —No. There's been no time like that in his schedule."

"Are they going to?"

Scary question. "Him, they don't need to, do they? He knows what he's doing."

"Just asking," Mitch said.

"Yeah," she said. "Well, whose would they give to him? Tell me that." Five on ten they made the same and only guess she could, and the idea scared hell out of her. "They took my mates into Testing. They told Dek report in. They didn't tell me an effin' thing. I'm either the only one right in the universe or I must be one of the problems." Which shaded closer to her private anxiety than she wanted. She got up, picked up her towel, for the showers. "So if you got any news, you owe me."

"Nothing," Pauli said. "Except a serious concern for the program. And Dekker."

Belters rarely said 'friend.' You didn't say, I care, I love, I give a damn. They wouldn't do that. But they came asking. Even that skuz Mitch. Made her think halfway better of Mitch, and that gave her another cause to worry.

"Yeah," she said. "Thanks. If I hear anything, either."

* * *

The door opened. Graff said, stone-faced, "The commander wants to see you."

"Yessir," Dekker said.

No questions. Graff was negotiating with an unreasoning, unreasonable son of a bitch and didn't need trouble from another source. He got up and walked in, saluted, and Porey said, all too quietly, "You may have had a problem, mister. This whole damn program may *have* a problem. So I want an answer, I want a single, completely straight answer: If you were second-guessing the Aptitudes, where would *you* have expected Pollard and Aboujib to fit in the crew profile?"

"Ens. Pollard's a computer tech, theory stuff." He had one sudden chance, maybe, to do something for Ben, which would drop the lot of them down the list, break Meg's heart and save all their skins. He debated a split second, then: "UDC Technical Institute. I'd have thought he'd be handling the computers. —To be honest, sir, I'd have thought he'd go somewhere up in Fleet Ops—they were going to send him to Stockholm. He's got—"

Porey snarled, "We've got *enough* UDC hands in this operation right now. What about Aboujib? Co-pilot?"

He didn't know what all this was about. Not enough to maneuver with. "Ben taught her numbers. I'd expect she's good. Longscan or armscomp. She's—" He flashed on Sal's frustration with the scan assignment. "I don't know— don't know. What she wants—is the fire button." His mind was on what Porey had said about Ben. He thought he might have done Ben harm, bringing in the Stockholm business. He made a desperate, uninvited counter. "Sir, I haven't got any doubts about Ben Pollard. He went UDC because they had his program, but he's Belter. He wouldn't do anything but a hundred percent for his partners."

Porey left a cold, cold silence. He didn't know what he was arguing for or against, or who was on trial. Porey just stared. "If," Porey began, and the phone beeped. Porey grabbed up the handset, snarled, "This is a conference, damn you—'' and the face went expressionless while Dekker had time to think, Something's happened . . .

Graff was paying the same kind of attention. Porey said, "Procedures. Stat. —Estimate," and looked grim as he hung up and stood up. "Pod's hung."

"God." Dekker thought Porey wanted the door—grabbed for the switch.

"Dekker!"

"I can help, sir, . . ."

"No!" Porey said. And there was no argument.

Meg hauled clothes on, still wet—damn sweater hung on an earring. She finessed it loose the painful way and got her head through—

Mitch, the skuz, was standing in the locker room door.

She jerked the sweater down. "Getting your thrills, Mitch?"

"Serious talk, Kady. Question. Couple of touchy questions."

Private, the man wanted. Hell of a way to get it; and time was, Mitch didn't get two seconds, but Mitch didn't look like trouble, Mitch looked like business, and curiosity was killing her. "So? Give."

"What is their damn *hurry* with Dek, do you get any feel?"

She bit her lip. Shook her head. "Neg. No. What are you asking?"

"Is Ben on our side?"

"Absolute. *No* question, and Sal and I fly with him."

Mitch ducked his head, looked up with the straightest eye contact she'd ever had out of him. "Ben made a phone call last night. Dek got pulled this morning. You know about that?"

"Yeah. Ben could have slipped it to the lieutenant—about two jumps ahead of me, you want the truth."

"That schedule of his. Did he set it? Is it his choice? Or is Porey doing it?"

"Much as I know it's his schedule." It was sensitive

territory. She wasn't sure she wanted to discuss any crew business with Mitch, who was Dek's competition in this place. But Dek had her scared to hell, that was what she had said to Sal and that was what made her confess now. "I can believe Ben might have stopped him. I just hope it didn't land either of them in trouble."

"Second touchy question. You apparently aren't too damn bad. How much of it do you think is tape?"

"I was *good* before I came here, mister."

Mitch held up a hand. "No offense. Straight q & a—they're talking about shoving it on the rest of us, I want to know from the ones that know—does that damn thing really work?"

Sounded like an honest question. "Different way to learn, same way you guys learn, what I hear, this Neural Input stuff. I don't know what's the difference, except we trank deeper—by what I hear. How could I tell? I don't get the other kind."

"Rumor is they're running you guys up to mission level sims. They're saying they're using you guys for guinea pigs because you came in cold, as far as these boards. That if it works with you—we're next and we got no choice. Now they're hauling Pollard and Aboujib back into Testing? Makes the rest of us damn nervous, Kady."

Made her nervous when he put it that way.

"You *know* anything about Pete Fowler, you ever have any—weird feelings off that stuff?"

"I'm not *being* him, Mitch, I'm not any damn dead guy. That's not what's going on. . . ."

"He was twenty-nine, he was a good, fast thinker, he was regular for Elly Sanders—she was the longscanner. You want any more? Pete's faults? His virtues? I can tell you. He was a nit-picking sumbitch about the checklist. . . ."

"I'm telling you I don't know anything about Pete Fowler. I damn sure haven't got a fix on Sal and I always was a stickler for doing—"

"Mitch!" somebody yelled, out in the sims. "They got a pod hung!"

"Oh, *shit*," Mitch said, and he was running—*she* started running after him, scared as hell, no idea what they could do, why they were going—but it was somebody she knew in that damned thing, and she moved.

"What's the status?" Porey asked, leaning over a tech—Security ops had eight monitors and four of them were black, except for green letters showing CORE-21, that was the sims area, anybody who worked up there knew that section, and Dekker knew it, made a guess what those black monitors showed before Porey got his answer.

"They cut the power, sir," the ops tech said, "Chief Jackson got the spin shut down. Cameras are working, they're on another generator, but all the pods are full crewed and frozen out there til they get power back on."

The core was totally dark, even the access areas—requests for personnel movement going out over com, the same sequence that must have attended his own accident, Dekker thought glumly—like standing off and watching it happen to him.

"Do we have a recovery team out there?" Porey asked, and the tech answered that they were still trying to organize that—only way they had to haul you back if a pod had to totally crash was suit up and go out there; the construction workers that formed the rescue squad were coming in from their off hours and from work around the carrier—

"Too damned long," he said, he didn't care if he was out of turn: "I know the systems, sir, I'm used to a suit—"

"You're *not* going out there," Porey said, and adjusted the com in his ear, scowling, eyes showing the least anxiety while he listened to something elsewhere. "—You have one?" he asked someone invisible. "Suiting now?"

They'd found somebody closer. Dekker drew a controlled breath, then, still wanting to *do* something; but rescue was evidently getting into motion. Black monitors. No emergency lights—the fool engineers had put the viewport shutters on the main power. Power was cut, completely, complete black in the chamber, no ventilation in the pod, no heat, no filtration for anybody out there. God hope the mags weren't all crashed.

"Patch through the suitcom," Porey said. Graff said to the tech at the boards in simulation Control, "Give us audio, here. Are we getting anything out of the pod?"

"We don't get anything. Whole core section's on that generator."

"What the hell kind of engineering is that, dammit to bloody *hell*, what kind of operation do we have here?"

"An old one," Graff said. "Lot of patch-jobs."

"Piece of junk," Porey muttered. "Nothing moves, does it?"

"Not the shutters, not the internal lights—there's a requisition to get them on another circuit, but the engineers have found a problem doing that."

"Can they power up with the rest of those pods sitting out there?"

"Should be able to," Graff said, while Dekker kept his mouth shut. Should be able to, once they got the one pod clear. If it didn't, if they were all crashed, everybody was in trouble. Imminent trouble.

"One man's not enough out there," he said tautly. "They've got no locators, those are all killed with the power. . . . Sir, in all respect, I know what I'm doing. . . ."

"Shut *down*, Dekker, you're not going up there."

A dim seam of light showed at the edge of one monitor— lock door, he figured, on a leech and hand-battery. Audio cut in, unmistakably a suit com, heavy breathing, little else, and a white star appeared in both monitors: suit-spot shining in all that black.

Sim chief's voice, then: *"You're going across the chamber, zenith climb about ninety meters . . . sensor range within . . ."*

"Copy that." Female voice, unexpectedly. Familiar voice

that sent a sinking feeling to the pit of his stomach as the star shot off at a fair speed. Scary speed.

"Don't hurry it, don't hurry it . . ." from the chief. *"Dammit, slow down."*

Meg didn't. Meg was hotdogging it, scaring hell out of him and the sim chief—miner showout, but habitual: a miner knew his distance without his eyes, by reckonings they didn't teach in construction, and she wouldn't miss: blind in the dark, she wouldn't miss: that was the push she was used to—and she was counting and calcing.

"Shouldn't argue with her," Dekker muttered, sweating it. "She knows her rate, she's feeling it . . . tell the chief that."

"Is that Kady?" Graff asked. "Dekker, is that Kady out there?"

"Yessir."

"Get her the hell out of there!" Porey said into the mike. "This is Comdr. Porey. Get her out of there. *Now!*"

Took a little relaying of instructions. Meg developed a problem with her mike. Didn't fool Porey, didn't fool anybody, but there wasn't a thing Porey could do from here. Meg was closing into sensor range, you could hear the pings on audio and see the rate drop.

Then number two monitor showed a faint haze of detail. Chamber wall and a pod directly in Meg's suit spot, he'd bet his life on it.

"She's all right," he said, feeling the shakes himself. "Sir, she knows her business."

Porey wasn't saying a thing about the transmission difficulties, wasn't giving any orders now, he just muttered, "Kady's on notice with me, you make that clear, Mr. Graff."

"Yes, sir," Graff said.

Word came from another channel that the Pod Rescue Unit was being deployed. At least some of the rescue squad had gotten there, and was launching the track-guided equipment that could tow the pod.

Meanwhile an engineer was giving instructions and Meg started identifying and freeing up the bolts that released it from its track.

"*Shit . . .*" came over the com; and froze his heart.

"*What's the matter?*" the chief asked; but he could see it for himself, the pod's number decal—number three. The pod they'd been scheduled for.

"That's Jamil," he said, to whoever cared, and looked for a chair free. But there wasn't one. "Jamil and his guys took our slot—said they could use the time . . ."

Didn't take much calc to find a lighted, open hatch, and Meg beelined for it, braked and took a shaky bent-kneed impact, another showout miner-trick, with a hand-up catch at the rim of the lock to stop the rebound. She cycled the lock on battery power, breath hissing with shivers—it wasn't cold coming through the suit, not this fast, it was shock starting to work, in the loneliness of the airlock. Let the rescue crew do the maneuvering with the PRU, the chief had said, they wanted her out of there and that lock shut before they powered up the mags and she agreed, she didn't know shit about the tow system: it was on now, it was moving, bound for a pod access lock where meds were waiting, and they weren't going to need her unless the mags were definitively crashed.

Moment of intense claustrophobia then, just the ghostly emergency light, then a door opened into a brightly lit ready-room full of guys willing to help with the suit.

She got the helmet off, drew a breath of icy clean air and got a first welcome bit of news—power-up was proceeding, pods were answering; they for sure weren't going to need her again out there, and she could unsuit and take the lift out to gravitied levels and the lockers. Good job, they told her, good job, but they were busy and she got herself out of the way, let them tend the suit, unaccustomed luxury for a miner-jock, and boarded the lift out of there.

* * *

Slow, slow business in the recovery of the pod, and they could only watch, in 1-deck Security ops. Dekker hung at Graff's back and Porey's, listened to the output from the rescue team on the open speaker.

They were working into dock now, at access 3. *"That's copy,"* he heard a voice say, and flashed on cold, on dark, on inertia gone wild—

Enjoy the ride, Dekker. . . .

"That's him," he said of a sudden—had everyone's attention, and he looked to Graff, who understood what he meant, Graff surely understood.

"ID that man," Graff snapped, "isolate that voice. —Mr. Dekker—" as he headed for the door. "Hold it."

"Dekker!" Porey said atop Graff's order, but he'd already stopped and faced them.

"I want you to listen," Graff said. "I want you to pick out that voice, all the voices that might be involved."

"Is he meaning the attack on him?" Porey wanted to know, and Graff nodded, leaning over the master com in ops. "Yes, sir, that's exactly what he means. —Play it back, ensign."

"That's copy," the recording said, among others, and Dekker said with absolute conviction, "Yes. That one."

"Who's carded to that area right now?" Porey asked. "Nobody's leaving that area without carding out, hear me?"

"Yes, sir," the com tech said; and relayed to Fleet Security.

"Not everybody's carded in," Graff said. "They probably let medics and techs in wholesale—anybody with a security badge . . ."

"Sir," the tech said, "I think I've got it pinned. That output's on e-com, I've got the serial number on the unit."

"Track it."

Time to indulge the shakes and the unsteady breathing, alone in the lift. *"They're getting telemetry,"* Meg heard, on the com track that was probably going out to every speaker in the mast. *"Four heartbeats."* Best news yet. Thank God, she thought, queasy in the steady increase of *g* against the deep fast dive the car was taking. She clenched her teeth and collected herself, watched the level indicator light plummet until the car came to rest and the door opened on warm air and bright light.

She expected Mitch and a handful of guys; but the room was packed, everybody who could cram themselves in, all wanting news. "Four heartbeats," she told them, which they might have heard, she couldn't tell if the com was feeding through, there was so much racket. She wasn't prepared to be laid hold of, wasn't expecting Mitch of all guys to pat her heavily on the shoulder and say how miner-jocks had their use—other guys did the same, and all she could get out was a breathless, desperate: "Jamil. Jamil took our sim slot   anybody seen Dek?"

Nobody had. She was shaking, embarrassing herself with that fact, but she couldn't stop the chill now. A big guy whose name she didn't even know threw his arm around her shoulders, hugged her against his side, and yelled out to get a blanket, she was soaked with sweat.

I'm all right, she tried to say, but her teeth kept chattering. Seeing that number out there had put a shock reaction into her—she wasn't used to shaking; wasn't used to *time* to think when she was scared, or, worst, to knowing there wasn't a damned thing she could do personally to help those guys or Dek. . . .

The blanket came around her. "Tried to kill us," she said between shivers. "Wasn't any fucking accident, Dek was supposed to be in that pod . . . That was *our slot* Jamil took . . ."

"Sims tech Eldon A. Kent," Graff said, reading the monitor, "out of Munich, trained in Bonn . . ."

"I want a piece of him," Dekker said. God, he wanted it, wanted to pound the son of a bitch so fine the law wouldn't have pieces left to work with. "Just let me find him."

"Certainly answers the questions about access," Graff murmured, reading over the data on the monitor. "Free access to the pods, a lot of the techs let each other through, never mind the rules. He's Lendler Corp, he comes and goes—what were you *doing* up there suited, Dekker? What were you doing with the mission tape?"

Piece suddenly clicked into place. Bad memory. Whole chunk of memory. "Wanted to look at the tape, just wanted to look at it—" The disaster sequence. The maneuver Wilhelmsen had failed to make. "Damned set piece. They wanted it to work, they kept training us for specifics. I told them that, I . . ."

"They."

"The UDC. Villy."

"So you went to the ready room, or up to the access?"

"The ready room. To run it on the machine there. They wouldn't let me in the labs, I was off-duty. I just wanted to *look* at the sequence—"

"Where did this Kent come in?" Porey asked.

"While I was running the tape."

"Alone?"

He shook his head. "Guy was with him. I know the face, I can't remember the name—"

"And they came in while you were reading the tape. What did they say?"

"They said they were checking out the pods, they were looking for some possible problem in the sims. They wanted me to go up to the chamber and answer some questions . . ."

Graff asked: "Did you suit to fly? Was that your intention?"

"I—I hadn't—no. I just had the coveralls. I hadn't brought a coat."

"You suited because of the cold, you mean."

"Yes, sir."

"You went up there," Porey said. "What happened?"

"They said put the tape in, I did that, they hit me from

the back. Said—said—'Enjoy the ride.' Sir, I *want* these guys . . .''

"Absolutely not," Porey said. "You don't go after them. That's an order, mister."

"Commander, they're up there right now with Jamil and his guys, they've got their asses to cover—"

"Mr. Dekker."

"They're with Jamil!"

"Mr. Dekker, shut *up* and believe there are reasons more important than your personal opinion. We have a program with problems, a ship with problems, and what happened to you and what happened up there isn't the only thing at issue. They're Lendler Corp technicians; and they didn't take a spontaneous dislike to you, do you read that, Mr. Dekker? Lendler Corp has a multitude of Fleet contracts, which has UDC contracts, which leaves us with serious questions, Mr. Dekker, does it penetrate your consciousness that there may be issues that have a much wider scope than your need for vengeance or my personal preferences? If things were otherwise, I'd turn you loose. As is, you keep your mouth shut, you keep it *shut* on this and let Security handle it. We'll get them. It may take time, but we'll get them. We want to know whether there's a network, we want to know if there's any damage we don't know about, we want to know if there *is* a connection to you personally or if you just have incredible luck, do you understand that, Mr. Dekker?"

"Yessir," he said, past a choking anger. "Yessir, I understand that."

"Then you see you keep your mouth totally shut about what you know. You don't even tell your crew; and believe me I mean that. —Mr. Graff?"

"Sir."

"Escort Mr. Dekker to my office. I'm not through with him."

"Walk slowly," Graff said, on the way out of ops. Porey was back there on com calling in senior Security, he was well sure: Fleet Police already had the pod 3 access as secured as it could be with medics at work; they had the answer they'd been looking for and the mess only got wider, with tentacles into God knew what, Lendler, any *other* corporation. You didn't take a highly educated technical worker and suddenly turn him into a saboteur and hand-to-hand murderer, not overnight, you didn't; which meant Kent was other than a peaceful citizen, Kent was skilled and malicious, and *somebody* in Lendler Corp had gotten him credentials and arranged for him either to get here or to stay here, at the time a lot of Lendler Corp had transferred out—Porey was right on this one. They had, as Villy was fond of saying, pulled a string and got a snake. Potential faults in the equipment, faults in the programming, faults in the assignments, and Porey still hadn't closed on the monumental coincidence of his pulling Dekker from the test today in the first place, *why* he'd had sudden misgivings on this day of all days . . .

The message that had turned up in his personal file, with no identifying header *or* record, damned sure hadn't been a spontaneous generation of the EIDAT system, and his stomach was increasingly upset, with guilt over the concealment of that security breach, and the conviction exactly who had inserted that message—along with a cluster of Testing Labs files nobody outside highest security clearances should have been able to access at all.

Bias in the tests, Earth-cultural bias in the Aptitudes, consequently in the choices and reactions trained into the UDC *and* the Shepherd enlistees—a bias that didn't want aggression on the fire-button or command decisions out of the pilots: he'd only to run an eye down the questions being asked and the weight given certain answers to see what was happening; and before the accident phone calls had already been flying back and forth between Sol One and B Dock: Porey had already invoked military emergency on Intellitron in as fine a shade of a contract clause as a merchanter could manage—demanding access to programs Intellitron had held secret thus far: Pending mission. Medical question. Emergency. Credit Edmund for the nerve of a dockside lawyer . . . and meanwhile, aside from the possibility of active sabotage, they had to wonder how many *other* examples of misassigned crews they were going to find, they had a clear notion *why* the UDC crews had had problems, and knew, thanks to Pollard, why the whole program might have a serious problem—which he couldn't, for Pollard's sake, confess.

Friendliest Edmund Porey had ever been to him, after he'd broken the news and Porey had absorbed it. And, dammit, he didn't want Porey's kind of friendship—he didn't want Porey deciding he could help Porey look good, and putting in a request for him on staff, God help him, even if it meant a promotion. Not at that price. And it looked that way now, it looked increasingly that way, with no word from his own captain, no evidence Keu was still in charge over at FSO.

Be careful, Demas had told him last night. Don't succeed too conspicuously.

"Mr. Dekker."

A breath. "Yessir."

"Coincidence in this instance is remotely possible."

"Yes, sir."

"You don't believe it."

"No, sir. I absolutely don't."

"You're probably asking yourself why you were so lucky—why I pulled you from tests."

Another breath. Maybe Dekker hadn't gotten that far. Maybe Dekker was still tracking on the past, pulling up damaged memory—maybe Dekker was thinking of revenge, or Porey, or the multitudinous accesses corporate connivance could infiltrate that a Fleet pilot wasn't educated to suspect . . .

"The reason I did pull you—we found a bias in the Aptitudes. I'm telling you something that's classified to the *hilt*, understand. If it gets to the barracks the wrong way, with no fix, it could affect performance. Fatally. You understand me? We're on a knife's edge here, right now. We don't need loose talk. On any topic.''

A worried glance. "Yessir.''

"I'm telling you this because I suspect one of your crew made the discovery and communicated it to me, secretly, which is *also* not for general consumption, and when the commander briefs you, don't let him know you know either—*how* I heard could bring one of your crew before a court martial, do I make myself absolutely clear on that?''

"Yessir.'' Dekker's voice was all but inaudible.

"The public story has to be that, having experience with this ship, we're going to be re-evaluating certain crews for reassignment—''

"Break crews? Is *that* what we're talking about?''

Damnable question. Touchy question, considering the Wilhelmsen disaster. He paused in the corridor short of the marine guards outside Porey's office, outside their audio pick-up, he hoped, or their orders to eavesdrop on an officer. "Not by fiat. I'm asking for any crews who might want assignments re-evaluated—in the light of new data. No break-up of existing crews unless there's a request from inside the crew. We recognize, believe me, we recognize the psychological investments you have.''

"Why in hell—'' Dekker caught a breath, asked, in bewildered, betrayed tones: "Why didn't you catch it before this?''

"Mr. Dekker, when we began this program, in an earlier, naive assumption of welcome here, we *trusted* the UDC to know Sol mindsets better than we did. We were absolutely wrong. We didn't understand the prejudice involved, against the people we most needed. And your crew is the most foreign to their criteria. More so than Shepherds. Maybe that explains how it turned up with your group. But what I've told you can't go any further. Hear me?''

Dekker drew a shaky breath. "Yessir.''

"I have to take your word, Mr. Dekker. Or, understand me—court-martial Ben Pollard."

"I'm giving you a two-day stand-down, Mr. Dekker," Porey said, the friendliest Dekker had ever seen the man, the quietest he'd ever imagined him. It still didn't include warmth. "I don't want you *near* the labs for forty-eight hours."

Graff said, from the side of the room, "I'd recommend longer."

Frown from Porey, who rocked back in the desk chair. "We haven't got longer. You have a mother a great deal in the news . . . which you know. You may *not* know there's a special bill proceeding through a JLC committee, that requires the military to surrender personnel indicted for major crimes, are you aware of that, Mr. Dekker? —Does that concern you?"

A complete shift of attack. Another assault on memory. Sometimes he thought he lost things. "My mother, sir, . . ."

"He's not gotten the headlines," Graff said. "His schedule's been non-stop for days . . ."

"Your *mother*, Mr. Dekker, has a battery of very expensive peacer lawyers, your mother is a cause that's burned a police station in Denmark and gotten a MarsCorp chartered jet grounded in Dallas on a bomb threat—do you know that?"

No, he didn't. He shook his head and Porey went on,

"The whole damned planet's on its ear, there's a lot of pressure on the legislative committee, and you're essential personnel, mister. Your crew is an essential, high-tech experiment that through no particular fault of yours, has taken a direct hit from a damnably persistent woman and a nest of lying political *fools* in the UDC, who are in bed and fornicating with the politicians who appointed them to their posts, the same politicians who are fornicating with the shadow parliament and the peacers in Geneva. That bill is a piece of currency in this game. We have to avoid you becoming another piece of currency in this affair, a damned media circus if they extradite you, and that means getting anything done with this project has assumed a sudden certain *urgency,* do you follow me?''

He saw the lieutenant out of the tail of his eye. Graff wasn't looking at him. Hadn't told him . . . God, *how* much else had Graff kept from him?

Porey said: ''We're talking about a fault in the Aptitudes, and I want your well-considered opinion here, Mr. Dekker, whether you want a go-with as-is, or whether you personally want to make a personnel switch. *Both* your crewmembers are demonstrably capable in the seats they've trained for— but 'capable' is a fragile substance in a Hellburner crew, you understand me?''

''Yes, sir,'' he managed to say. ''Extremely well. Pollard and Aboujib?''

''Exactly.''

''Can I talk to them?''

THUMP of Porey's hand on the desk. ''You're the pilot! Gut decision! Which?''

An answer fell out. ''I'd ask them, sir.''

''Correct answer,'' Graff muttered, looking at the floor.

Hard to argue with Porey. Hard to think in Porey's vicinity. But there was Graff. Graff agreed with him . . . Graff handed him secrets that could mean Graff's own career; and Graff had failed his promise to tell him if there was news from Sol One . . .

Porey said, ''Then we'll put the decision up to them, since that's where you want it. No preferences. You've lost one crew. Let's see if this one's worth the investment. Meanwhile, Mr. Dekker, do some thinking about your own responsibilities—like executive decisions. Do you make executive decisions, Mr. Dekker?''

''Yessir.''

''Do you remember your instructions, regarding what you've seen and heard?''

''Yes, sir.''

"What are they?"

"Silence. Sir."

A hesitation. A cold, cold glance, as if he were a morsel on Porey's plate. Then a casual wave of the hand. "Dismissed. Two-day stand-down."

"Yessir." Anger choked him of a sudden, out of what reserve of feeling he wasn't sure. But it wasn't at Graff. He refused at gut level to believe Graff had deliberately lied to him. The service had. The out-of-reach authorities had, and not for the first time in his life. He saluted, turned and reached for the door.

"Mr. Dekker," Graff said, from the side of the room. "Excuse me, sir. —Mr. Dekker, outside, a moment."

"Yessir." He wasn't enthusiastic. He didn't want to talk. But Graff followed him outside, between the guards.

"Mr. Dekker, I failed a promise. —Do you want the information, on your mother's whereabouts?"

He nodded. Couldn't talk. He was acutely conscious of the guards on either hand; and Graff steered him well down the corridor, toward the corner, before he stopped. "Your mother is on Earth at the moment—everything funded by the Civil Liberty Association, as far as we can tell."

"Why?"

"The peace movement finds the case useful—the Federation of Man, for starters—as I warned you might happen; there is a financial connection between certain of these organizations, the CRA, the Greens and a number of other organizations—"

"It doesn't make sense! She's not political!"

"I'm afraid it's rather well left the original issue. It's the power of the EC that's in question. There've been demonstrations at the Company offices in Bonn, in Orlando, Tokyo, Paris—"

More and more surreal. "I don't believe this. . . ."

"There's a great deal of pent-up resentment against the Company, economic resentments, social resentments—so Saito tells me: mass population effect: the case came along, it embodied a concept of Company wealth and power against a helpless worker. The Company is understandably anxious to defuse the situation; they've offered a settlement, but concession seems to have encouraged the opposition. Salazar's plane was forced to land in Dallas because of a bomb threat, that's what the commander was talking about: whether that was a peace group or a random lunatic no one knows. I can't overstate the seriousness of what's happening downworld."

"She's never been on Earth. She can't have any idea what's going on . . ."

"We certainly wish she had decided against going down."

"Did she ever call back?"

"No: my word on that, Mr. Dekker, I swear to you. Most probably her lawyers advised her against it. Most probably— considering who funds them."

"I've got to call her! I've got to talk to her—"

"Reaching her, now, through the battery of bodyguards and security around her, on Earth—I earnestly advise against it. I don't think you can get through that screen. If you do it's almost certainly going to be monitored, very likely to be placed back on the news, by one side or the other in this affair."

"God. Where is she—right now, where is she?"

"Bonn, as of this morning. Mazian is in the same city. There are peacer riots and demonstrations. The news-services are crawling all over the city. If you want to communicate with her, you just about have to do it through news releases, and it's not the moment for it. We're imminently concerned about this extradition bill getting through. We don't want the maneuvering going public, and it could if you make a move. One believes the legislators aren't stupid. No one is spelling out to the media what effect the bill will have, no one is saying outright that it's aimed at you in specific, incredibly the news-services haven't put it together yet or don't even know about it. It's all proceeding in committee, so far; Salazar publicly making speeches on the fear of some 'criminal element' with a finger on the fire button. Earth is extremely worried about that point.''

"Do they know what we are? Do they understand this ship?''

"The general public knows now it's no missile project: no one believed we could maintain cover after the hearings, yes, it's leaked, what it is—senatorial aides, company representatives, nobody's sure exactly what; but we're completely public; and the program, with what we've found out in the last three hours, is in such disarray we can't *take* another round of hearings. The coalition that put command of this facility in our hands is extremely shaky—as I understand it. If political reputations are threatened by the wrong kind of publicity, certain key votes could shift—and we could be massacred in the legislative committee. That, aside from your personal welfare, is why the Company and Fleet Command are extremely anxious to stop that bill; certain citizen lobbies are very fearful of wildcat attacks from the Fleet provoking a military strike at Earth; and even *knowing* it's a certain faction in MarsCorp pushing that bill, certain key senators desperately need a success in this program to play against it or they can't—politically—stand the heat of standing against the bill.''

"What do they want from us? I'm not a criminal! Jamil and his crew aren't criminals! I want to know who's trying to kill me that doesn't fucking *care* if they get my crew along with me! Nobody's going to do a damned thing about those guys that did this, are they—are they, sir?''

"Keep your voice down. The guards have audio. We don't even know at this point that it wasn't a simple mechanical. Those systems have been under heavy use. But I'll grant you we don't think that's the case. That's one problem. And I'll tell you between us and no further, I had a real moment of doubt at the outset whether to make an issue of the Aptitudes with your crew or let it ride the way it was. The temptation to let it stand and save this program one more major setback was almost overwhelming— but I know, and I think you know, this system is operationally too sensitive and strategically too critical to accept half right. I hate what happened to Jamil. I wish I'd ordered a general stand-down—but hindsight's cheap. As it is, the pod sims are in stand-down, we've got a question of other sabotage possible—what you've given us is very valuable; but we're running short of time to develop a case, and we're going to have to find answers for a pack of legislators, it's dead certain. Right now I don't want you to think about any of this. I want you to take the stand-down, get a night's sleep, and remember what you know is dangerously sensitive. You understand me on that point?''

"Yessir."

"I have confidence in you," Graff said, turned and walked him back to the marine guards, "Corporal. One of you take Mr. Dekker where he wants to go. Get him what he needs. —I suggest it's a beer, Mr. Dekker. I strongly suggest it's a beer. Tell galley I said so. Check with me if they quibble."

"Yes, *sir*," the marine said. "This way, sir."

"Beer, sir," the guard said, had even gotten it for him and brought it to him at a table back in the galley, quiet refuge in a flurry of cooks and a clatter of pans around them—and in consideration of the Rules around this place, and politeness, and the damned regulations—Dekker shoved the kid's hand back across the table, with: "Sip, at least. Where I come from—fair's fair."

"Nossir," the corporal said, and shoved the beer into his hand. "We can, any evening, and you guys can't, and, damn, you guys earn it."

Misted him up, he'd had no expectation of that, and he hid it in a sip of beer. Guy he didn't know. Young kid who was going to ride that carrier out there with two thousand other guys and get blown to hell if he made a mistake.

Guy's name was Bloomfield, T.

And if Graff could have done anything personal for

him—he was grateful to the lieutenant for Cpl. Bloomfield, who didn't know him, had no personal questions, didn't chatter at him, just let him sip his beer. He felt the alcohol go straight for his bloodstream and his head: after months of abstinence he was going to be a serious soft hit. He thought about going back to barracks and catching some sleep, he thought about his crew and Jamil and the guys he knew; and he wanted quiet around him, just quiet, no one to deal with, and when they got to the changes they were going to make in assignments—that wasn't going to happen.

He wondered where Meg was, most of all, finally said to Bloomfield, "You have a com with you. You think you guys could locate a female about my height, red hair, shave job, Fleet uniform . . . ?"

"*That* one," Bloomfield said reverently. And kept any remark he might have to himself. "Yessir." And got on the com and said, "This is Bloomfield. Anybody on the com know where the redhead is?"

Remarks came back, evidently. Bloomfield listened to something on the earplug, struggled for a sober face, and asked, looking at him: "You want her here, sir?"

He managed a laugh. "Tell her it's Paul Dekker asking. Cuts down on casualties."

CHAPTER

16

YOU knew it was bad, Mitch put it, and trez correctly so, Meg thought—when they gave the whole barracks a beer pass, and brought cans and chips into the sacred barracks to boot. Pod sims were severely crashed, mags could be down a week, if sabotage *wasn't* the cause, as was the running speculation in the barracks: in which case, plan on longer.

Beer helped the mood, though: the ping-pong game got highly rowdy, a couple of armscompers not quite in their best form, but at least everybody was laughing. Word from hospital was guardedly optimistic—the meds weren't talking about life and death with Jamil and the guys now, but how long they'd be in hospital, about the percentage they could expect to come back and how soon. Jamil was conscious, Trace was. In the ruckus around the table, nobody questioned Ben and Sal slipping late into barracks. Ben just settled down soberly on Dek's other side with: "Heard the news. Bad stuff," while Sal went for beers.

"Meg pulled them out," Dek said. "Got to them fast as

anybody alive could. And the sim chief was on fuckin' duty this time, didn't have to *stop* to get fuckin' Tanzer's fuckin' authorization, he just braked the other mags and cut the power, was all. The worst part's the stop. I can tell you that. —They go on and switch you guys, or is somebody going to tell me what they did, or what?''

Dek had had considerably more than one beer, not a happy drunk, but direct.

''Yeah, they switched us. Damned right they did.''

At which Dek looked at Ben and Meg recognized it was a good thing Sal came back with the beers.

Dek asked: ''Why in *hell* didn't you tell me?''

Ben took his beer and Meg held her breath. Ben said: ''Because they could've said no deal. And you already knew.''

''I didn't know.''

''Yes, you did. Give me armscomp, hell, I don't want the guns . . . why'd they give me the guns? I'm a numbers man. So Sal said, 'Want to trade?' and I said, 'You friggin' got it, give me the comp and I'll get you the fire-tracks . . .' ''

''Bull*shit*, Ben.'' Dek's voice wobbled of a sudden. ''What are they going to do about it, then?''

Like he *didn't* know. Like he hadn't told her, in a couple of minutes during which Cpl. Bloomfield had been calling the hospital, checking on Jamil.

''Come on, cher.'' Sal squatted down with her beer and patted Dek on the knee. ''Screw the regs. Ben's the numbers, Ben's always been the numbers—''

Ben said, ''Armscomp and longscan's integrated boards, what's the difference, who's punching up, who's punching in? They ran us switched, as a pair, didn't have an iota of trouble with the sim—Sal's got to get the feel for the ordnance, but she's on it . . .''

''It's not a free lunch, Ben.''

''Close as. I got my hands on that *system,* Dek-boy, I got a system runs like it's friggin' elegant—''

Ben was in serious lust. Dek looked at him. Dek was

going to hit him, Meg thought, poised to grab. But Dek didn't.

Sudden *quiet* from the ping-pong match. Rapid fall-off of noise from the door inward, and she looked, where, God, it was *UDC* uniforms incoming, senior guys; and the lieutenant was with them. Guys were coming to their feet. They did.

"Villanueva . . ." Dek murmured. The redoubted Captain Villy, then.

"At your ease," Graff said—official voice, that. *Something* sure as hell was up. Nobody moved. "Personal message first," Graff said. "Jamil says he's coming back. Says he and Dekker are in a race."

Fly-by was a show-out, but, God, that was good news: he was no cheap write-off and neither was his crew. Cheers at that. A faint laugh out of Dek.

"As you know," Graff continued, "the mag interfaces took damage in shut-down, repair crews can handle that . . . but the larger question is what caused the pod to hang, and we are not putting crews back into the moving sims until we can pinpoint a cause and ensure operational safety. This does not, however, mean the program is at stand-down."

Whole room must be breathing in unison, Meg thought. Good on everything they'd heard so far. But there were the UDC uniforms.

—Just hope to God they aren't putting us back under Tanzer.

"—Lab-sims will continue as scheduled. We have also made selection of Fleet crews for a carrier operations exercise—"

"Test run," Dekker muttered, at her side. Translation from a lot of sources, to the same effect.

"—starting within the hour." Quiet settled. Quickly. "In the meanwhile we are taking steps to integrate Fleet and UDC instructional *and* operational personnel. You will see UDC personnel in Fleet areas, eventually in barracks: on which matter I want to say something specific—"

Rising murmur of dismay. The lieutenant waited, frowning.

"There was an incident reported to me, out of rec-hall, an attempt from a UDC crew to meet this company halfway, which was reciprocated with good grace. As a pilot myself, I appreciate the criticality of operational confidence in fellow personnel—let's be blunt: confidence of that kind was a casualty of the Wilhelmsen run.

"But what went wrong with this program does not serve this program; and when you're heads-up and hands-on, what doesn't serve this program doesn't serve *you* or the carrier you're defending. I don't have to spell out to you the reality for the future: that you will be working with UDC crews, whose lives will be equally at risk, including the lives of personnel aboard your carrier. Competition is well and good where it brings out extreme effort. But the relationship between the four core crewmembers of this ship will be extended eventually to the complete thirty-member support team aboard, who will rely on core crew: in the same way, a carrier's four Hellburner crews will have to rely on each other, and on that carrier and its internal support crew, for survival. There is no more serious business. Those of us from merchanter background have never quarreled with your style or your customs—and we refuse to quarrel with the personal customs of our sister service out of the inner system. *Whatever makes a crew work,* is that unit's business and only their business: that's the position we've always taken. That's the position we expect you to take now, because when you're out there in the wide dark, friends, your personal *style,* and whether you're from Sol's inner or outer system, doesn't make a damn bit of difference. The reliance you have on the crews making up your defensive envelope—that's all you've got. Those are your brothers and your sisters. And the uniform will not matter."

Murmur from the barracks, worried murmur.

Graff cut it off with: "The *names* of the pilots . . ." and got instant quiet. ". . . of the three crews selected, given alphabetically: Almarshad, . . . Dekker, . . . Mitchell. Those crews: pack immediately and board ECS4 within the hour; your quarters in this barracks will remain in your name, sacrosanct. You have no mass limit for this particular run: the carrier's engines will not notice your handweights or your case of soft drinks, for that matter; but remember that all electronics aboard must be listed with the duty officer, and alcohol and medications of any sort must be dispensed by carrier staff only.

"Other crews will keep listed schedules. That's all, guys, have a good evening. We'll have a further briefing after breakfast call."

"Lieutenant!" Mitch called out. "Is that as in—*test flight?*"

"It's as in keeping this program going, Mr. Mitchell. You'll get more specific briefings after you're aboard. That's all I can tell you. I won't be making this trip. You'll be under the orders of Comdr. Edmund Porey, specifically. Goodbye, good luck, good outcome."

"Porey!" Sal breathed.

"What in hell are they doing?" Ben muttered, which was what *she* was thinking. "They're crazed," Dek said, and called out, "Lieutenant!" started across the room.

And stopped, still, arms at his sides, just stopped, for no reason she could see. The lieutenant was still standing there, looking straight at him with a worried expression, but Dek didn't ask his question and the lieutenant didn't give his answer.

"Shit!" Sal said, and went for Dek before she had the brains to, as Graff walked out with Villanueva, and guys were coming up and accosting her and Sal and Ben with congratulations—noisy and excited gatherings around Almarshad and Mitch and their guys, speculation flying . . . upbeat: the whole program had crashed on them, and now everything was moving faster than anyone thought.

"Dek." She got his attention and he looked sane—sane and a little shaken. Ben overtook and asked: "What are we *doing* in this sort-out?"

"We have to pack," Dek said for an answer, which meant, to an old Company hand, We can't discuss it here.

Another time-glitch, the station's smooth pale surfaces to the carrier's spartan corridors, foam steel and color codes, lights that worked only when there was presence, hand-lines rigged every which way, and déjà-vu on every surface. The rigging crew had been kind enough to supply a hand-line with a color cue and Dekker followed it, herding the duffle along, the head of his little column, Mitchell's group and Almarshad's. Long, long way from the entry to the rider loft: the lifts wouldn't take them where they wanted to go so long as the carrier core was crashed, and the rules wouldn't let you do miner tricks, not on Porey's ship, he had that by experience. You slogged it the hard way, and expected sore arms.

Ship's officer was ahead, check-in point. "Welcome aboard," they got; and a copy apiece of the ship's internal regs; and the standard information on alcohol, volatiles, explosives, electronics, and live animals or plants.

"*Inner perimeter take-hold for power up . . .*" rang out on the speakers—inner perimeter didn't mean them; which he knew, but not everyone seemed sure of on the instant; and the petty officer said, "Core's going to engage for you. You can take the lift, captain's compliments."

Captain's compliments. He took a breath, exchanged glances with his crew, thinking, Bloody hell . . . because extravagant gestures from Porey were highly suspect. The man *liked* causing pain: he'd met what he'd taken for examples of the type, but cheap talent, compared with Porey's position and intelligence and potential. He didn't want to be on this ship, he didn't want to be under Porey's command, even feeling as he did now that Porey was a competent commander—he knew in his mind that they were aboard for security reasons, not because of the test; and they weren't mission candidates, he'd said as much to his crew in the privacy of their quarters, but the way this was starting out, this move on Porey's part—was Porey in games mode. You bet your life on your nerves and your skill, and they had Porey jinking like this to start with, yanking them out, putting UDC into the barracks when he damned well *knew* they were worried about UDC security? A dozen guys with combat nerves, trained to deal with this kind of thing, and what in hell was Porey up to, making maneuvers on the ones trying to make his program work?

Snake, he thought as he punched the lift call. It's politics, it's damned, stinking politics, that's what it smells like— he's afraid I'll talk, he wants me where he can control com, where I can have another accident if it comes to that— man'll do anything, nothing in him you can get hold of, nothing gets to his eyes except when people squirm—he enjoyed it this morning, when he knew he'd got a hit in, and I hadn't done anything, he's *that* kind . . .

The siren blasted the thirty-second warning. Surreal sound, one he'd heard a handful of times in his life, when he'd ridden out from the Belt.

"Helluva surprise," Almarshad muttered. "Nobody sets foot on this carrier but the commander's own staff, what any of us have heard, not even the lieutenant. Don't they trust each other or what?"

Almarshad wasn't thinking about surveillance. Wilson wasn't, either, who said, "Wish the lieutenant was going," as if Porey wouldn't eavesdrop. Dekker felt a cold fear, of a sudden, that not all of them might come back down this particular lift again. Mitch's crew and Almarshad's: the mission team and the backup, that was the order of things he could see, and he had a sudden claustrophobic sense he couldn't go through with this, couldn't watch this, couldn't stand another watch in mission control while something went wrong . . .

The deck vibrated with the engagement of the core. The lift door opened to let them in.

Motion instead of thinking—a moment of dumping thoughts and negotiating the door, null-*g*. He got himself and his crew and their baggage in with two other teams, grabbed the take-hold in the corner next to the lift controls and stared at the panel, read the instruction and warning stickers on monofocus and didn't blink, because he could lose himself right now, lose where he was, and when this was, and what he had to do . . .

G increasing. "Hold on," he said, as the indicator approached the loft exit. The car hit the interface, jolted into lock with the personnel cylinder. The door opened . . .

Wood and sleek plastic. Carpeted burn-deck . . .

Looked like the Shepherd club on R2. Like exec offices.

"My Gawd," Meg breathed at his back. "Is this us or Porey's cabin?"

"It's us," he said in shock, "it's evidently us."

Wasn't real wood, it was synth, but it was good synth. There was a tended bar, an orderly with trays of food and null-capped liquor—there were more orderlies to take their duffles and carry them away . . .

"Shee-it," came from Sal. And Ben:

"Class *stuff*, here."

Reality was completely slipping on him. He gave up his baggage to the orderly who caught a look at his nametag and took the duffle away—no wide spaces, the whole huge loft was diced up into safer, smaller spaces, by what he could see from his vantage; it hadn't been like this the last time he'd been aboard. Bare girders on the ECS5—no paneling, no carpet, no interior walls and no orderly with cheese and crackers and margaritas and martinis. The Shepherds were right in their element: Mitch said, "All *right*," and moved right in on the bar; and Ben didn't blink, Ben had been living the soft life on Sol One; Meg and Sal had been with the Shepherds—

But he hadn't. This wasn't real. Not for him. It wasn't ever supposed to be for him . . . there were people who had luxuries and people who didn't have, by some rule of the universe, and he couldn't see himself in a place like this . . .

"As you were." Porey's voice, deep and live. He looked

around at the outer-corridor entry, as the commander walked in. Porey strolled past Mitch to the bar and picked up a cheese and cracker, popped it in his mouth. Nobody moved. Nobody thought to salute. It was too bizarre, watching Porey walk a tour of the very quiet area.

"We had a problem. We still have a *problem*, gentlemen. —Ladies. —We have sims down—again. We have one of our best teams down—again. This wasn't your fault. Fixing it, unfortunately, is your responsibility. Seeing you have time and opportunity to focus on the job at hand—is mine. I've pulled you out here, and I am pulling this carrier out of station. Our final Hellburner prototype is mated to the frame, we're proceeding with deliberate speed, we've advised the necessary powers that there will be a test, and we are, frankly, using the time to make our final selection. Three units will be using traditional lab sims, which we can manage aboard this ship, and using sims *in* the actual prototype, daily, shift after shift. Mr. Dekker's unit will be using something different in addition, which we are watching and evaluating. Selection will be solely on the basis of scores and medical evaluations.

"Alcohol is not a prohibition during this watch. It will be available from time to time as schedules permit; but I suggest you not have a hangover in the morning: schedule will start with orientation to the library, the loft, the prototype—

"About which, remember you people are the best of the best—a carrier's survival and the accomplishment of its objectives is in large part your mission. You will live very well here, as you can see: core crews and technicians will occupy these quarters, with adequate staff to assure your undivided attention to your duty, which is solely the operation of your craft, the protection of your carrier and the achieving of strategic and tactical objectives. Additionally, privilege is extended in special facilities to your maintenance personnel, your library research technicians, and your communications and analysis personnel—you will sit at the top of a pyramid of some seven hundred staff and crew, with information gathering and processing facilities interfaced and cross-checked with the nerve center of the carrier itself. Everything you need. Anything you reasonably request. And, yes, *tactical* and targeting decisions will be part of your responsibility, in consultation with the captain of this ship. You will learn to make those decisions in close cooperation with carrier staff, decisions which were not, until now, your responsibility. Command believes your expertise in gravity-bound interactions and object location is an invaluable resource; and you will no longer receive cut-and-dried mission profiles. You will construct them yourselves. This is a policy change reflecting a change in the source of policy: how long we can maintain that control of policy rests directly on your successful completion of this mission.

"In the meanwhile, enjoy yourselves, ask the staff for anything within reason, and consult your individual datacards for further briefings." The second half of the cracker and cheese. Porey walked slowly toward the exit. And stopped. "Enjoy yourselves, gentlemen. Ladies."

Scared hell out of a guy—Porey, as Meg would put it, doing courtesy.

"Shit," Ben said, closing ranks with him and Meg; and Sal said, close after, "So that's Porey up close."

"That's Porey," Dekker said.

"Po-lite chelovek," Meg said. "Nice place, and all. . . . You wouldn't ever think it, would you? Son of a bitch."

A massacre, a slaughter of the innocent. Graff braced his finger against his lips, watched the vid in dismay, the crowd, the peacers shouting, the blond woman with the stringing hair looking distractedly left and right over the crowd like something trapped. Reporters asked, "Is your son the model they're basing this tape on? Are you in communication with him?" Ingrid Dekker shook her head in bewilderment, saying, "I don't know. I don't have anything to do with him, nothing he did has anything to do with me . . . it's never had anything to do with me . . ."

God.

He sat there, watching the alien scene, steps of some ornate building, a cathedral, they said, in London, the placards and banners, the sheer mass of human beings . . .

À bas la Compagnie, they were yelling. Down with the EC.

And elsewhere on Earth's life-rich surface, a UDC spokesman was claiming that the attitudes of the rab movement were infiltrating the Fleet, that the real aim was to disarm Earth's local forces, that the Earth Company was attempting to use the Fleet and the whole construction push in the Belt to take political control of the UDC and establish a world dictatorship . . .

Disaster. Utter political disaster.

"The tape is the damning thing. Someone's given out details. Someone in a position to know what we're doing—"

Saito said, "Don't discount Tanzer. The UDC has those records at their disposal, a lot of damaging data. We had to accept the UDC structure in place, and after the takeover, we knew it was a bomb waiting to go off."

"What side are they on, Com, for God's sake? Do they think it's a bloody game we're playing?"

"Their power is in question. Their sight has unquestionably shortened. The question whether or not they're in control of the EC or whether the EC is in control of Earth's policy—it's a very large, a very sensitive, issue in this system. The EC has enormous power, a constituency spread over the stations and the refineries and worlds outside this system. And we outsiders only know the EC. But there are governments, many governments on Earth, that consider the situation out there solely the EC's war."

"But it *is* the EC's war. Do any of us doubt it's the EC's war? The EC's cursed emigration restrictions created the mess, *they* motivated the dissidents to move out, *they* insisted on micromanaging at lights distance. Every stupid decision they ever compromised their way into created this war, but the fact is something very foreign is coming *here*, that's the point. They're worried about tape-training off a rab model because the *rab* movement is foreign? The rab isn't azi. The rab isn't designed personalities. The rab isn't an expansion into space so remote we don't know what may come out of it or what in hell they're going to provoke ... *Belters* are foreign? They should worry about me, Com. *I'm* foreign. *I'm* more alien than anything they've ever met!''

"Maybe they do worry. Maybe that's what that mob in Geneva is really saying. Give us back our control over things. Make it stop. Make it the way we always thought it was.''

"It never was. Not for one moment was the universe the way they imagined.''

"Of course it wasn't. But they thought they knew. They thought they controlled it all. Now they know they don't. And that poor woman—is the symbol of their outrage.''

"Alyce Salazar has to be the EC's greatest internal liability. Why in *hell* do they go on letting her take the offensive?''

"Principally because Mars wants its independence. Because Mars has gotten quite different, quite alien from Earth. That's what I've turned up on the Salazars.''

"Cyteenization?''

"Something like. Something like the Belt—with nostalgic conservatism as the engine, instead of the radical reform that drove the rab to the Belt. They cling to an Earth that never existed. They're the pure article, more Earther than Earth is—maintaining the true opinion, the true Earthly tradition. Never mind the outbackers are eccentric as they come. The corporate management runs the government, quite conservative, quite protective of their personal interests and their family influence.''

"I thought that was illegal.''

"It is. But it's the driving force in Martian society— who's in whose camp. Understanding what the daughter's desertion meant to Alyce Salazar—simplistically, face-saving has to be a large part of her motive, by what we've turned up. The girl escaped her mother's authority by literally slipping through customs and eluding her mother's personal security: that was one blow to the Salazar corporate image; more extravagantly, she embarrassed her mother by dying, quite publicly, quite firmly associated with Belter rab in a fullscale Company disaster. The daughter was clearly a dynastic hope on her part—a bid to extend Salazar's influence into another generation. A lot of Salazar alliances were built on that assumption."

"Which had to be revised at the daughter's death."

"Which to a Martian corporate, was a major disaster. A threat to her immediate control. It's radicalized the Salazar influence: she's—certain people think, calculatedly—offended certain elements that oppose the Company. The consensus I'm getting from intelligence is she's not mad, she calculatedly created a cause and an opposition to force the EC itself down her path in a move to come out of this more powerful than she was. That's what we're dealing with. She's maneuvering for power equal to the EC president—and the EC so far is paralyzed, because of who's backing her. They can't betray the conservatives in Bonn, or it erodes a structure they've built up over decades. The conservatives there are in fear for their lives over the radical resurgence. And *that* promotes Company hardliners, like Bertrand Muller. Muller is for the war, incidentally. He wants us to 'recover Cyteen.' "

"My God."

"He calls it a colony. What do you want? He's ninety years old, he formed his current opinion on his fortieth birthday, and he says the Company police who fired on the rab were defending civilized values."

"We're in the hands of lunatics."

"Of financiers. Far worse."

17

H IT it, hit it, hit it—"
    Breathless dive down the handlines for the seats,
one, two, three, four... in place, switches up...
    Launch. Surreal burst of static while the screens
and the V-HUD spieled numbers and lines...

"Shit!" from Ben. You couldn't cure him—or Sal; and
there wasn't a miracle, they'd screwed the first run, the
second and the third, but damn, Meg thought with half a
neuron to spare, it felt better of a sudden... wasn't garbage
she was screening, it was starting to shape itself—

Objective wasn't *there*, God, intelligence gaffe—

Time to sweat. Ben was on it, logicking his way for the
current location. Dek said, "What the hell?" and Ben
confirmed a fire-zone. Virtual ordnance blasted out into
virtual reality and she figured—yes!

"Got it, got it, got it—"

"Watch that mother!"

Fan of junk in the carrier path. Dek repositioned and gave
Sal the window on a roll to the main objective, and Meg

input him the latest calc in long vision, new definition to the
hostile fire-paths he was ready to see, more precise positions she was inputting to Sal and to him.

Feeling too good, too damn good, you didn't cut a rip
like that, couldn't sustain it . . .

Couldn't get overconfident, the damn sim kept throwing
them targets and you couldn't *believe* you were getting
them, effin' sim had to be playing with them . . .

Couldn't go on this way—she was the only one in the
crew who had time to worry, worry was the job description,
taking the long view, mission objective, degree of criticality,
sight and target, sight and target, priority was seen to, ride
home couldn't be this—

"Shit!"

Whole list of hits. It had felt too good all the way
through, and Dekker shook his head, looking at the outcome, all of them gathered around the table, getting the
same news. Objective achieved, path cleared, flock of
surprises locked and taken out . . .

"Too soft," Ben muttered. "Too soft, this thing. I don't
like it. It's not supposed to fall down like this . . ."

Dekker rocked his chair on its hinge, propped a knee
against the table and surveyed his crew, the chart-table with
its windowed displays—not the stuff they'd worked with in
the station, not the hard plastic chairs and the scrub-boards
and the antique display system: anything they wanted, Porey
said, and for himself he still had crises of disbelief.

And moments of slipping reality—like this one, that
showed him faces he knew with reactions that just weren't
wrong . . . Pete and Elly and Falcone riding in the cockpit
with them an hour ago, if he wanted to be spooked about it;
but that *wasn't* really what had happened: the carrier had
that tape lab down the corridor, the way the carrier had a lot
else it hadn't let out, and his crew spent hours there, but
they didn't drug deep anymore, they didn't need to, that was
the story from the tape-techs. Done was done and their

sessions were simply reaffirming the synched reactions, making sure—Meg said—they didn't pick up any bad habits in live practice. . . .

Live practice. Hell of a way to word it, considering.

They ran the sims in the prototype itself up to four hours a day, its V-HUD and instruments linked realtime to the carrier boards and the sims library, thanks to what Ben called the effin' difference between the UDC's EIDAT and the Fleet Staatentek. Ben seemed personally vindicated in that—what it all meant, he wasn't sure, but it ran.

And they did, not the first time, damned sure, the screw-up had been what Meg called egregious and Sal called words he'd never heard. Until, this sim-run . . .

This run, he looked at the result and the fact Ben had psyched that relocated target right and laid the probability fan right *over* the son of a bitch, dead center—that was a fluke, but Ben swore he'd had a good hunch—which was what Elly had used to say. Same words. That was a spook-out, too; but it was another fluke. The cockpit wasn't haunted and his crew didn't see spooks in the mirror. He slept with Meg with no illusions it was Pete Fowler, hell if, Meg would say. You didn't confuse one with the other . . .

And that still wasn't what worried him. It was what Ben said, it wasn't supposed to fall down this easy. They were out here on no other reason than keeping *him* away from the media, he told himself that once a day and he managed to relax and worry about Mitch and Almarshad, who were the ones in jeopardy—*still* catching glitches; and the crew who was dogging it and trying to come up from scratch and a couple of total disasters pulled a hundred percenter?

He'd thought he knew the answers, he'd eased off, kicked back, taken it for granted he was just going to steer while everything was going to go to hell and they started handing him stuff that fit together.

Adrenaline had come up, hold-it-steady had become tracking-on, this last run; he was still hyped and on his edge and he hadn't been this alive down to the nerve-ends since—

Since he'd screwed the sim. You knew all along something was wrong with our set-up, Ben kept insisting. And by comparison, now it wasn't wrong, and he couldn't sit still and couldn't help remembering how it felt to be a hundred percent On, and right . . .

With a crew he *cared* about, dammit, more than he'd ever cared about human beings in his life, and too damn many deaths and too many lost partners, with a chance to make runs *they'd* plotted, the way the UDC hadn't let them do it, and that perfect run lying on the table saying . . . Can't do it twice. Complete fluke. Can't pull it off again . . . System can't be that perfect. Something's wrong.

His gut was in knots and his suspicion began to be, in two blinks of an eye and the work of an overhyped brain, that it could be working because his team had come in with miner-experience, something the lofty Shepherd types with their fancy tech hadn't had, or—

Or the tape off his dead partners worked, and Porey *hadn't* given up when they'd had to downgrade the crew to basics—it wasn't basics anymore. They'd either pushed the sim to the limit—or it had lied to them. And he didn't put that past Porey, he didn't put anything political past Porey, if he wanted to prove something to some committee in charge of finance . . .

They were on the damned *list*, that was what, they always had been, that son of a bitch had jerked him sideways and just kept going with his crew. What was it, a confidence-building exercise? Another damned psych-out for more damn political reasons? He felt sick at his stomach.

"You all right, Dek?"

He looked at Meg, realized everybody was looking at him.

"Dek," Ben said, "you aren't spooking on us, are you?"

He shook his head solemnly. "It's August eighth, Ben."

"Huh?" Sal said. Meg frowned. But Ben said;

"It better be, Moonbeam. It had effin' better be."

* * *

"Yes, sir," Graff said, at the table, hands folded, looking straight at two very anxious senators and a busy background of senatorial aides. There was a committee, inevitably if there was a glitch, there was a committee, thank God currently meeting at Sol One, in the comfort of class 1 accommodations: it wanted answers and this was the forerunner, the shockwave.

"*Why* is a junior lieutenant left in command of this base? What in *hell* does your base commander think he's doing taking that carrier out? We give you the authority you ask for, and immediately the program goes to hell in a handbasket, while the officer in charge removes a carrier and declares he's going to test, without notifying the UDC or the Joint Committee, *with* a highly controversial figure aboard, conveniently unavailable to an ongoing investigation, while a distorted version of the whole damned training program leaks to the media? What kind of circus are you running here?"

His stomach was in knots. He missed certain of the references. Demas and Saito had advised him certain things to say, certain points to make, the direction he should go with these men. But Demas and Saito didn't know one truth he knew. Neither did Porey and neither did the captain.

"Sir," he began on that track, "with all respect, I deny that the breach was in our Security."

"Are you suggesting the UDC leaked it? What about Dekker's phone call to Sol One? What about other phone calls from other Fleet personnel?"

He hoped to hell there wasn't a recorder going. "Let me explain, sir. Fleet personnel are contained in a security cocoon within the former administrative apparatus. Our personnel are issued cards which do not work with civilian accesses, which can't access BaseCom or the internal phone system without going through FleetCom, which is physically aboard the carriers, if there were anyone outside this facility for them to call, nearer the Belt. The one exception was Dekker, who—'' They began to interrupt and he kept going. ''—who made his only call to his mother in my office, on my authorization, and I recorded the call in its entirety in case any question arose about that contact. The UDC system is run through BaseCom, which is linked by other means to station central. Those are the principal routes information can take. There is the shuttle, and there is contact between human beings who can walk from one place to another. If information flowed from this facility, it took one of those routes.''

On which they had evidence, except a member of a Fleet unit also had accesses he wasn't supposed to have ... that Fleet Command didn't know about ... which, if he confessed it now, was damning to him, to the Fleet, to Dekker's crew at minimum, to the Fleet's credibility and their support from the legislative committee, at worst.

While at least at some level the UDC and potentially the legislature knew about Pollard's security clearance—and might possibly know he'd somehow retained system access—if Pollard himself weren't under higher orders.

God, he should never have held his information source secret from Porey. Never.

''I suggest you use the channels you have to find *out* what's going on, lieutenant. *Somebody* in your command with real authority had better get his ass into this station, find out where the leak is and get this program off the evening news. You're public as *hell*, reporters are demanding to come over here in herds, we've got a very fragile coalition that worked hard to give you what you asked for, and let me tell you very bluntly, lieutenant, if anything goes wrong with this rumored upcoming *test* you've lost the farm. You cannot disavow another failure, your captains can't pass the buck to junior officers. Do you understand that? Am I talking to anyone who remotely understands the political realities of this situation?''

''*Yes*, sir, I do understand.'' No temper. ''I am thirty-eight unapparent years of age, sir, and older than that as you count time. I was in command of this base during the last hearings, I was lately the director of personnel in this program, I *am* currently in charge of this facility and the testing program, and of the investigation, and we do have an answer, at least to what happened to Jamil Hasseini and his crew." He reached in his pocket and held up a yellow plastic washer. "This caused the so-called accident."

He had their attention. At least.

"How?"

"Operations records showed a hangup in an attitude control. This plastic washer turned up to block the free operation of the yoke. In a null-*g* facility, you may know, maintenance has to be extremely careful to log and list and check every part, down to the smallest screws and washers, that they take into the facility. These are experienced null-*g* workers. We don't know by those records how long this little part has been there—whether it was there from the time the pod was assembled and it by total accident floated over a course of years undetected into the absolutely most critical position it could take in the control system—or whether it was placed there recently."

"Sabotage, in other words."

"We view it as more than suspicious. Paul Dekker was assigned to that pod."

"So we've heard."

"How much have you heard?"

"Maybe you'd damn well better tell us what there is to hear. We hear Dekker was assigned there and pulled at the last minute. Again. Why? How?"

"By my order, as chief of personnel. I made a routine final check on the crew stats: they were coming out of a period of orientation and lab sims. I felt we might be rushing it, in terms of fatigue levels. A stand-down under those circumstances is routine. Routine—except that this was the time his replacement crew was going into sims with him. Except that the same individuals we suspect of sabotage had access to that area. Civilian employees: Dekker's given a positive ID on one of them as guilty of assault in the last so-called accident. We're talking about deliberate sabotage and premeditated murder committed on Dekker—"

"With what motive?"

"I doubt it was personal. We've two employees of Lendler Corp under surveillance. We don't know all their contacts, yet. But they had access on both occasions."

Frowns. "Can you prove anything?"

"We're developing a case. But you see the problem we've been working against."

"Your security is supposed to be on top of things. People come and go where they like here, is that the way it works?"

"People with security clearances, yes, sir—in this case clearances granted by the UDC, interviewing people on Earth, where we have no screening apparatus. We're reviewing the systems, and the clearances, but there are 11338 civilians on B Dock, hired by the UDC and overseen by various offices. We're naturally giving Lendler Corp a higher priority in our review, but that doesn't mean information can't go out of here through another route."

"Meanwhile Dekker is unavailable."

"He is unavailable."

"And you have no proof of this sabotage."

"Their access. Dekker's testimony. The washer. Circumstantial evidence placing them in the area."

"You know what that's worth."

"A good reason not to let out what we know or make charges we can't substantiate. We're gathering evidence."

"Meanwhile these purported saboteurs are at work on this station."

"Yes, sir. Of necessity, they are."

"And Paul Dekker's out there on that carrier. —Is he in any way involved in the upcoming test?"

"Certainly he'll be in observation and advisement. All

crews have that assignment during a run. Whether he'll be assigned the run or not—that's dependent on evaluations.''

"He *can't* be the one to take the controls. That name can't be prominent in this program. —Have you *no* comprehension?''

"Senator, political decisions in crew choice caused the last disaster to this program. And I can't believe I'm hearing this all over again.''

"I can't believe what I'm hearing from the junior command officer on this base. I can't believe your persistence in putting this man into the glare of publicity. Let me make it clear to you, lieutenant, careers are going down in flames if there's a second disaster. We've backed you, we've delivered votes in the JLC, we've patched together the coalition that gives you what you asked for and damn you, you serve us up Dekker for a witness to sabotage and Dekker for the representative of your program, and leak to the press, while you're 'developing a case' you daren't bring to court. Are you aware what's happening on Earth? Are you *aware* of the fire-bombing at the EC headquarters? Are you aware of the bill pending in committee?''

"The extradition bill? Yes, I'm aware of it. And both acts of sabotage were aimed at him—by people who didn't even know him. This is no personal grudge on the part of the saboteurs, senator, it's politically motivated murder, the same as the substitution that killed his crew was politically motivated, by people who may not have known where their orders came from. Now we have another coalition, as I understand it, part of which is working for this bill, but somebody else clearly doesn't want him in court—somebody in a position to obtain security clearances wants him dead, and if we break the Lendler case into the open right now, it's going to be a string that reels more and more information into the spotlight—it's as explosive as the Dekker case and for identical reasons. *That's* why we haven't expelled these individuals. We know where they are. We suspect who they work for.''

Temper. Saito had warned him. He got it under control. He faced the senators and the busily note-taking aides with a cold stare, and saw anger and consternation on both senatorial faces.

"I also want to know," he said, "how this exact information about Dekker's being pulled from the sim got to the Joint Committee. Was it out of Stockholm?"

Silence for a moment. The other senator said, harshly, "Through the media, lieutenant. Not the way we prefer our briefings."

"Haven't you the power to find out those sources?"

"No. We haven't. There are *laws*."

"To cover illegal activity? I find that incredible."

"We want to know who made this decision to test. *Is* there a test? Or is this whole maneuver a cover for this Dekker person?"

"There assuredly will be a test."

"With Dekker's crew?"

"Possibly."

"Let me tell you what this looks like to us. It looks like a do or die proposition, a harebrained go-for-broke damned stupid risk, on your senior captain's perception that the Fleet's losing prestige in Europe and your facility here is shut down! We can't *get* you another ship to wreck, lieutenant, we can't continue our support in the face of this stupid risk of lives and equipment!"

Senior captain? Mazian? "The program is *not* shut down, sir. If you perceive that, you've been misled."

"The simulators are wrecked, you're vulnerable to sabotage, you're sending out crews who aren't ready—"

"No, sir. I'm delighted to report that all necessary equipment is functioning. There's been no hiatus in the program. All our crews are at work, including the UDC teams, integrated with ours."

A silence. Doubt, curiosity, and deep offense. He had his own doubts, of these men Saito called essential and friendly and to be trusted with the truth, these fools who wouldn't so much as talk to Saito, because *Saito* wasn't a command officer and *Saito* wasn't in charge.

"This doesn't agree with our information."

"I hope I have better news, then, sir. Our crews are keeping schedules, we are bringing our other senior crews, including UDC personnel, up to mission-ready; and when they're ready they will go. Officially, I know nothing about the upcoming test. I won't know the time until I'm told. But assuredly it will go. And any media attention to this facility will find everything in operation."

A modicum of respect, perhaps. A reassessment, a reevaluation what situation they were dealing with, certainly.

"Maybe you'd better explain yourself, lieutenant. With what equipment? With this *tape* you've come up with? Are we brainwashing our crews?"

"Crews at mission ready have to practice daily to maintain those skills. With the damage to the sims, Fleet Command opted to use the Hellburner prototype, patched to the shipboard simulators."

"When was that authorized?"

"The patch?"

"The shipboard facility. The chamber."

"Not chambers, sir, nothing like. I'm not privy to the details, but this is equipment we brought with us into the system, that we regularly use. Combat crews on stand-by also have to practice, virtually daily, to keep their edge. We certainly can't stop a carrier's operations or use its physical self for exercises. Naturally we have the equipment."

"Then why in *hell* haven't we been using it all along? Why spring it now? Why this whole damned, accident-riddled program?"

"Politics, sir." He hoped he kept all satisfaction off his face. "As the situation was told to me, we were ordered at the outset, over our captains' explicit protests, to submit our trainees to the UDC Systems Test protocols, to their aptitude criteria, their rules and their existing equipment during testing of the prototypes. As I believe, there was a major policy battle over that point in the JLC, and we lost.''

Total quiet in the room. The clicking of the aides' keys had stopped.

"You never said explicitly," the other senator put in, "that you *had* the equipment."

"There was some fear," Graff said, "that the UDC might use its position to demand control of that equipment. In a situation in which we are not to this hour solely in control of communications system accesses, in which we've had sabotage, attempted murder of our personnel, assignment of flight personnel on criteria purely ideological in nature—plus the security breach—we are trusting your discretion on this point and we trust there will not be another leak. What we train on is a very dearly held piece of information. If our enemy knows what equipment we have—we are, in the vernacular, screwed. We protested, through every channel we trusted, that the station facilities here are a hundred fifty years old, with maintenance problems that eat up funds for improvements we asked for. The decision to put the rider training into the hands of the UDC, to use Lendler's data conversion system for the pods in the first place—was as I understand, a purely political decision. We asked to review the software. We were not trusted to make that input. *We . . . were . . . not . . . trusted.*''

Another silence. An angry silence on both sides. But it wasn't productive anger. Graff shifted back in his chair. "I'm not a diplomat. My captain left other officers here who are. But they aren't command track by UDC rules. So I pass their word on to you. As for the operational crews of all the ships—you gave us a requirement to have carriers on standby to defend this system—and I can tell you with absolute certainty I would be grossly irresponsible to take that carrier's controls after months of total stand-down. We're in constant training, all ops crews and staffs are in training during any stand-down; and the UDC has never provided carrier control sims. It's certainly no secret."

"Where did you obtain this other equipment?" Anger. Still, a genuine offense, and he answered with careful exactness:

"I haven't been on that carrier and I honestly don't know the source."

"Where would you expect that carrier to obtain it?"

"The black market."

"Whose black market?"

The question seemed naive. "The one out *there,* sir. Outside this solar system. There's very good equipment available."

"I find this outrageous. *Union* equipment? Is that story true?"

"We have manufacturers. We're not primitives looking for Earth's expertise, my God, senator. We *provided* the designs that are making your corporations money."

'Are you using Union equipment?''

"Senator, we don't look for the label. If it works, if it's better, we use it. If we can get our hands on Unionside equipment, we're delighted, and they'd be extremely upset, if they knew it. They don't want us using their programs."

"Are you creating tape?"

"Of course. They're creating tape over in the UDC. In TI. They're creating tape in Houston, for physical rehab patients—"

"You *know* what we're asking. These people with their fingers on the fire button—are you saying, lieutenant, that the tape training your crews are being given is being adjusted to the personality of some single individual, and among those individuals may be Paul Dekker?"

"Physical reaction tape doesn't affect personality. That's a complete misapprehension."

"It's a public perception. Truth doesn't matter. Public perception does! You're going to use a rab agitator, a man linked to riots in Bonn and Geneva—"

He held his voice steady and his hands from clenching. "A young man who knows nothing about riots in Bonn, who was qualified for a pilot's license before his enlistment, which one would hope the ECSAA doesn't do for criminals—"

"Oh, come on, lieutenant! The ECSAA licensed every miner in the Belt!"

"Dekker was a pusher pilot at Sol One, in your own space, by your certifications. He's an outstanding young officer who's distinguished himself by his work and his dedication to this program. And if he meets mission criteria, he will be a source for training material. Skill—"

"He's too politically sensitive. It's already too public. God! Why do you people persist in shoving this man in our faces? Are you actively *challenging* the legislature?"

He shook his head. "Your creativity, sir, with all respect. Any choice made on political and not operational grounds reduces this ship's chances of survival. If this test fails, the EC has no alternative and no further resources to offer us. I'm authorized to tell you we will have no choice at that point but to pull out entirely and abandon our defense of the motherworld. That's precisely where it stands."

"Dammit!"

"Yes, sir. I agree with you. But no one but our predecessors had a choice."

Things kept on surreal, so far as Dekker was concerned, time-trip to a place he'd never been, and the little things got to you: the moment in the shower you couldn't remember where you were: the split-second during mission prep the whole scene seemed part of the station, not the carrier. Nothing felt safe, or sure. You ran the prep, you ran the sims, you scribbled away on your plans, you ran the sims, and every once in a while they gave everybody a day down and you could put your feet up, play cards and enjoy a light beer, because the carrier pilots were using the equipment, but the whole thing cycled endlessly.

You could believe at times you were in the war, the other side of the Hinder Stars. Or in Sol Station's carpeted corporate heart, where orderlies served you food you didn't even recognize, arranged in pretty patterns on the plates. Your bed turned up made, your clothes turned up clean and the bar when it was open served free drinks. Wasn't so bad a life, you could get to thinking. But debt for this had to come due, either to Porey or to God, or to somebody.

Hit two hundred-percenters, back to back, and he started thinking, the sims are lying to us. They're jerking us around, trying to give us confidence—

They want their damn theory to work, they're targeting the tape they're giving us at the exercises, that's why we're getting scores like that, that's why it's not happening to the other teams—

Some damned fool in an office somewhere could believe a lie and put us out there, when it's all lab stuff that looks good . . .

"Dek, what are you guys having for breakfast?" Call from the end of the narrow room, down by the display.

Damn, they'd posted the scores.

Lot of guys went and had a look. "Hell," he groaned, but it wasn't ragging this time, it was a rueful shake of heads and a:

"Dek, looks like you got the run."

"Not yet," he said to Almarshad.

"No, I mean you got the run. You're posted. Mitch is back-up one, we're two, half a point between us."

Blood went to his feet. He sat there, with his crew, who weren't celebrating, who just looked at him; and got up as Mitch and Almarshad came over and congratulated him, not looking happy, not taking it badly either. It was too serious for that, too damned uncertain for that.

"Not a thorough surprise," Mitch said. "Sounds like we're headed for girl-tape for sure." Ragging it a little close to the edge, that. But he took Mitch's offered hand, and Meg let him lay a congratulatory hand on her shoulder after. "Kady. Class job, you guys. Sincerely."

Meg looked as if she'd swallowed something strange. Sal just looked smugly satisfied, and gave Mitch a kiss on the cheek.

Ben said, "I can't believe this. I can't believe this. What am I doing here?"

CHAPTER

18

HIS mother had said often enough, You don't care, Paul, you just don't care about people, there's got to be something basic missing in you—

Maybe there was. Maybe he didn't feel things other people did. Maybe machines were all he came equipped to understand, all that was ever going to make sense to him, because he couldn't stay away from them . . . he honestly couldn't live without doing this . . .

He couldn't turn it loose. When he was away from the ship, he could think reasonably about it, and know that it was a cold way to be, and that if he could be something different and he could be back in the Belt with people he cared about, doing nothing but mining, he could be happy— he'd *been* happy there; he could have been again, in the right company . . .

But when he got up here in null-*g*, in the rider loft, with the four Hellburner locks staring him in the face, and the ship out there, behind number 1, then everything was different, every value and priority was revised. The ship was different, every value and priority was revised. The ship was a presence here. Was waiting to be alive; and he was, in a way he wasn't in the whole rest of his life. He was scared down in the gravitied quarters, scared out of his reason, and he realized he'd gotten everyone who cared about him in one hell of a mess; but up here—

Up here he knew at least *why* he'd made the choices he had, right or wrong, he knew why he'd kept going, and why the pods made him afraid—just that nowhere else was this. Nowhere else had the feel this did. It didn't altogether cure being scared, but it put the fear behind him.

This was where he would have been on that day, dammit, except for Tanzer, except for Wilhelmsen being put in the wrong place, at the wrong time . . . it felt as if his whole life had gone off-line since then, and he was just now picking up again where it should have been, with the people he should have had: time that had frozen on him, was running again, the mission was in his pocket, and right now the only thing he was honestly afraid of up here was being pulled from the mission again—

But nobody in command would mess with him—not now. It wasn't Tanzer in command. He was too valuable. He was somebody, finally, that people couldn't shove aside, when all through his life people had been trying, and they couldn't do that again. If he did this—if he lived through it—

If he made good on everything he'd promised.

"Dekker."

Porey's voice, echoing over the speaker, making his heart jump.

"Sir?"

"Mission dump has gone to your files. We have incoming."

Cold hit his gut, raw panic negated every reasoning. It couldn't happen. It wouldn't happen, it wasn't true . . .

"I said incoming, Dekker. Get your ass into library! Fast!"

He grabbed a new grip on the zipline for the lift and hit the inner lift wall, *damn* the drilled reaction, he didn't believe it, damn, he didn't believe it. *"We're not betraying position,"* the voice from the speakers said. *"We're allowing forty minutes, that's all we can allow, for library access, plot, and confirm. Get with it."*

"You're lying! Sir! This is a test run, this is the damn *test,* you don't have to pull this on us!"

Silence from the lift speaker. Lift crashed into the frame, jolted him and the whole compartment around to plus 1 *g,* and he caught a grip on the rail.

"Damn you!" he yelled at the incommunicative com. "Damn you to hell, commander, —*sir!* Where's this incoming?"

But nothing answered him.

"I swear to you it wasn't our guys," Villy said on the way to the officers' conference room, to a meeting Graff would as soon have skipped. "That's official from the colonel. He didn't leak it, nobody on staff did that he can trace. That's what he wants me to say."

"What do *you* say?" Graff asked.

"He's not lying." Villy didn't sound offended by the question. Villy's eyes, crinkled around the edges with a lot of realtime years, were honest and clear as they always had been. You wanted to believe in Alexandro Villanueva the way you wanted to believe in sanity and reason in the universe. But Villy quoted Tanzer at him and it was suddenly Villanueva's own self Graff began to worry about, now, about the man who, over recent weeks, he'd worked with as closely and as cooperatively as he worked with his own staff—sorting out the tempers, the egos, the simple differences in protocols: they'd mixed the staff and crews in briefings and in analysis sessions, they'd given alcohol permissions in rec on one occasion, holding the marine guards in reserve—and nobody'd been shot, nobody'd been taken to the brig, and no chairs had left the floor. More than that, they had a remarkable sight ahead of them in the hall, that was Rios and Wojcak in UDC fatigues and Pauli in

Fleet casuals and station-boots, engaged in conversation that involved a clipboard waved violently about.

No combat. Sanity. Cooperation, if a thin one. There was a secret, highly illegal betting pool going among the crews, odds on *which* crew was going to draw the test run, and a sizable pot, from what Fleet Police said, the UDC crews leaning heavily toward solid, by-the-book Almarshad and the Fleet tending to split between Mitchell and Almarshad and no few still betting on Dekker as the long shot. He hadn't taken the action on that pool that regulations demanded; Villy hadn't, more remarkable, Tanzer hadn't, if Tanzer knew, which he personally doubted—Tanzer didn't know everything that was going on these days, Villy directly admitted there were topics he didn't bring up with Tanzer, and it was too much to hope that Tanzer had learned anything about dealing with the Shepherds or changed his style of command. It was Villy's discretion he leaned to—had been leaning to it maybe more than he should have. Maybe he'd only been naive, looking too much for what he hoped and too little for the long years Tanzer had built up a network in this place.

Fact was, same as he'd told the committee, there were too many chances for leaks, too many contractors, too many technicians, too many station maintenance personnel with relatives in Sol One or, God knew, in Buenos Aires or Paris. It was worth their jobs to talk, the workers knew that, they'd signed the employment agreements, but they were human beings and they had personal opinions, not always discreetly.

Shuttle was coming in—approaching dock. They might be rid of the senators, but they had reporters incoming, FleetCom had broken the news of the impending test. The senators had no wish to get caught here, they were packing to leave, had their last interviews with the Lendler personnel today (God hope they didn't give anything away) and the shuttle would be at least six hours in maintenance and loading, latest report.

None too soon to be rid of the lot, in his book.

"We have any new data on the hearings at One?" Villanueva asked him. "Anything from the JLC or the technical wing?"

"Nothing. Not a thing yet."

Steps behind them in the hall, rapid, as they reached the briefing room. Late arrival, Graff interpreted it, turned to glance and met an out-of-breath Trev, out of FleetCom. Evans handed him a printed note.

It said: Reporters are on the shuttle. All outbound system traffic on hold. Test is imminent.

Hell, he thought. And: Why didn't the captain warn us? FSO has to have known, FSO has to have signed the press passes . . .

"Reply, sir?"

"None I want in writing. Tell Com One I said so and what in hell. Those words. Stat."

"Yessir," Trev said, and cleared the area at max speed.

Which left Villy's frown and lifted eyebrow.

"Reporters, on the inbound shuttle," he told Villy. "The test's been announced, I don't know by whom . . . System traffic is stopped. We're stuck with the shuttle, the senators, and the reporters."

Villy's look couldn't be a lie. "They've been inbound for three damned *days!* This isn't a leak, this is a damned publicity set-up! What kind of game are you guys running over at FSO?"

"That's what I'm asking FleetCom. Bloody *hell,* what are they doing to us?"

"Damn mess," Meg muttered, in the ready room, looking at the lighted plot-screen—Dek was a bundle of nerves, holding to the hand-grip beside her and memorizing that chart with the only drug-training he'd ever had, the bit that helped you focus down and retain like crazy. Ben was swearing because he hadn't got his specific numbers out of carrier Nav yet, Sal was talking to the ordnance clerk; and

Meg muttered her own numbers to voice-comp, while suit-up techs tugged and pulled at her in intimate places. You didn't even do that basic thing for yourself, you just memmed charts fast as you could and talked to the systems chiefs and techs who you hoped to God had done their job.

The helmet came down over her head, and other hands twisted the seal. 360° real-HUD came active, voice-link did. She evoked her entry macro, that prepped her boards long-distance, dumped her touch, her patterns, her mem-marks on the plot-screen fire-path to the Hellburner systems.

Mitch's crew and Almarshad's were in flight control, two beats of argument between them whether it could possibly be real, whether they might actually have a realspace system entry launched at high v from far out; or whether intelligence reports foretold something about the drop in—the consensus was test, set-up, but *they* couldn't take it as a test run, didn't dare believe the ordnance that would come at them was anything but real. The sketchy fire-track was running right past Earth's moon, not the kind of thing Sol System traffic control was going to like, and that meant a wide-open track with a shot at Earth that if they didn't get a fast intercept on that incoming ship—the doomsday scenario: they could lose the whole motherwell in less than ten minutes, that was what shaped up on their data. Billions of people. All life on earth. The enemy wouldn't *do* that. They were human beings . . .

But life in the Belt and the gossip from Fleet instructors argued there were minds out there more different than you ever wanted to meet. And you could never, ever bet on them doing the logical—

Siren went off, the board and take-hold. "Hell!" Ben cried, because they were going, there was no more time, the carrier was going to hit the mains and the next input they got was going to be off carrier ops, the carrier's longscan/com team that was their data-supply and their situation monitor, them and the back-up teams doing *her* job for the sixty-minus seconds it was going to take them to board and belt.

She grabbed the dismount line behind Dek, in crew-entry order, hindmost, and hung on as the door slammed wide and the line meshed with the gears, hell of a jerk on the arm. You held on, was all, as the singing line aimed you for the mounting bars at the hatch, one, two, three, four, tech lines ringing empty, the Hellburner's tech hatch open, but receiving no one. Carrier technical crew shouted good wishes at them as they shot past and one after the other hit the stop, pile-up of hand-grips—inertia carried them in—she hit the cushions last, heard the hatches shut when she flipped the toggle, both ports, confirm on the seal by on-panel telltales as she was snapping the only manual belt; second toggle and they went ops-com, linked with the carrier, sending and receiving a blitz of electronic information. "We're go," Dek said, and instantaneously the carrier mains cut in with a solidity that shoved them harder than the pods ever had, 10+ in a brutal, backs-downward acceleration.

Carrier was outputting now, making EM noise in a wavefront an enemy would eventually intercept in increasing Doppler effect, and to confuse their longscan they were going to pull a pulse, half-up to FTL and abort the bubble, on a heading for the intercept zone—that was the scary part. That was the time, all sims aside, that the theoretical high v became real, .332 light, true hellride, with herself for the com-node that integrated the whole picture.

They tranked you down for jump. They didn't for this move. They told you what it was going to be, they pulled disorientations and sensory assaults, and learned the mem-techniques from the starship crew, and hoped you could get the threads back when you came out—but meanwhile you just kept talking to the computer and the carrier and moving your markers with the joystick, laying the strike and the strategy as if you were seeing it tamely on the light-table instead of on monitors, with numbers and grids floating in glowing colors. Reality became hyper-extended vision, into mathematical futures, chaos of nature, two intersecting presence-cones of human action that had to narrow at a proximity to Luna that was truly harrowing.

Hard to breathe. The flight-suit squeezed the ribs in efficient pulses, oxygen flowed—damned sure not the pod this time. This was real—this was—

Moment that the brain skipped . . . moment that they weren't—anywhere, and all the data left the brain void. A voice said, like God, *Stand by sep, Hellburner;* she recalled that procedure, scanned her crew's LS, TAC and STAT data glowing gold at the upper periphery of her midrange vision and said, mechanically as any machine, "Sep go, that's go, go . . ."

Bang!

"We have absolutely identical interests," Villy said to the gathered reporters, while Graff folded his arms and leaned against the wall by the door. Captain Villy rested elbows against the podium and said in that voice that had to be believed: "Let me explain where the UDC stands. Yes, there've been problems in the past. As a test crew, in this facility, we've seen ideas that worked and we've seen ideas that didn't—we've worked with a lot of bright-eyed young pilots and techs that came in here all impatient to be trained in equipment we ran when it didn't have all the buttons they put on it—who never gave a damn about what we knew so long as the buttons worked. That's the truth. And I'll tell you, having the future operational crews shoved in here to be part of the testing procedures—that's been a hell of an adjustment for us—but the Fleet did call this one right. The physiological demands of this equipment are hell; and the crews that can fly this baby are going to be so scarce in the general population they're probably going to give some of us a chance to be honest working crew."

Tidbit of real News. Graff pricked up his ears, saw Optex record lights like so many blinking eyes among the reporters.

"They say the other guys have to grow 'em in vats, and

eighteen years from now we're going to see their hand-raised clone pilots in the cockpit. That eighteen years is the lead we have, because they tell us the merchanters that won't take our side, won't take the Union side either. Union doesn't have the insystem crews we do—they're a lot more mechanized, their mining equipment's state of the art, a lot of robots. Their miners sit on big ore-collectors, they don't have our antique equipment and consequently they never developed the pool of experienced insystem crews like we drew in from our asteroid belt—''

"What about this tape?" a reporter asked, out of turn. "What about this Union mind-tape?"

"It's not Union," Graff said from near the door, and drew an immediate concentration of steady red lights. "It's ours, and it works only on the reflexes, a glance left or right at the panels, mathematical formulae and routines, nothing as organized thought or attitudes . . . It covers the same kind of memorizations you do in school—'' He trusted they did such things in schools. These reporters were Earth's equivalent of com and he doubted they had any experience in common. He wanted Saito down here, but Saito was on the carrier, where FleetCom with a test proceeding mandated she be; Demas was God knew where—Demas had taken refuge in Ops, he was willing to lay bets . . .

Com said in his ear: *"Mission is go-for with Dekker. Rider is sepped. We're coming up in station systems."*

"I copy," he told the bone-mike. "I'm on my way to mission control."

Reporters were still looking at him. Optex lenses were all turned his way, and Villy was watching him from the podium.

"Mission's away," he said, removed the uncomfortable security com from his ear, and added, with a certain suicidal satisfaction, "Team leader *is* Dekker," and watched all chaos erupt.

"All *right!*" Ben sounded finally satisfied with the numbers and Dekker gave a little breath of relief—a relief that

Ben probably wouldn't understand. Smug, that was Ben when he relaxed; but Ben wasn't smug now, he was On and anxious, all the way.

"We just keep running quiet a while, Dek-boy. A real hold-steady here, minimum profile, just keep us out of their acquisition long as we can—carrier's gone up ahead, going to fire a decoy and brake hard."

The carrier's vane-config showed clear, that was the immediate worry on this maneuver—the carrier was going to pull an axis roll: a thing the size of some space stations was going to do a total reverse, pass them again at close range, rotate a second time and tail them at a distance . . .

"This is a set-up," Meg complained, "we got too many numbers on this, Ben. It's got to be a set-up . . ."

"Dekker a murderer?" Graff said, tracking past the spex windows of mission control to the profile screens and the working teams and his own trainees at the boards. They'd established the reporters in the viewing area, gotten the senators a secure spot in a VIP observation point, and on the displays in mission control a situation was unfolding neither party yet comprehended. "No. He happens to be the survivor of three documented attempts on his life, two of which put him in hospital, one of which killed Cory Salazar."

Not the loudest voice, but the one he chose to hear: "That contradicts what Councillor Salazar charges—"

Probability fans were changing color on the screens, rapidly narrowing. "It is, nevertheless, the truth. The evidence against Paul Dekker was fabricated by the identical agencies responsible for covering up a strike-breaking police action that took seventeen other lives documented in 2304 sworn affidavits and complaints."

"From Belters?" Bias dripped from the question, and sharpened focus and temper for a split-second.

"From civilian and military eyewitnesses and victims living and dead in Earth Company records. There are *no* grounds for the charges against Paul Dekker—they're old history, investigated and officially dismissed when the agencies that made the charges were dissolved by legal action for corruption, wrongful death, and labor abuses. As for the culpable parties, they were relieved of command and stripped of their licenses, but unfortunately that was the *only* action taken. I suggest you ask Ms. Salazar why she's never named them in her pending suit.''

''Why didn't she?''

''I couldn't speculate on her motives.''

Ten and twenty questions at once. Riot, as reporters a moment ago drifting along the spex wall suddenly elbowed each other to get Optex pickups to the fore. *Let* the Company raise hell, let the Fleet ship him to the battle zone— please God, ship him to the zone, away from reporters, cameras, Edmund Porey, and self-serving senators demanding dinner in the VIP observation area.

Then someone shouted, from the hall, ''They're releasing the separation footage!'' and bedlam surged in the other direction, reporters trying to get into mission control, jamming in the doorway. Two stayed to ask:

''Who authorized this test, lieutenant?''

''Not in my need-to-know, I'm afraid. Insystem traffic near Luna shows lift delayed for thirty minutes on the monitor up there. That has to come from very high levels.''

''Who can authorize it?''

''Sol One Stationmaster, for the lowest level.''

''If—''

The barrage of questions and dicing of information kept up. He stood there with his gut in knots. It was go now, no likely recall of the rider. Mission parameters were showing on the screens, dopplered transmission from the carrier, and from the rider, via the carrier. Course was laid for intercept from the ecliptic, of a zenith system entry shielded from the carrier by Earth's own security zone . . .

Worst-case scenario in system defense—an attack coming into Earth's vicinity, and not a damned thing on the transmissions to say the case wasn't real . . . worse, there was an incoming showing on the one screen his eye knew for real-case. Something *was* inbound or they'd gotten insystem traffic management to lie, and it didn't. Ever.

Ship felt good, felt *good* all the way, zero no-calls and zero glitches on the boards. Clean, wide sep from the carrier and for a while they would keep the carrier's rate inside its shields, pretending to the enemy that separation was still to come. Attitude assemblies were all answering test-calls. Dekker lost himself in the internal config-confirms, in the numbers that were the immediate future—Meg was there to tell him where he was, Ben was shaping further future, and Sal was working up the fire-path, armaments taking program, talking to Meg's boards which would talk to his V-HUD when the time came. Right now body-sense was expanded into the ship, time was cut loose and independent of circumstance—the track and the fire-points were shaping up further and further into the diagrams spread in his far vision—but he was only generally aware of that: he was seeing that interval as leisurely information-building minutes diving toward a split-second hype-point, where he had to be ready to execute a sequence of immaculately timed moves to confuse the enemy, position the fire platform, and get their asses safely past a line of answering fire scarily close to Luna, with a *v* that overrode both Luna's pull— and the available energy of their own missiles.

Which was all Sal's problem.

They aren't *doing* anything, the reporters objected with increasing frustration, even anger, and Graff said, finally, with a heart going faster and faster, eyes fixed on the monitors beyond the spex panes: "Oh, yes, they are. They're maintaining output silence. The carrier's doing all the transmission, noisy as it wants to be. They launched something on either side before they braked, one's a decoy, one's the rider, and the rider doesn't want to be seen yet, that's the name of the game—even we don't know which it is, because they haven't told us and motion hasn't started."

Questions broke out, a shouted confusion.

"Yes, we have no doubt they're still conscious. See the four dots on the screen, all doing fine . . ." Trajectories were widening their perspective on the screens and one reporter noticed the obvious. "That's going straight through Luna space—is that Luna space?"

"All system traffic's suspended. The firepaths will have been cleared and safed."

"What if—"

Chatter kept up. Media seemed to abhor a thinking silence.

He watched the situation on the screens, thinking, Damn, who's feeding them their orders? But he heard no calculations emanating from FleetCom. He suspected the carrier armscomper had primed them for this—set up the incoming *and* the response: he personally suspected that anything and everything Porey did was with mirrors; but he kept his mouth shut and hoped to God no reporter got onto that question.

And the firepaths *were* damned close to Luna . . . the reporter was right, they were terrifyingly close, from the viewpoint of civilians not used to starships at entry and exit *v*—close, and with a maneuver that, if they did it—damn, it was Russell's Star, replayed—

Long, long time on a hold-steady. Easy to become hypnotized, if not for the nuisance chatter on internal com. Dekker did the small breathing exercises that kept him aware of time—nothing but freefall at fractional light, minimal signature, nothing noisy, no output at all, no input but the passive recept of the carrier and its boards that advised them things they couldn't output to see.

Couldn't prove it wasn't real, what they were receiving. You couldn't assume it, daren't assume it.

"What we're going to do imminently, Dek-boy, we're

about to do a little round the corner shot at this sumbitch. Luna's shadow's your boost point, God, I hope you get it right . . ."

"Copy that," he muttered. "Do your own job, Ben."

"Ordnance up," Sal said. "Meg. Dek, that's your plot-points, you copy?"

Dots and lines were multiplying in his midvision now, floating in space, designating essential fire-points, orientation, mass decrease. Considerable decrease: Hellburner was 90% fuel, engines, ablation surface, and ordnance.

"He's got it," Meg said. "Here we go, guys. —Initiate."

Pulse of the main engines. Missiles launched with a shock through the frame, one and two away. . . straight toward the moon. Adrenaline stretched time and distances.

"T-1," Ben was saying, calling out the major coordination points.

Second pulse, high-g RO, intermittent accel and launches directly down their backpath toward their carrier, staccato hammer of missiles away, Hellburner's mass diminishing fast.

Second RO, braces engaged. Had to hold the track with immaculate numbers—crossing the carrier firepath now, edge on, minimum profile.

"Son of a *bitch*," Ben yelled, as the emissions recept picked up launch, but their four missiles had kicked off the frame on the mark and Dekker swung into his scheduled Profile RePosition with an instant eighth less mass and a violence that blurred vision. "Track!" Ben yelled at Sal. "Track!"

"Got it, got it, got it," Sal cried, onto a steady stream of profanity, as their chaff gun opened up down the hostile firetrack straight for the incoming. "Burn it!" Ben yelled, and Dekker shoved it to +10.5 instant gs ahead, on the instant, rotated sideways as they were.

Countered. Graff watched the fire bursts, listened to the dispassionate voice of FleetCom confirm the intercept.

It looked so slow on this scale—so incredibly slow. But his heart knew the speed at which things were moving, his gut was in knots, he wanted his own hands on controls, he wanted that with every breath he took—

They were on. God, God, they were making it. So had Wilhelmsen—this early on. Another ReOrient and they were still throwing fire . . .

But, damn! the lines intersected, and of a sudden—missiles near Luna were off the scope of a sudden—

Range safety? or hostile action?

"Test stop," came over the speakers. *"The test has been terminated . . . this is FleetCom mission control . . ."*

Disaster? Graff felt cold all over. Couldn't have. The plot was still tracking.

"The incoming is confirmed as EC militia merchanter Eagle, proceeding at V to maintain effect shields against inert chaff which will not, repeat not, intersect civilian traffic. Luna-vectored ordnance was destroyed by the range safety officer. At no time was this ordnance capable of reaching the lunar surface: technical explanation will follow. The remaining ordnance is being cleared from the area by destruct commands issued by range safety. Rider ordnance trajectories have been computed as intersecting Eagle presence and moment with three major strikes, sufficient to have eliminated the incoming threat. This concludes a successful test of the Hellburner prototype. In-progress System traffic will resume ordinary operations in fifteen minutes . . ."

Impossible to hear in the spectator gallery, after that. Crews and techs inside mission control were out of their seats, pounding each other on the backs with complete disregard of uniform or gender. "Damn *on!*" Villy roared from the other side of the spectators, Optexes were going, reporters were shouting questions—a few of them loudly incensed about the apparent proximity to the moon.

God, he just let it go. Gave fragments of answers, how he felt—damned happy; had he been nervous—wanted to be *out* there, he said, all the while tracking on the screens, the celebrations, the communications from FleetCom telling Hellburner 1 there was no need to brake, the carrier was on direct intercept, and from UDC System Defense saying that lift traffic would resume in areas declared cleared, starting with alpha zone, near Earth's atmosphere.

Was it an unwarrantable risk to Luna? a reporter wanted to know. He said, tracking on the politics as well as the damned brilliant straight-line shot, "In the first place, it was never going to hit the moon. It was moving past the moon faster than it was moving toward it. By the laws of physics it absolutely couldn't hit the surface."

"If something had gone wrong with the missiles—"

"They didn't have enough fuel to reach the moon soon enough to hit it. It's absolutely impossible."

"But they could reach the carrier."

"The carrier could run into them. The range officer got it well within the safe zone. If it had failed to detonate, there were two back-up systems; and, I reemphasize, the ordnance was not infalling Luna, no more than the ship itself was. The armscomper knew exactly what she was doing."

"She," a reporter pounced on the question, but another shouted:

"Was it a successful test, when the duration was half an hour *less* than the Wilhelmsen run, at a slower speed?"

"The rider *eliminated* the threat. It had nothing left to shoot at. There's no point in continuing beyond mission accomplished."

"But could they have kept going?"

"No doubt whatsoever. And let me point out, they were slower, but their target was moving at system entry speeds. Wilhelmsen's targets were only randoms, from known fire points, nothing this real-time. But he gave us data that helped us. It wasn't a pointless sacrifice—never a pointless sacrifice." Tanzer had just shown up in mission control, Tanzer accepting handshakes of his staff, beyond the sound-damping spex, and the whole press corps was suddenly trying to figure out how to get where they weren't going to be admitted. Villy clapped him on the shoulder in passing and escaped the intercepts, while another Optex pickup arrived in his face with,

"Ms. Salazar has denounced the choice of Paul Dekker as the source of tape for the program and called for the disfranchisement of the Fleet. How do you feel about that?"

"My answer? If that incoming had been Union, that ship and that young pilot and crew would have prevented global catastrophe. A single barrage of inert matter falling on Earth at half light would create ecological disaster." Stock answer, stock material, the science people had calc'ed it years ago: he knew not a damned thing about climates, truth be told.

A reporter followed up: "Earth was not in actual danger."

"Earth was in deadly danger if that had been a Union ship. But Hellburner demonstrated its ability to deflect any such attack. Their course was right on intercept with that incoming militia ship, you can see it on the display up there. This was a live ordnance test, but nothing at any time was aimed at Earth or Luna."

"What if it went off-track?"

"That's why there are range safety officers." He didn't want to say what he suspected, that if the destruct sequences for the rider's missiles hadn't been dumped to *Eagle*'s computers by the Sol system buoy on entry, the range safety officer on the ECS4 had to have had a few extremely anxious moments once the shots went around the limb of the moon. That volley had come very close to sending the missiles out of communication with the carrier. But the crew hadn't pulled any punches. No crew could afford to think in those terms. Ever.

"Lieutenant, lieutenant, do you think—"

"Excuse me. . . ." He was getting a burst of new information off FleetCom on the screens and over the PA, and another line of comflow in his ear from Saito, saying . . .

Panic over much of Europe, assumption the test was real, public reactions yet uncertain . . . But Mazian was in front of the cameras in Bonn, with pronouncements of what a Union strike would have meant for Earth, . . . calling Paul Dekker

and his crew phenomenally skilled, heroes of Earth's own
defense forces, a combined Fleet-and-*UDC* crew...

"Good run. Still room for improvement."
Porey's voice; and Dekker wanted to tell him go to hell
for the trick they'd pulled. Destruct the ordnance, damned
right they'd had to, he'd been scared as hell they might hit a
friendly ship; but a Belter didn't *have* ordinary nerves, and
he'd not been a hundred percent convinced until they'd
gotten the congratulatory communication from FleetCom
that it had been the scheduled test.
Didn't know what to do with the nerves now, things were
still dragging along, interminable time stretch: not so hard a
job, this run, but that was the problem, wasn't it? You didn't
get the hellish repositions and redirects when you were working with Ben and Sal when your co-pilot was thinking ahead
of the pilot's problems so he didn't get called on for those
moves—only *one* of those shifts he'd had to rip, they'd hyped
the *v* sideways hard after Sal's best shot and Ben was still
muttering about realspace feeling real, and soreness setting in.
Meg said, "We're in the pocket, right in the pocket, now,
Dek, you don't have to do a thing til the bow-shock.
—Incidentally, compliments from Capt. Kreshov, on *Eagle*,
he says it was a damn pretty job, his words. —Thank you,
sir. The team appreciates the compliment. —We got a drink
offer from his armscomper..."
"Sounds good," Ben said. "Yeah!" from Sal.
Himself, he wasn't highly verbal, just tracking on the
approaching carrier—Ben decided it was a frigging party, all
of a sudden, Sal and Meg evidently had; and he could
strangle Ben. They weren't through until they'd been through
the realtime shields, nothing virtual about it this time:
carrier coming up like a bat behind them, Baudree's showing out, no different than the rider jocks, except Baudree
was carrying multiples of their mass, and when he contemplated
dock after what he'd been through he felt sweat running on
his forehead and a tension cramp knotting his leg.

Meg switched him out of the FleetCom loop to carrier-com, then, the range blip and the docking schematic a total preoccupation in his 360° V-HUD compression, carrier Helm talking to him now, wanting his attention, while he left Meg and Ben to watch elsewhere.

"Just hold steady and we've got you."

Moment of panic. Hard to shift time-perception. It wasn't going fast now. Everything took forever and a tiny bobble was disaster. You didn't screw it at this stage. Didn't, please God, didn't.

"Bow shock in 43 seconds."

"Copy that. Go." He couldn't afford to think they'd done it . . .

Not yet.

"That's capture and dock," FleetCom's dispassionate voice said. *"Thank you, Mr. Dekker. Excellent job."*

Graff found himself breathing again.

"We're going into our checklist." Dekker's voice. The reporters had gotten to recognize it. Had picked up on the tension in mission control and Villy had finally gotten it through, the shift the pilot had to make between nanosecond events and docking at relatively slow docking approach. "We had two funerals getting this down pat," Villy muttered. "It's no piece of easy the kid's working—hell of a buffet when you cross the shields."

Another flurry of technical questions. Graff looked for an escape, saw the door to the VIP area open and the two senators walk out—instant recognition from the press, instant convergence in that direction. Shouts and questions.

"We were invited to observe this test." The senior senator, Caldwell. "To see how the taxpayers' appropriations have been spent. I must say we've had a compelling demonstration of the effectiveness of the technology, outstanding performance . . ."

"J-G," Demas said, in his ear. *"Bonn. Our suspect did work for MarsCorp."*

He ducked for the corridor, deserted Villy and the senators for a small nook near a couple of marine security guards. "Say," he asked the security unit. "Have we got a case?"

"I don't know if we have a case, but he has former close associates in the Federation of Man, and the UDC background check didn't go that deep, he was passed in under Lendler security, and hear this, J-G, the UDC 'took Lendler's word for it,' unquote. 'All their personnel have to have a clearance.' Unquote. MarsCorp is 45% of Lendler's business: the atmospherics softwares, for a start."

Bloody hell, he thought. The information had hit his brain. The implications were still finding sensitive spots in his nervous system. 'Took Lendler's word for it.' 'All their personnel have to have a clearance.' Political implications, far beyond the Dekker affair.

"You're serious."

"Mars is threaded all through this. But so is the Federation of Man. Eldon Kent has two cousins in that association. Lendler's records on him are so-named classified—which we can't penetrate without filing charges."

"Not yet. Not yet. God."

Saito cut in on the channel. *"J-G. The carrier is returning to dock."*

"We're deep in reporters. Tell the commander that."

"I'm sure he knows," Saito said.

Damn! he thought, but he kept it off his face, he hoped, at least. He stood very still for a moment, heard Caldwell saying, inside, ". . . a tribute to the skill and dedication of Earth's industry and innovation—"

MAINS cut in, hard, and Dekker gave himself up to the force, just breathed the way one had to and trusted, figuring at this point if the carrier hit a rock or took them to hell, he wasn't afraid any more, he just stared at the blank, black VR in front of him, sensory deprivation... they were planning to fix that, arguing about what a crew wanted, coming off hype, whether they wanted anything at all but a VR off the carrier's boards, but Dekker personally voted just for the vid of the carrier surface, that was the only thing he wanted to see, he was convinced of it now, only thing a rider crew was going to want was constant reassurance that they were snugged up against the frame and locked, and that the clanks that rang through the hull were the auto-service connections and the ordnance servos, ready to shove ordnance up into the racks if there were a need to launch the prototype a second time immediately, which, thank God, there wasn't, and the servos didn't.

Tired, now, just tired. The carrier pulsed down to system

speeds, and announced a reposition on a new vector. Slow as humans lived, now, Dekker supposed, but things were moving faster than he could track or understand—

Which was the universe at ordinary, Meg would say, if Meg was talking, but none of them seemed to have the energy to talk right now, just trying to ride through the braking and not think, he supposed, all of them coming down off hype, and exhausted.

Second accel. He made the deep sustained breaths and shut his eyes. Black around them and black inside: reality had caught up to him, and Cory was dead. Long time back. Another life. Pace the breaths and count, the way you had to with a shove like that, to keep conscious. Hotdogging from Baudree, far as anybody could do that with a mass like this—

"What in hell's he doing?" Ben asked plaintively. "Where are we going?"

"Going back to base," Meg said.

"You got read-out?"

"Nyet. But you *feel* the direction, rab."

"Come off the mystic stuff. Nobody 'feels' the direction."

"Hey. There's ways and ways to feel it, cher, we did it. Where else they got to take us? —And there's those of us that feel the sun. Those that lived close to her—"

"Hell if, Kady."

"Nothing mystic. We got magnetics. Science boys say so."

"That's shit."

"Dunno. But the sun's starboard by 15 and high by 5."

"Trez garbage, Kady."

"Hey. Trez mystique, Pollard."

"Could get us a comlink," Sal grumbled. "Bloody damn hurry, they could let us come aboard. I got a serious bet on with Mitch's guys. And we're alive to collect . . ."

"*What'd* you bet?"—Ben, alarmed.

Familiar voices in the dark. He was safe here. Porey was outside, Porey who wanted him to make decisions, when

Ben and Meg were the ones who decided—exactly the way Graff said about merchanter crews, and he couldn't understand why Porey expected him to follow UDC rules; he didn't *want* the say, just fly the ship, that was all, and he'd done that, hadn't he? He'd done the part he wanted, and for his part, he didn't care where they went from here, whether Meg was right or whether they were going to turn up somewhere out in real combat, he wanted to talk to Mitch and the guys, just a real quiet chance at the crews they'd worked with, chance to store it down, debrief—forget the things he'd been through.

But that wasn't the way it worked. God, that was still to go through, the meds were going to haul them in and go over them with a microscope. And he'd gotten spoiled, he wanted the massage, the stand-down and the beer and somebody else to make up his bunk, the kind of treatment you got on the carrier, that was what, he'd gotten spoiled . . .

But the barracks was where he lived. He looked forward to messhall automat cheese sandwiches . . . french fries and a hamburger and a shake, one thing Porey's fancy cooks couldn't come up with, not with the right degree of grease. You had to have things like that or you didn't know you were alive, and not in some passing dream . . .

Eyes were watering, tear tracks running down his face. He didn't know why. He just listened to carrier ops, com chatter between base ops and here, and traffic control; and Meg was right, they were routed in.

Did it, he kept telling himself, the dark was proof of that, the feel of the ship was proof of that. He'd done what he wanted to do, the most outrageous thing he'd ever planned to do, and he didn't know what was left but to be free to do it.

Didn't even have to teach how. Tape would do that. He just had to get it together for the next time they let him fly. . . .

"We find—" Graff said, to the gathering of Optexes, "when we bring in an integrated crew—the sum of the one is reliably the sum of the rest. People in this profession, given the chance to pick their own partners, sort themselves, I don't know how otherwise to express it. You don't work with anybody under your ability, where you know your life is on the line. Yes, they're all four that good . . ."

"This *crew* is tape-taught," a reporter said. "What does that say about human skill?"

"Let me explain for any of you who're thinking of tape in the classic sense, the *tape* we're referring to is really the neural net record: you go in with what you did before, matched to a performance you want; and the neural assist system shapes itself around you—that's why we work with just four people at this stage. They're physically programming the systems."

"By their feedback."

"Exactly. The tetralogies won't do what these people do. They brought instincts and experience no tape can teach. The experts and the computers all have to ask *them* what the right reaction is—*that's* what the tape is, that's all it's doing, recording and learning from the humans in control . . . storing all the responses as a norm some other human being just may exceed. . . ."

The reporters liked that idea. You could see it in the mass mark-that orders to the Optex loops, the shouted questions, the sudden comprehension on their faces. They wanted a confirmation of themselves, *that* was what they wanted for their viewers, another human yearning, a sense of synch with the chaos systems around them. "You're saying there's something unquantifiable, something about the human factor . . ."

"The human component governs the computers, that's the way it is in the starships, that's the only way this ship is going to do what it was created to do. That's what the whole design fight has been about and that's what this crew's just proved."

A vid byte they could use. The carrier was in dock.

Presumably the rider crew and the backups were on their way down and the reporters were ready; he was theoretically the sacrifice, stalling and pacifying the reporters with running commentary, but, damn! he'd scored a point.

On the viewscreens and the monitors, images of Bonn and Paris and London, demonstrations by the Federation of Man and the leading peace groups, claiming Earth itself had been at risk, never mind high-v ordnance was aimed the other way: that same fear of near-c in system that discouraged the trade they might have had—people were frightened, stunned by the rapid approach, reporters already asking (personal applications always chased a new idea) why they languished three days on a shuttle ride that the carrier could cover in thirty minutes . . .

They had more questions. He saw the lift indicator showing operation, and nodded in that direction. "They're coming onto station."

Attention deserted him for the lift area: marines and Fleet Security had an unbreachable line of athletic bodies setting up a clear area, through which Villy, on similar advisement, showed up with Tanzer and the senators in tow, trailed by a still ecstatic crowd of Fleet and UDC crews from mission control—a complete media show-out, Graff thought with an uneasy stomach; and damned Porey to bloody hell for the decision to come straight in—but what else was it all for, after all? Risk Dekker, risk the prototype, risk *Eagle* with its thousand-member crew, for that matter, not to mention oversetting local regulations and stirring up the peacers with what they thought was a burning issue—

"Lieutenant." Tanzer arrived on his left hand.

"Colonel. We seem to have done it."

Tanzer shot him a look as if he were weighing the courtesy 'we' that he hadn't even considered in saying. The senators were in earshot. He'd delivered Tanzer an unintended, face-saving favor and Tanzer looked as if he were trying to figure what he wanted in exchange.

"We *have* done it," Tanzer said, as the lift doors opened.

Dekker and his crew walked out still in their flight gear, all pale and tired-looking, but cheerful till they confronted the shockwave of reporters, questions, and Optexes—nobody, dammit, had even warned them what was waiting: Porey had let them walk into it. Graff dived forward; and the other core crews surged through and grabbed them, slapping backs and creating a small island of riot inside the cordon of security He hung back a little, let the crews have their moment—saw Dekker both dazed and in good hands, the reporters not getting past the guards, just jostling silently for position with the Optexes as he finally took his turn with the crew, shook hands and congratulated them. There was glaze in their eyes. The four of them were still hyped and lost and not coping with the timeflow—he knew the look, he felt it, he ached to insulate them from this, get them quiet and stability. . . .

"Good job," he said. "Good job, all of you."

"Thank you, sir," Dekker breathed, and looked past him where—he turned his head—the vids showed riot in Bonn and Paris, just wide-tracking, lost.

"Ens. Dekker," the reporters shouted, "Ens. Dekker, how do you feel right now?"

Dekker turned his head to look at the reporter, honestly trying and failing, Graff read it, to accept one more slow-moving attention track. "I—" he began.

A reporter said, "Ens. Dekker. Ens. Dekker. There's a news crew standing by with a link to Bonn. Your mother's with the crew. Are you willing to speak to her, tell her how you feel at this moment?"

Damn! Graff thought, and shot another glance at the vids, where placards and banners called for peace, where a blond woman with a look as lost as Dekker's gazed into the lenses and then to the side, probably toward a monitor.

"Talk to her," the reporter said, "you can talk, she'll hear you—do you hear us, Ms. Dekker?"

"Yes," Ingrid Dekker said. *"Yes, I hear you. . . ."*

"I hear you," Dekker said faintly, and the whole area shushed each other to quiet.

"Paul? Paul? Is that you?"

"Yes." God, he was going to fracture—Graff saw the tears well up, saw the tremor. "Are you all right, mother? Are they treating you all right?"

Ingrid Dekker bit back tears. *"I wanted to return your call."*

"I wanted to call again. They said the lawyers wouldn't—"

Somebody shoved between Ingrid Dekker and the interviewer, said, *"That's enough."*

"Let her alone!" Dekker cried. "Damn you, take your hands off her—"

The picture jolted, the broad shadow of peacer security for a moment, Ingrid Dekker's voice crying, *"Paul, —Paul, I want to go home!"*

Kady got hold of Dekker. Aboujib did; and Pollard said, on Optex, "Those sons of bitches."

"We'll see if we can get Ms. Dekker back on," the interviewer was saying; and addressed his counterpart in Bonn. "Can you get to Ms. Dekker to ask—?"

Dekker was in shock, reporters shoving Optex pickups toward him, marines under strict orders not to shove back. That face was magnified on monitors all around the area, pale and lost, then Senator Caldwell's face was on the screens, reporters asking him his reaction.

Caldwell said, gravely: *"It's clear Ms. Dekker had something more to say, and the Federation leadership didn't want her to say it. I see enough to raise serious questions about how free Ms. Dekker is, at the moment..."*

Serious questions, Graff thought, choking on his own outrage. Serious questions whether Porey's timing for noon in Bonn, when Mazian was there, with the peace demonstrators, was anything like coincidence.

—God, run the test right past Luna in a move the peacers were bound to protest, have the reporters set up, the questions primed—

Then send Dekker and a crowd of excited crews head-on into the media for a reaction, when Porey damned well *knew* he was spaced?

He couldn't pull Dekker out directly, couldn't order Security to oust the reporters, daren't look like censorship on *this* side of the issue. He went in, took Dekker's arm with Optexes on high gain all around him. "Someone will do something." Which rang in his own ears as one more damned promise he didn't know how he was going to keep.

Dekker gave him a bleak, blank stare. "I don't want to leave, sir. If they can get her back I want to talk to her."

The mikes got that, too. Kady said, out of turn, "They don't want her loose. That's clear."

But all that showed on the Bonn monitors was a shut wooden door, and a reporter outside it, with no sound going out, talking, while demonstrators elbowed and shoved.

And all that showed on theirs was Dekker's stricken face, Dekker saying, dazedly, "They lied to her. They lied to her all the way..."

"It's playing," Demas said, leaning against the counter, "it's playing over and over again, around the planet, as the world wakes up. Dekker's a handsome kid, doesn't at all hurt his case. Or ours."

Graff wanted to break something—Demas' and Saito's necks, if he didn't recognize in Demas' glum expression an equal disgust. He looked at the vid, seeing Ingrid Dekker's bewildered distress, her son's—"Let her alone!" Over and over again.

As a weapon, Ingrid Dekker had turned in the hands of her wielders, and bit to the bone. Dekker was no longer the faceless Belter exile, he was the pilot who'd pulled a spectacular success with the Hellburner, he was a kid with a human grievance and a mother held prisoner by causes and politicians, and the demonstration organizer who had shoved Ingrid Dekker away from the reporters was under heavy condemnation and refusing questions.

Demas was right: it didn't hurt that Dekker had the face of a vid star and sincerity that came through the body language. The crew hadn't played badly either: the rumored split in the UDC/ Fleet ranks, Ben Pollard with his UDC insignia on his flightsuit, Kady and Aboujib in flash and high tech, all of them profoundly concerned and angry at a human issue.`. . .

While on the evening and morning news around the world, Alyce Salazar was doing damage control, covering her partisans, claiming that the Fleet had manipulated the media (truth) and that, quote, the important issues were being ignored in a rush to sympathy for a lying scoundrel who'd conned her daughter. . .

Dekker might be seeing it—he'd ordered open media access for appearances' sake while reporters were here, if no other reason; and had no argument from Porey. The vid was going out over all the station, their local authority doing no screening whatsoever.

"J-G," Demas said, "honestly, *I* didn't know until they ordered me to take charge of Security, right when the test started. They did query Saito, early on, for an assessment of Dekker's personnel record, his cultural makeup—"

"They. Did the captain know?"

"I don't know what there is to know. My guess is, Mazian sent Porey in here to figure the odds. If it was good enough, go, shove the best team in the ship and make the run; and if it turned out to be Dekker, meet the political chaff head-on, no hiding it, aim him straight for the cameras and damn all Salazar could do."

"Pardon me, Nav, but the *hell* the timing was random! High noon in Europe, in Bonn? Mazian's there. He knows the schedule. He *knew* it would draw instant fire!"

"I don't think he planned the scene with Dekker's mother."

"I don't put it past him."

"I think you give him too much credit. Some things just drop into your lap. But Mazian did want the protests—according to Saito. He wanted to solidify the issue, Saito says, so that it has substance, and then shoot that substance to hell. Make the peacers take a specific position and prove them wrong.''

''Dekker's mother.''

''Dekker's mother is a side issue. An opportunity I'm sure they'll take advantage of. Not mentioning Salazar. The EC wants Salazar stopped, in such a way it *won't* break Mars out of the union . . . and we have the Kent business with MarsCorp's fingerprints all over it.''

''And daren't use it, dammit, we daren't even arrest Kent and Booten, we don't know—''

A stray thought crossed his mind.

''What?'' Demas asked in his silence. ''Don't know what?''

He leaned back in his chair and looked at the vid, where another instant opinion poll was playing. A radical shift in the numbers in the last 5 hours, plus or minus 3 points of accuracy. People believed the things they'd seen. 45% believed Paul Dekker was innocent and 46% now believed there was a significant threat of the war reaching Earth.

He said to Demas, apropos of nothing previous, ''I want a statement prepared, a public relations version of Dekker's file. In case. I don't like unanticipateds, Nav.''

''You've got it. But the Company will black-hole it. Salazar is too sensitive an issue. And far too powerful. She's using the issues, she's *not* the grieving mother, she's a politician. Kent . . . has got to be a professional. And if we've got him, there'll be others—inside the Earth Company offices, for all we know.''

''All the same,'' he said.

He offered Demas a thin smile, and Demas took himself and his securitied briefcase back to the carrier, to Saito, to whatever lines of communication they were using to reach the captain with or without Mazian's knowledge.

They knew now what had killed Wilhelmsen: Ben Pollard had put them onto it and Porey's question to Dekker had shown it plain as plain. Wilhelmsen had been UDC command track. Pete Fowler had been the shadow behind

Dekker's status, the real decision-maker—and the UDC had put them into the same cockpit. But they couldn't put that story in the release to the media—they dared not confuse the issue. Dekker was the point man, the—what had Saito said—the face the public knew? Dekker was the command officer of record in both crews; and that was the way the story was going to Earth.

Himself, he put on his jacket and went to evening rec, where there was a general liberty in force, with most of the reporters packed in with the senators on the shuttle, about six hours distant from the crews, thank God.

Thanks to some other agency, he was trapped with eight of them on station for at least a week. And damned if he was going to deal with them blind.

Beer and vodka were permissible; and Mitch and the UDC's Deke Chapman were doing a *v*-vid arcade game, noisy and rude, with bets down and the marine guards in on it, when a command officer walked in on it unannounced . . .

"Graff," Meg said, the whole room drew a breath, seemed to decide it was a friendly tour, and went back to an abated roar; Vasquez offered the lieutenant a beer.

"Sip," Graff said, in the way of a Shepherd who was on duty; so Graff got his sip to a cheer from all about, then said, quietly, "Pollard. Word with you. Outside."

Quick frown from Sal.

"No trouble," Graff said. "Just an operational. As you were, everybody."

Jokes on that score, no disrespect at all, just guys on an R&R from death and destruction. Meg slid into her chair again, caught Dek's hand, because he was looking spaced again—

Letdown, she understood that. Only thoroughly happy moment he'd had in his life, by all she knew; and they'd hit him head-on with that business with his mother and the peacers. He looked her in the eyes now as if she had the answers—as if, as the rab would say, she was the word and the knowhow.

And maybe she had been that, once, for a lot of people—maybe she'd been more, once, than she ever let on to those who checked on such things—but the generations changed, the whole human race spun and raced toward tomorrow after tomorrow, and if you were twenty-five now you didn't know the rab that had been the young and the foolish and the seekers after personal truth. The rab is, they'd used to say—after the Company man had said, No dealing with rabble. The rab is, and the rab will be, and screw the corp—

Was it lover or her personal tomorrow—looking into her eyes and hanging on the words?

"She'll get out," she told him, because she knew it was his mama he was brooding about; and maybe Cory. He didn't have many tracks left when he got this far down. She hit his arm, and said, "Rab is and rab does, jeune fils. And they shot us down. Don't forget that. Shot you down. I got nothing to teach you about being screwed."

"She never *cared* about politics, Meg!"

"We got to do, got to do, jeune fils. Life is, death is, and that's all; but we're here and they got to deal with that. They got to deal with us."

Dek had been a kid when the rab had lost its innocence, and the blood had run on the Company steps. Severely young, Dek still was, in some ways. She couldn't be, again; and she told it cold and plain as she'd learned it herself: "There's no *luck,* jeune rab, things don't brut *happen* for no damn reason, and you aren't it, forgive, cher. But nobody at this table, not me and not you and not Sal, is that important, that God is going to screw up somebody else's life to get you. I dunno who, I dunno why, but we've eliminated God as a suspect. . . ."

Dek managed a laugh, a grin, and picked up his beer with his hand shaking. He drank a sip without spilling it. At least.

"Hey," Sal said, "They got the whole UN Human Rights Commission asking to talk to your mama. . . ."

"But if they get her out she's not safe, Salazar's people tried twice to kill me and got Jamil—"

"Cher rab, are they going to risk stirring things up now? They got their ass on the line. They want quiet, soon as they can hush this up. When the corp-rats get caught, they always want a real quick silence."

He let go a sigh, shook his head.

Sal elbowed him. "Take you on, cher. Billiards or poker?"

Poker, it was. Ben pulled a chair back, set his beer down, said, cheerfully, "Deal me in," and collected looks from his crewmates. He kept the smugness off his face—the reason was for Sal's ears, for Dekker and Meg once the stuff went public—as would happen, he was sure, when Security found out what to do with the file that had landed in their laps.

Dekker asked, "What did they want?"

"Oh, nothing."

"Come on," Sal said.

"Oh," Ben said, picking up cards, "just a little tekkie stuff." *Good* hand, it was. There were nights a guy was On, and this was it.

Damn, there was stuff going to hit the news tomorrow.

"Tekkie stuff, hell," Sal said. "What was it?"

"Just a little advice." And access numbers and a nailpolish-sealed card. He laid down chips.

Didn't have to go to Stockholm to prove the Staatentek over the damned EIDAT, damn no. *Elegant* equipment, they had on that carrier.

"What advice?"

He smiled, thinking about the morning news, and MarsCorp, and Salazar's personal memo file, and the wonderful, damning things it held.

"Don't buy stock in EIDAT, Lendler or MarsCorp. Even at discount."

"What have you got?" Dekker asked sharply.

Wider smile. "A winning hand, Dek-boy, odds are—a winning hand."

By the year 2000, 2 out of 3 Americans could be illiterate.

It's true.

Today, 75 million adults... about one American in three, can't read adequately. And by the year 2000, U.S. News & World Report envisions an America with a literacy rate of only 30%.

Before that America comes to be, you can stop it... by joining the fight against illiteracy today.

Call the Coalition for Literacy at toll-free **1-800-228-8813** and volunteer.

Volunteer Against Illiteracy. The only degree you need is a degree of caring.

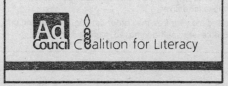

Ad Council C oalition for Literacy